Etienne-Jules Marey

Animal mechanism

A treatise on terrestrial and aerial locomotion

Etienne-Jules Marey

Animal mechanism
A treatise on terrestrial and aerial locomotion

ISBN/EAN: 9783742811493

Manufactured in Europe, USA, Canada, Australia, Japa

Cover: Foto ©Andreas Hilbeck / pixelio.de

Manufactured and distributed by brebook publishing software
(www.brebook.com)

Etienne-Jules Marey

Animal mechanism

THE
INTERNATIONAL SCIENTIFIC SERIES.

TABLE OF CONTENTS.

BOOK THE FIRST.

FORCES AND ORGANS.

CHAPTER I.

OF FORCES IN THE INORGANIC KINGDOM AND AMONG ORGANISED BEINGS.

Matter reveals itself by its properties—When matter acts, we conclude that forces exist — Multiplicity of the forces formerly
admitted ; tendency to their reduction to one force in the inorganic kingdom—Indestructibility of force ; its transformations
—Vital forces, their multiplicity according to the ancient
physiologists—Several vital forces are reduced to physical
forces—Of laws in physics and in physiology—General theory

CHAPTER II.

TRANSFORMATION OF PHYSICAL FORCES.

To prove the indestructibility of forces, we must know how to
measure them—Units of heat and of mechanical work—Thermo-dynamics—Measure of forces in living beings—Successive
phases of the transformation of bodies ; successive development
of force under this influence—Thermo-dynamics applied to

CHAPTER III.

ON ANIMAL HEAT.

Origin of animal heat—Lavoisier's theory—The perfecting of this
theory—Estimates of the forces contained in aliment, and in
the secreted products—Difficulty of those estimates—The force

CHAPTER IV.

ANIMAL MOTION.

CHAPTER V.

CONTRACTION AND WORK OF THE MUSCLES.

CHAPTER VI.

OF ELECTRICITY IN ANIMALS.

CHAPTER VII.

ANIMAL MECHANISM.

CHAPTER VIII.

HARMONY BETWEEN THE ORGAN AND THE FUNCTION.— DEVELOPMENT HYPOTHESIS.

CHAPTER IX.

VARIABILITY OF THE SKELETON.

BOOK THE SECOND.

FUNCTIONS: TERRESTRIAL LOCOMOTION.

CHAPTER I.

OF LOCOMOTION IN GENERAL.

CHAPTER II.
TERRESTRIAL LOCOMOTION (BIPEDS).

CHAPTER III.
THE DIFFERENT MODES OF PROGRESSION USED BY MAN.

CHAPTER IV.
QUADRUPEDAL LOCOMOTION STUDIED IN THE HORSE.

CHAPTER V.
EXPERIMENTS ON THE PACES OF THE HORSE.

Double aim of these experiments ; determination of the movements
under the physiological point of view, and of the attitudes with

CHAPTER VI.
EXPERIMENTS ON THE PACES OF THE HORSE.
(Continued.)

BOOK THE THIRD.
AERIAL LOCOMOTION.

CHAPTER I.
OF THE FLIGHT OF INSECTS.

CHAPTER II.
MECHANISM OF THE FLIGHT OF INSECTS.

LIST OF ILLUSTRATIONS.

—◆—

PAGE

TRACINGS.

TRACINGS OF THE MUSCLES.

TRACINGS OF HUMAN LOCOMOTION.

TRACINGS OF THE LOCOMOTION OF THE HORSE.

TRACINGS OF THE FLIGHT OF INSECTS.

ANIMAL MECHANISM:

TERRESTRIAL AND AERIAL LOCOMOTION.

INTRODUCTION.

LIVING beings have been frequently and in every age compared to machines, but it is only in the present day that the bearing and the justice of this comparison are fully comprehensible.

No doubt, the physiologists of old discerned levers, pulleys, cordage, pumps, and valves in the animal organism, as in the machine. The working of all this machinery is called *Animal Mechanics* in a great number of standard treatises. But these passive organs have need of a motor; it is life, it was said, which set all these mechanisms going, and it was believed that thus there was authoritatively established an inviolable barrier between inanimate and animate machines.

In our time it is at least necessary to seek another basis for such distinctions, because modern engineers have created machines which are much more legitimately to be compared to animated motors; which, in fact, by means of a little combustible matter which they consume, supply the force requisite to animate a series of organs, and to make them execute the most various operations.

The comparison of animals with machines is not only legitimate, it is also extremely useful from different points of view. It furnishes a valuable means of making the mechanical phenomena which occur in living beings understood, by placing them beside the similar but less generally known phenomena, which are evident in the action of ordinary

machines. In the course of this book, we shall frequently
borrow from pure mechanics the synthetical demonstrations
of the phenomena of animal life. The mechanician, in his
turn, may derive useful notions from the study of nature,
which will often show him how the most complicated problems
may be solved with admirable simplicity.

Animal mechanics is a wide field for exploration. To
every function, so to speak, a special machinery is attached.
The circulation of the blood, the respiration, &c., may and
ought to be treated separately, so that we shall limit this work
to the study of one single, essentially mechanical, function,
locomotion in the various animals.

It is easy to demonstrate the importance of such a subject as
locomotion, which, under its different forms, terrestrial, aquatic,
and aerial, has constantly excited interest. Whether man has
endeavoured to utilize to the utmost his own motive power,
and that of the animals; whether he has sought to extend
his domain, to open a way for himself in the seas, or to rise
into the air, it is always from nature that he has drawn his
inspirations. We may hope that a deeper knowledge of the
different modes of animal locomotion will be a point of
departure for fresh investigations, whence further progress
will result.

Every scientific research has a powerful attraction in itself;
the hope of reaching the truth suffices to sustain those who
pursue it, through all their efforts; the contemplation of the
laws of nature has been a great and noble source of enjoyment to those who have discovered them. But to humanity,
science is only the means, progress is the aim. If we can
show that a study may lead to some useful application, we
may induce many to pursue it, who would otherwise merely
follow it from afar, with the interest of curiosity only.
Without pretending to recapitulate here all that has been
gained by the study of nature, we shall endeavour to set
forth what may be gained by studying it still further, and
with more care.

Terrestrial locomotion, that of man, and of the great mammals, for instance, is very imperfectly understood as yet. If
we knew under what conditions the maximum of speed, force,

or labour which the living being can furnish, may be obtained, it would put an end to much discussion, and a great deal of conjecture, which is to be regretted. A generation of men would not be condemned to certain military exercises which will be hereafter rejected as useless and ridiculous. One country would not crush its soldiers under an enormous load, while another considers that the best plan is to give them nothing to carry. We should know exactly at what pace an animal does the best service, whether he be required for speed, or for drawing loads; and we should know what are the conditions of draught best adapted to the utilization of the strength of animals.

It is in this sense that progress is being made; but if we complain with reason of its slow advance, we must only blame our imperfect notion of the mechanism of locomotion. Let this study be perfected, and then useful applications of it will soon ensue.

Man has been manifestly inspired by nature in the construction of the machinery of navigation. If the hull of the ship is, as it has been justly described, formed on the model of the aquatic fowl, if the sail has been copied from the wing of the swan inflated by the wind, and the oar from its webbed foot as it strikes the water, these are but a small part of nature's loans to art. More than two hundred years ago, Borelli, studying the stability and displacement of fish, traced the plan of a diving-ship constructed upon the same principle as the formidable *Monitors* which made their appearance in the recent American war.

In modern navigation the dynamic question still leaves several points in obscurity. What form should be given to a ship so as to secure its meeting with the least possible resistance in the water? What propeller should be chosen in order to utilize the force of the machine to the best advantage? The most competent men in such matters avow that these problems are too complex to admit of the conditions most favourable to the construction of ships being determined by calculation. Must we wait until empiricism, by dint of ruinous guesses, shall have taught us how a problem of which nature offers us such diverse solutions, should be solved? Ingenious constructors have already attempted to imitate the natural propellers; they have fitted up small boats with machinery which works like the tail of a fish, oscillating with an alternate motion. And it has been found that this apparatus, although still imperfect, already constitutes a powerful propeller, which will perhaps be preferred hereafter to all those which have hitherto been used.

Aerial locomotion has always excited the strongest curiosity among mankind. How frequently has the question been raised, whether man must always continue to envy the bird and the insect their wings; whether he, too, may not one day travel through the air, as he now sails across the ocean. Authorities in science have declared at different periods, as the result of langthy calculations, that this is a chimerical dream, but how many inventions have we seen realised which have also been pronounced impossible. The truth is, that all intervention by mathematics is premature, so long as the study of nature and experiment have not furnished the precise data which alone can serve as a sound starting point for calculations of this kind.

We shall then attempt to analyse the rapid acts which are produced in the flight of insects and of birds; afterwards we shall endeavour to imitate nature, and we shall see, once more, that by seeking inspiration from her we have the best chance of solving the problems which she has solved.

We may even now affirm, that in the mechanical actions of terrestrial, aquatic, and aerial locomotion, there is nothing which can escape the methods of analysis at our disposal. Would it be impossible for us to reproduce a phenomenon which we understand? We will not carry our scepticism so far.

It was considered for a long time that chemistry, all-powerful when it was a question of decomposing organic substances, would always remain incapable of reproducing them. What has become of this disheartening prediction?

We hope that the reader who follows the experimental researches detailed in this book will draw from them this conviction, that many of the impossibilities of the present, need only a little time and much effort to become realities.

BOOK THE FIRST.

CHAPTER I.

FORCES AND ORGANS.

Of forces in the inorganic kingdom and among organised beings—Matter reveals itself by its properties—When matter acts, we conclude that forces exist—Multiplicity of forces formerly admitted; tendency to their reduction to one force in the inorganic kingdom—Indestructibility of force; its transformations—Vital forces, their multiplicity according to the ancient physiologists—Several vital forces are reduced to physical forces—Of laws in physics and in physiology—General theory of physical forces.

WE know matter only by its *properties*, which we could not conceive of apart from matter. The word property does not answer to anything real : it is an artifice of language ; thus, the expressions, weight, heat, hardness, colour, &c., attributed to various bodies in nature, mean that these bodies manifest themselves to our senses by certain effects which have been made known to us by daily experience.

When matter acts, that is to say, when it changes its state, there occurs what we call a phenomenon, and by a new application of language we call the unknown cause which has produced this phenomenon, *Force*. A body which falls, a river which flows, a fire which warms us, the lightning which flashes, two bodies which combine, &c., all these correspond to manifestations of forces which we call gravity, mechanical force, heat, electricity, light, chemical affinities, &c.

In the first ages of science the number of forces was almost infinitely multiplied. Each particular phenomenon was regarded as the manifestation of a special force. But by degrees it was recognised that divers manifestations might result from a single cause; and thenceforth the number of forces which were admitted diminished considerably.

Weight and attraction were reduced to one and the same force by Newton, who recognised, in the falling of the apple to the ground, and the retention of the star in its orbit, the effects of an identical cause—universal gravitation. Ampère reduced magnetism to a manifestation of electricity. Light and heat have long since been regarded as manifestations of an identical force, an extremely rapid vibratory motion imparted to the ether.

In our own time a grand conception has arisen, once more to change the face of science. All the forces of nature are reduced to one only. *Force* may assume any appearance; it becomes, by turns, heat, mechanical work, electricity, light; it gives rise to chemical combinations or decompositions. Occasionally, force seems to disappear, but it has only hidden itself; we can find it again in its entirety, and make it pass anew through the cycle of its transformations.

Force, which is inseparable from matter, is, like it, indestructible, and to both the absolute principle, that in nature nothing is created and nothing is destroyed, is applicable.

Before we enter upon a detailed exposition of this great conception of the conservation of force and its transformations in the inorganic world, let us see whether any analogous generalisation has been arrived at in the science of organised bodies.

The living being, in its manifestations of sensibility, intelligence, and spontaneity, shows itself to be so different from the inert and passive bodies of inorganic nature; the generation and the evolution of animals are so peculiar to themselves; that the earliest observers traced an absolute boundary between the two kingdoms of nature.

Particular forces were imagined, to which each of the normal phenomena of life was attributed, while others, like malignant genii, presided over the production of the maladies by which everything that has life may be attacked.

The complexity of the phenomena of life hindered observers for a long time from discerning the link which united them, and prevented their referring to one and the same cause these manifold effects, and thus reducing the number of forces which had at first been admitted. Man ended by taking the fictions of his imagination for realities. Little by little, the charm of the unintelligible exercising fascination over him, he at last denied that physical laws had any influence upon living beings. This extravagant mysticism represented certain animals as capable of withdrawing themselves from the influences of weight; according to it, animal heat was of another essence than that of our hearths; subtle and impalpable spirits circulated in the vessels and the nerves.

Time has not even yet disposed of all these absurdities; but we can prove that the science of life tends at present to undergo a transformation as complete as that of the physical sciences, whose development we have just sketched. Physiology, guided by experience, seeks and finds the physical forces in a great number of vital phenomena; every day sees an increase in the number of cases to which we can apply the ordinary laws of nature. That which escapes them remains for us the unknown, but no longer the unknowable. Among the phenomena of life, those which are intelligible to us are precisely of the physical or mechanical order.

In the living organism we shall find those manifestations of force which are called heat, mechanical action, electricity, light, chemical action; we shall see these forces transforming themselves one into the other, but we must not hope to arrive immediately at the numerical determination of the laws which regulate the transformations of these forces. The animal organism does not lend itself to exact measurements, its complexity is too great for valuations, to which physicists attain with great difficulty by making use of the simplest machines.

Each science, according to its degree of complexity, is approaching more or less surely to the mathematical precision at which it must arrive sooner or later. A law is only the determination of numerical relations between different phenomena; there is then no perfect physiological law. In the phenomena of life it is scarcely possible to determine and to foresee anything except the manner in which the variation will be produced. Hitherto, the physiologist has reached only that degree of knowledge which the astronomer would possess, who

knew, for instance, that the attraction between two heavenly
bodies diminishes when their distance increases, but who had
not yet determined the law of inverse proportionality to the
square of distances. Or, he is like the physicist who has proved
that compressed gases diminish in volume, but who has not
found the numerical relation between their volume and the
pressure.

Without doubt, however, there are numerical relations
between the phenomena of life; and we shall arrive at the
discovery of them more or less speedily, according to the
exactitude of the methods of investigation to which we have
recourse.

If physicists had limited themselves to establishing that
bodies dilate as they become heated, and if they had not
sought to measure the temperature of those bodies and the
volume which they assume with each variation of the temperature, they would have had only an imperfect idea of the
phenomena of the dilatation of bodies by heat. For a long
time physiologists confined themselves to pointing out that
such or such an influence augments or diminishes the force of
the muscles, causes the rapidity of their motions to vary,
increases or diminishes sensibility and motive power. Science,
in our time, has become more exacting, and already the
rigorous determination of the intensity and duration of certain
acts, of the form of different movements, of the relations of
succession between two or several phenomena, the precise
estimation of the rapidity of the blood, or of the transference
of the sensitive or motive nervous agent; all these exact
measures introduced into physiology, lead us to hope that
from more scrupulous measurement better formulated laws
will soon result.

In the comparison which we are about to make between
the physical forces and those which animate the animal
organism, we shall take it for granted that the fundamental
notions recently introduced into science, and by which all those
forces tend to reduce themselves to one only, that which
engenders motion, are known; and shall, therefore, confine
ourselves to a rapid sketch of the new theory.

The value of a theory depends on the number of the facts

which it embraces; that of the unity of the physical forces tends to absorb them all. From the invisible atom to the celestial body lost in space, everything is subject to motion. Everything gravitates in an immense or in an infinitely little orbit. Kept at a definite distance one from the other, in proportion to the motion which animates them, the molecules present constant relations, which they lose only by the addition or the subtraction of a certain quantity of motion. In general, increase of motion enlarges the orbit of the molecules, and widening their distance from each other, increases the volume of the bodies. By this rule, heat is proved to be a source of motion. Under its influence the molecules, becoming more and more separated, cause bodies to pass from solid to liquid, and then to a gaseous state. These gases become indefinitely dilated by the addition of fresh quantities of heat. But that force which lends extreme rapidity to the motion of the molecules, that force which is admitted in theory is rendered tangible by experiment; its intensity is measured by opposing to the dilatation of a body an obstacle which it will have to surmount. Thus it is that the molecules of gases or vapours imprisoned in the cylinder of machines, communicate to the partitions and to the piston the pressure which is employed in producing action by machinery. This mechanical action is, in its turn, transformed into heat if the conditions of the experiment be reversed; if, for example, an external force, thrusting back the piston of an air-pump, restrains the molecular motions by violent compression.

The new theory has thrown light upon certain hypotheses, those, among others, which claimed admission for the latent heat of fusion, or of vaporisation of bodies, the latent heat of dilatation of gases. It has suppressed others; for instance, the discovery of atmospheric pressure has banished the hypothesis which has now become ridiculous, that nature abhors a vacuum.

Although the theory accommodates itself with less ease to the interpretations of luminous and electric phenomena, it admits, according to the great analogy between these phenomena and heat, of supposing that they themselves are only

manifestations of motion. Besides, the transformation of
motion into heat, into electricity, into light, may be proved
experimentally.

Fig. 1 represents the details of the experiment.

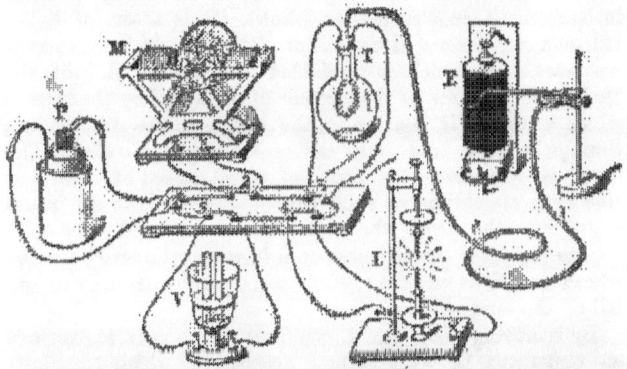

FIG. 1.—Showing the transformation of the electricity of a battery into mechanical action, into heat, light, and chemical action.

Various instruments are so arranged upon a table that an
electric current, engendered by a battery P, may be made to
pass through them.* The current is conducted in an elliptic
circuit, on a small square board, represented in the centre of
the figure. This circuit is formed of a thick copper wire;
at certain points this wire is interrupted and dipped into
cups of mercury, from which other wires communicate with
the various apparatus through which the current is to be conducted. In Fig. 1, the metallic bridges 1, 2, 3, 4, 5, connect
the cups of mercury, and form a complete circuit, which the
current may traverse without passing through the various
apparatus placed around it.

If we take away loop No. 1, the current which passed
through that loop is forced to traverse the elliptical circuit
without passing through the surrounding apparatus. But if we

* Instead of the single element represented in the Figure, it is necessary
to employ a series of Bunsen's cells, to realise the experiments perfectly.

afterwards remove loop No. 2, the current must traverse the apparatus M, which is an electro-magnetic motor. This apparatus will begin to move and will produce mechanical action.

Let us at the same time remove loop No. 3, the current must also traverse a registering thermometer. [That instrument is constructed as follows. It is a sort of Reiss' thermometer, formed of a spiral of platinum, which the current traverses, and which is conducted into a flask full of air. Under the influence of the heating of the spiral by the current which traverses it, the air in the bottle dilates, and passes, through a long tube, into the registering apparatus. The latter is composed of a drum of metal, closed on the upper side by a membrane of india-rubber. When the air penetrates into the drum, the membrane swells, and lifts up a registering lever, which traces on a turning cylinder E, a curve whose elevations and depressions correspond with the rise and fall of the temperature.]

By removing loop No. 4, we force the current to traverse an apparatus L, with carbon points, in which electricity gives birth to the bright light with which every one is acquainted. When it passes through the voltameter V, the current produces decomposition of the water. The intensity of the current is measured by the quantity of water decomposed, i.e., by the volumes of hydrogen and oxygen which are disengaged.

We see, in the first place, by means of this apparatus, that electricity can become successively mechanical work in the motor M, heat in the spiral of the thermometer T, light between the carbon points L, and chemical action in the voltameter V.

But we also recognise that the electricity which undergoes one of those metamorphoses is taken away from the current whose energy is thus diminished. If, for example, we make the motor M work, we shall see that the register marks a diminution of heat in the thermometer. If we stop the electro-magnetic motor with the hand, an increase in the temperature becomes immediately apparent; the registered curve rises.

When the electro-magnetic motor is working, we see the

intensity of the light diminish, and the decomposition of the water in the voltameter grow less. All these phenomena resume their pristine energy as soon as we suppress the production of mechanical action.

During this time, all the force expended in these various forms of apparatus is disengaged from the battery under the influence of a chemical action: the transformation of a certain quantity of zinc into sulphate of zinc. Thus, in the furnace of a steam engine, the combustion of the coal, that is to say, the oxidation which transforms carbon into carbonic acid disengages heat, which is afterwards converted into work.

But this force, disengaged from bodies, was contained in them when the zinc was in the condition of metal, and the carbon in the state of coal; these bodies had employed in their formation the same quantity of force which they have yielded up in passing into another condition. Thus it would be necessary to restore to the sulphate of zinc and to the carbonic acid as much electricity or heat as they have thrown out, in order to reproduce the metallic zinc or the carbon in a pure state.

According to the modern theory, force which manifests itself at a given moment is not created, but only rendered sensible, from being latent.

Here in *tension* is that potential force, which, stored up in a body, waits the opportunity to manifest itself. Thus a *stretched* spring will at the end of an indefinite time give back the force which has been used to stretch it; and a weight, lifted to a certain height, will restore, the instant it falls, the work that has been employed upon raising it.

CHAPTER II.

TRANSFORMATION OF PHYSICAL FORCES.

To prove the indestructibility of forces, we must know how to measure them—Units of heat and of mechanical work—Thermo-dynamics—Measure of forces in living beings—Successive phases of the transformation of bodies; successive throwing off of force under this influence—Thermo-dynamics applied to living beings.

WE have just seen that force, in the different states which it presents, may be now latent, or potential, or again in action, in the form of heat, electricity, or mechanical activity.

To follow this force through all its different transformations, to establish that no portion of it is lost, a means of measuring it under all its forms is necessary. The chemist can prove the indestructibility of matter, by showing, with a balance, that a gramme of matter will preserve its weight through all the changes of condition that can be imposed upon it. Let that matter be weighed in the liquid state, in the solid state, or in the gaseous state, the weight of a gramme will always be found under the most various volumes and aspects.

A measure is then necessary for the different manifestations of force. Every quantity of heat, of electricity, or of mechanical work ought to be compared with a particular unit, as every weight ought to be compared with the unit of weight.

Unit of heat. The sensations of heat and cold which we experience at the contact of different bodies do not correspond with the quantity of heat which those bodies contain. Thermometrical apparatus are not in a condition to give us the measure of the quantities of heat, since different bodies, presenting to our senses and by the thermometer the same temperature, may yield very unequal quantities of heat. But, to warm the same weight of a body to the same number of degrees, the same quantity of heat will always be necessary.

Now, according to the agreement which has been come to in France and in many other countries, the unit of heat or

calorie is the quantity of heat necessary to raise a kilogramme
of water from zero to one degree centigrade.

Unit of work. Mechanical force has been accurately defined only since the notion of work has been introduced into
science. The unit of mechanical work admitted in France
is the *kilogrammètre;* that is to say, the force necessary to
raise the unit of weight—the kilogramme—to the unit of
height, the metre.

Electric force is measured by one of its effects, the decomposition of water, for it is demonstrated that to decompose
the same volume of water the same quantity of electricity will
always be requisite.

These measures of forces in *action* furnish, in their turn,
the means of estimating the quantity of potential force contained in a body. Thus, it will be demonstrated that in a
kilogramme of coal, and in the quantity of oxygen necessary
to transform that coal into carbonic acid, there were in tension
7000 units of heat, since by combining all the heat disengaged by combustion, a mass of water of 7000 kilogrammes
shall have been heated.

But a substance which burns is not always completely
oxidized; hence, it does not put in action the totality of the
force which it contained in tension. A kilogramme of carbon,
for example, may undergo only a first degree of oxidation, and
thus becoming oxide of carbon it yields only 5000 units of
heat. This oxide of carbon burning in its turn, and becoming
carbonic acid, will then yield only the remaining 2000 units
of heat.

Transformation of physical forces takes place, as we have
said, without any loss of the transformed force. To demonstrate this, it must be proved that a certain number of units
of heat transformed into work, will furnish a constant number
of kilogrammètres, and inversely, that this work in becoming
heat again, will restore the primitive number of units of heat.

The science which explains the relations between heat and
mechanical work, and fixes the value of the *mechanical equivalent
of heat is called thermo-dynamics.* This conception, which is
the complement of the theory of the transformation of forces,
and which proves that in their transformation they lose

nothing of their value, is justly considered the most remarkable of modern times.

Partly seen by Sadi-Carnot, clearly formulated by R. Mayer, demonstrated brilliantly by the experiments of Joule, the notion of the equivalence of forces is now admitted by all physicists. Each day furnishes a fresh confirmation of this doctrine, and leads to greater precision in the determination of the mechanical equivalent of heat. The value now generally admitted for that equivalent is 425, that is to say, that work equal to 425 kilogrammètres must be transformed into heat to obtain a unit, and inversely, that the heat capable of heating to one degree one kilogramme of water at zero, if it be transformed into work, can, in its turn, lift a weight of 425 kilogrammes one metre.*

But one restriction must be placed upon the estimation of thermo-dynamic transformations. Carnot suspected, and Clausius had clearly established that in the case of heat being employed to produce work, the heat cannot transform itself altogether, and that the greater part remains still in the state of heat; while in the inverse operation the whole of the work applied to that effect may be transformed into heat. This does not exclude the law of equivalence, of which we have just spoken; for if it be true that, in a steam engine for instance, there is only to be found under the form of work a small quantity, about 12° of the heat produced by the furnace, it is no less true that the quantity of heat which has disappeared furnishes in work the exact number of kilogrammètres which corresponds to its mechanical equivalent.

These notions had no sooner been introduced into science than the physiologists endeavoured to use them for the clearing up of the obscure question of heat and work produced by animals. The assimilation of living beings to thermal machines was already in the state of vague conception. We shall see what light has been thrown upon it by the new theory.

---

* Some experiments made by Regnault on the rapidity of sound, and on the expansion of gases, give as the true value of the equivalent the number 439.

We have said that forces are produced within the organism. All living beings give out heat and produce work. The disengagement of these forces is caused by the chemical transformation of food.

In the living being it is possible to measure approximately the quantities of heat and work produced, and even to estimate the quantity of force contained in food; in order to do this it is sufficient to apply the methods which physicists have employed in the estimation of inorganic forces.

Thus, a man placed for some time in a bath will yield to the water a certain number of units of heat, which may be easily measured. Applied to the moving of a machine, the force of a man or an animal will produce a number of kilogrammètres no less easily to be measured. If the aliment be subjected to the experiments which determine the heating power of different combustibles, it will be found that each of them contains a certain quantity of potential force. Favre and Silbermann have supplied most valuable information, attained by great labour, on this point; and Frankland has continued their investigations. We now know the calorific power of almost all the alimentary substances, it is, therefore, possible to calculate what free force their complete oxidation will yield either under the form of heat or under the form of work.

But, as we have seen with respect to combustibles employed for industrial purposes, the oxidation is not always complete. Coal partially consumed, gives solid or gaseous residues, such as coke and oxide of carbon, which, being oxidized in a more complete manner, furnish a certain quantity of heat. In the same way, the residues of digestion still contain non-disengaged force. All these forces ought to be estimated if we want to know how much of their force in tension has been lost by the alimentary matters in passing through the organism, and how much ought consequently to be found again under the form of force in action. The urinary secretion also eliminates incompletely transformed products; the urea and the uric acid contain force in tension, which ought to be taken into account in calculations.

The watery vapour which saturates the air as it comes out of the lungs removes from the organism and carries away with it a certain quantity of heat; the same thing takes place in the boiler of a steam-engine, as well as in cutaneous evaporation.

This complication in the measure of force among organized beings shows what difficulties await those who are endeavouring to verify the principles of thermo-dynamics in animals; yet, nevertheless, it would be illogical to admit without proof that, in living beings, the physical forces do not obey natural laws. Several *savants*, firmly convinced of the generality of the laws of thermo-dynamics, have attempted to demonstrate them upon the animal organism.

J. Béclard was the first who endeavoured to prove that in the muscles of man heat may be substituted for mechanical work, and *vice versâ*. For this purpose he examined the thermometrical temperature of two muscles, both of which contracted, but one worked, that is to say, raised weights, while the other did not work. It might have been expected that less heat would have been found in the first muscle, because a portion of the heat produced during its contraction ought to have been transformed into work.

The idea which governed Béclard's experiments was assuredly correct, but the means at his disposal for ascertaining the heating of the muscles were altogether insufficient. A thermometer was applied to the skin at the level of the muscle, in order to give the measure of the heat produced; thus the variations of temperature obtained by Béclard according as the muscle worked or not, were so slight that no real value could be attached to them.

Herdenheim obtained clearer results by operating upon frogs' muscles, which he made to contract with or without the production of work, ascertaining their temperature by means of thermo-electric apparatus.

Hirn was bolder in his experiments, for he sought to determine the equivalent of mechanical work in animated motors.

In order to make Hirn's experiment comprehensible, let us consider the simpler case of a mechanician desiring to establish the thermal equivalent of the work of a steam engine, knowing how much fuel it has burned, what heat has been given out, and what quantity of work has been produced.

First, he will estimate the heat which should correspond

with the combustion of the coal which he has burned; he will
prove that the heat which he has obtained is less than this,
which is made evident by the disappearance of a certain
number of units; this disappearance he will attribute to the
transformation of heat into work. Now as he knows the
number of kilogrammetres produced by the machine, he will
only have to divide this number by that of the units of heat
which have disappeared, in order to find the number of
kilogrammetres equivalent to each of them.

Hirn believed that the combustion effected, the heat given
out, and the mechanical work produced by a man could be
estimated at the same time. He enclosed the subject in a
hermetically closed chamber, and made him turn a wheel
which could, at choice, revolve with or without doing work.

The air of the chamber being analysed, showed what
quantity of carbonic acid had been given out; from thence
were deduced the combustion produced and the number of
units of heat to which that combustion ought to have corresponded.

The heat given out in the chamber was ascertained by the
ordinary calorimetric processes; it was, in proportion to the
work produced, sensibly inferior to that which ought to
have been found according to the quantity of carbonic acid
exhaled.

This disappearance of a certain number of units of heat
was explained by their transformation into mechanical work.

From these experiments Hirn deduced a valuation of the
mechanical equivalent of heat for animated motors; but the
number which he obtained differed considerably from that
which has been established by physicists. This difference is in
no wise surprising when we think of all the causes of error
which are united in such an experiment. There may have been
an error concerning the quantity of carbonic acid exhaled; an
error concerning the nature of the chemical actions which
disengaged this carbonic acid, and therefore respecting the
quantity of heat which ought to have accompanied the disengagement; an error in the estimation of the heat diffused
through the calorimetric chamber; finally, an error as to the
quantity of mechanical work produced by the subject. In

fact, while it is relatively easy to estimate the work of our muscles when employed in lifting a burden, there are other muscular actions which constitute an important sum of work and which we do not yet know how to value with precision; we allude to the movements of the circulation, and especially to those produced by the breathing apparatus.

The remarks which we have made upon the greater number of the physiological experiments from which it has been sought to establish numerical data, apply to that of Hirn. But though it cannot furnish an exact determination, this experiment at least enables us to perceive the manner in which the phenomena vary; it shows that a certain quantity of heat always disappears from the organism when external work is produced. No greater precision could be obtained in the measure of thermo-dynamic transformation in the greater number of steam-engines, and yet nobody disputes that in these motors heat and work are substituted for one another in equivalent relations.

CHAPTER III.

ON ANIMAL HEAT.

Origin of animal heat—Lavoisier's theory—The perfecting of this theory —Estimates of the forces contained in aliments, and in the secreted products—Difficulty of these estimates—The force yielded by alimentary substances is transformed partly into heat and partly into work—Seat of combustion in the organism—Heating of the glands and muscles during their functions—Seat of calorification—Intervention of the causes of cooling—Animal temperature—Automatic regulator of animal temperature.

DURING a long period, animal heat was considered to be of a peculiar kind, distinct from that which is manifested in the inorganic kingdom; this arose from certain conditions under which the living tissues become hot or cold, without its being easy to discover how this heat appears, or how it disappears. It was almost natural to admit that heat is

connected with influences of nervous origin, when it was
seen that certain violent emotions produce icy coldness in
human beings, whereas others bring into the countenance
sudden heat. Now all these facts have found an explanation
in which there is nothing to infringe the ordinary laws of
physics. In order to comprehend them thoroughly we must
pass under our review the production of heat and its distribution throughout the various parts of the organism.

It has long since been established that aliment is indispensable in the living being for the production of heat, as well
as of muscular power. Inanition, at the same time that it
reduces the strength of the animal, produces profound cold
in it. We owe to the genius of Lavoisier the comparison
of the living organism to a grate which burns or incessantly
oxidises substances taken from without, by borrowing from
the atmosphere the oxygen requisite for these transformations. This theory has triumphed over all the attacks which
have been made upon it, and their only result has been the
perfecting of its details.

Let us reduce to its true proportions the comparison of the
living organism with a burning grate. In both, an oxidable
matter finds itself placed in relation with oxygen; but while,
in a grate, the natural gas comes in contact with the combustible previously raised to .an elevated temperature, in the
organism the gas dissolved in the blood comes in contact with
materials which are themselves dissolved in that liquid, or
which have deeply entered into the tissue of the organs.
Thus, the circulation transports into every part of the
organism the elements which are necessary to the disengagement of force. These bodies remain in contact, without acting
one upon the other, until the moment arrives when a specific
action brings about their combination. This office, analogous
to that of the spark which kindles the flame, or to that of
the cap which discharges gunpowder, belongs to the nervous
system.

When the oxidation is at an end, and the forces necessary
to the functions have been set at liberty, there remain in the
tissues certain products which have become useless, and which
may be compared to the ashes in the grate and to the gases

which go up the chimney. These products must be eliminated. Again, the circulation undertakes this office; the blood dissolves the carbonic acid and the salts which are the ultimate products of organic oxidation, and then carries them, in its perpetual course, to the eliminating organs, the lungs and the glands.

So long as it remained unsuspected that heat and mechanical work could be substituted for each other, an attempt was made to account for all the combustions which take place in the living organism, by estimating the quantity of heat discharged by an animal in a given time. Physicists and physiologists made great efforts to determine this illusory equality between the theoretical heat, which corresponded with the combustions which take place in the organism, and the quantity of heat furnished by the animal under experiment.

Just as a machine, when it is working, furnishes less heat to the calorimeter than would be given out by a simple grate consuming the same quantity of combustible matter, so the living being gives out less heat in proportion as it executes more mechanical work. We have seen, by Hirn's experiments, that it is solely according to the difference which exists between the heat experimentally obtained and that theoretically estimated, that we now endeavour to find the value of the equivalent of mechanical work in living beings.

Whatever may be the varied manifestations of force in the organism, a certain portion of that force always appears under the form of heat, and this it is which gives to animals a higher temperature than that of the medium in which they live.

May we not, by ascertaining the temperature of the different parts of the body of the animal, discover the points at which heat is formed, and define the actual seat of those combustions of which we establish only the distant results?

It is now demonstrated that the lungs, by which the oxygen of the air penetrates into the organism, are not the seat of combustion, because the blood which comes out of that organ is, in general, colder than that which has gone into it. If two thermometers or thermometrical needles be introduced

into the heart of an animal, in order to ascertain the temperature of the blood which is returning through all the veins
of the body into the right cavities, and that of the blood which
is coming into the left cavities from the lungs, we find that
the blood of the right-hand side of the heart is the warmer;
so that it follows that heat is principally produced along the
course of the great circulation.

If we would more particularly localize the origin of heat,
we must take a special organ and investigate, in a comparative manner, the temperature of the blood which comes
to it through the arteries, and goes out of it through the
veins.   Thus it has been recognized that the muscles, in
action, and the glands while they are secreting, are organs
for the production of heat; and in them the most energetic
chemical action takes place.

But we must not expect, when examining all the muscles or
all the glands at the moment of their action, to find an un-
varying elevation in the temperature of their venous blood.
A third element enters into the problem; it is the loss of
heat which takes place while the blood is passing through the
organ.   Now, all portions of the body are not equally subjected to loss of heat; the most superficial are the most
exposed to them, while the deeper organs are sheltered
against the causes of cold.*   Under these conditions every disengagement of heat in the glands ought to be represented by
an elevation of temperature in the venous blood.   If, on the
contrary, we lay the sublingual gland bare, in cold weather,
and investigate the temperature of the blood in the veins of
that gland, we shall find the blood colder than that which
has entered through the arteries.   Must we conclude from
thence that there has been no disengagement of heat in that
gland?   In no wise.   We must simply admit that the loss
of heat has exceeded its production. ·

In short, heat appears to be produced in all the organs,
but in various degrees, according to the intensity of the

* When we wish to ascertain the increase of temperature of the blood
in the glands, we must choose, for this investigation, the blood of the
veins of the liver or the kidneys, organs sheltered from cooling influences.

chemical action which takes place in them. The temperature
of an organ necessarily results from the heat supplied to it
by the blood, from that which has been produced in its
interior, and from that which it has lost. Thus it is that
certain veins, those of the limbs, for example, bring back
blood colder than that of the corresponding arteries; whilst
others, like the sub-hepatic veins which leave the liver, bring
back blood warmer than that which has entered the hepatic
gland. In fact, after all compensations are made, the heated
venous blood predominates in the living organism over the
cooled blood; so that it re-enters the heart $1\frac{1}{4}°$ warmer than
when it came out of it.

This leads us to study the question of the *temperature of
animals*.

Among the different animal species, some, while producing
heat, are subject to the variations of the surrounding temperature, so that they have been called *cold blooded*. They are
now called animals of variable temperature, which is more
exact. As for the animals called *warm blooded*, they possess
the singular property of having the blood in the deeper
portions of their bodies almost always at the same temperature, notwithstanding the variations of the external heat.
Thus, a man, sailing from the polar regions to the equator,
may be subject, in a few weeks, to changes of 30° in the
surrounding temperature, but his blood remains at about
38°.

It is easy to understand that in the midst of incessant
variations in the production of heat inside the organism,
and of the no less great variations in the causes of its
waste, such uniformity can only be obtained by means of a
regulator of the temperature. We shall now proceed to certain
developments of the wonderful functions of the regulator of
the animal temperature.

Human industry has often found it difficult to provide fixed
temperatures, or at least to counterbalance the causes of ex-
cessive heat and cold. A hot-house must neither fall below,
nor rise above a certain temperature. But this problem is
relatively a simple one; the hot-house is always warmer
than the external air; it can only be subjected to more or less

intense causes of cooling, which may be compensated by a
suitable variation of heat. Bunsen's regulator solves this
problem satisfactorily, by regulating the supply of gas which
serves as a combustible, augmenting it if the inclosed air
tends to grow cold, diminishing it in the opposite case.

In the animal economy, two orders of influences tend incessantly to cause variation of temperature in its production
and in its expenditure. Causes of loss of temperature exist,
as in the instance just mentioned. The temperature of the
surrounding air, against which our clothing protects us more
or less efficiently, on the one hand, and the more or less
easy evaporation by means of cutaneous perspiration, according to the hygrometrical state of the atmosphere on the
other; the action of the wind, or of air-currents; the temperature of the baths which we take, all these different
causes tend to increase or diminish the waste of heat to
which the body is subject. To these influences must be added
those of the hot or cold food which we eat; of the hot or
cold air introduced into our lungs by respiration, &c. All
these constitute in general the causes of loss of heat.

Another variable element in the establishment of the
animal temperature is the production of heat which takes
place in the interior of the organism, and which, as well as
its loss, varies under numerous influences. The aliments of
which we partake, act, through their nature and quantity, on
this production of internal heat; the activity of the glands
causes a discharge of caloric; and the case is the same with
respect to muscular action, which cannot be produced without
the heating of the muscle.

It is true that within certain limits our senses warn us to
restrict the production of heat, or to promote it, according as
external influences diminish or augment its waste. Thus,
the amount of food taken varies with climate, so that the en-
forced sobriety of the dweller in hot countries has no *raison
d'être* in cold ones. Obligatory idleness during the heat
of the day under a burning sky is one manner of diminishing
the production of heat; the Northmen, on the contrary, endeavour to compensate, by muscular activity, for the cold to
which they are subjected.

But these are not the true regulators of the animal temperature. Our will commands all those actions whose influence may be favourable to the regulation of our temperature; but, in general, Nature, in order to secure the indispensable functions of life, removes them from the control of our will. It is in an *automatic* apparatus that we shall find the real regulator of temperature.

This apparatus must obey external and internal influences at the same time, it must retain heat when it tends to be dissipated too rapidly, and, on the other hand, it must facilitate its decrease when it is produced too abundantly within the organism.

This double end is achieved by a property of the circulatory system: the blood vessels, animated by nerves whose action has been revealed by M. Cl. Bernard, close under the influence of cold, and open under the effect of heat. This property regulates the course of the blood in each of the organs, and at the same time the temperature throughout the entire economy.

Let us take an animal which has just been killed; the circulation of the blood is stopped, and with it all the functions. This animal, if placed in a low temperature, becomes cold. According to physical laws, the extremities of the limbs and the surface of the body will lose heat in the first instance, while the central portions will still remain very hot, being sheltered by the more superficial layers against the causes of loss of heat. This corpse will resemble an inert body which has been heated, and is growing cold. The circulation of the blood opposes itself, during life, to the unequal partition of heat over the various points of the organism; bringing the arterial blood, at a temperature of nearly 38° (centigrade), to the superficial portions, it warms them when the external temperature tends to chill them. On the other hand, if, in the living animal, the production of heat has been augmented, the circulation opposes the indefinite heating of the central regions of the body; it brings that heat to the surface, where it is lost in contact with the external colder medium.

The effect of the circulation of the blood is therefore to

render the temperature of the organism uniform. But this
uniformity is never complete; in fact, except in the case of the
animal's being in a vapour bath at 38°, and losing none of
its heat, the surface of the body is always colder than the
interior, but no ill effect is produced by the chill, which does
not act upon the essential organs.

If the circulation of the blood were of equal swiftness in every
part, such a uniformity would not result in the preservation of
the uniform temperature necessary for the internal regions of
the body; we should then merely see it exposed to more general
elevations and depressions of temperature, according to the respective predominance of causes of heat or the loss of it. To
produce uniformity of central heat it is indispensable that some
influence should augment the rapidity of the circulation
each time that the organism produces more heat, or that the
elevation of the surrounding temperature diminishes the causes
of cooling. Circulation in the superficial portions of the body
is extremely variable, as we may ascertain by observing the
varying aspects of those portions, which are sometimes red,
hot, and swollen, sometimes pale, cold, and shrunken, according to the more or less abundance of the blood which circulates in them. This variability depends upon the contraction
or the relaxation of the little arteries, whose muscular sheaths
obey special nerves. When, under the influence of these nerves,
named vaso-motors, the vessels contract, circulation slackens,
while by a contrary action, the relaxation of the vessels ac-
celerates the course of the blood. Now, it is the temperature itself which most generally acts in regulating this state
of contraction or relaxation of the vessels, so that the animal
temperature possesses in reality an *automatic regulator*.

Every one has observed the influence of heat and cold on
the circulation in the skin. If we dip one hand in hot, and
the other in cold water, the first will grow red and the second
pale; heat has, therefore, the effect of relaxing, and cold of
contracting the vessels. In other words, according to what we
have already seen, heat, by its action upon the circulation,
favours the loss of heat; while cold acts in an inverse sense,
and tends to diminish the intensity of the chilling process.
And it is not only under the influence of the variations of the

external temperature that these effects are produced; they are equally observed when the animal heat varies in its production. The heating of the organism which accompanies muscular activity, or which results from taking very hot drinks, produces the acceleration in the superficial circulation, which throws out this excess of heat to the surface. Inanition, muscular repose, the drinking of iced waters, &c., slacken the circulation near the surface and check its cooling action.

Such are, as far as we can explain them in a short chapter, the origin and the distribution of heat in the animal organism. The part played by the circulation of the blood in the distribution of heat, perhaps demands more ample details; and, indeed, we have treated it more fully elsewhere.* In the present chapter we have studied heat only as manifestation of force, and have merely designed to show that, notwithstanding all appearances, heat is of the same nature in the inorganic world and in organised beings.

CHAPTER IV.

ANIMAL MOTION.

Motion is the most apparent characteristic of life; it acts on solids, liquids, and gases—Distinction between the motions of organic and animal life—We shall treat of animal motion only—Structure of the muscles—Undulating appearance of the still living fibre—Muscular wave—Concussion and myography—Multiplicity of acts of contraction—Intensity of contraction in its relations to the frequency of muscular shocks—Characteristics of fibre at different points of the body.

MOTION is the most apparent of the characteristics of life; it manifests itself in all the functions; it is even the essence of several of them. It would occupy much space to explain the

---

* *Physiologie médicale de la Circulation du Sang.* Paris, 1863; and *Théorie physiologique du Choléra, Gazette Hebdomadaire de Médecine.* 1867.

mechanism by which the blood circulates in the vessels, how
air penetrates into the lungs, and escapes from them alternately, how the intestines and the glands are perpetually
affected by slow and prolonged contractions. All these movements take place within the organs without the exercise of the
will; frequently even the individual in whom they occur is
unconscious of them; these are the acts of *organic life*.

Other movements are subjected to our will, which regulates
their speed, energy, and duration; these are the muscular
actions of locomotion, and the different acts of *the life of relation*. We shall treat specially of this order of phenomena,
which are more easy to observe, and to analyse. Suffice it
here to say that the absolute division between the acts of
organic life and those of the life of relation ought not to be
accepted unreservedly. Bichat, who established it, based it
upon anatomical and functional differences which are of less
importance now than they were in his time. The muscular element of organic life is unstriped fibre obedient to the
nerves of a particular system called the *great sympathetic*,
on which the will has no action; motions produced by this
kind of fibre are manifested some time after the excitement of
the nerve or of the muscle, and continue for a considerable
time. In fact, the object of those acts which are intended to
maintain the life of the individual imprints upon them a
special character. The muscular element of the life of relation consists of a fibre of striated appearance, whose action,
under the control of the will, is dependent upon nerves
emanating directly from the brain or from the spinal marrow.
These movements become evident rapidly as soon as they are
provoked by excitement; they are of brief duration, and are,
generally, not indispensable to the maintenance of the life of
the animal.

Although this distinction is, in a general way exact, it is
plain that it is too arbitrary, and that numerous exceptions
to the anatomical and physiological laws which it tends to
establish may be quoted. Thus, the heart, an organ directly
indispensable to organic life, and not under the governance of
the will, is a structure which much resembles the voluntary
muscles. Certain fishes of the genus *tinca* have striated muscles

in the large intestine, as Ed. Weber has pointed out. Very often, on the other hand, the will has no power over certain muscles which, by their structure, and by the nature of the nerves which animate them, belong to the system of the life of relation. Habit, besides, by repeated exercise, appears to extend the action of the will over the muscles, almost indefinitely. The young animal shows, by the awkwardness of his movements, that he is not in full possession of his muscular functions; he seems to have to study the simplest acts, and performs them badly; while the gymnast, or the skilled piano forte-player executes prodigies of agility, strength, or precision, without any apparent effort of the will proportionate to the result obtained. Many physiologists think, and we are of the same opinion, that there exist in the brain, and in the spinal marrow, centres of nervous action which acquire certain powers, by force of habit. They attain to the command and co-ordination of certain groups of movements without the complete participation of that portion of the brain which presides over reasoning and the consciousness of our actions.

Let us lay aside these questions, which are still under investigation, and examine into the production of motion in a voluntary muscle. The organ which generates motion is composed of several elements. Simple as it is supposed to be, it requires the intervention of muscular fibre, of the blood vessels, which unceasingly convey to it the chemical elements at whose expense the motion is to be produced, and finally, of the nerve which excites motion in the fibre.

When the physiologist desires to analyse the actions which take place in the muscles, he does not deal, in the first place, with voluntary motions, whose complexity is too great. The operator isolates a muscle, and induces motion in it, by bringing to act upon its nerve artificial excitements which he has under his control.

To give an idea of the part played by each of the elements of the motive apparatus in the production of movement, it is sufficient to operate upon the leg of a frog. By laying bare and severing the sciatic nerve, the influence of will upon the muscle may be suppressed, so that the latter will only execute

such motions as are produced by excitation, electric or
otherwise, applied to the portion of the nerve which remains
in communication with it. On the sides of the sciatic nerve
are an artery and a vein. Compression of the artery will
prevent the blood from reaching the muscle; compression of
the vein will produce stagnation of the blood. The influences
which different states of circulation produce upon the muscular
function may then be observed; and, finally, by making an
incision in the skin of the foot, the muscle will be laid bare,
and cold, heat, or the various poisonous substances by which
its action is modified, may be brought to bear directly upon it.

When the nerve of a frog thus prepared is excited by an
electric discharge, a very brief convulsive movement in the
muscle is produced; this motion is called *Zuckung* by the
German physiologists, and we propose to call it *shock*, in
order to distinguish it from true contraction. It is so rapid
that its phases cannot be distinguished by the eye, so that, to
appreciate its characteristics aright, recourse must be had to
special instruments. Registering apparatus only can supply
this need, for they faithfully render all the phases of motion
communicated to them. The general disposition of these forms
of apparatus, which for a long time were used almost exclusively
in the service of meteorology, is generally known. The
indications of the barometer, of the thermometer, of the force
or the direction of the wind, of the quantity of rainfall, &c.,
register themselves under the form of a curve which, according
as it is elevated or depressed, expresses the increase or
diminution of intensity of the phenomenon to be registered.
The time during which these variations are accomplished may
be estimated by the length occupied by the curve upon the
paper, which travels in front of the marking pen with an
ascertained and perfectly regular speed.

The use of instruments of the same kind has been introduced
into physiology by Volkmann, Ludwig, and Helmholtz. We
have endeavoured to extend the employment of them to a great
number of phenomena, and we have constructed many instruments whose description would be out of place here. The
apparatus which registers muscular motions bears the name
of *myograph*; it shows the disturbance of the muscle by

means of a curve which readily allows us to study its phases. We have fully explained elsewhere the nature of this instrument, the experiments for which it is suitable, and the results which it gives.* At present we shall limit ourselves to a summary description of the chief results of myography.

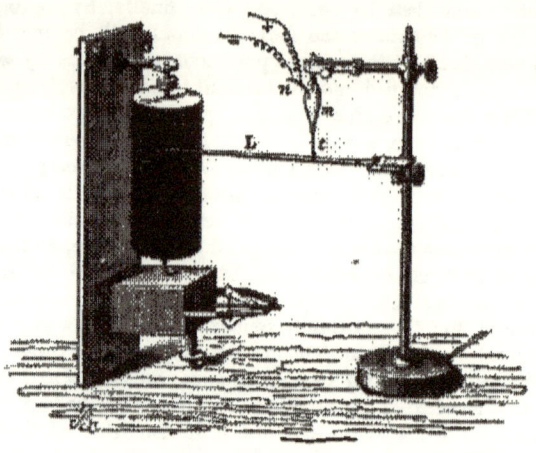

FIG. 2.—The Myograph.

In order to explain thoroughly the function of the apparatus, let us reduce it in the first place to its essential elements. Fig. 2 shows a muscle of the calf of a frog's leg, *m*, suspended by a clip by means of the bone to which the upper part of the muscle is attached. The tendon, *t*, of the muscle has been cut and then tied by a thread to the lever, L, one end of which can be raised or lowered while the other is fixed ; the nerve, *n*, is susceptible of electric excitement, which produces certain contractions followed by relaxations in the muscle, that is to say *shocks*. Each of these movements of the muscle is communicated to the lever, which is raised or lowered, ampli-

* *Du Mouvement dans les Fonctions de la Vie.* Paris, 1867 : G. Baillière.

fying at its extremity the motions which it has received. This lever, which ends in a point, traces on a turning cylinder certain curves, which, when they are raised, indicate the contraction of the muscle, and when they are lowered, show its return to its primitive length.

With the arrangement which we have made in the myograph a muscle may be operated upon without being detached from the animal, which allows of the organ being left in the normal conditions of its function.

In Fig. 3 the frog is represented in the experiment, fixed, by means of pins, on a piece of cork.

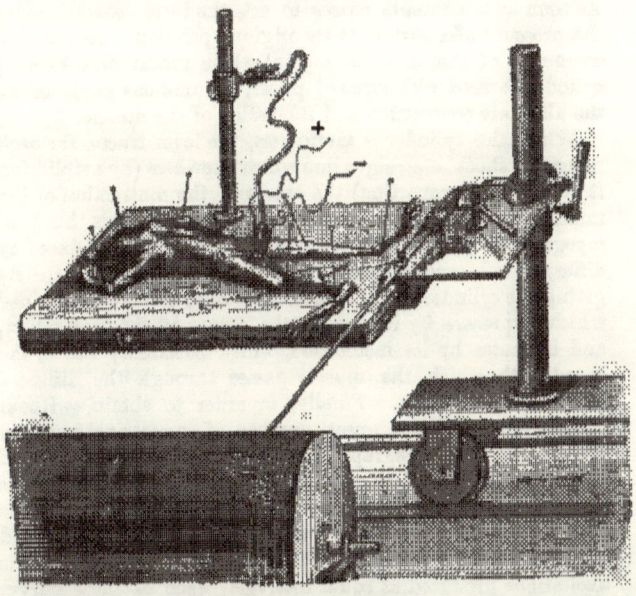

Fig. 3.—Marey's Myograph.

The brain and spinal marrow have been previously destroyed, so as to extinguish all voluntary movement and sensibility. Although, to all appearance, the animal is dead, it will nevertheless retain for several hours the circulation of the blood, and the power of motion under the influence of electric discharges. An electric excitator conveys the current from an induction coil to the nerve of the frog.

In order to register these movements and to depict them by curves which express their different phases, they are transmitted to the myograph in the manner already described. The tendon of the muscle is cut, and connected by a wire which is fastened at the other end to the lever of the registering apparatus; the latter moves in a horizontal plane, when the contractile force of the muscle is exerted upon it. As soon as the muscle ceases to act, the lever returns, under the pressure of a spring, to its original position. At the free extremity of the lever is a point which traces, on a turning cylinder covered with smoked paper, the motions produced by the alternate contraction and relaxation of the muscle.

When the cylinder is motionless, the lever traces, for each muscular shock, a straight line which expresses (by amplifying it in a known proportion) the extent of the contraction of the muscle. Several authors limit themselves to this kind of myography, by which they ascertain the variations produced by different influences in the intensity of muscular action. By giving the cylinder a rapid rotatory motion, a curve is obtained which expresses by its height the extent of the contraction, and indicates by its inclination, which constantly varies, the speed with which the muscle passes through the different phases of the shock. Finally, in order to obtain, without confounding them, a great number of successive tracings, the foot of the myograph is placed upon a little railroad which works parallel to the axis of the cylinder. The writing point then traces an indefinite spiral all round the cylinder, and on this spiral a number of regularly graduated curves (Fig. 5) are traced, answering to a series of electric excitations produced at equal intervals; each of these curves corresponds with one of the electric shocks.

If the speed with which the cylinder turns be augmented or diminished, a change ensues in the appearance of the curves, which necessarily occupy a greater or less space on the paper, but if a uniform speed in the rotation of the cylinder be maintained, the curves retain the same form so long as the muscle gives the same movements.

Not only are shocks produced in the muscle by acting upon its nerve by electricity, but also by applying electric excitement to the muscle itself. Pinching, percussion, and cauterization of the nerve are also excitants which provoke shocks of the muscle.

The character of these movements changes under certain influences. Fatigue of the muscle, the cooling of that organ, the stoppage of circulation in its interior, modify the form of the shock, diminish its force, and augment its duration. Under these influences the myographic curve passes through different forms, such as 1, 2, 3, Fig. 4.

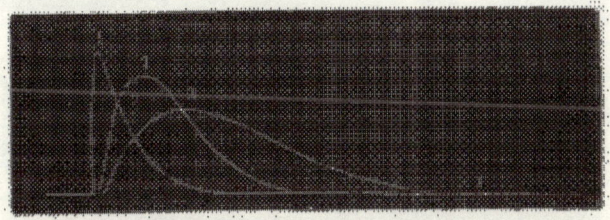

Fig. 4.—Character of the shock, according to the degree of fatigue of the muscle: 1, muscle fresh; 2, muscle a little fatigued; 3, muscle still more fatigued.

Among the different species of animals, the durations of the shock vary considerably; in the bird they are very brief (two to three hundredths of a second). In man they are longer; in the tortoise and hybernating animals longer still. Certain poisons modify the characteristics of this movement in so special a manner, that the slightest traces of those poisons introduced into the circulation of the animal may be discovered in the form of the tracings.

By Fig. 5, we may judge of the successive forms which will be assumed by the shocks of the muscle of a frog, under the influence of a gradual absorption of veratrine.

These experiments still reveal only one fact: it is that the muscle is shortened or lengthened by a movement whose

phases vary under the different influences which we have just
described.

If we endeavour to pursue the study of this phenomenon of
the contraction of the muscle, we see that it is only a change
in the form of that organ, and that the diminution of length
is accompanied by a corresponding dilatation which might
be expected in a sensibly incompressible tissue. 'But the
manner in which this dilatation is produced is curious.

Fig. 5.—Successive transformations of the shock of a muscle becoming
gradually poisoned by veratrine. Underneath to the left of the figure
are shown the first effects of the poison.

It has been long since observed that there are formed upon
living muscles at the points where they are excited, lumps or
nodosities which run along the whole length of the muscle,
with more or less rapidity, like a wave on the surface of the
water. Aeby* has shown that this is a normal phenomenon,
and, under the name of *muscular wave*, he has described this
movement, which, from the excited point, passes to the two
extremities of the muscle at the rate of about a metre in a
second. By means of an apparatus, which we have called

* *Untersuchungen uber die Fortpflanzungsgeschwindigkeit der Reizungs in
der quergestreiften Muskelfasern.* Braunschweig : 1862.

myográphical clips, the reality of this movement of the wave may be verified in the living animal.

When the wave appears in the muscle, it produces contraction. During the whole of its passage the contraction continues, and when, having reached the end of the muscular fibre, the wave vanishes, the contraction disappears with it.

These facts resemble those which the microscope reveals in living muscular fibre. Let a bundle of muscular fibres be taken from an insect, and placed under the objective of the microscope (the feet of coleoptera are well suited for this purpose); we first observe the beautiful transverse striation of these fibres, and then we perceive on their surface an undulatory movement often alternating, which resembles the motion of waves on the surface of water. On examining this phenomenon more closely, we see that the transverse striæ of the fibre are, at certain points, very close together, which is shown in the figure by a dilatation of the fibre. This is the wave shown by the microscope; the longitudinal condensation of the muscle at this point gives it greater opacity than in the other portions (Fig. 6.) This opaque wave travels

FIG. 6.—Appearance presented by a wave in muscular fibre.

through the length of the fibre. In other words, the points at which the striæ approach each other are not always the same, the longitudinal condensation disappears in one place whilst it is produced in the contiguous parts.

Since the contraction of the muscle is accompanied by its transverse dilatation, we may study the characteristics of the motion produced in a muscle, according to this expansion. We have succeeded in registering these changes in the volume of the muscle, as we have registered the changes in its length. Under these conditions we might study muscular action in man himself, because there is no need of mutilation.

Let us suppose a muscle held between the flattened ends of

a clip; at each of its dilatations the muscle will force open the clip, and this movement may be registered. This method enables us to study the phenomenon of the muscular wave, and the speed with which it travels throughout the whole length of the muscle.

Fig. 7 exhibits a bundle of muscle held at two points of its length between the myographical clips, 1 and 2. These instruments are so constructed that when their ends are pushed apart by the dilatation of the muscle, the move-

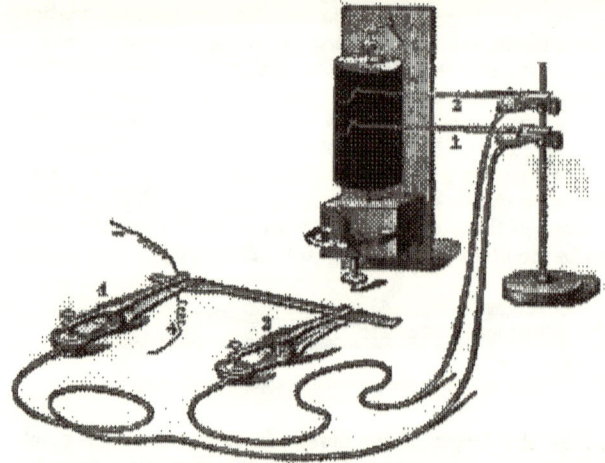

FIG. 7.—Disposition of a bundle of muscle between two pairs of myographical clips. Clip No. 1 holds the electric excitators of the muscle. A wave is represented at the moment when it has just crossed each of the clips.

ment compresses a sort of little drum which sends a portion of the air which it contained through an india-rubber tube into a similar little drum. Fig. 7 shows two of these instruments fixed upon a foot. The expansion of the membrane lifts a registering lever, and thus gives notice of the dilatation of the muscle at the point where it is compressed by clip No. 1. The movement is shown upon the tracing by a curve analogous to those which we have already seen.

Let us suppose that the muscle is electrically excited at the level of the first clip; notice is given of the formation of the wave at that part of the muscle, but clip No. 2 does not yet give its signal. In order that it may act, the wave, as it passes along the muscle, must reach it. As this occurs, clip No. 2 gives the signal in its turn, and it is shown by the tracing, that this second movement is later than the first by a certain space whose duration may be estimated according to the speed of the rotation of the cylinder.

The influences which modify the intensity and the duration of the muscular shock have appeared to us to modify the intensity and the speed of the propagation of the wave. Thus the two lower curves represented in Fig. 8 show that the transference of the wave is retarded by cold.

Fig. 8.—Two determinations of the speed of the muscular wave.

The experiment has been made upon the muscles of the thigh of a rabbit. The clips were placed as far as possible apart, about seven centimetres. Electricity was applied to *the lower extremity of the muscle*, and the two upper curves of Fig. 8 were obtained. The interval which divides those curves marks the duration of the transference of the muscular wave. After the muscle had been chilled with ice the curves at the bottom of the figure were obtained. We see that the transference of the wave is slackened, for there is a longer interval between these curves than between the first.

Production of mechanical force in the muscle.—We have seen that chemical action is the source of muscular force; through

what media does this force pass before it becomes mechanical
work?

In steam engines, heat is the necessary medium between
the oxidation of the fuel and the developed mechanical work.

It is very probable that the same
thing takes place in the muscles.
The chemical action produced by
the nerve within the fibre of the
muscle disengages heat from it :
this heat in its turn is itself
partially transformed into work.
We say partially, since according to the second principle of
thermo-dynamics, heat cannot be
entirely transformed into mechanical work.

Certain facts seem to justify
these views : thus, by warming
a muscle, we change the form of
it, and may see it contract in
length as it expands in breadth.
These effects disappear when the
muscle is cooled.

Muscular fibre is not singular
in its power of transforming heat
into work. India-rubber, for instance, has an analogous property,
and this substance may be made
to imitate the muscular phenomena to a certain degree. If
we take a strip of india-rubber
(not vulcanised), and, drawing it
between the fingers, stretch it out
to ten or fifteen times its original
length, we see that it becomes

Fig. 9.—Transformation of heat into
work by a strip of india-rubber.

white, and of a pearly lustre. At the same time the strip
will become sensibly warm, and it will tend energetically to
return to its original condition, so that if we let go either of
its ends, it will instantly resume its former length, and fall to

its original temperature. According to our view, the sensible
heat has disappeared and become mechanical work. If we
plunge the strip when extended into water, so as to deprive it
of its heat, it remains, as it were, congealed in its extended
state, and does not develop any mechanical work. But if we
restore to the elongated strip the heat which it had lost, it
will recover its elasticity with considerable force. Fig. 9
represents a strip of india-rubber thus pulled out and cooled.
It has been laden with a weight that it may have no tendency
to recover itself. But, if we take the strip between our fingers,
we feel it swell and shorten at the same time that it lifts the
weight; there is again production of mechanical work.

If we thus heat the strip at various points we create a
series of lateral expansions, each of which raises a certain
quantity of the weight. Lastly, if we heat it throughout all
its extent, the strip returns to its original dimensions, with
the exception of the slight elongation produced by the suspended weight.

Strong analogies exist between these phenomena, and
those which take place in muscular tissue. The identity would
be perfect if the wave which heat produces on the strip of
india-rubber were transmitted to each end. This transference
implies, in the muscular fibre, the successive propagation
of the chemical action which disengages the heat. It is thus
that if we light a train of powder at one point, the in-
candescence spreads throughout its entire length.

These analogies have struck us as being remarkable: they
seem to us to open new views of the origin of muscular
action.

CHAPTER V.

CONTRACTION AND WORK OF THE MUSCLES.

The function of the nerve—Rapidity of the nervous agent—Measures of time in physiology—Tetanus and muscular contraction—Theory of contraction—Work of the muscles.

, THE experiments described in the preceding chapter show us the muscle under artificial conditions, which may, perhaps, induce us to suspect the results which they furnish. Can this electrical agent, which has been employed to excite motion, be assimilated to the unknown agent which the will sends through the nerves to command the muscles to act? And these artificially-produced movements, those brief shocks, always similar if the conditions of the muscle be not changed, in what do they resemble the motions commanded by the will, which are so varied in their form and their duration? These objections deserve at least a brief discussion.

The function of the nerve. When a nerve is excited by an electric discharge, the electricity employed does not always pass to the muscle in which the reaction takes place. The shock is produced equally well when all propagation of the electric current along the nerve is prevented, and it exhibits itself equally when excitants of a quite different nature are employed, for instance, pinching or percussion. Thus, the excitant employed only excites in the nerve the transference of the agent which is proper to that organ. Is not this nervous agent itself electricity? Notwithstanding the able labours of the German physiologists, and especially of M. Du Bois Reymond, science has not yet decided on that subject. We know that electric phenomena are produced in the nerve when it has been excited in a certain way, and that their propagation throughout the nervous cord seems to have precisely the same speed as that of the transference of the nervous energy itself. How has this speed been measured?

Helmholtz had the boldness to undertake this measurement, and, by determining the speed of the nervous agent, he has furnished physiologists with a method which enables them to measure the duration of other phenomena connected with the nervous or muscular functions. Thus the experiment described above, in which we have measured the speed of the transference of the wave in a muscle, is only an application of the method of Helmholtz.

In order to make the conditions of this experiment thoroughly comprehensible, let us make use of a comparison. Let us suppose that a letter is despatched from Paris to go to Marseilles, and that, being resident in the latter town, we should be informed of the precise instant at which the postal train leaves Paris, while we have nothing to warn us of its arrival at Marseilles except the knowledge of the moment at which the letter is delivered there. How can we, according to these data, estimate the speed of the mail train? It is clear that the instant at which we receive the letter does not indicate that of the arrival of the train; for between that arrival and the distribution, many preliminaries take place, the sorting of letters, delivery, &c., which require a certain time not within our knowledge. In order to have an exact idea of the speed of the train which carries the mail, we must receive a signal of the passage of that train through an intermediate station between Paris and Marseilles, Dijon, for instance; then we shall see that the distribution of letters takes place six hours sooner after the departure from Dijon than after the departure from Paris. Knowing the distance which separates these two stations, we may ascertain from the time employed in traversing it, the speed of the train. By supposing this speed to be uniform, we shall know the hour at which the train will have arrived at Marseilles, which will give us knowledge of the time consumed in the sorting and distribution of the letters.

Helmholtz, in experimenting upon the nervous motive agent, first excited the nerve at a point very distant from the muscle, and noted the time which elapsed between the excitement which despatched the message carried by the nerve, and the appearance of motion in the muscle. Then acting on a point of the nerve very near to the muscle, he ascertained that under these new conditions the motion followed the excitement more closely.   The difference of time which he observed in these two consecutive experiments measured the duration of the transference of the nervous agent along the known length of the nerve, and consequently expressed its speed, which varied from 15 to 30 metres per second. It is feebler in the frog than in warm-blooded animals.

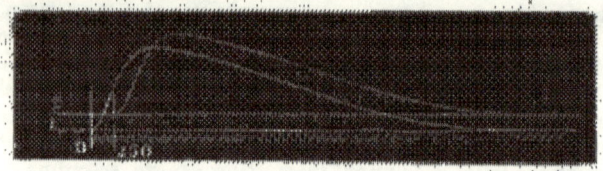

Fig. 10.—Determination of the speed of the nervous agent in man.   1. Shock produced when the nerve has been excited very close to the muscle. 2. Shock produced by the excitement of the nerve at a farther distance of 30 centimetres. D, Vibration of a chronographic tuning-fork vibrating 250 times in a second, serving to measure the time which corresponds with the interval of the shocks.

Now, it results from the experiments of Helmholtz, that all the time which elapses between the excitement and the motion is not occupied by the transference of the nervous agent; but that the muscle, when it has received the order carried by the nerve, remains an instant before acting.   This is what Helmholtz calls *lost time*.   This time would correspond, in the comparison which we have employed above, with the duration of the preparatory labour between the arrival of the letters and their distribution.

Physiologists have repeated the experiment of Helmholtz with some improvements.   In fig. 10 tracings may be seen which we have ourselves obtained while measuring the speed of the nervous agent.

Two muscular shocks are successively registered upon the same cylinder, care being taken that the nerve shall be excited in the two experiments, at different points, but at the same instant with regard to the rotation of the cylinder; for example, at the precise moment at which the point of the *myograph* passes over the vertical which corresponds with the origin of the lines 1 and 2.

In the experiment which regulated the shock of line 1, the nerve was excited very near the muscle. In that which was traced by the shock of line 2, the nerve was excited 30 centimetres farther off. As the cylinder turns with a uniform motion we can estimate the time corresponding with the distance which separates the two shocks. To facilitate the measurement of this interval, the vertical lines indicate the starting points of these shocks; in fig. 10 the interval which separates them corresponds with a hundredth of a second, during which the nervous agent has passed over 30 centimetres of nerve, which corresponds with a speed of 30 metres per second. In order to measure this time with very great exactitude, we use a method invented by Duhamel. It consists in making the cylinder trace the vibrations of a chronographic tuning-fork provided for this purpose with a very fine style, which scratches on the sensitive paper. We have recourse to this method in all our experiments.

Let us return to fig. 10. If the interval which divides the starting points of the two shocks corresponds with the time which the nervous agent has taken to pass along 30 centimetres of nerves, there is a much more considerable time, which, for each of the lines 1 and 2, is measured between the signal of the excitement marked by the first of the three vertical lines and the first shock. This is the *lost time* of Helmholtz; it represents more than a hundredth of a second in this experiment.

The greater number of authors think that the speed of the nervous agent varies under certain influences; that heat augments it, while cold and fatigue diminish it.

It seems to us, on the contrary, that this variability of duration belongs almost exclusively to those still unknown phenomena which are produced in the muscle during the *lost time* of Helmholtz.

Just as the *employés* of the post, fatigued or chilled by cold, cause delay in the distribution of despatches, without there having been any change in the speed of the train which has brought them, so the muscle, according to whether it is rested or fatigued, heated or chilled, executes more or less rapidly the movement dictated by the nerve.

Besides this, all the influences which cause variation in the moment at which the shock of the muscle appears, cause variation of speed in the propagation of the wave in its interior; which proves that the conditions which accelerate or retard chemical actions, the first causes of all these phenomena, are solely concerned.

Of the contraction of the muscle. Hitherto, we have applied to the nerve only one single excitation, to which one single motion responded, the *muscular shock.* Notwithstanding its brevity, this shock has an appreciable duration; in man it takes 8 or 10 hundredths of a second for the muscle to accomplish its contraction; then a longer time for it to resume its normal length; after which, if it receives a new order from a nerve, it gives a fresh shock. But if the excitations of the nerve succeed each other at such short intervals that the muscle has not time to accomplish the first shock before it receives a second, a special phenomenon is produced; these movements are confounded and absorbed into a state of permanent contraction, which lasts as long as the excitations go on succeeding each other at short intervals.

Thus the shock is only the elementary act in the function of the muscle; it plays therein, after a fashion, the same part as a sonorous vibration plays in the complex phenomenon which constitutes sound. When the will ordains a muscular contraction, the nerve excites in the muscle a series of shocks which follow one another so closely that the first has not time to end before a second begins, so that these elementary movements combine together and coalesce to produce the contraction.

Volta pointed out, in a letter to Aldini, this singular fact, that a frog which receives a series of excitations, by the reiterated contacts of two heterogeneous metals applied to his nerve, does not react at each of these contacts, but undergoes a sort of permanent contraction. Ed. Weber shows that the action of successive induced currents is of the same kind, and he has given the name of *tetanus* to the state of the muscle thus excited. Helmholtz perceived that the muscle vibrates in the depths of its tissue under these conditions of contraction, because the ear applied to this muscle hears a sound whose acuteness is exactly determined by the number of the electric excitations sent to the muscle in a second.

By means of a very sensitive myograph, we have been able to render visible the vibrations of the muscles under the influence of tetanus-producing shocks.

Fig. 11 shows how this fusion of shocks is manifested by a contraction of the muscle, permanent in appearance, but in which the tracing reveals vestiges of vibrations. Vibrations may be found in the tetanus which strychnine produces in the muscles of an animal, as well as in that which is caused by the irritation of a nerve by heat and chemical agents.

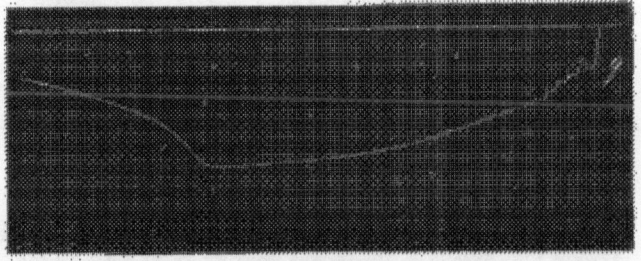

Fio. 11.—Gradual coalescence of the shocks produced by electric excitations of increasing frequency.

In short, these voluntary contractions seem to be only a series of shocks, combining together by the rapidity of their succession.

It has long been known that by applying the ear to a muscle in a state of voluntary contraction, we can hear a grave sound, whose tone several authors have sought to determine. Wollaston, Houghton, and Dr. Collongue are almost agreed upon this tone, which would correspond to a frequency of 32 or 35 vibrations per second. Helmholtz thinks that this tone of 32 vibrations per second is the normal sound given out by the muscle in contraction, and according to his experiments in electric tetanization, he regards this number as the minimum necessary to produce the state of apparent immobility of the electrically tetanised muscle.

If voluntary contraction, studied with the aid of the myograph, furnishes no trace of vibrations, we must not be surprised, since the essential character of that act consists in the coalescence of shocks. But the existence of the sound which accompanies the contraction of the muscle sufficiently proves the complexity of this phenomenon. Let us add another proof in favour of this theory. When a muscle receives excitations of equal intensity, the contraction which results from them is all the stronger in proportion to their frequency. Now, in contracting the muscles of the jaws with more or less force, we have been able to convince ourselves' that the acuteness of the muscular sound increased with the energy of the effort. We may thus obtain variations of a *fifth* in the tone of the muscular sound.

We shall also see hereafter how the electric state of the muscles in contraction proves still more the complexity of this phenomenon.

The conclusion at which we have arrived is, that during voluntary contraction, the motor nerves are the seat of successive acts, each of which produces an excitation of the muscle. The latter, in its turn, causes a series of acts, each of which gives birth to a muscular wave producing a shock. It is in the *elasticity* of the muscle that we must seek for the cause of the coalescence of these multiplied shocks; they are extinguished just as the jerks of the piston of a fire-engine disappear in the elasticity of its reservoir of air.

Of work done by the muscles. After having seen how mechanical force is produced, let us try to measure it—that is to say, to compare it with the kilogrammetre, the unit of measure of work. If we suspend a weight to the tendon of a muscle which we cause to contract, we easily obtain the measure of work by multiplying this weight by the height to which the muscle raises it.

In animated motors, the measure of work is less easy to obtain. Sometimes, indeed, the strength of an animal is utilized in the lifting of a weight, but the greater part of the acts in which the strength of animals is employed can only be estimated by enlarging the definition of mechanical work. Thus, a horse which tows a boat, a man who planes a board, a bird which strikes the air with its wing, does mechanical work, and yet they do not lift weights. In order to reduce cases of this kind to a general definition, we must admit as the expression of work, *the effort multiplied by the space traversed.* This effort, besides, may always be compared with the weight, the lifting of which would necessitate an equal effort, so that we say of a traction or an impulse, that it corresponds with 10 or 20 kilogrammes. When a workman planes or turns a piece of metal, if the tool which he drives into it penetrates only on condition of receiving an impulse of one kilogramme, the workman, in order to have effected a kilogrammetre of work, ought to have detached from the mass a shaving of a metre in length. A horse which tows a boat with 20 kilogramme force, will have employed a force of 20,000 kilogrammetres when he has gone 1,000 metres.

But still that is not yet sufficient to be applied to all the forms of mechanical labour. If, for example, force be employed to displace a mass, the effort necessary for the movement will vary with the speed which is given to that mass. Let us imagine a block of stone suspended freely at the end of a very long rope; the lightest pressure applied to this block for a few instants will produce movement in it, while the strongest blow of the fist will scarcely cause any sensible displacement, because the force requisite to displace masses increases according to the square of the speed which is communicated to them.*

A force of very short duration applied to a mass, produces only a shock incapable of displacing it. But this same shock, if it be exerted by means of an elastic medium, is transformed into an act of longer duration, and without having added anything to the quantity of motion, becomes capable of producing work.

This elasticity intervenes in the animal economy to permit the utilization of the very brief act which constitutes the formation of the muscular wave. The formation of the wave,

* This action is expressed by $\frac{m\,v^2}{2}$.

which lasts only for some hundredths of a second, represents
the time of application of each element of the force of the
muscle. At each new wave, there would be produced a true
shock if the elasticity of the fibre did not extinguish this
abruptness, and transform these jerky little contractions into a
gradual increase of tension which constitutes the prolonged
effort of the muscle.

A motor only works on the double condition of developing
an effort, and accomplishing a motion. Thus a muscle which
contracts, performs no external work, except while it is contracting; as soon as it has reached the limit of its contraction,
it ceases to work, whatever may be the effort which it
develops. When we sustain a weight after having lifted it,
the act of sustainment does not constitute work.

But, in these conditions, to maintain the elastic force of the
muscle, the same acts are produced in its interior as during
the work; the muscular waves succeed each other at short
intervals, and heat is disengaged by chemical action. Now,
this heat, which cannot transform itself into action, ought
to remain in the muscle, and heat it strongly. This is precisely what we observe, so that in the malady called tetanus,
which consists of a permanent tension of the muscles, it
is ascertained that heat is produced with an exaggerated
intensity, the temperature of the entire body rising several
degrees.

CHAPTER VI.

OF ELECTRICITY IN ANIMALS.

Electricity is produced in almost all organised tissues—Electric currents
of the muscles and the nerves—Discharges of electric fishes; old
theories; demonstration of the electric nature of this phenomenon—
Analogies between the discharge of electrical apparatus and the shock
of a muscle—Electric tetanus—Rapidity of the nervous agent in the
electrical nerves of the torpedo; duration of its discharge.

MOST of the animal or vegetable tissues are the seat of
chemical actions, whence result an incessant disengagement
of electricity. In this way, the nerves and muscles of an

animal furnish manifestations of dynamic electricity. Matteucci has discovered the manner in which the muscular
current is usually produced. Du Bois Reymond has added
much to our knowledge of this current, of its intensity, and
of its direction in every part of a muscle. Treatises on physiology give copious details of experiments relative to nervous
and muscular electric currents. This study has been the
more eagerly pursued because the proximate cause of the
function of the nerves and muscles was expected to be found
in these electric phenomena.

The most interesting fact connected with muscular electricity, with respect to the transformation of force, appears to
be the disappearance of the electrical state of a muscle at the
moment when it contracts, or when it is tetanized. It appears
then that the chemical actions of which the muscles are the
seat, are entirely employed in the production of heat and
motion.

To observe these phenomena, we must make use of a very
sensitive galvanometer. Suppose a muscle connected with one
of these instruments; it gives its currents, and deflects the
magnetic needle a certain number of degrees. When this deviation has been effected, and the needle has become stationary
in its new position, it is only necessary to produce tetanus in
the muscle, and immediately the needle retrogrades towards
zero. This is what Du Bois Reymond calls the *negative variation* of the muscular current. The same phenomenon is
observed in the voluntary contraction of the muscles.

The interpretation of the negative variation is very important. Du Bois Reymond having remarked, that for a
single muscular shock no deflection of the needle from zero is
obtained, concluded that this is on account of the short duration of the electrical disturbance accompanying a shock. In
tetanus, on the contrary, a series of modifications in the
electrical condition of the muscle correspond to the series of
shocks produced—their accumulated influence deflects the
magnetic needle.

This phenomenon is familiar to physicists. It is known
that the needle of a galvanometer subjected to a frequently-
interrupted current, takes a fixed position intermediate be-

tween zero and the extreme point which it would have occupied if the current had been continuous.

In the muscles in which the shock is protracted, as in the tortoise, a very prolonged change in the electrical state is produced; and therefore these muscles can by each of their shocks cause a deflection of the magnetic needle. It is the same with the movements of the heart; each of these appears to be only a *shock* of the cardiac muscle, and yet it deflects the magnetic needle in the same manner as tetanus of an ordinary muscle. This fact, that a negative variation is equally seen in a muscle which is contracted voluntarily, is of the greatest importance. It confirms the theory which assimilates contraction with tetanus, that is to say, with a discontinuous or vibratory action.

One point which has been long under discussion relative to the manifestations of muscular electricity, is whether the negative variation is caused by a change of direction in the muscular current, or by a transitory suppression of this current. The latter hypothesis has been rendered extremely probable by the numerous experiments in which the needle of the galvanometer has never been seen to retrograde beyond the zero point. Thus the phenomenon of negative variation seems to prove the principle which we laid down at the commencement of this article, that force is manifested in the muscles in a different manner during activity and repose, and that the manifestation under the form of mechanical work is substituted for that under the form of electricity.

Electric fishes.—Animal electricity appears in a much more striking form in the discharges produced by certain fishes. In this case the special organs have for their object the production of electricity; nevertheless, by their structure, their chemical composition, and their dependence on the nervous system, these organs remind us of the conditions of the muscular apparatus.

The number of species provided with electrical organs which was formerly restricted to five,* has been remarkably

* The five species formerly known were the Raya torpedo, the Gymnotus electricus, the Silurus electricus, the Tetraodon electricus, and the Trichiurus electricus.

increased since Ch. Robin has shown that all the species of
the genus ray have electrical apparatus and functions in a
more or less rudimentary condition. Besides, the analysis
of this singular act, which is called the *electric discharge*, has
been better studied, as physicists have themselves learned the
different properties of the electric agent.

In the 18th century, they said, when speaking of the torpedo,
that "this fish when it is touched throws out a kind of
venom which paralyses and benumbs the hand of the fisher-
man." Muschenbroeck, in the last century, ascertained the
electrical nature of the torpedo's discharge. Walsh, in 1778,
saw plainly that the numbness produced by this animal differs
in no respect from that which is caused by the discharge of an
electrical machine. He proved by a great number of experiments, that the effect produced by this fish is manifestly
electrical. He subjected the discharge to a series of trials,
in which it had the same effect as the electricity developed by machine. For instance, he showed that the animal
might be touched with impunity, by taking as a medium of
communication non-conductors of electricity. Besides, he made
the discharge pass through a chain of individuals holding each
other by the hand, and all felt the same singular effect which
is produced by the Leyden jar.

At a later period Davy obtained with the current of the
torpedo the deflection of the galvanometer, the magnetization
of steel needles placed within a spiral of brass wire traversed
by the discharge, and the decomposition of saline solutions.

Becquerel and Breschet verified the same facts in the wire
of the galvanometer, the current circulating from the back to
the belly of the animal.

The demonstration of the spark came still later. Father
Linari and Matteucci obtained this spark by breaking in
various ways a metallic circuit through which the current of
the torpedo was passing. The most ingenious process is that
of Matteucci, who made use of a file in the following manner :
A metallic plate attached to a brass wire is fixed under the
belly of the torpedo; on its back is placed a file on which the
end of a metallic wire rubs. The animal is then irritated,
and one or even several sparks are seen in the dark to pass

between the wire and the file. The production of the spark is probably effected when the circuit is broken at the precise moment of the passage of the torpedo's current.

The use of the file is clearly seen, since the friction causing the circuit to be closed and broken at very short intervals, some of them will necessarily coincide with the discharge, as it has but a short duration. Let us observe, in passing, that the production of two sparks during the discharge of the torpedo, shows very clearly that it has an appreciable duration, measured at least by the time which has elapsed during the passage of the wire across two successive teeth of the file.

A. Moreau succeeded in collecting this electricity on a condenser which allowed him to measure the variation of the intensity of the discharge by the indications of a gold leaf electroscope. We have seen how our acquaintance with the electrical phenomena of the torpedo has passed through many successive stages, and how the progress of physical inquiry has, on this subject, invaded the domains of physiology.

Nevertheless, the discharge of the torpedo, as the above-mentioned experiments have shown, seems like a kind of hybrid phenomenon, in which the effects of tension machines appear to be confounded with those of a galvanic battery. We must, by new researches, endeavour to assign the place in the series of well-known manifestations of electricity, which the discharge of electric fishes ought to occupy.

Considered in a physiological point of view, this phenomenon possesses another kind of interest. The most recent discoveries tend to assimilate the function of this electrical apparatus with that of a muscle. If, for example, we compare the action of the nervous system on the electrical organs of certain fishes, with that which the nerve exercises over the muscle, we are struck with the following analogies :—

The electrical discharges, like muscular shocks, can be produced under the influence of the will of the animal ; they may also be considered as reflex phenomena ; excitation of the electric nerve produces the *discharge*, as that of the motor nerve produces, the *shock* of a muscle ; an entire paralysis of the electrical apparatus takes place when the nerve is cut, as

in a muscle when its nerve is divided. This paralysis takes
place also under the influence of *curare*, although this poison
appears to act more slowly on the electric nerves than on the
greater part of the nerves of motion. Indeed, the *electric
tetanus*, to employ the happy expression of A. Moreau, is
manifested, not only when the nerve of the torpedo is subjected to excitations very rapidly succeeding each other, but
also when the animal is poisoned with strychnine or any
other tetanizing substance.

It was natural enough to compare the different cells or
laminæ of the electrical apparatus in fishes, with the elements
of the voltaic pile, and following up this idea, to inquire what
was the electro-motive power of each of these little elements,
and what were the effects of tension resulting from the
association of these pairs. The following is the result of the
experiments of Matteucci.

A portion of the electrical apparatus of the torpedo, placed
en rapport with the extremities of a galvanometer, gives
birth to a current of the same order as that in the apparatus
of which it formed a part. The longer the prism thus
detached, the more numerous must be the elements of this
kind of animal pile, and the greater the deflection of the galvanometer at the moment of its discharge; this is produced
by exciting the nervous fibre which corresponds with the
small portion of the electrical apparatus of the torpedo placed
on the pads of the galvanometer. Thus far, the analogy of
the electric apparatus with the pile is perfect, since the effects
of tension increase with the number of elements which are
employed. This analogy holds good with all the electrical
fishes, when we endeavour to compare the intensity of the
currents obtained in different parts of the apparatus.

In the torpedo it is found that the discharges are at their
maximum when we touch the two surfaces of its apparatus on
the inner side, that is to say, at the thickest part, which contains the greatest number of discs superposed on each other.
In the gymnotus, whose electrical prisms have so great a
length, it is found that the discharge is stronger still, on
account of the greater volume and number of the elements.
It is proportional to the extent of space contained between the

two points which receive this impulse. In the silurus it is
the same; a much greater impression is made on us when
we touch different points of the animal at a greater distance
from each other.

In fact, we may receive a discharge from a single surface
of the electric apparatus of the torpedo, by touching unsym-
metrical parts, that is to say, points where the number of
the elements of the pile is not so great, because of the
different length of the prisms which compose it.   Thus,
although the polarity may be identical on the same surface of
the apparatus, the fact of the inequality of electric tension
on the different points of this surface suffices to create the
possibility of a current, and to determine its direction.

As to the origin of the electric force, we think that no one
can now see anything in it but the result of chemical actions
produced in the interior of the apparatus

But before they arrived at this opinion, physiologists advanced many hypotheses as the source of animal electricity.
Thus, when Du Bois Reymond had shown that the nervous
tissue possesses an electro-motive force sufficiently powerful,
and that there exists in living nerves a current in a constant
direction, it was thought that the voluminous nerves which
belong to the electrical apparatus of fishes carry electricity
to it, as the blood-vessels supply blood to the organs.   Matteucci has demonstrated that a large lobe of the brain of the
torpedo is the origin of the nerves belonging to its electrical
apparatus.   He has observed that it is possible to remove all
the rest of the brain, without depriving the animal of the
power of giving voluntary or reflex discharges; but that it
can no longer do so when this lobe is destroyed. He has for
this reason named this the electric lobe of the torpedo.

When a dying animal no longer gave spontaneous discharges, it was sufficient, said Matteucci, to touch the electric
lobe in order to obtain discharges more violent than those
which the animal gave voluntarily during the state of perfect
activity.

Nevertheless, the notion of Matteucci has been exaggerated,
when this thought was attributed to him, that electricity is
formed in the brain of the torpedo, and is conveyed by its

nerves. It is as much as to say that the motive force is created in the brain and conveyed to the muscles by the nerves of motion. The electricity of the torpedo has its origin in the special organ of this fish—as mechanical work is originated in a muscle. When we see the phenomena of electricity or of motion produced, the motive or electric nerves fulfil only the duty of transmitting the order received from the brain; but the electricity which circulates in the nerves is not that which is manifested so energetically in the discharge of the apparatus. It is, says Matteucci himself, as if we were to confound the effect of the gunpowder with that of the priming which has been used in order to fire the charge.

Thus, the most probable theory is that which assimilates the electric nerves to those of motion, the discharge to a muscular shock, the series of discharges to tetanus.

In order to verify this theory, we have endeavoured to ascertain* whether the nerves of the torpedo carry out the commands of the will with the same rapidity as the nerves of motion; if, when the electric apparatus has received the order transmitted by the nerve, it hesitates, like the muscle, an instant before it re-acts (*lost time*), in fact, whether the discharge of the torpedo, contrary to those given by tension machines, possesses a certain duration which may be compared to that of the shock of a muscle.

It has been seen, that heat, cold, the ligature of the arteries, and the action of certain poisons modify considerably the form and duration of the muscular shock. If experiment showed that as to its retardation, its duration, and its other phases, the torpedo's discharge corresponds with the shock of a muscle; if it is proved, that in both cases, the same agents produce the same effects, we should be right in assimilating still more completely the electrical phenomena with those of motion; the physiology of the former would illustrate, in many points, that of the latter.

During a stay of a few weeks at Naples we have been able to sketch out this mode of inquiry, which has furnished

* See, for the details of these experiments, "Journal de l'anatomie et de la physiologie." 1872.

results as yet incomplete, but which tend to assimilate the
electrical with the muscular action.   These results are as
follow :—

1. The rapidity of the nervous agent in the electrical nerves
of the torpedo seems evidently to be the same as that of the
nervous agent producing motion in the frog.

2. The phenomenon called by Helmholtz *lost time* exists
also in the electric apparatus of the torpedo, and lasts about
the same time as in the muscle.

3. The discharge of the torpedo is not instantaneous, like
that of certain kind of tension electrical apparatus, but it
is prolonged about fourteen hundredths of a second ; which is,
in a remarkable degree equal to the duration of a shock in a
frog's muscle.

We cannot enter here into the details of the experiments
which have furnished these results, but we will endeavour, in
a few lines, to explain the method which we employed.

Registering apparatus measure the slightest intervals of
time ; this we have seen in speaking of the estimated rapidity
of the nervous agent.   But, in order to employ the graphic
method, we must have motion to give the required signal.

Thus, in the experiment of Helmholtz, the muscular shock
itself announced that the order of movement which the nerve
had to convey had arrived at its destination.

In order to obtain the signal of the electric discharge, we
have employed it to excite the muscle of a frog, the shock of
which was inscribed on the registering cylinder.

The trace furnished by the *frog-signal* is somewhat delayed,
it is true, after the excitation has been produced ; but this
delay is a known quantity, and it can easily be taken into
account.

The following is the method adopted to measure with the
ordinary myograph the duration of the different acts which
precede the discharge of the torpedo.

In a preliminary experiment (fig. 12) the nerve of the frog
was directly excited, and a note was taken of the time (*s g*)
which elapsed between the instant (*s*) of the excitation, and
the signal (*g*) given by the frog.

In a second experiment the torpedo was excited, still at the

instant (*e*), and the electricity of its discharges was collected
by means of conducting wires which sent it to the nerve of
the *frog signal.* This would give its shock at the point (*t*).

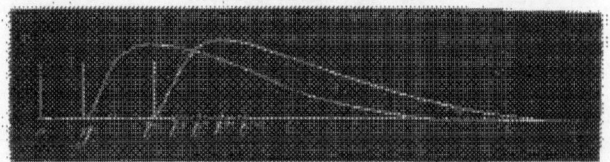

FIG. 12.—Measure of the time which elapses between the excitation of
the electric nerve, and the discharge of the torpedo.

The difference (*g t*) would express the time consumed by
the torpedo between the excitation of its nerve and the discharge. By varying the experiment, as we have done for the
motive nerves (page 43), we obtain the measure of the
rapidity of the electric nervous agent, and that of the *lost time*
in the torpedo apparatus. *

Finally, in order to measure the duration of the electrical
action, we had recourse to a method which consists in collecting this discharge during a very short time (1-100th of a
second) to send it to the *frog signal,* and varying gradually the
instant at which the electricity of the torpedo was collected.
It was thus ascertained that starting from the point (*t*) one
might, during 14-100ths of a second, obtain a series of signals
from the frog—*t′, t″, t‴, t‴′,* but that beyond that time the
frog gave no signals, thus proving that the discharge had
terminated.

We have not been able to follow out farther the comparison of the electric with the muscular action ; but, according
to the results already furnished by experiment, we can foresee

* Deprived of appropriate apparatus, we have been obliged to construct
for ourselves a kind of registering instrument which should measure short
intervals of time with sufficient precision. We refer the reader, for the
real arrangement of the experiments, to the "Journal de l'anatomie et de
la physiologie," loc. cit. Fig. 12 represents tracings which one would
obtain with the registering instruments already known.

that new analogies will still show themselves between these two manifestations of force in living beings, mechanical work and electricity.

CHAPTER VII.

ANIMAL MECHANISM.

Of the forms under which mechanical work presents itself—Every machine must be constructed with a view to the kind of work which it has to perform—Correspondence of the form of muscle with the work which it accomplishes—Theory of Borelli—Specific force of muscles —Of machines; they only change the form of work, but do not increase its quality—Necessity of alternate movements in living motive powers—Dynamical energy of animated motors.

If we have lingered long over the origin of heat, of mechanical work, and of electricity in the animal kingdom, it was in order to establish clearly that these forces are the same as those which are seen in the inorganic world. Certain evident differences must have struck the earlier observers, but the progress of science has shown, more and more clearly, this identity, which is now disbelieved only by those whose minds are still under the influence of obsolete theories.

Mechanical force, to which our attention must now be exclusively directed, has hitherto been studied only in its origin; we must follow it through all its applications to work of different kinds which it executes in animal mechanism.

In all the machines employed in the arts we must have *organs* which serve as media between the forces which we employ and the resistance which are required to be overcome. This word *organ* is precisely that which anatomists use to designate the portions which compose the animal machine. The laws of mechanics are applicable as well to animated motors as to other machines; this truth, however, has to be demonstrated, but, like many others, it was for a long time unrecognized.

Of the forms of mechanical work.—When we have at our
disposal a certain quantity of force, it is necessary, in order to
utilize it, to collect it under conditions which vary according
to the nature of the effects which we desire to produce.

We have seen that the measure of work actually employed
is the product of the resistance multiplied by the space
through which it has to pass. Such a measure, being the
product of two factors, may remain constant if the two factors
vary inversely. So that a considerable weight, raised to a
slight height, will give the same result of work as a light
weight raised to a greater height.

These will be two different forms of the same quantity of
work ; but, in this case, the form is of extreme importance.
In order that the *work applied* should be available, it is necessary that its form should be the same as that of the
resisting force—that is, of the work *required to be done*.

If we have as a moving power a piston of a steam engine
of large diameter and short length, capable of lifting 100
kilogrammes to the height of a centimetre, and that it is
necessary with this generator of force to lift one kilogramme
to the height of a metre, which equally represents a kilogrammetre of work, the motive force in this machine cannot
be utilized directly ; for at the end of the stroke of the piston
the weight of a kilogramme will only have been lifted
one centimetre, and $\frac{99}{100}$ of the force at our disposal will remain unemployed. Every machine, therefore, must be constructed with a view to the special form under which the
resistance to be overcome presents itself.

It is true that by means of certain contrivances, levers or
wheel-work properly combined, it is possible to cause a certain quantity of work to pass from one form to another, and
to apply it to the resistance to be overcome. But this will
be the object of ulterior study. We have only to consider at
this moment the case in which the force is directly applied
to the obstacle which it has to surmount, which is a very
frequent condition in animated motive powers.

Let us return, then, to the hypothesis in which the moving
force of the piston of an engine must be applied directly to
overcome resistance. Under these conditions the constructor

will be careful to give to the surface of the piston such an area, that the pressure on this surface may be precisely equal to the resistance which it has to overcome; then he will give to the cylinder such a length that it will allow the piston to travel just as far as the resistance ought to move. It is only under these conditions that the machine will do the desired work, and utilize all its moving power. On the contrary, in the case in which work answering to a kilogrammetre must be done by lifting 100 kilogrammes to the height of a centimetre, the cylinder must be made so large that the pressure of steam on the surface of the piston will develop an effort of 100 kilogrammes, and such a length only must be given to the cylinder, that the movement of the piston may be merely a centimetre.

One cannot substitute one of these forms of cylinder for the other, for in one case the force would be insufficient, and in the other, the range would be too restricted.

The only thing which is equal in both is the amount of work that the two machines can do, that is to say, the product of the force employed multiplied by the space passed through; this is again the product of the surface of a section of the cylinder multiplied by its length, or, in other terms, it is the volume of steam contained in each machine, this vapour being supposed to be at an equal tension.

This proportion of the volume of the matter which works to the work performed, is found in every case in which a moving force is employed.

Two masses of lead falling from the same height will do work proportionate to their volume, or, which is the same thing, to their weight. Two threads of india-rubber of the same length, both of which have been stretched to the same degree, will do work proportionate to their transverse sections, and, consequently, to their respective weights. Lastly, two threads of the same diameter, but of unequal lengths, after having been subjected to the same elongation in proportion to their original lengths, will, as they contract, do work proportionate to their respective lengths, that is to say, to their weight.

This leads to the consideration of muscle, which conforms

rigorously to the general laws which we have just enunciated.
The larger a muscle is, that is to say, the more extensive is
its surface, the more susceptible it is of considerable effort.
But, on the other hand, a muscle contracts only in proportion
to its own length.   We may estimate that the mean shortening
of a muscle while contracting, when it is not detached from
the animal, is about a third of its length when in repose. It
follows that the work done by a muscle will be in proportion
to its length and its transverse section; that is to say, to its
volume or to its weight.

Thus, it is possible to ascertain, according to the anatomical characters of a muscle, what is the force which it possesses, relatively to that of other muscles of the same animal,
and what is the form under which its work is done.

The substance of the muscles, that is to say, of red flesh,
presents the same density in the different parts of the animal
frame; in consequence of which the weight is the most exact
and the most expeditious method of estimating the relative
importance of two masses of muscle, and of predicting the
quantity of work which they are able to execute.

As to the form under which muscular work must be produced, it is deduced not less easily from the form of the
muscle. If it be thick and short, it should produce a strong
effect multiplied by a short range; if it be long and slender
it will have a more extended range, but will only develop
feeble energy.

There are many examples in proof of this law which
regulates muscular action—the sterno-mastoidal, the sartorius, and the rectus abdominis, are muscles of a long range,
or, as it may be otherwise expressed, having a great extent of movement; they have a fleshy portion of greater
length. The large pectoral muscle, the gluteus maximus,
or the temporal muscle are large and short muscles, that
is to say, capable of a considerable effort, but of slight
contraction.

Borelli already understood the laws of muscular force;
without the intervention of the *notion of work*, which was not
introduced into mechanics at the time when he lived; he
made a very clear distinction between these two opposite

characteristics of the action of a muscle according to the impulse of its volume or its length. And as a theory is always required to satisfy the mind, this author sought to interpret these different effects by a theory of the structure of the muscles.

Let us imagine, said he, a minute chain of metal formed of circular elastic rings, and that an extensile force should be exerted on this chain. Each ring will change its shape and assume an oval form, and the whole chain will be lengthened in proportion to the number of its rings. When it recovers itself, under the influence of elasticity, the chain will grow shorter again in proportion to its length. The minute chain of Borelli is the primitive fibre revealed to us in the animal economy by the microscope. But, said Borelli, if we form a bundle of a great number of these chains, each one of them will resist the extensile force in proportion to the elasticity of its rings, that is to say, the thickness of the bundles, and the force with which the extended bundle will recover itself will be in the same ratio.

We do not reason otherwise now that histology has shown us, in a muscle, a bundle of fibres whose actions are combined like the chains suggested by the Naples professor.

Passing to other considerations, this author studied the influence exerted by the direction of the fibres on the force which they develop. He remarked that the muscles whose fibres converge obliquely on the same tendon, like the barbs of a feather on the central shaft, afford neither a range nor an effort proportionate to their length and their sections. We have no modification to make of this estimate of the composition of forces in the muscular organ.

Of the specific force of muscles.— In the machines constructed by man, it is not enough to measure the longitudinal and transverse dimensions of the cylinder, in order to know what quantity of work each stroke of the piston will develop; we must also know under what pressure the steam acts. That is estimated by the number of atmospheres it can lift as it escapes. At other times the force of the steam is measured by the number of kilogrammes of pressure which it exerts on every square centimetre of the surface of the cylinder. In every case it is an estimate of the specific force of a certain volume of steam which is to be determined.

In the same manner, in hydraulic machines, we must know the charge of water or its pressure, in order to ascertain the work which the machine can perform.

Physiologists have also sought to determine the specific force of muscular tissue in different animals, and to compare with the unit of transverse section of muscle the effort which it can make. In this manner they have estimated that the muscle of the frog would develop an effort of 692 grammes (E. Weber) for each square centimetre of section ; that human muscle would develop 1087 (Koster). In the bird the force would be about 1200 (Marey) ; in the insect it would be still greater (Plateau).

According to Straus Durkheim, a muscle of the stag-beetle weighing 20 centigrammes would carry, if we measure the moment of power and that of resistance a weight of seven kilogrammes.

By such estimates as these, we might compare animated moving powers with machines working under variable pressures. The frog, we might say, works with a pressure less than one atmosphere, man with a pressure greater than one atmosphere. There would be a greater pressure in the bird, and still greater in the insect.

Of machines.—When mechanical force cannot be directly utilized, because it is not in harmony with the form of work which it ought to effect, various means are employed in the arts to transform it. Machinery known under the names of wheels and levers are continually used for this purpose. In the animal organism contrivances are also found which change the form of the work of the muscles. The lever is almost exclusively used by nature for this purpose. The arrangement of the bony levers which form the skeleton is so generally known that it needs no explanation here ; but there is a very common error on this point, even among physiologists, which it is necessary to point out.

Almost all the levers which are found in the organism belong to the third order, that is to say, where the muscular force is applied between the fulcrum and the resistance. Under these conditions, the effort that can be developed at the extremity of the lever is less than that of the muscle; but the space passed through by this extremity of the lever is proportionately increased, so that the product of the force multiplied by the distance remains the same.

Thus, we find in a great number of standard treatises, a sort of accusation brought against nature, for having entirely wasted a great part of the force of our muscles by causing them to act under a disadvantageous leverage. It is true, that to extenuate this fault, they are willing to grant that this arrangement, unfavourable in an economical point of view, gives to our muscles an elegance which they would not have possessed, if for example, a long muscular band had extended from the sternum to the wrist. These mechanical and æsthetic notions ought to give place to more correct ideas. We must, above all, remember that a muscle produces work corresponding to its volume or its weight, whatever may be the proportions of the lever to which it is attached. The effect of the latter is only to regulate the form under which it produces the work, without adding to it or subtracting from it. An error of the same kind is often committed in considering the part played by levers made use of by man in his work. It often happens that human force is unable to raise certain weights; we have recourse in these cases to levers of the first or second order, in which we increase the power of the arm in the ratio of the longer to the shorter arm of the lever.

In this manner we utilize a motive force which could not produce external work if we endeavoured to bring it to bear directly on the resistance to be overcome. But a lever which amplifies the force exerted, diminishes as much the extent of the work produced; it adds nothing to the work executed by the motive power.

Before the notion of work had been introduced into mechanics, and when it was not clearly understood that it was impossible to increase by mechanism the amount of force at our disposal, many false ideas were entertained with regard to the part played by machinery. When we consider those gigantic masses of stone the pyramids of Egypt, or those

enormous blocks, called dolmens, which our forefathers
erected in prehistoric times, it was admitted that these
Titanic works pre-supposed a very advanced knowledge of
mechanism. Even now it would require an immense time,
or an army of workmen, to execute similar works by employing only the force of man and that of animals.

We must not imagine that the old Gauls or ancient
Egyptians were able to escape from the inevitable necessity of
employing many men or an enormous lapse of time in these
labours at the period when the only source of mechanical
work was that derived from living beings.

But we live under new and better conditions, thanks to
the invention of machinery which develops mechanical work.
In addition to the utilization of natural motive powers, such
as water courses and wind, man is now able to employ steam
engines, by means of which a small quantity of fuel does the
work of a great many animals. It is by these means that
Egypt has succeeded in a few years in cutting through the
Isthmus of Suez, an enterprise which, four thousand years ago,
would have absorbed the efforts of many generations.

Necessity of alternate motion in living motive powers.—When
the piston of a machine has reached the end of its stroke, the
steam which impelled it must escape, and the piston must
return in the opposite direction to accomplish fresh work.
In the same manner, the muscle, after having contracted,
must be relaxed in order to act afresh. But mechanicians
have found that in the alternate movements there is a loss of
work. When a heavy object impelled forward with rapidity
has to be brought back in the opposite direction, it is necessary first to destroy the work which it contains, so to speak,
under the form of active force. Precisely in the same manner,
when a limb suddenly extended is required to be rapidly bent,
the momentum acquired must first be destroyed; to do which
requires an expenditure of work.

To guard against this loss of motive power, mechanicians
have recourse, as much as possible, to the employment of
circular movements instead of motion to and fro. Thus, man
who is so often inspired in his inventions by the arrangements of which nature offers him examples, deviates in this

case from his model; he endeavours to surpass it, and he is right. To make this understood we cannot do better than quote a passage in which L. Foucault compares the screw-propeller of ships to the organs of swimming in fishes:—

" In our machines," said he,[*] " we have usually a great number of parts entirely distinct one from the other, which only touch each other at certain points; in an animal, on the contrary, all the parts adhere together; there is a connection of tissue between any two given parts of the body. This is rendered necessary by the function of nutrition which is continually going on, a function to which every living being is subject during the whole of its existence. We can, besides, understand the absolute impossibility of obtaining a continued movement of rotation of one part on another, while still preserving the continuity of these two parts."

Thus, a profound difference separates mechanisms employed by nature from those invented by man; the former are subject to special requirement from which the latter can be freed. The muscle can only act under the condition of being attached by its vessels and nerves to the rest of the organism. No portion of the body, not even the bones themselves, which have the least vitality, can be free from this necessity.

One might find, in the animal organism, many other mechanical appliances, the arrangement of which resembles that of machines invented by man, but with differences ever of the same kind as those which we have just described.

For instance, the circulation of the blood is effected in living beings by a veritable hydraulic machine, with its pump, valves, and pipes. But the fundamental difference between this complicated mechanism and machines constructed by man, arises from the absence of independent portions, and especially of the piston. The heart is a pump without a piston, and its variations of capacity are obtained by the contractility of the coats of the vessels themselves. With the exception of this difference, we find perfect analogies between the circulatory apparatus of animals and hydraulic motive powers. The function of the valves is identical in both in spite of apparent differences.

* " Journal des Débats," Oct. 22, 1845.

We have formerly noticed in the circulation of the blood an influence which regulates and increases the effective work of the cardiac pump; it depends on the elasticity of the arteries.[*] In like manner, in hydraulic machines, man has recourse to the employment of elastic reservoirs, to utilize more fully the work of pumps, and to render uniform the movement of the liquid, notwithstanding the intermittent character of the motive power. This effect may be compared to that which we have before remarked in the elasticity of muscles.

Dynamic energy of animated motors.—Animated motive powers and machines are subject to the same estimation of work; it is the dynamic energy of the former as compared with the latter.

The production of external work corresponding to 75 kilogrammetres per second, has been called the *horse-power*, or, in more general terms, the motive power of one horse, it being supposed that one horse could develop the same amount of work.

But animal motors cannot work incessantly, so that the horse-power would represent at the end of the day a much greater amount of work than the animal could have produced, had it been employed as a motive force.

Man is estimated much lower as to his dynamic energy, ($\frac{1}{7}$ of a horse-power), and yet, if we only require from the muscular force of a man an effort of short duration, it will furnish dynamic energy exceeding that of a horse-power. In fact, the weight of a man is often more than 75 kilogrammes; each time that the body is raised to the height of a metre per second, in mounting a staircase, the man has effected during this second the work adequate to one horse-power. And if, during several instants, he can give to his ascent the speed of two metres per second, this man will have developed the work of two horse-power.

Thus, in our estimate of the work done by the greatest or the smallest animals, we must consider it as a multiple or a fraction of the ordinary measure of horse-power.

---

[*] "Physiologie médicale de la circulation du sang."

CHAPTER VIII.

HARMONY BETWEEN THE ORGAN AND THE FUNCTION.—
DEVELOPMENT HYPOTHESIS.

Each muscle of the body presents, in its form, a perfect harmony with the nature of the acts which it has to perform—A similar muscle, in different species of animals, presents differences of form, if the function which it has to fulfil in these different species is not the same—Variety of pectoral muscles in birds, according to their manner of flight—Variety of muscles of the thigh in mammals, according to their mode of locomotion—Was this harmony pre-established?— Development hypothesis—Lamarck and Darwin.

THE comparison between ordinary machines and animated motive powers will not have been made in vain, if it has shown that strict relations exist between the form of the organs and the characters of their functions; that this correspondence is regulated by the ordinary laws of mechanics, so that when we see the muscular and bony structure of an animal, we may deduce from their form all the characters of the functions which they possess.

It is known that the transverse volume of a muscle corresponds with the energy of its action; that the athlete, for instance, is recognized by the remarkable relief in which each of his muscles stands out under the skin. But less is known concerning the physiological signification of the length of the muscles, that is to say, the less or greater length of their contractile fibres. And yet Borelli has already given the true explanation. In his opinion, as we have seen, this length of red fibre is proportioned to the extent of movement which the muscle is fitted to produce.

This distinction between the contractile or red fibre and the inert fibre of the tendon is of the utmost importance. Experiment has shown that the muscles when they contract are shortened to an extent which represents a constant fraction of their length. We may, without erring from the truth, estimate at $\frac{1}{4}$ of their length, the extent to which a muscle

can contract. But, whatever may be the absolute value of
this contraction, it is always in proportion to the length of
red fibre; that is the result of the nature of the phenomena
which produce work in the muscle.

Thus, every muscle whose two points of attachment are
susceptible of being much displaced by the effect of contraction, must necessarily be a long muscle. On the contrary,
every muscle which has to produce a movement of short
extent must of necessity be a short muscle, whatever may be
the distance which separates the two points of attachment.
Thus, the flexors of the fingers and toes are short muscles;
but they are furnished with long tendons, which convey even
to the phalanges of the fingers or toes the slight movement
originated at a considerable distance at the fore-arm or the leg.

It is easy to estimate, in the dead body, the extent of the
displacement which a muscle can exercise on its two points of
attachment. By producing the movements of flexion or
extension in a limb, we can ascertain with sufficient exactness the extent by which they separate or draw together the
osseous attachments of its muscles. In a recent skeleton we
can also judge with sufficient accuracy of the amount of these
movements by the extent to which the articulated surfaces
can glide over each other.

In examining the muscular frame of man we are struck
with the extreme length of the *sartorius* muscle; it is easy
to be seen that no other can displace to such an extent its
points of bony attachment. The sterno-mastoidal and the
magnus rectus abdominis are, after this, the longest muscles;
these also are muscles which have very extensive movements.
We might thus cause all the muscles of the organism to pass
under review, and in them all we should see that the length
of the red fibres corresponds with the extent of the movement
which this muscle has to execute. But, in the study, we
must be on our guard against a cause of error which would
tend to arrange certain short muscles among those which are
longer.

Borelli himself has noticed this cause of error; he has
shown how *penniform* muscles, that is to say, those whose
fibres are inserted obliquely into the tendon, like the barbs of

a feather into the common shaft, are short muscles which appear like long ones. These considerations are indispensable when we wish to understand the action of the various muscles of the organism; it is only by this means that we can estimate the real length of their contractile parts.

Though the harmony between the form and the function of different muscles is revealed everywhere in the anatomy of the human frame, this harmony becomes much more striking if we compare with each other different species of animals. Comparative anatomy shows us, in species closely allied to each other, a singular difference in the form of certain muscles whenever the function of these muscles varies. Thus, in the kangaroo, essentially a leaping animal, we find an enormous development of the muscles of leaping, the *glutei*, the *triceps extensor cruris*, and the *gastrocnemial* muscles.

In birds the function of flight is exercised under very different conditions in different species; so, also, the anatomical arrangement of the muscles which move the wing, the *pectoral muscles*, varies in a very decided manner in different species. To show the perfect harmony which exists between the function and the organ, it would be necessary to enter into long details of the mechanism of flight. The reader will find, farther on, explanations on this head. We will content ourselves with giving in a few words the differences which have been observed in the movements of the wing, and in the form of the muscles which produce them.

Every one has remarked that birds which have a large surface of wing, as the eagle, the sea-swallow, &c., give strokes of only a slight extent; that depends on the great resistance which a wing of so large a surface meets with in the air.

Birds, on the contrary, which have but very little wings, move them to a great extent, and thus compensate for the slight resistance which they meet with from the air; the guillemot and the pigeon belong to the second group. If it be admitted that the first-mentioned birds must make energetic but restricted movements, and that the second must move with less energy, but with greater amplitude of stroke, the conclusion arrived at must necessarily be that the first ought to have large and short pectoral muscles, while in the

second, these muscles should be long and slender. This is
precisely what takes place; we can be assured of this, by the

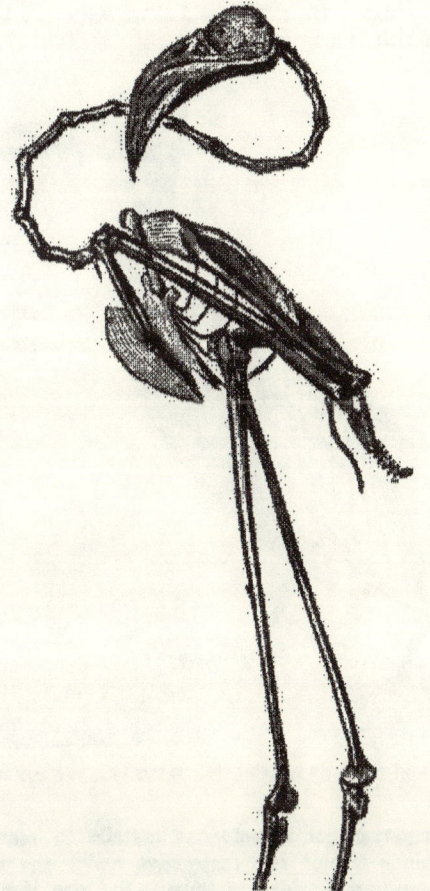

Fig. 18.—Skeleton of a flamingo (after Alph. Milne-Edwards); the wing
is very large, the sternum very short and deep, which indicates the size
and the shortness of the pectoral muscles.

simple inspection of the sternum in different species; for this bone measures, in some degree, the length of the pectoral muscles which are lodged in its lateral cavities. Thus, birds with long wings, have a wide and short sternum; the others have one which is long and slender.

Fig. 14.—Skeleton of a penguin; sternum very long, wing very short.

The comparison of homologous muscles in mammals of different kinds is not less instructive under the aspect in which we are now considering them. But one is often embarrassed in this comparison by the difficulty of recognizing the homology. The discrepancies are sometimes so striking

that anatomists have described under various names the same
muscle in different species.

Still, in the greater number of cases, the homology is not
doubtful; it is implicitly admitted by the fact of an identical
designation being applied to certain muscles in different
species. These are precisely the muscles which we shall take
for an example, to show the harmony which exists between
the function and the organ.

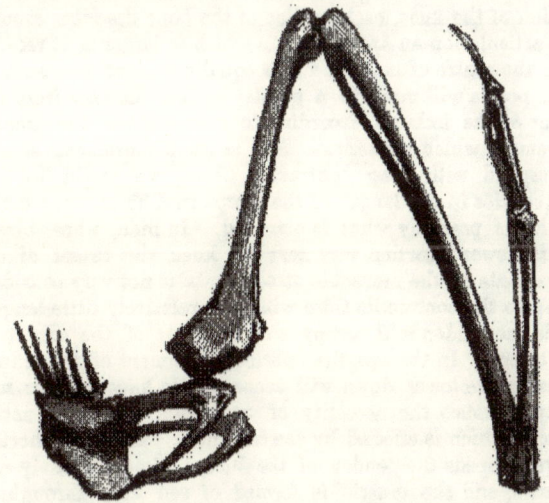

Fig. 15.—Skeleton of the wing and sternum of the sea-swallow (Hirundo
marina)—showing the extreme shortness of the sternum, and the great
length of the wing.

Thus the *femoral biceps* is easily recognized in all mammals; and it varies considerably, especially in its lower attachment. In certain quadrupeds it is inserted all along the leg,
almost to the heel; in these animals the leg is never extended upon the thigh; in animals which have the power of
leaping, the lower attachments of the biceps is more elevated;
it is still more so in the simiœ, which can almost extend
the leg upon the thigh and stand upright. In man the biceps

is inserted high in the perinæum. If one can rely on the anatomical plates of Cuvier and of Laurillart, the negro has the perinæal insertion of the biceps not so high as in the white man, thus approximating to its position in the ape.

Neglecting at present the question why there should be this variety in the attachment which regulates the motion of the biceps, let us content ourselves with considering the consequences which this arrangement may have upon its function. It is clear that during the movement of the flexion and extension of the knee, each portion of the bone describes around this articulation an arc of a circle which is larger as it recedes from the centre of motion. It is equally evident that each of these points will move to a greater or less distance from the femur or the ischium, according to the extent of the circular movement which it executes. And as great movements should correspond with long contractile fibres, we ought to find inequalities in the length of the biceps in different mammals.

This is precisely what is observed. In man, whose biceps has its lower insertion very near the knee, the extent of the movements of the moveable attachments is not very considerable; so the contractile fibre will have relatively little length, while the tendon will occupy a certain part of the extent of the biceps. In the ape, the inferior attachment of the muscle taking place lower down will consequently have greater mobility; whence the necessity of a greater length of active muscle, which is effected by the tendinous part being shorter. In quadrupeds the tendon of the biceps almost entirely disappears, and the muscle is formed of red fibre throughout almost all its extent.

The *rectus internus* muscle of the thigh presents the same variability in its attachments and its structure. If we observe its arrangement in man (fig. 16), we see at once that the attachment of this muscle to the leg is very near the knee, and that its tendon is very long. Let us examine the same muscle in an ape (figs. 17 and 18), we find that its tibial attachment is much farther from the knee, and as a consequence of the more extended movements which this attachment executes, we find that the muscular fibre gains length at the expense of that of the tendon, which is extremely short.

This variability in the point of attachment is still very noticeable in the *semi-tendinosus* muscle, which derives its name from the fact that in man, about half of the length

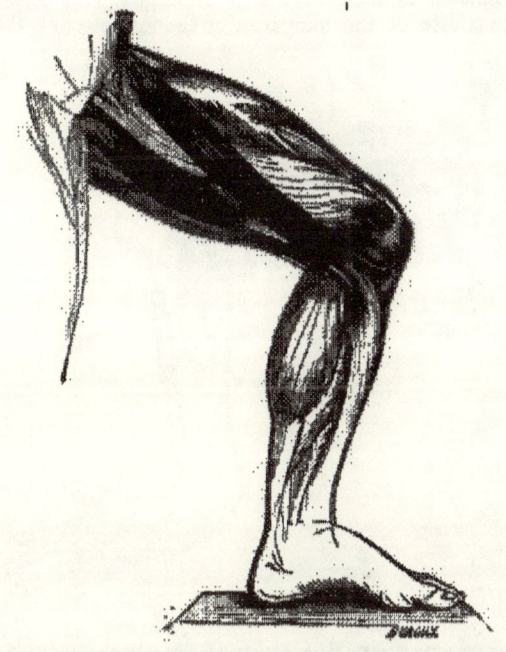

Fig. 16.—Muscles of the thigh in man. The *sartorius* muscle (above) and the *rectus internus* (below), are darkly shaded, that they may be more easily recognised. The rectus internus is, at its lower extremity, provided with a long tendon; its fleshy part is short, which is in harmony with the slight extent of movement in this muscle, the attachment of which is very close to the knee. The sartorius muscle is provided with a short tendon at its inferior attachment.

of the muscle is occupied by the tendon. In fact, the inferior attachments of the *semi-tendinosus* in man is very close to the articulation of the knee, but in apes, where it is attached lower down, the muscle has almost entirely lost its tendon; it is altogether lost in the greater part of other mammals, in the Coaïta, for example.

We might multiply indefinitely examples which prove the perfect harmony between the form of the muscles and the characters of their functions. Everywhere the transverse development of these organs is associated with strength, as in the triceps of the kangaroo, or the masseters of the lion ·

Fig. 17.—Muscle of the thigh in the Magot ; rectus internus muscle almost entirely formed of red fibres ; the attachments of this muscle being at a considerable distance from the knee, give it a great extent of movement in bending the leg upon the thigh. Sartorius muscle, having a very short tendon.

everywhere also, the length of muscle is connected with the extent of movement, as in the examples which we have just cited.

Is this harmony pre-established, or rather is it formed under the influence of function in different creatures? In the same manner as we see the muscles increase in volume by the habit of employing energetic efforts; we also observe them,

under the influence of more extended movements, acquire a
greater length ?   Can we see a displacement of the tendinous
attachments of the muscles to the skeleton, under the influence
of changes in the force of muscular traction ? Such is the second
problem which we propose to ourselves, and which experiment
should be called on to determine.

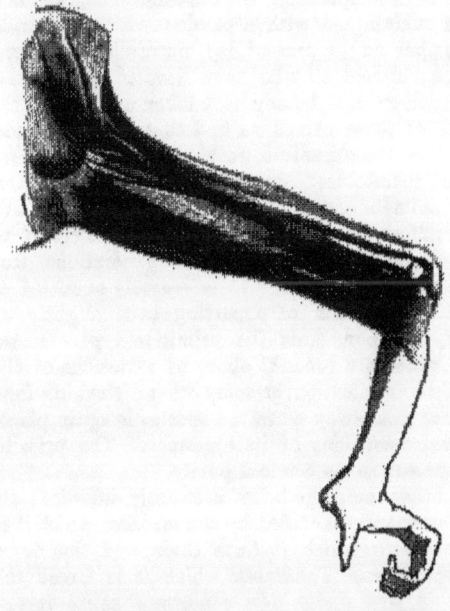

Fig. 18.—Muscles of the thigh of the Coaita. Rectus internus, inserted
at a distance from the knee, almost entirely without tendon. The
sartorius having its superior attachment very far from the coxo-femoral
articulation, has very extended movements ; it possesses in consequence
a great length of red fibre, and not of tendon.

THE DEVELOPMENT THEORY.

The natural sciences have derived at the present day a
great impulse from the influence of the ideas of Darwin.

Not that the opinions of the illustrious Englishman are yet universally accepted; it has been recently seen with what vehemence the defenders of the prevalent theory reject the development hypothesis. But the appearance of the Darwinian theory has excited long discussions; to the arguments which Lamarck formerly brought forward in favour of the variability of living beings, many others have been added by the partizans of development. On the other side, the old doctrine has been maintained with a passion which was little anticipated, so that at the present day, naturalists are divided into two camps; almost all who have devoted themselves to the study of zoology or of botany have taken one side or the other.

In one of these camps we find that the old school, those who consider the organized world almost unchangeable, have retrenched themselves. According to them, the very numerous series of animals and plants is limited to a certain number of *species*, unalterable types which have the power of transmitting themselves through successive generations, from their origin to the end of time. It is scarcely admitted that the species has the power of departing even slightly, and in a temporary manner, from the primitive type. Those slight changes, which are brought about by variations of climate or of food, by domestication, or some other disturbing force of the same order pass away when the species is again placed under the normal conditions of its existence. The primitive type then re-appears in its original purity.

In the other camp the belief is entirely different; the living being is incessantly modified by the medium which it inhabits, the temperature which it finds there, and the nourishment which it procures. The habits which it is forced to assume in order to live under new conditions cause it to acquire special aptitudes which modify its organism, and change the form of its body. And because hereditary descent transmits to descendants, within certain limits, the modifications acquired by their ancestors, the *species* is modified by degrees. Lamarck was the author of this theory of *development*, to which Darwin and his followers have recalled the attention of naturalists. Darwin adds to these external influences, which can modify the species of animals, another cause which maintains and increases these modifications continually, when they are advantageous to the species. This cause is *natural selection*.

If the chances of birth have given to certain individuals a slight modification which renders them stronger or more active, as the case may be, but altogether more fitted to maintain *the struggle for existence*, these individuals are destined by that very circumstance to reproduce their kind. Not only does their physical superiority increase their chance of longevity, and give them by that means more time to multiply, but, according to Darwin, the very existence of a physical superiority in an animal causes it to be preferred above others, for the purpose of reproduction. Thus the entire species would be improved by successive acquisitions of new qualities every time that an individual happened to be born with better endowments than the other representatives of this species.

The struggle between the old school and that of development threatens to endure yet a long time, without either side finding a victorious argument to overcome the other. Every one knows the reasons which have been alleged on both sides, and for which, in their turn, geology, archæology, zoology, and agriculture have been laid under contribution. When and how will the strife end? No one can as yet answer this question. Yet, if one might venture a prediction as to the issue of the combat, founded on the actual attitude of the adverse parties, one might predict the defeat of the old school. Their ranks are, in fact, thinned every day; they evidently grow discouraged, and seem to avow their inability to furnish proofs of a scientific character, by sheltering themselves under an orthodoxy that has nothing in common with the dispute.

One objection might perhaps be brought against both systems—that of keeping too much to generalities in their discussions, and not bringing sufficiently into relief the prominent points of the debate.

Thus, we must allow that Lamarck is much too vague in his explanations, when he attributes to outward circumstances the changes in the living organism. Between a need which is manifested and the appearance of a form of organ which corresponds to that need, there is a hiatus which his theory has not filled. He tells us that the animal species which we now see, so admirably adapted, each to the kind of life which it leads—provided, according to their necessities, with claws or hoofs, wings or fins, sharp teeth or horny beaks—have not always lived under this form; that they have gradually acquired these diverse conformations, which are at present in perfect harmony with the conditions under which they live. But, when we ask him to show us a modification of this kind in process of accomplishment under an external influence, the author of the "Philosophie Zoologique" has little wherewith to furnish us, except modifications of slight importance; he objects that scientific observation does not go far enough back into the ages of the world. If we open the tombs of Memphis and show Lamarck the skeletons of animals identical with those which live in Egypt at the present day, he replies without being disconcerted: "It is because these animals lived under the same conditions as those which exist at the present time." The answer is as good as the attack, but proves nothing. We might carry on the discussion for ever on such grounds as these.

Darwin is more precise when he pleads in favour of *natural selection*. There is no one at the present time who does not admit the enormous power of selection in modifying the type of organized beings. Breeders have produced the most curious transformations in the animal kingdom, by choosing continually for the purpose of reproduction, individuals possessing in a high degree the physical characteristics which they desire to impress on the race. Selection produces in the vegetable kingdom transformations of a similar kind; so that Darwin has, without giving way too much to hypothesis, attributed the principal part in transformation to a selection which is made naturally, for the reasons that have just been given. But Darwin, as well as Lamarck, only considers under a restricted point of view the causes of the transformation of organized beings. Each of the two chiefs of this doctrine gives the greatest prominence to the cause of variation which *he* first has pointed out.

The new school which, by a judicious eclecticism, endeavours to make a due partition between these two kinds of influences, in order to explain by successive transformations

the surprising variety of living beings, has already furnished
important arguments in favour of development. But many
savants look with suspicion on these studies; they consider
that the immutability and variability of animal species belong
to the domain of insoluble questions.

It is true, that if we ask the partizans of development to
prove experimentally the reality of their doctrine; if we
require of them, for example, to transform the *ass* species into
the horse or anything analogous to it, they are forced to avow
their inability, and they reply that it is necessary, in order
to effect this, to exercise modifying influences during millions
on millions of years. It must indeed have been by very slow
transitions that the variation of species has been effected, if it
indeed has taken place. Consequently, in the absence of an
experimental solution, the development hypothesis can neither
be proved nor refuted.

Learned men, whose minds are habituated to rigorous demonstration, are not interested in such questions; they have
no scientific value in their estimation. And yet science meets
with such every day. When an astronomer studies the influences which may cause the heavenly bodies to move more
slowly; when he predicts a modification of the orbit of the
earth after the lapse of some millions of years, or a lengthening of the period of rotation of our planet—changes which
would affect all the inhabitants of the earth with a mortal
chill—this philosopher is listened to. When he speaks of a
cause, however slight it may be, of the retardation of a
planetary movement, every one understands that if this cause
should continue during many ages, its effects will be exaggerated by the lapse of time. No one tells this astronomer
to wait till some millions of years have proved the accuracy of
his reasonings.

Why should we be more unjust to the theory of development? It cannot, it is said, bring before our eyes the transformation of one animal into another. This is true, but it
may show us some tendency to this transformation. However
slight it may be, yet accumulating more and more during
many ages, it may become as complete a transformation as
we can imagine.

But what we have a right to demand of the advocates of development, even now, is that they should show us this tendency; that they should bring it before us under the form of a slight variation in the anatomical characters of individuals when exposed to certain influences, which continued from generation to generation, would in the end produce the most important modifications in the species. No one denies that the morphological characteristics of individuals are transmitted in different degrees to their descendants. The point which is to be demonstrated is the manner in which an external cause acts in order to impress on the organism the primary modification. Researches of this kind belong to experimental physiology, and this science may even now furnish us ,with some reliable arguments.

At the time when Lamarck lived, scientific logic was not very exact in its requirements. In his opinion, a want which was felt, originated the organic conformation suited to satisfy it.

A certain bird which was in the habit of seeking its food at the bottom of the water, made constant efforts to lengthen its neck, and its neck grew longer; another bird wished to advance as far as possible into the waters of a pond without wetting its plumage; the efforts which it made to extend its legs gradually gave them the proportions observed in the wading birds (Grallatores). The giraffe, attempting to feed on the foliage of trees, gained by this exercise cervical vertebræ of a surprising length.

Lamarck, certainly, attributed to hereditary descent the function of accumulating continually for the profit of the species that which each individual had acquired for his own benefit ;.but he did not show what the slight acquisition was which was made by the individual himself, under the influence of external circumstances, and of the habits which he was forced to acquire. J. Hunter reasoned in a similar manner in sciences of a different order. When he wished to explain the cicatrization of wounds and the consolidation of fractured bones, he recognized the necessity that new tissue should be supplied by the blood; but why did the blood carry these elements to the parts which needed them ? "It was," said he, "in virtue of the *stimulus of necessity.*"

We seek at the present day to state with precision the relation between causes and effects, to ascertain the gradual transitions which the animal or vegetable organism is able to pass through when it finds itself placed under new conditions. We have a glimpse of the influence which function exercises over the organ itself which produces it. The short and pithy formula of Mons. J. Guérin, " *Function makes the organ,*" expresses in a general manner the modifying action of function. This formula will acquire additional force when supported by individual examples.

It must be shown how the bones, the articulations, the muscles are modified in various ways by the effect of functions of different kinds; how the digestive apparatus, yielding to very varying kinds of food, passes through transformations which adapt it to new conditions; how a change effected in the circulatory function produces in the vascular system certain anatomical modifications which may be predicted before they take place; how the senses acquire new qualities by exercise, or lose by desuetude their former powers. These changes of function under the influence of the function itself are accompanied by anatomical modifications in the apparatus, physiologically modified.

The first demonstration to be furnished will be to ascertain one of these transformations, and to show that it is always produced in a certain manner under certain circumstances. And if, in the second phase of the experiment, it can be proved that hereditary descent transmits even the least part of the modification thus acquired, the development theory will be in possession of a solid starting-point.

This seems to be the true course to follow, if we desire to obtain a solution of this important question. During several years serious efforts have been made in this direction. Having been ourselves for a long time conversant with the problems of animal mechanism, we have often been induced to reflect on the reciprocal relations of the organs of locomotion and of their functions. We will therefore attempt to show how the skeleton and the muscular apparatus harmonize with the movements of each animal under the ordinary conditions of its existence.

CHAPTER IX.

VARIABILITY OF THE SKELETON.

Reasons which have caused the skeleton to be considered the least variable
part of the organism—Proofs of the yielding nature of the skeleton
during life under the influence of the slightest pressure, when long continued—Origin of the depressions and projections which are observed
in the skeleton—Origin of the articular surfaces—Function rules the
organ.

Any one who examines the skeleton of an animal, and holds
in his hands its osseous portions as hard as a stone; who knows
how these bones have survived the destruction of all the other
organs, and how they can remain, after the lapse of thousands
of ages, tho only vestiges of extinct animals, may naturally look
upon the skeleton as the unchangeable part of the organism.
This skeleton, he argues, is the framework of the body, and
the soft parts are grouped around it as best they may, reposing
in its cavities, spreading over its surfaces, but always obey-
ing a law stronger than their own, and arranging themselves
in tho spaces which have been allotted to them among the different portions of the bony structure.

The observer, however little he may be acquainted with
anatomy, soon perceives on the surface of the bone a thousand
curious details; he sees there numerous small hollows, little
abodes which seem to have been destined to receive or to shelter
some organ that has disappeared. These hollows correspond
with the origin of the muscles which adhered at these points to
the excavated bones. Elsewhere there are deep rounded grooves
which remind one of the channels found in the curbstones of
ancient wells. A cord has also passed in that direction; it was
the tendon of a muscle which incessantly glided along that bone.
But at the two extremities of this humerus the bone is polished
as if by friction; in the upper part it is rounded like a
sphere, and it is lodged in a cavity of the shoulder-blade which
it exactly fits. One would say that the movement of these

bones had worn the surfaces smooth; the humerus continually
changing its position, and turning upon its axis, seems to
imitate the action we employ when we wish to obtain by
means of friction a body of a spherical form.

It is thus, for instance, that opticians produce the forms
and the polished surfaces of convex and concave lenses. At
its lower end the shoulder-bone shows the trace of the same
phenomenon, a small spherical projection articulating it with
the radius; it shows also that there existed movements of
two kinds, and close by, we meet with a surface cut like
the' groove of a pulley; this, in fact, only contributed to the
flexion and extension of the fore-arm.

If we examine the skull we meet with fresh surprises; here
every want is foreseen. Deep cavities lodge in their interior
the brain and the organs of sense.

The nerves have conduits which allow them to pass through;
each vessel creeps along a furrow which forms a canal for it,
and is ramified with the minute arteries whose rich foliation it
delicately traces out.

If the bone were not so hard, one would really suppose that
it had been subjected to external force, of which it bears, as it
were, the *impression*. But it is in vain to press a bony surface; it resists absolutely the force which is applied to it. It
is necessary to use a saw or a gouge if we wish to make a
channel in it. How could the pressure of soft parts hollow
out these cavities which are sometimes so deep?

The foresight of nature has prepared everything in the
skeleton so that it may be disposed in the best possible manner
to receive the organs to which it offers its solid and invari-
able support. Such is the natural argument of all those
who have not seen, with their own eyes, these osseous changes
take place, and these channels hollowed out. The anatomist
as well as the zoologist have necessarily reasoned in this
manner. They have considered the skeleton as the unalterable
element of the organism, and therefore they have derived from
it the greater part of the specific characters in zoology.

It must be very difficult to oppose an opinion which has
been for a long time received. Thus, when Mons. Charles
Martin, carrying out and rectifying the ideas of Vic. d'Azir,

has shown that the humerus of a man or of an animal is the homologue of the femur, but of a femur twisted on its axis, so that the knee turned behind becomes an elbow, zoologists have replied that this torsion was purely *virtual*. Instead of being the effect of a muscular effort, whose slow and gradual action has reversed the axis of the bone, this singular form is, in their opinion, the result of a pre-established arrangement of the organism; for the embryo shows a contorted humerus, before muscular action has been sufficiently developed to produce such a modification of its skeleton.

We might, with greater show of reason, argue in a directly opposite manner.

No one denies at the present day that the bony system is perfectly yielding in its character. These organs, which are so compact and so hard in the dead skeleton, are, on the contrary, essentially capable of being modified while the organism is living. If we exert upon a bone a pressure or a tension, however slight it might be, yet if prolonged for a considerable time, it can produce the strangest changes of form; the bone is like soft wax which yields to all external forces; and we may say of the skeleton, reversing the proposition to which we have just alluded, that it is completely under the influence of the other organs, and that its form is that which the soft parts with which it is surrounded permit it to assume.

We are indebted to medicine and surgery for the knowledge of important facts, of which many examples could easily be given. Thus, when an aneurism of the aorta is developed, and it happens to meet in its course the sternum or the clavicle, it does not stop at this barrier of bone, but perforates it in a few months. The substance of the bone is absorbed and disappears under the pressure of the aneurism; it certainly resists less the effort of the invading tumour than do the softer parts—the skin, for example.

But this pressure of the aneurism differs in no respect from that of the arterial blood; the force with which the aneurismal sac compresses and perforates the bones, is present in every part where an artery touches a bone. The same absorption of the bony material still goes on, so that the artery hollows out for itself a furrow in which it lodges with its dif-

ferent branches, an example of which is seen in the internal
surface of the parietal bones of the human skull. Even a vein
is able to form a considerable hollow in a bone. The abnormal dilatation of those veins which are called *varicose*, and
which is usually produced in the legs, is accompanied with a
change of form in the anterior surface of the tibia ; the bone
wears the impress of the dilated veins. We cannot say that
these osseous furrows enter into the pre-established plan of
nature ; that the skeleton had originally these furrows in
order to provide for the swollen state which should hereafter
be produced. Surgeons know that these hollows are formed
in the bone of an adult, which was in a perfectly normal state
before accident had caused the varicose dilatation of the veins.

It is a similar mechanism which forms along the bones the
furrows imprinted by the muscles, and which gives to the
perinœum, for instance, the prismatic form by which it is
characterized.

The hollows in which the tendons are lodged are not formed
beforehand in the skeleton ; it is the presence of the tendon
which has hollowed them out, and which still maintains them.
Should a luxation take place and change the position of the
bone with respect to the tendon, the former furrow which is
now empty is gradually effaced ; at the same time a new
furrow is formed, and by degrees assumes the necessary depth
to allow the tendon to repose in its fresh place.

But, it may be said, that the articular surfaces, so perfect
in their structure, so well adapted to the movements which
they carry on, are certainly organs formed beforehand. Here
the bony surfaces are clothed with a polished cartilage
moistened with a synovial fluid which facilitates their movement still more ; all around them, fibrous ligaments prevent
the bones from passing the limits allotted to them, and the
surfaces from separating from each other. So perfect an apparatus could not be formed by the function alone.

We have here at least a proof of the foresight of nature
and of the wisdom of her plans.

Let us turn once more to surgery, which will show us that
after dislocations, the old articular cavities will be obliterated
and disappear, while at the new point where the head of the

bone is actually placed, a fresh articulation is formed, to which nothing will be wanting in the course of a few months, neither articular cartilages, synovial fluid, nor the ligaments which retain the bones in their place. Here again, according to the expression which we used just now, function has produced the organ.

So much for the furrows formed in the bone. But how can we attribute to external influences those decided prominences which we observe everywhere on the surface of the skeleton, those apophyses, as they are called, to which each muscle is attached.

The answer is not less easy; it is sufficient to account for the formation of projections on the face of the bone, if we call into play an influence contrary to that which we know to be capable of hollowing out the indentations. We must admit that traction has been exercised on the portion of the bone where the projection is observed.

The existence of traction on all the points in the skeleton to which muscles are attached is absolutely evident; it is clear that the intensity of these tractions is proportional to the force of the muscles which produce them. Thus, it is precisely in the tendinous attachments of the stronger muscles that we find the more projecting apophyses; a proof that the prominences in the bone are intimately connected with the intensity of the effort acting upon them. The right arm, more frequently used than the left, acquires more decided projections on its bony structure. When paralysis of a limb suppresses the action of the muscles, its skeleton is no longer under the influence of muscular power, and the apophyses become less prominent; in fact, if paralysis dates from birth, the bone remains nearly in its fœtal form, which function has not supervened to modify.

Comparative anatomy also confirms this general law that the longer the apophysis is, the greater energy it reveals on the part of the muscle which was inserted into it.

Mons. Durand de Gros has clearly shown the influences of muscular function on the form of the torsion of the humerus in different species of fossil and recent animals. Thus the humerus in the mole, the ant-eater, and several other burrowing animals is scarcely recognizable, so thickly is it studded with ridges and projections, each of which gave insertion to a powerful muscle.

The skull and the lower jaw in the carnivora bear the traces of a powerful muscular action. In the skull a deep hollow retains the impression of enormous temporal muscles; all around the temporal depression, decided ridges were the solid points of attachment of the muscle; again, a strong and long apophysis by the side of the lower jaw shows the violent tractile force to which it has been subjected in the efforts of mastication.

If the effects of muscular actions on the bones augment with the intensity of the force of the muscles, they do not vary less in proportion to the duration of their action. From infancy to old age, the modification of the skeleton goes on more and more, and even allows us, to a certain degree, to determine the age of the subject.

Mons. J. Guérin has shown that in the old man the vertebræ have longer apophyses, the ribs more angular curves, &c. Compare the cranium of a young gorilla with that of an adult animal; the form will appear to you so different that unless you had been told that the two skulls belonged to animals of the same species, you would scarcely have believed it. Of a rounded form in the young gorilla, it changes its shape in the adult; it assumes a kind of ridge like the crest of a helmet; this is the apophysis into which the temporal muscles are inserted. We should never finish if we were to point out all the modifications to which the skeleton is subjected in different species of animals; modifications which from the beginning to the end of life become more and more marked.

Medicine, in its turn, furnishes us with curious information as to these questions, by showing us the sudden development of accidental apophyses which are called *exostoses*. In certain maladies which attack the entire body, we see the skeleton covered, in a great number of points, with accidental osseous projections; and almost all these prominences are developed at the points of attachment of the muscles, and as they increase, they extend especially in the direction in which muscular traction is applied.

The curvature of the bones, or their contortion on their axis, is a phenomenon which is frequently observed. I have mentioned that Mons. Ch. Martin has demonstrated that in all the mammalia, the humerus is a contorted femur, whose axis has made half a turn upon itself; this contortion, according to Gegenbaüer, is less in the fœtus than in the infant, and becomes still more marked in process of age. It is therefore partly effected by causes which are in action during life; and if it be true that every fœtus brings into the world a contorted humerus, it is not less true that this form may be considered as the effect of muscular action accumulated from generation to generation in terrestrial mammals.

Articular surfaces are particularly interesting to study when we wish to ascertain the influence of function over the organs. If we admit that the friction of these surfaces has polished them, and given them their curvature, it is easy, when we consider the movement which takes place in each articulation, to foresee the form which these surfaces ought to possess.

The surfaces whose curvature has the greater number of degrees, will correspond with the more extensive movements. Moderate movements, on the contrary, will only produce surfaces whose curvature will correspond with an arc of but few degrees. As a necessary consequence, the radius of curvature in the articular surfaces will be very short, if the movements are very extended; it will be very long if the movement is moderate.

Let us examine, from this point of view, the articulations of the foot in man; we see in the tibio-tarsal articulation a curvature of small radius, on account of the considerable movement of the foot on the leg. In the tarsus the radius of the curvature increases in proportion as the mobility of the bones diminishes. The scaphoid shows articular surfaces of a great radius; the radius increases still more in the tarso-metatarsal articulations, in which the movements are very limited; then it diminishes again in the articulations of the metatarsals with the phalanges, and of the phalanges with each other, at which point there is great mobility.

Everyone knows that if the articular movement is only effected in one direction, the surfaces will curve only in that direction; such are the trochlear surfaces, of which the articulation of the elbow, the condyles of the jaw, &c., are examples. But if the movement is executed in two directions at once, the surfaces will present a double curvature, and in the case of an inequality in the amplitude of the movements, the radii of these curvatures will be unequal. Thus, in the wrist there exist movements of flexion and extension which are considerably extensive, but the lateral movements are restricted. The result of this is that in the elliptical head formed by the carpal bone, there is a curvature of small radius in the direction of the movements of flexion and extension, while, in the lateral direction, the curvature belongs to a circle of much greater radius.

It is still more interesting to observe the articular surfaces of a series of animals in different classes and species. Similar articulations present movements of very different kinds, which must bring about no less important differences in the articular surfaces.

Let us take, for example, the head of the humerus, and follow the changes of its form, in man, in the ape, the carnivora, the herbivora, the birds. We shall see that the perfect equality of movement in every direction which can be executed by the human arm corresponds with a perfect sphericity to the head of the humerus—that is to say, a curvature of the same radius in every direction. Among apes, those which in walking throw a part of their weight usually on their anterior limbs, have the head of the humerus flattened at the upper part, as if by the weight of the body. Besides this, the movements which are required in walking being more extended, the curvature of the head of the humerus in these animals presents its least radius in the antero-posterior direction. This modification is more marked still in the carnivora, and above all in the herbivora, the head of whose humerus, flattened above, presents its short radius of curvature in the direction of the movements which serve for walking, and which predominate in this articulation.

Birds possess, in the articulation of the shoulder, two movements of unequal extent. One, by which they spread and fold their wings, and which carries the elbow sometimes

near to the body, and sometimes very forward; the other,
usually more restricted, is made in a direction perpendicular
to the former; it is that which constitutes the stroke of the
wing.

Curvatures of different radii correspond, therefore, to these
two movements of unequal amplitude; to the greater movement of stretching and folding the wing a curvature of short
radius corresponds; to the less extensive movement which
raises and lowers the wing during flight, there is a corresponding curved surface of very long radius. The result of
this is that the head of the humerus in birds' assumes the
form of a very elongated ellipse, at the level of the articular
surface.

But the movements of flight present in different species
great variations of amplitude. Birds which have sail-like
wings give but very small strokes with them, while the
pigeon, at the moment when it takes flight, strikes its wings
one against the other above and below, producing a clapping
noise, which is familiar to every one.

To these variations in the extent of the movements correspond varieties of surface in the head of the humerus, which
in birds with sail-like wings has a very elongated elliptical
surface; but in the pigeon it tends to the circular form, and
very nearly attains it in the spheniscus, an aquatic bird found
in southern seas, and closely resembling the penguin.

From all this we may gather, that in the form of the bony
structure, everything bears the trace of some external influence, and particularly of the function of the muscles. There
is not a single depression or projection in the skeleton,
the cause of which cannot be found in an external force,
which has acted on the bony matter, either to indent it, or
draw it forward. It was not, therefore, a metaphorical exaggeration to say, that the bone is subject, like soft wax, to all
the changes of form which external forces tend to impress
upon it; and that, notwithstanding its extreme hardness, it
resists less than the most supple tissues the efforts which tend
to change its form.

And will this new form, acquired by means of function,
disappear with the individual? Will he not transmit even

the slightest trace to his descendants? Will hereditary
descent make an unique exception with respect to these acquired characters? This appears very improbable, and yet
we must admit it, if we negative the development theory.
We must bring forward a contrary hypothesis, which would
reverse the ordinary laws of hereditary descent, if we refuse
to certain anatomical characters the power of becoming trans-
missible.

VARIABILITY OF THE MUSCULAR SYSTEM.

We have stated that the bony system is subject to external
influences, and especially to those of the muscles, which impress on each bone the form which we observe in it. The
great variety of forms in the skeletons of different animal
species corresponds, therefore, with the diversity of their
muscular systems. Thus, whenever in animals of different
species we find resemblances in certain bones, we may affirm
that the muscles which were attached to these bones were
also similar. Whenever we observe in an animal, on the
contrary, a bone of a peculiar form, we may feel assured of
a peculiarity in the muscles which were attached to it.

But if the muscle and the bone vary simultaneously, what
can be the cause which influences them both? It is understood that the skeleton, as it is modified, plays a passive part;
that it is subject to the form imposed upon it by the muscle.
But what gives to the muscle itself, an organ eminently active,
and the true generator of the mechanical force by which
the skeleton is in some degree modified, the particular form
which is revealed to us by anatomy?

We hope to demonstrate that the power to which the muscular system is subjected belongs to the nervous system. The
nature of the acts which the will commands the muscles to
perform, modifies the muscles themselves, in their volume and
their form, so as to render them capable of performing these
acts in the best possible manner. And, as this *necessity*
which determines all the actions of animal life, governs the
will, it is this, which, according to the external conditions
under which every living being is placed, influences its form,

and regulates it according to the laws which we must now
endeavour to make known.

Nothing in the organic form is under the dominion of
chance. The specific varieties of living beings have been too
often compared to the fancies of an architect, who, while
adhering to an uniform plan, invents a thousand varieties of
details, as a musician composes a series of variations on a
given theme.

In our present inquiry we may say that the great variety
which is found in the muscular apparatus, whether in the
different parts of the body of an animal, or in the homologous
parts of animals of different species; for instance, varieties
in the volume or the length of muscles; the very unequal
partition of the red contractile fibre, and the inert, white,
glistening fibre of the tendon; that all this is entirely subject
to the dynamic laws of muscular function.

Adaptation of the form of muscles to the requirements of function.
Normal anatomy can only furnish us with examples of the
harmony which exists between the form of the organs and
their habitual function. Experiment alone can show us that,
by changing the function, we may bring into the form of the
organs modifications which may harmonize them with the
new conditions which may be imposed upon them. It will
be easy to make experiments for this purpose. From the
moment when we know in what direction the modification
ought to be produced, in order to adapt the organ to the
function, the changes effected in animals placed by us under
conditions of peculiar muscular function, will derive an important significance. But while we wait for the realization of
this vast series of experiments, there are some which we can
employ even now. Experiments made ready to our hand are
furnished by pathological anatomy.

Medicine and surgery are full of information on this interesting subject. They show us, for example, that it is
movement itself which keeps up the existence of the muscle.
A long repose of this organ brings about first the diminution
of its volume, and soon a change in the elements which compose it. Fatty corpuscles are substituted for the striated fibre
which form its normal element; at last, those corpuscles,

becoming more and more abundant, invade the entire substance of the muscle. This phase of alteration, or fatty degeneration, is followed by an absorption of the substance of the
muscle, which disappears entirely at the end of a certain
time.

Thus, not only does the volume of the organ increase or
diminish according as the necessities of its habitual function
require a greater or less force, but it wholly disappears when
its function is entirely suppressed. This effect is observed in
paralysis, where all nervous action is destroyed; in certain
cases of dislocation, which bring closer together the two insertions of a muscle, so as to render its action useless; sometimes
even in fracture and anchyloses, which, by an abnormal connection, render the two extremities of a muscle immovable,
and prevent any contraction of its fibres.

But what will happen, if the muscle, instead of losing all
its function, only experiences a change with respect to the
extent of the movements which it can execute? After certain
incomplete anchyloses, or certain dislocations, we see the
articulations lose more or less of their movements; as the
muscles which command flexion and extension only need, in
such cases, a part of the ordinary extent of their contraction.

If the theory just enunciated be correct, these muscles ought
to lose a portion of their length. In order to verify this fact,
we have only to make a short excursion into the domain of
pathological anatomy.

A warm discussion arose, some twenty years ago, as to the
transformation which the muscles underwent in those patients
who were afflicted with the deformity commonly known by the
name of *club-foot*. Sometimes the foot is twisted upon the
leg, so that the surface which should be uppermost is next
the ground; sometimes the foot is so forcibly extended that
the patient walks continually on its extremity. In all these
cases the muscles of the leg have only a very limited play;
they undergo, therefore, either fatty or fibrous transformation.
Among these muscles, those which have no longer any action
undergo fatty degeneration, and then disappear; while those
whose action is partly preserved, present only a change as to
the proportion of red fibre and tendon. In the latter case

the contractile substance diminishes in length, and is replaced by tendon, which often assumes a considerable development.

J. Guerin, when pointing out the fibrous degeneration of the muscles, thought that he saw in it the proof of a primitive muscular retraction, which would ultimately have produced dislocation of the foot. This eminent surgeon also thought that the alteration of the fibre was the only lesion of the muscles in club-foot. Scarpa maintained, on the contrary, that in the greater number of cases the luxation of the foot was the original phenomenon.

As to the nature of muscular change, all surgeons at present agree in admitting that it may have two different forms, and that sometimes the muscle undergoes fatty degeneration, and in other cases it is transformed into fibrous tissue. We are especially indebted to the beautiful works of Cuvier, for our knowledge of the conditions under which each of those changes in the muscular substance is produced.

An example will illustrate how the muscles are affected according as their function is suppressed, or simply limited in extent.

The muscles of the calf of the leg, or gastrocnemians, are two in number; their attachments and their functions are very different. Both are inserted below in the calcaneum, by the tendon of Achilles, and are, consequently, extensors of the foot on the leg. But their superior insertions are different; the *soleus*, having its insertion exclusively in the bones of the leg, has no other office than that of extending the foot, as we have said before. The twin gastrocnemii, on the contrary, being inserted in the femur, above the condyles of that bone, have a second function, that of bending the leg upon the thigh.

Let us suppose that anchylosis of the foot has been produced; it entirely suppresses the function of the soleus, which passes through the fatty degeneration, and disappears. The two gastrocnemii are in a different condition; if their action on the foot has ceased, there still remains their function of bending the leg on the thigh; these muscles have, therefore, only one of their movements reduced in amplitude. Con-

x

sequently, under such conditions, the twin muscles lose only
a part of the length of their fibres; they undergo what surgeons call partial fibrous transformation, a modification which
is only a change of proportion between the red fibre and the
tendon.

Those who are accustomed to regard pathology as a complete infraction of physical laws, will perhaps be astonished
to see us search among these cases of dislocation and anchylosis for the proofs of a law which regulates the form of the
muscular system in its normal state. It would be easy to
show that these scruples have no foundation; but it will be
better still to bring forward other examples which may not lie
open to the objections so often urged against the applications
of medicine to physiology.

It is again from J. Guerin, that we must quote the facts
of which we are about to speak.

When we examine the muscular system at different periods
of life, we find that it varies greatly in its aspects. It seems
that the muscles have distinct ages, and that, formed at first of
contractile substance, they lose by degrees, as they grow
older, their red fibres, which are replaced by the white and
glistening fibres of the tendon.

Thus, the diaphragm of a child is principally muscular,
while in the old man the aponeurotic centre, the true tendon
of the diaphragm, is extended at the expense of the contractile fibre. The substitution of tendon for muscular fibre is
still more marked in the muscles of the leg in infancy; they
are relatively much more rich in contractile substance than
during adult age. In the old man, in fact, the tendon seems
to invade the muscle, so that the portion of the calf of the leg
which remains is placed very high, and is very reduced in
length. The muscles of the lumbar and dorsal regions present
the same character; in old age they are poorer in red fibre,
but richer in tendon.

What then, is the change which takes place in the muscular
function during the different periods of life? Every one knows
that, except in the very rare cases in which the man keeps up
the habit of gymnastic exercises, the muscular function becomes more and more restricted—at least, as far as the extent

of movement is concerned. The articulations of the limbs, and those of the vertebral column, undergo normally a sort of incomplete anchylosis, which continues to lessen more and more the flexibility of the trunk.

Look at a young child tossing about at his ease: one of his movements is to play with his foot; to take it in his hands and carry it to his mouth appears to him very natural, and as easy as possible. In the adult, the muscular force attains its maximum; but the movements are not so extensive as in infancy; man has no longer, as is well known, the same flexibility in his limbs.

The old man can neither stoop readily nor completely draw himself up; his vertebral column has lost its suppleness; he takes only short steps; to sit down on the ground, with the knees raised, is to him extremely difficult; and if we examine the extent of flexion and extension in his foot, we find that it has become very limited.

The function of the muscles, therefore, changes with the different periods of life, and becoming more and more restricted, employs continually less contractile fibre. It is thus that the muscular modification of which we have been speaking is naturally explicable. This modification, which consists in the increase of the tendinous element at the expense of red fibre, may be prevented by keeping up the extent of muscular movements, by means of suitable exercise.

Let us now return to comparative anatomy. Since it shows us perfect harmony between the form of the muscles in different species of animals and the characters of muscular function in the same species, the most natural conclusion seems to be that the organ has been subjected to the influence of function.

If the race-horse is modified in its form by the special exercise which is called training, is it not an evident proof of the influence of function on the anatomical characters of the organism? And if a species, thus modified artificially, returns to the primitive type when replaced under the conditions from which it had been taken, is it not the counter-proof of the theory which assigns to function the office of a modifier of the organ?

H 2

These very facts are, however, interpreted in an opposite
sense by the partisans of the invariability of species; they
seem to find an unanswerable argument in support of their
cause, in the return to the primitive type, when the modifying
influences have ceased.

· To what conclusion can we come when we meet with these
contrary opinions? It must be that the partisans of development have not completed their task, and that they ought to
add new proofs to those which they have already given. It
is to experiment that the principal part belongs, while theory
is not without its importance; by causing us to foresee in what
manner a certain kind of function ought to modify a muscle,
it will give its proper value to the modification which may
subsequently be obtained. Indeed, without theory, the experimenter can seldom recognize the modification which he
has observed. We seldom find in anatomy anything but
that which we seek for, especially when we have to do with
slight variations like those which we might hope to produce
in the organism of an animal.

The experiments to be tried are tedious and troublesome;
their plan, however, is easy to trace.

If man, adapting to his necessities the domestic animals,
has already succeeded in modifying their organization within
certain limits, he has produced these changes, as we may
say, fortuitously. Only intending, for example, to obtain
draught horses or racers, it was not necessary to place
the species under conditions entirely artificial. This must,
however, be done, if we aim at elucidating the problem of
which we speak, and of carrying to the farthest possible
limit, changes in the conditions of the mechanical work of
animals.

Man has utilized the aptitudes of different animals, rather
than sought to give them new ones. It would be necessary
to do violence to the habits of animals, and to constrain
them gradually to perform acts to which their organism is
but slightly adapted. If, in order to get its food, a species
with an organization unsuitable for leaping, should be compelled to take leaps of gradually greater height, everything
leads us to suppose that it would acquire at length great

facilities for leaping. If the descendants of these animals retained any of the power of their ancestors, they might perhaps, in their turn, develop still more this faculty of leaping. Graduating thus the effort imposed on this particular species, no longer in a utilitarian point of view, which there would be no inducement to surpass, but requiring indefinitely more force or greater extent in the play of the muscles, we might hope that the anatomical development would increase indefinitely, and that we might obtain something analogous to that which is now called the passage of one species into another.

What we have said of the muscular function applies to all the rest. By modifying in a gradual manner the conditions of the food of animals, as well as those of light and darkness, temperature, and atmospheric pressure under which they may be made to live, we may impress upon their organism modifications analogous to those which zoologists have already observed under the influence of climate, and of the various atmospheric conditions and different altitudes in which animals have been placed by nature. These changes, brought about by well-managed transitions always tending to the same end, would have a chance of producing considerable transformations in animal organization, provided that, by persevering determination, these efforts were indefinitely accumulated; as in the case of breeders of animals, who use similar means for the production of selected kinds of stock.

We will proceed no farther in the field of hypothesis, but we will, in conclusion, make an appeal to zealous experimentalists. Many who have been convinced of the great importance of this enquiry seem already to be engaged in this enterprise. What question, in fact, can more nearly concern the human race than this: *Can our species be modified?* According to the tendency which may be given to it, can it be directed either towards perfection, or degradation?

BOOK THE SECOND.

FUNCTIONS: TERRESTRIAL LOCOMOTION.

CHAPTER I.

OF LOCOMOTION IN GENERAL.

Conditions common to all kinds of locomotion—Borelli's comparison—
Hypothesis of the reaction of the ground—Classification of the modes
of locomotion, according to the nature of the point of resistance, in
terrestrial, aquatic, and aërial locomotion—Of the partition of muscular
force between the point of resistance and the mass of the body—Production of useless work when the point of resistance is movable.

THE most striking manifestation of movement in the different species of animals is assuredly locomotion : the act by
which each living creature, according to its adaptation to outward circumstances, moves on the earth, in the water, or
through the air. Therefore it is more convenient to study
movement with regard to locomotion, for we can thus observe
it under the most varied types.

At the commencement of these studies we ought to consider
the general characteristics of the function which is to occupy
attention, and to point out the general laws which are to be
found in all the modes of animal locomotion. But what can
be more difficult than to ascertain the common features which
unite acts so different as those of flying and of creeping, as
the gallop of a horse and the swimming of a fish? Still this
has been frequently attempted. Borelli has endeavoured to
represent the various modes of terrestrial locomotion, by the
different methods which a boatman employs to direct his boat.

This comparison may, with some additional developments,
serve to explain the mechanism of the principal types of locomotion.

Let us suppose a man seated in a boat in the midst of a tranquil lake. Under these conditions, his skiff will remain perfectly motionless. If he wishes to advance, he must find what is called a point of resistance. Suppose him to be furnished with a pole, he will plunge it towards the bottom of the water till it reaches the ground; then, making an effort, as if to drive from him this resisting body, he will cause his boat to move in the opposite direction. This progression with the point of resistance on the ground is similar to the ordinary conditions of terrestrial locomotion.

If the boatman be provided with a boat-hook, he will get his point of resistance under different conditions. Laying hold of the branches of trees, or the projections of the shore, he will drag his pole towards himself, as if to bring near to him the bodies to which it is fastened; and if these bodies resist his efforts, the boat alone will be displaced and drawn towards them.

Here are then two opposite modes of progression with bearings on solid bodies; in one the tendency is to repel, in the other, to draw them nearer: the effect is the same in each case.

But if the lake be too deep, or if the shores be too distant to furnish the boatman with the solid fulcrum which he had used before, the water itself will serve as a medium of resistance. The boatman, armed with a flattened oar, endeavours to drive the water towards the stern of his boat; the water will yield to this impulse, but the boat, impelled in an opposite direction, will go forward. The various kinds of paddles for steam-boats, the screw, in fact, all nautical propellers, present this feature in common, of driving the water backward, in order to produce in the boat an impulse in the contrary direction, and to cause it to advance.

Instead of an oar acting on the water, we may suppose the boatman provided with a much larger paddle with which he might drive back the air at the stern; he will propel his boat on the surface of the lake. He might make progress also by turning a large screw like the sails of a windmill, or by agitating at the stern some large fan which would drive the air in the direction opposed to that in which he desired to force his boat.

In all these modes of locomotion a force is expended which impels in opposite directions two bodies more or less resisting; the one is the fulcrum, the other the weight to be displaced.

Old writers called the force acting on the boat *re-action*—they considered it as an effort emanating from the soil, the water, or any resistance whatever to which the effort of the rowers was applied. We can now understand clearly that all the motive force is derived from the boatman. This force can have as its result, either the repulsion of two points to which it is applied, or their approach to each other. In these two cases one of the points may be fixed, it is then the other which will be displaced; or the two points may be movable, and then, according to their unequal movability, one of them will be displaced more than the other.

This general principle can be applied to all cases of locomotion: it will be sufficient for us to notice that which is essential in all the types which we shall consider.

The most natural classification seems to be that which is based on the nature of the point of resistance; accordingly, we may distinguish three principal forms of locomotion —*terrestrial, aquatic,* or *aërial.* But in each of these forms, what a variety of mechanism we shall meet with!

If it be true that walking and creeping are the two principal types of terrestrial motion, that swimming corresponds with the more habitual mode of aquatic locomotion, and flight with aërial locomotion, it is not less true that in certain media many kinds of locomotion are employed. Thus, walking and creeping are used both on the earth and in the water; flight is habitually performed in the air, and yet certain birds take a decided flight in the water.

In fact, if we were compelled to assign to every animal its particular type of locomotion, our embarrassment would be as great as if we were classifying these movements. Some, indeed, move with an equal facility on the earth, the water, and in the air. We will not therefore attempt a strictly methodical classification of the different modes of locomotion of which we are about to take a rapid survey.

Terrestrial locomotion furnishes two principal types: in one the effort consists in pressing on the ground in the direction opposite to the intended movement; this is the more usual mode of locomotion; walking, running, leaping, belong to this first form. For this purpose the limbs serving for locomotion are composed of a series of rigid levers, susceptible of change in length; they can be shortened by the angular flexion of the articulations, and they grow longer by being drawn up. If the leg when bent touches the ground at its extremity, and if a muscular effort be made to produce the extension of the limb, this can only be effected by removing to a greater distance from each other the ground on which the extremity of the leg rests and the body of the animal which is united to the base of this limb; the ground offers resistance, and the body, yielding to the impulse, is displaced. Sometimes the displacement in terrestrial locomotion is effected, not by a change in length, but by a simple change of the angle formed between the limb which causes the motion and the body of the animal.

In the second type, namely *creeping*, a tractile effort is produced; the animal lays hold by a part of its body on an external fixed point, and then drags the mass of its bulk towards this point. Let us take a snail, and place it on a piece of transparent glass; at the end of a few moments the animal begins to crawl. If we turn the glass over, we shall see through the plate the details of its movements. Throughout all the length of its body appears a series of transverse bands, alternately pale and deeply coloured, opaque and transparent. These bands are transmitted by a continual motion, from the tail to the head of the animal; they seem like the spirals of a screw which turns incessantly in the same direction. If we fix our attention on one of these bands in the neighbourhood of the tail, we see it pass towards the head, which it reaches in fifteen or twenty seconds, but it is followed by a continued series of bands which seem to spring up behind it as it advances. These bands remind us of the muscular wave and its progress through a contracting fibre, only with greater dimensions. Each time that a wave arrives at the cephalic region of the animal, it disappears, producing a forward motion of the head, which slips a little on the surface of the glass and advances slightly without any retrogression.

It appears that the cephalic region lays hold on the fixed
point towards which all the rest of the body is dragged forward.   In fact, in the posterior region an opposite phenomenon takes place; each new band which takes its rise there, is
accompanied by a backward motion of that region, which moves
as if it were drawn by a longitudinal retraction of the contractile tissue.

Other modes of creeping are not less curious; that, for
example, which takes place in the interior of a solid body;
as a worm, when it advances in the tubular cavity which it
has hollowed out in the ground.   The hinder part of the body,
soft and extensible, is assuredly of much less size than the
cavity of the hole from which we endeavour to pull it, and
yet the worm resists the force of traction, and breaks rather
than be drawn out.   This is because, within the ground,
the anterior portion of the body, shortened but swollen, dilates
within the passage, and finds there a solid point of resistance.
If we let the worm go we shall see it rapidly shorten its
body, and withdraw the rest of it into the ground, being
dragged backward towards the anterior portion which has a
firm hold on the soil.

By the side of the action of creeping we may naturally
place that of *climbing*, in which the anterior limbs seek to lay
hold of some elevated projection, and as they bend raise the
rest of the body of the animal.   The hinder part then fixes
itself in its new position, and the anterior limbs, thus set free,
seek, higher up, a fresh resting place to make a new effort.
What different types in these two modes of terrestrial locomotion!   The varieties are so great that we can scarcely give
an exact idea of them, except by describing the mode of progression adopted by each particular animal.

Locomotion in water presents a still greater diversity.   In
one case, we see a fish which strikes the water with the flat
of its tail; in another, a cuttle fish or a medusa, which, com-
pressing forcibly its pouch full of liquid, drives out the water
in one direction and propels itself in a course directly opposite;
the same phenomenon is produced when a mollusk closes rapidly
the valves of its shell, and projects itself in the direction opposed
to the current of water which it has produced.   The larvæ of

dragon-flies expel from their intestines a very strong jet of liquid, and acquire, by this means, a rapid and forcible impulse.

The *oar* is found in many insects which move on the surface of the water. A contrivance is employed by other animals, which resembles the action of an oar used at the stern of a boat in the process called *sculling.* To this latter motive power may be referred all those movements in which an inclined plane is displaced in the liquid, and finds in the resistance of the water, which it presses obliquely, two component forces, of which one furnishes a movement of propulsion. This mechanism will require some explanation; it will be found in its proper place, with all the developments which it affords.

Aërial locomotion. This mechanism is still the same; the motion of an inclined plane, which causes motion through the air. The wing, in fact, in the insect as well as in the bird, strikes the air in an oblique manner, repels it in a certain direction, and gives the body a motion directly opposite. With the exception of certain birds which spread their wings to the wind, and which, hovering thus without any other effort than simply steering, have received the picturesque name of hovering or sailing birds (oiseaux voiliers), all animals move forward only by an effort exerted between two masses unequally movable. It can be easily understood that if one of these points where the force is applied is absolutely fixed, the other alone will receive without diminution the motive work developed; such is the condition of terrestrial locomotion on soil perfectly solid. But we can understand also that the softness of the ground constitutes a condition unfavourable to the utilization of the force employed, and that the extreme mobility both of the air and the water offer still less favourable conditions for swimming or flight.

But this mobility of the point of resistance varies with the rapidity of the movement; so that a certain stroke of the wing or the oar, which would be without effect if produced slowly, would become efficacious by its very rapidity.

In different kinds of locomotion, the resistance which it is necessary to overcome in order to displace the body, does not vary less than that which serves as an external point of

resistance. This variability depends on many causes. Thus,
different kinds of animals, when they move, have not to
struggle with the same effort against their weight. The fish,
which is of nearly the same specific gravity as water, finds
itself suspended in it without having to exert any force;
and if it wishes to move in any direction, it has only to
overcome the resistance of the fluid which it is necessary
to displace. The bird, on the contrary, if it desires to sustain itself in the air, must make an effort capable of
neutralizing the action of its weight. If it moves forward
at the same time, it must perform, in addition, the work
which is consumed in overcoming the resistance of the air.

*Partition of muscular force between the points of resistance and
the mass of the body.* When, in physiology, we seek to estimate the work of a muscle, we fix it firmly by one of its
attachments, and we ascertain the extent passed through
by its movable extremity. If we know the weight which
this muscle can raise as it contracts, and the extent through
which that weight is raised, we have elements by which we
can estimate the work effected. But these are almost ideal
conditions, which are scarcely ever found in terrestrial locomotion; nor can we observe them in animals which move in
the water, and more especially in those which fly through the
air. Let us only compare the effort necessary to walk on a
movable soil, on sandy dunes, for instance, with that required
in walking on firm soil. We shall see that the mobility of
the resisting surface presented by the sand destroys a part of
the effort necessary for the contraction of our muscles; in
other words, that a greater effort is necessary to produce the
same useful work, when the point of resistance is not stable.

This amount of work is easy to be understood, and even to
be measured.

When a man, while walking, places one of his feet on the
ground, the corresponding leg, slightly bent, draws itself up,
and pressing on the ground below, gives at the same time an
upward impulse to the body. If the ground entirely resist
this pressure, all the movement produced will be in the
direction of the trunk of the body, which will be raised
to a certain height, three centimetres for example. But if

the ground sink two centimetres under the pressure of the foot, it is evident that the body will only be raised one centimetre, and the useful work will be diminished by two-thirds.

The compression of the soil under the foot certainly constitutes work, according to the mechanical definition of this word. In fact, the soil, as it yields, offers a certain resistance. This resistance must be multiplied by the extent to which the soil is indented, in order to ascertain the value of the work accomplished in this direction. But this work is absolutely useless with respect to locomotion: it is an entire loss of the motive force expended.

When a fish strikes the water with his tail, in order to drive himself forward, he executes a double work; a part tends to drive behind him a certain mass of fluid with a certain velocity, and the other to drive the animal forward in spite of the resistance of the surrounding water. This last work alone is utilized; it would be much more considerable if the tail of the animal met with a solid point of resistance instead of the water which flies from before it.

Is it possible to measure the diminution of useful work in locomotion, according to the greater or less mobility of the point of resistance?

If the ground on which we walk resist perfectly, it must be admitted that no part of the muscular work is lost; but in every case in which a displacement of the resisting surface exists at the same time as that of the body, it is necessary to determine the law according to which this partition is made. A principle established by Newton regulates the science of mechanics; this is that "action and re-action are equal." Does this mean, in the case before us, that half of the work is expended on the resisting surface, and the other half on the displacement of the body of the animal? This cannot be true, if we may judge by the many cases in which a force acts on two bodies at the same time.

Thus, in the science of projectiles, the motive force of the powder—that is to say, the pressure of the gases which are disengaged in the cannon, acts at the same time on the projectile and on the piece, giving these masses a velocity in opposite directions. Thus, the *momentum* (M.V.) is equally divided between the two projectiles, so that the mass of the cannon and of its carriage, multiplied by the velocity of the recoil which is communicated to it, is equal to the mass of the projectile multiplied by the velocity of propulsion which it receives. As the cannon weighs much more than the ball, the velocity of its recoil is much less than that communicated to the projectile.

As to the *work* developed by the powder against the cannon and against the ball, it is divided very unequally between these two masses.

In fact, the work produced by an active force being proportional to the square of the velocity of the mass in motion (its formula is $\frac{mv^2}{2}$), calculation shows that this work, when the piece weighs 300 times more than the ball, would be 300 times greater for the ball than for the cannon.

We shall return to these questions, when in considering the particular kinds of animal motion, we enter on the investigation of human locomotion.

CHAPTER II.

TERRESTRIAL LOCOMOTION (BIPEDS).

Choice of certain types in order to study terrestrial locomotion—Human locomotion—Walking—Pressure exerted on the ground, its duration and intensity—Its-actions on the body during walking—Graphic method of studying them—Vertical oscillations of the body—Horizontal oscillations—Attempt to represent the trajectory of the pubis—Forward movement of the body—Inequalities of its velocity during the time occupied by a pace.

ACT OF WALKING IN MAN.

THE types of terrestrial locomotion are so various that we must, for a time at least, confine ourselves to the study of the most important among them. For locomotion among bipeds we will take as a type that of man. The horse will be chosen as the most important representative of the method of walking adopted by quadrupeds. As to other animals, they will be studied in an accessory manner, and especially with reference to the resemblances and differences which the modes of their locomotion present when compared with the types which we have chosen.

Many authors have already treated on this subject; from the time of Borelli to that of modern physiologists, science has slowly advanced: it seems to us that it can now resolve all obscure questions, and determine them definitely, by the employment of the graphic method.

While observation employed alone furnishes only incomplete and sometimes false data, the graphic method carries its precision into the analysis of the very complex movements concerned in locomotion. We shall see, when we treat of the paces of the horse, that the disagreement we find among writers on this subject shows clearly the insufficiency of the methods hitherto employed.

Human locomotion, though much more simple in its mechanism, is still very difficult to analyse; the works of the two Webers, though considered as the deepest investigation of human locomotion that have yet been made, show many omissions and some errors.

The most simple and usual pace is *walking*, which, according to the received definition, consists in that mode of locomotion in which *the body never quits the ground*. In running and leaping, on the contrary, we shall see that the body is entirely raised above the ground, and remains suspended during a certain time.

In walking, the weight of the body passes alternately from one leg to the other, and as each of these limbs places itself in turn before the other, the body is thus continually carried forward. This action appears very simple at first sight, but its complexity is soon observed when we seek to ascertain what are the movements which concur in producing this motion.

We see, in fact, that each movement of the limbs brings under consideration a phase of impact and one of support in each of these; the different articulations bend and extend

alternately, while the muscles of the leg and the thigh, which
produce these movements, pass through alternations of contraction and relaxation.

The intensity of the pressure of the feet on the ground
varies with the rapidity of walking and with the length of the
step. Besides this, the body passes through periodical oscillations, the re-action of the impact of each foot on the ground;
and the different parts of the body are subject to this re-action
in various degrees. These oscillations are produced in different directions; some are vertical, others horizontal, so that
the trajectory which follows any point of a body is a very
complex curve. In addition to this, the body is inclined and
drawn up again at each movement of one of the legs; it
revolves as on a pivot round the coxo-femoral articulation, at the
same time that it is slightly bent following the axis of the
vertebral column; and, under the action of the lumbar muscles,
the pelvis moves and oscillates with a sort of rolling motion.
At the same time the anterior limbs, exerting an alternate
balancing power, lessen the influences which, at each instant,
tend to cause the body to deviate from the straight course
which it strives to maintain.

All these acts have been analysed with much sagacity by
one of our pupils, Mons. G. Carlet,* from whom we quote some
of the results which he has obtained.

The motive force developed in walking, its pressure on the
ground in one direction, and its propelling effects on the mass
of the body on the other hand, are the three elements which
will at first occupy our attention.

Motive force. This is found in the action of the exterior
muscles of the thigh, the leg, and the foot. The lower limb
forms, as a whole, a broken column, whose angles are rounded
off, and whose return to the perpendicular is effected by pressure on the ground below, and on the body above. This is all
that we can say on this head, which, if treated more at length,
would require considerable amplifications.

Pressure on the ground. This pressure, equal, as we have
before seen, to that in the opposite direction, which tends to
impel the body forward, must be studied in its *duration, its*

* G. Carlet, Étude de la Marche. Annales des Sciences naturelles, 1872.

phases, and its intensity. The registering apparatus enables us to do this perfectly; an experimental instrument placed under the sole of the foot is connected with a lever which gives the signals of the impact and of the rising of the foot, as well as the expression of the force with which the foot is pressed upon the ground. We call this first instrument the *experimental shoe,* which may be thus described :—

Under the sole of an ordinary shoe is fixed with heated gutta percha a strong sole of india-rubber 1½ centimetres in thickness. Within this sole there is an air chamber, which in fig. 19 is represented by dotted lines.

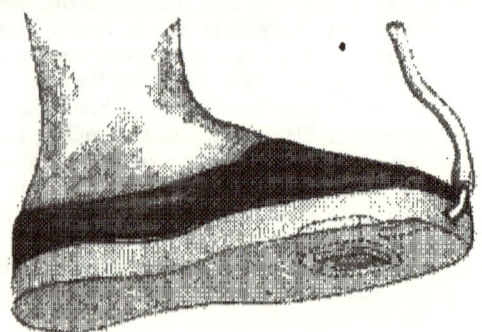

ΙΟ. 19.—Experimental shoe, intended to show the pressure of the foot on the ground, with its duration and its phases.

This chamber, having upon it a small piece of projecting wood, is compressed at the moment that the foot exerts its pressure on the ground. The air expelled from this cavity escapes by a tube into a *drum with a lever* attached, which registers the duration and the phases of the pressure of the foot.

Let us suppose that the experimenter is provided on both feet with similar shoes, and that he walks at a regular pace round a table which supports the registering apparatus; we shall then understand the arrangement of the experiment.

The registering instruments employed are already known to the reader; they resemble in all points those which have

ι

served for the investigation of the muscular wave (fig. 7, page 37). If we substitute in this figure an experimental shoe for each of the myographical clips 1 and 2, we shall have the arrangement of the apparatus necessary for the study of *footsteps* or *impacts* of the foot on the ground.

Fig. 20 has been furnished by an experiment in walking. Two tracings are given by the intermittent pressure of the feet on the ground. The full line D corresponds with the right foot; the dotted line with the left.

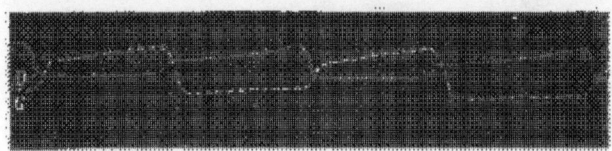

Fig. 20.—Tracings of the impact and the rise of the two feet in our ordinary walk.

Knowing the arrangement of the apparatus, we can understand that each impact of the foot on the ground will be represented by the elevated part of the corresponding curve. In fact, the pressure of the foot on the ground compresses the india-rubber sole and diminishes the capacity of the included air-chamber. A part of the contained air escapes by the connecting tube, and passes into the registering drum.

We see in fig. 20 that the pressure of the right foot, for instance, commences at the moment when that of the left begins to decrease; and that in all the tracings there is an alternation between the impacts of the two feet. The period of *support* of each foot is shown by a horizontal line which joins the minima of two successive curves.

The impacts of the right and left feet have the same duration, so that the weight of the body passes alternately from one foot to the other. It would not be the same with respect to a lame person; lameness corresponds essentially with the inequality of the impacts of the two feet.

There is always a very short period during which the body is partially supported by one foot, but when it already begins to rest on the other; this time is scarcely equal to the

sixth part of the duration of a single *impact* or pressure of
the foot.

Intensity of the pressure of the foot upon the ground.—The
curves traced by walking may also furnish the measure of the
effort exerted by the foot upon the ground. The *experimental
shoes* constitute a kind of dynameter of pressure; they compress the drum, less or more, according to the effort they
exert; and consequently they transmit to the registering lever
more or less extensive movements. In order to estimate,
according to the elevation of the curve, the pressure exerted
by the foot, we must substitute for the weight of the body a
certain number of kilogrammes. We see thus that, if the
weight of the body (75 kilogrammes, for example) is sufficient
to raise the lever to the height which it attains at the commencement of each curve, an additional weight will be required
to raise it to the maximum elevation which it attains towards
the end of its period of pressure.

That proves that, in walking, the pressure of the foot on
the ground is not only equal to the weight of the body which
the foot has to sustain, but that a greater effort is produced at
a given moment in order to give the body the movements of
elevation and progression which we have just been studying.

According to Mons. Carlet, this additional effort is not more
than 20 kilogrammes, even in rapid walking, but it is much
greater in running and leaping.

Reactions.—We shall designate by this name the movements
which the action of the leg produces on the mass of the body.
These movements are very complex; they are effected at the
same time in every direction, and give to the trajectory
which a point of the body describes in space, some very complicated sinuosities. The graphic method alone can enable
us, at least as yet, to appreciate the real nature of these
movements.

In the first place, what point of the body shall we choose
in order to observe the displacement caused by the act of
walking? Almost all authors have taken for this purpose the
centre of gravity, the point which Borelli places *inter nates et
pubim*. But if we reflect that the centre of gravity changes
as soon as the body moves, that in the flexion of the legs this

centre rises, that it is altered if we raise our arms, that, in fact, it describes within the interior of the body all sorts of movements, as soon as we cease to be motionless, it is easy to understand that it will be impossible to refer to this ideal and movable point, the reactionary movements produced by the pressure of the feet upon the ground. It will be better to choose a determinate part of the trunk of the body, the pubis, for example, in order to study its movements in the act of walking.

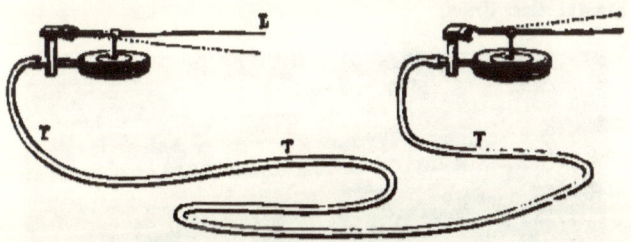

Fig. 31.—Transmission of an oscillatory movement to the registering apparatus.

The instrument which we have already employed will be applicable to the study of these displacements.

Let there be two *lever drums*, united by a long tube T T T. Let a vertical oscillary movement be given to one of these levers, so as, for example, to carry the lever L downwards into the position indicated by the dotted line, the other lever will be displaced in the opposite direction, and will assume the position also shown by the dotted line near it. Under these conditions the lowering of one lever corresponds with the elevation of the other, since the compression of the air in one of the drums must lead to its expansion in the other. If we wish to obtain from the two parts of the apparatus indications in the same direction, it would be necessary to turn one of the drums, so as to place its lever downwards.

Vertical oscillations of the body.—Let us suppose that one of these levers traces a curve on the registering apparatus, while the other rests, by its point, on the pubis of a man who is walking; all the vertical oscillations of the pubis will be registered.

But, in order that the *experimental lever* may receive and transmit faithfully the vertical oscillations which the pubis executes during the act of walking, the drum itself must be protected from these oscillations. For this purpose an instrument has been invented, composed of two horizontal arms, which turn on a centre. These arms can move only in a horizontal plane, situated at the height of the pubis of the person under experiment; to one of these arms is fixed the experimental *lever drum*.

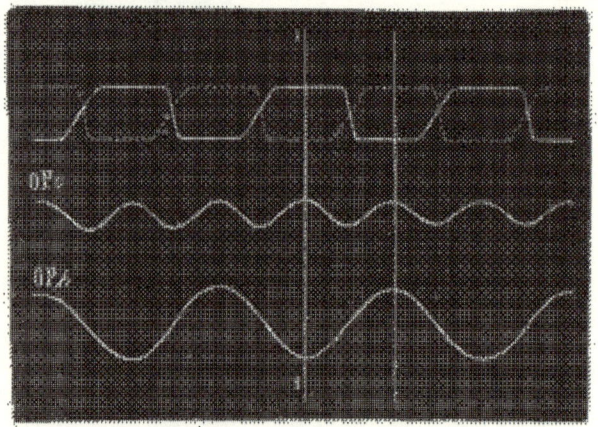

Fig. 27.—The upper curves, one in full line, the other dotted, represent the phases of the impact and of the rise of the right and left foot. Reading the figure from left to right, each rise of the curve denotes the commencement of pressure: the upper horizontal part corresponds with the duration of the pressure, and the descent with the rise of the foot. The lower horizontal part of the curve indicates that the corresponding foot is in the air. O Pv. Oscillations of the pubis from above downwards, that is, vertically. O PA. Oscillations in a lateral direction, or horizontally. It is evident that two oscillations in the vertical direction correspond with a single horizontal oscillation.

The person who walks, follows during this time a circular path, pushing before him the arm of the instrument, to which is fixed the apparatus which is to experiment on the vertical oscillations of the pubis. We get thus the tracing repre-

sented by the line O Pv (fig. 22). It is seen that the pubis
rises at the middle of the pressure exerted by each foot, and
sinks at the instant when the weight of the body passes from
one foot to the other.

The real amplitude of these oscillations is about 14 millimetres, according to Mons. Carlet. This movement, however,
varies with the length of the step; it increases with it, but
this increase does not depend on the maxima of the curve
being more elevated, but on its minima being lower.

We may explain these phenomena very easily. When the
body is about to quit the support of one leg, this limb is in
an inclined position, and the result of its obliquity is that its
superior extremity which sustains the trunk is at a less height.
The other leg, which reaches the ground at this instant, is
slightly bent; it will soon draw itself up, and thus raise the
body which is supported by it; but in this movement, the
leg describes the arc of a circle around the foot resting on the
ground; therefore, in the series of successive positions which
it occupies, the body rises more and more as the leg which
supports it approaches the vertical position; it sinks again as
the leg becomes oblique.

We can easily perceive that the length of the step lowers
the trunk, by increasing the obliquity of the legs. Indeed,
the constant character found in the maxima of the vertical
oscillations is explained by this fact, that the leg, when extended and vertical, constitutes necessarily a constant height
—that which answers to the maximum of the elevation of the
body.

Horizontal oscillations of the body.—The pubis, since that is
the point whose displacement we are now studying, is carried
alternately from left to right, and from right to left, at the
same time as it moves vertically. In order to register these
movements, we make use of a lever-drum arranged in such a
manner that the membrane is forced inwards and outwards
alternately by the lateral movements which are given to the
lever. During this time the registering lever, connected with
it by means of the tube, oscillates vertically, in which direction alone tracings can be made on the cylinder. If, in the
curve which is traced, the elevation corresponds with a trans-

ference of the pubis towards the right, the depression will express a deviation of this point towards the left.

The experiment gives the curve O P A (fig. 22) for the tracing of the horizontal oscillations. It is first to be observed that the number of these oscillations is only half that of those which take place in the vertical direction; so that the body is carried towards the right side at the moment of the maximum of elevation, which corresponds with the middle of the pressure on the right foot, and towards the left at the middle of the pressure on the left foot. This lateral swaying of the trunk is the consequence of the alternate passage of the body into a position sensibly vertical over each foot.

If we would give an idea of the true trajectory of the pubis under the influence of these two orders of oscillations combined with forward movement, we must construct a solid figure. With an iron wire bent in different directions, we may illustrate very clearly this trajectory. Fig. 23 is intended to represent the perspective view of this twisted iron wire; but we can scarcely expect the reader to comprehend clearly this mode of representation.

Fig. 23.—Attempt to illustrate, by means of a metallic wire, the sinuous trajectory passed through by the pubis. To understand the sketch of this solid figure, we must suppose the wire to be close to the observer at its left hand extremity, while it is removed from him at the right extremity. The amplitude of the oscillations has been greatly exaggerated to render them more intelligible.

In short, according to the formula of Mons. Carlet, the trajectory of the pubis may be inscribed in a hollow half-cylinder, with its concave portion upwards, at the base of

which lie the minima, and on the sides of which, the maxima
terminate tangentially.

Forward progress of the body.—It is clear that during the
act of walking, the body never ceases to advance; but the
forward movement has not always the same velocity. To
appreciate these alternate phases of acceleration and retardation, it is necessary to employ a method which would give the
measurement of the space passed through during each of the

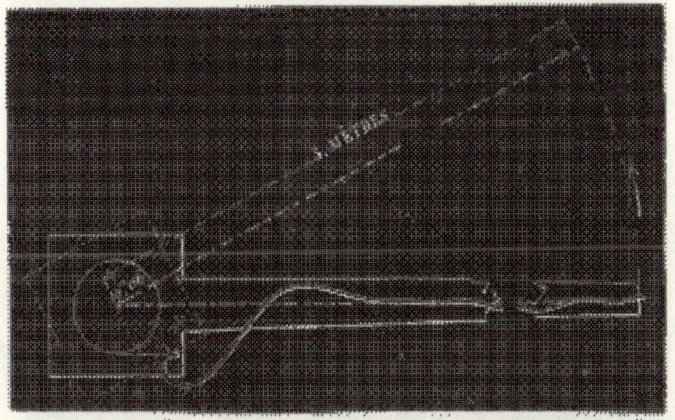

Fig. 24.—Showing two successive positions of the arm of the instrument,
and the corresponding positions of the tracing points of the levers. The
arm of the lever being three metres in length, and the radius of the
cylinder being only six centimetres, a similar angular displacement of
the person walking, and of the style which writes, will correspond with
spaces which will be to each other as 50 to 1.

movements in the act of walking, and which would also
express the time employed in passing through each of these
spaces. In order to obtain this double indication, we have
recourse to the following method :—

It is necessary, first, to ascertain how far the body advances
at the different instants of the act of walking. This measure
of the spaces passed through, is obtained by inscribing the
curves of locomotion, no longer on a cylinder turning with a
regular motion, but on an immovable one, on which the

registering levers are displaced by a quantity proportionate to the space passed through.

For this purpose the cylinder is placed on the axis round which the instrument turns, and on the central end of one of these revolving arms the registering instruments are fixed. The ratio of the radius of the cylinder to that of the circle described by the person walking, allows us to estimate in the tracings the length of the space passed through at each instant. This ratio was 50 to 1 in our experiments.

Thus, in the tracing obtained, if from one point to another we reckon an interval of a centimetre, this corresponds with 50 centimetres passed over on the ground by the person walking. This first notion would be but slightly interesting in itself, since it would teach us nothing more than what we learn concerning the intervals between two positions of the feet, as measured on the ground. The impressions left by our steps on soft ground would furnish in a very simple manner this measurement. But if, in addition to this knowledge of the space traversed, the tracing gives us the intimation of the time passed in traversing it, we are provided with a method of estimating the rapidity of the advance of the body at every instant.

Fig. 25.—D. Tracing of the impact and rise of the right foot, furnished by a lever subjected at the same time to 10 vibrations per second. It is seen that the vibrations occupy more space at the end of the pressure of the foot; this expresses the greatest rapidity of the advance of the body at this moment. The same acceleration is observed at the end of the period of support of the right foot; this is explained by the action of the left foot, which is, at this moment, at the end of its pressure.

Fig. 25 shows (line D) the tracings of the impact and rise of a limb, and those of the vibrations of a chronograph inscribed simultaneously. To obtain these tracings, we cause to converge at the same time, on the same lever-drum, two transmitting tubes, one of which conveys the variations of pressure to which the experimental shoe is subjected (fig. 19), and the other, ten vibrations per second furnished by a chrono-graphic tuning-fork of large size.

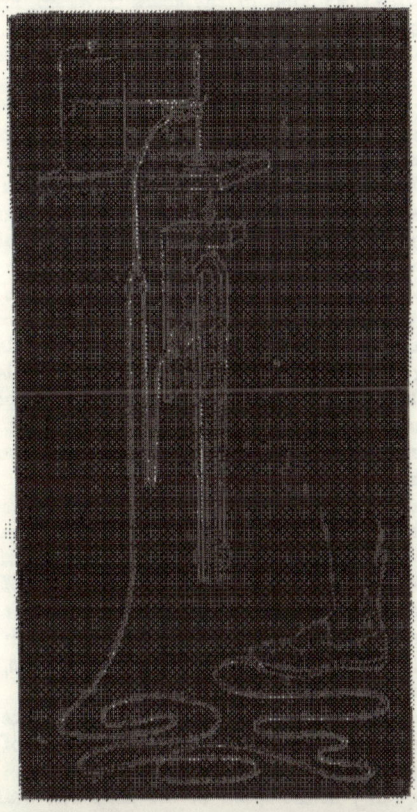

FIG. 20.—A large tuning-fork whose vibrations are reduced by means of lead to 10 per second, acts on the registering lever drum, by an experimental drum attached to one of its branches. This also receives at the same time, by a tube with two branches, the influence both of the impact and rising of the foot of the person who walks.

Fig. 20 shows how these instruments are arranged. It is seen that the drum will be affected by the double influence of the changes in the pressure of the foot on the ground, and of the vibrations of the tuning-fork; and this produces in a single tracing the interference of two movements, giving at the same time the notion of the space traversed, and that of the time employed in passing over it.

In order to analyse this tracing, let us consider only, in the first place, the sinuous curve which obeys at the same time the tuning-fork, and the experimental shoe on the right foot; and in this curve let us only examine the elevated part—that which corresponds with the pressure of the foot upon the ground. We see that, during the duration of this pressure, the style has passed through a space on the cylinder measuring about 2 centimetres; therefore, as the displacement of the style is fifty times less than that of the person walking, he will have advanced about one metre during the pressure of one foot. But while he traversed this metre, he did not advance with an uniform velocity; in fact, during the first half of this distance, the tuning-fork made about four vibrations, whilst in the second, it has scarcely made two and a half. Thus the foot which presses the ground with a force increasing from the commencement to the end of its impact, gives the body an impulse whose velocity equally increases.

During the rise of the foot, the line traced by the tuning-fork indicates also that the body of the person walking progresses with an accelerated motion. That is easily understood if we remember that, in walking, the rise of one foot corresponds exactly with the tread of the other. It is, therefore, the impact of the left foot on the ground which gives the body of the walking person an accelerated motion, which is observed during the rise of the right foot.

This method appears to us applicable to all cases in which it is necessary to measure the relative durations of different phases of movement.

The inequality in the speed of the man who walks brings with it an important consequence. When a man drags a load, the effort which he makes cannot be constant; at each foot-fall a redoubled energy is produced in the traction that is developed, and as this increase of effort has but a very short duration, a series of shocks, as we may call them, occurs at

each instant. But we know that these shocks are very unfavourable to the full utilization of mechanical force; we have
explained (page 49) the inconvenience which would arise
from them in the work of living motive agents, and the
manner in which these shocks are lessened by the elasticity
of muscular fibre.

Under the conditions in which a man dragging a load is
placed, if he is attached by a rigid strap to the mass which
he has to draw, the shocks of which we have spoken will be
produced, and he will feel their reaction on his shoulders. In
order to avoid these painful jerks, and to utilize more fully
the effort which he makes, we have placed between the carriage and the traction strap an intermediate elastic portion,
the effect of which has answered our expectations.

We are endeavouring to construct analogous contrivances,
which may be adapted to the traces of ordinary carriages, so
as to lessen the violence of the pressure on the collar, and to
utilize more fully the strength of the horse.

CHAPTER III.

THE DIFFERENT MODES OF PROGRESSION USED BY MAN.

Description of the apparatus for the purpose of studying the various modes
of progression used by man—Portable registering apparatus—Experimental apparatus for vertical reactions—Walking—Running—Gallop
—Leaping on two feet and hopping on one—Notation of these various
methods—Definition of a *pace* in any of these kinds of locomotion
—Synthetic reproduction of the various modes of progression.

THE principal modes of progression employed by animals,
are *walking*, which we have already described at some length
as far as it relates to man, *running* at different rates of speed,
the *gallop*, and *leaping* on one or two feet.

The act of walking varies according to the nature or the
slope of the ground; we shall have to treat of these different
influences.

In this new study it is no longer possible to employ the

apparatus which we have used in our previous researches. The circular and horizontal track on which the experimenter was obliged to walk must be exchanged for surfaces of every kind and of every slope.

If the new instruments to which we must have recourse leave the experimenter more liberty in his movements, they are, on the other hand, relatively less complete as to the indications which they furnish; therefore, we can only require from them two kinds of indications; those of the pressures of the feet on the ground, and those of the vertical re-actions which are communicated to the body by these pressures.

Fig. 27 shows a runner furnished with apparatus of the new construction. He wears the experimental shoes which we have already described, and holds in his hand a portable registering instrument, on which are traced the curves produced by the pressure of his feet. As the cylinder of this instrument turns uniformly, the curves will be registered in proportion to the time, and not to the space traversed during each of the acts by which this curve is traced.

In order to facilitate the experiment, and to allow the apparatus to assume a uniform motion before it traces on the paper, we have recourse to a special expedient. The points of the tracing levers do not touch the cylinder; but in order to bring them in contact with the paper, an india-rubber ball must be compressed. As soon as this compression ceases, the points retreat from the cylinder, and the tracing is no longer produced. In fig. 27 the runner holds this ball in his left hand, and compresses it with his thumb.

In addition to this, the runner, in order to obtain the tracings of the vertical re-actions, carries on his head an instrument whose arrangement is represented in fig. 28.

It is an *experimental lever-drum* fixed on a piece of wood, which is fastened with moulding wax on the head of the experimenter, as seen in fig. 27. The drum is provided with a piece of lead placed at the extremity of its lever; this mass acts by its *inertia*.

While the body oscillates vertically, the mass of lead resists these movements, and causes the membrane of the drum to sink when the body rises, and to rise when the body descends.

Fig. 27.—Runner provided with the apparatus intended to register his
                  different paces.

From these alternate actions a current of air results, which, transmitted by a tube to a registering lever, shows by a curve the oscillatory movements of the body.

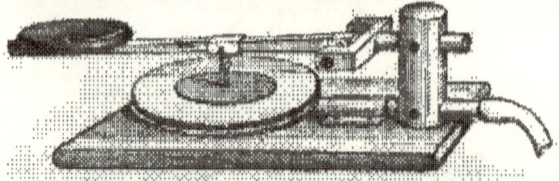

FIG. 38.—Instrument to register the vertical re-actions during the various paces.

We will not enter into the details of the experiments which have served to verify the exactitude of the tracings thus obtained; they consisted in adjusting the weight of the disc of lead and the elasticity of the membrane of the drum, until the movements given to the apparatus are faithfully represented in the tracing.

We will call *step-curves* each of the curves formed by the pressure of a foot upon the ground, and we will designate by the name of ascending or descending oscillations, the curve of the vertical re-actions on the body.

1. *Of walking.*—We have already pointed out the distinctive character of walking considered as one of the modes of progression in man. We have said that the body, in walking, never leaves the ground, and that the footsteps follow each other without any interval, so that the weight of the body passes alternately from one foot to the other.

But this definition cannot apply to walking on an inclined surface, on yielding soil, or upstairs. Being obliged to pass rapidly over these peculiar conditions of walking, we will only give the tracing which corresponds with the act of mounting a staircase (fig. 29).

It is to be remarked that the *step-curves* encroach on each other, showing that each foot is still pressing on the ground, when the other has already planted itself on the next step. Besides this, it is at the time of this double pressure that the lower foot exerts its maximum force; it is at this moment, in fact, that the work is produced which raises the body to the whole height of a step.

Nothing like this is observed in the descent of a staircase; the step-curves cease to encroach on each other, and succeed each other very nearly as in ordinary walking on level ground.

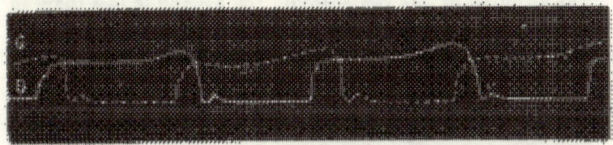

Fig. 29.—Tracing produced by walking upstairs. D. tracing of the pressure and rise of the right foot (full line). G. tracing of the left foot (dotted line). It is seen that the curves produced by the feet encroach one on the other, and that the maxima of the pressures of the feet correspond with the end of the pressures.

2. *Of running.*—This mode of progression, more rapid than walking, consists, like it, in alternate treads of the two feet, whose step-curves follow each other at equal intervals; but it presents this difference, that in running, the body leaves the ground for an instant at each step.

Accordingly, as running is more or less rapid, different names are given to it; those of the *gymnastic march* and the *trot* present no utility in a physiological point of view; they correspond, with but slight variations, to running at various degrees of speed. To ascertain the principal characters of this mode of progression, it is only necessary to analyse fig. 30.

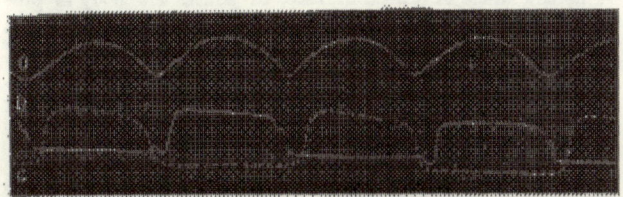

Fig. 30.—Tracing produced by running (in man). D. (curve formed by a full line), impact and rise of right foot. G. (dotted line) action of the left foot. O. oscillations and vertical re-actions of the body.

The pressures of the feet are more energetic than in walking; in fact, they not only sustain the weight of the body, but impel it with a certain speed both upwards and forwards. It is known that to give a mass a rising motion, a greater effort must be exerted than would be sufficient simply to sustain it.

The duration of the pressures on the ground is less than in walking; this brevity is proportional to the energy with which the feet tread on the ground. These two elements, force and brevity of pressure, increase generally with the speed at which a person runs. The frequency of the foot-falls increases also with the speed of the runner; but among the various kinds of running, there are some in which the extent of space passed over in a given time depends rather on the extent of each pace than on their number.

The essential character of running is, as we have said, *the time of suspension* during which the body remains in the air between two foot-falls. Fig. 30 clearly shows the suspension, by the interval which separates the descent of the curves of the right foot from the ascent of the curves of the left foot, and *vice versâ*. The duration of this time of suspension seems to vary but little in an absolute manner; but if we compare it with the speed of a runner, we see that the relative time occupied by this suspension increases with the speed of the course, for the duration of each tread diminishes in proportion to this speed.

How is this suspension of the body at each impulse of the feet produced? We might think, on first consideration, that it is the effect of a kind of leap, in which the body is projected upwards in so violent a manner by the impulse of the feet, that it would describe in the air a curve, in the midst of which it would attain its maximum elevation from the ground. In order to convince ourselves that such is not the case, let us make use of the apparatus which registers the re-actions or vertical oscillations of the body.

In fig. 30 is seen (upper line O) the tracing of oscillations in running. This trace shows us that the body executes each of its vertical elevations *during the downward pressure* of the foot, so that it begins to rise as soon as the foot touches the ground; it attains its maximum elevation at the middle of the pressure of this foot, and begins to descend again, in order to

K

roach its minimum, at the moment when one foot has just
risen, and before the other has reached the ground.

This relation of the vertical oscillations to the pressure
of the feet shows plainly that the *time of suspension* does not
depend on the fact that the body, projected into the air, has
left the ground, but that the *legs have withdrawn from the
ground* by the effect of their flexion; and this takes place at
the very moment when the body was at its greatest elevation.

We shall have again to recur to these phenomena when we
come to speak of the paces of the horse, in which a similar
suspension of the body exists, and which are called on that
account *elevated paces*.

The influence of the different inclinations of the ground
acts in nearly the same manner in running as in walking,
with this difference, that in running, their effects are generally
greater.

3. *Of the gallop.*—In the modes of progression described
hitherto, the movement of the limbs is regularly alternate, so
that the succession of steps is made at equal intervals.
These are the normal kinds of human locomotion; but man
can imitate, to a certain extent, by the movements of his feet,
those periodically irregular cadences which are produced by a
horse when he gallops. Children, in their amusements, often
imitate this mode of locomotion, when they *play at horses*.
This abnormal kind of motion is of no interest, except to
explain the mechanism of the gallop in quadrupeds.

By registering together the step-curves and the re-actions,
it is seen (fig. 31) that the foot placed behind is the first
which reaches the ground; that it exerts an energetic and
prolonged pressure, towards the end of which the foot in front
touches the ground in its turn, but during a shorter time;
after which there is a considerable period of suspension.
Thus, there is a moment when the two feet are in the air.

In this mode of progression, the re-actions are similar in
character, in some respects, to the pressures. In fact, a long
re-action (line O) is produced, in which we recognise the
interference of two vertical oscillations, the second of which
commences before the first has finished. After this re-action
there is observed a lowering of the curve, whose minimum

corresponds with the moment when the two feet are in the air.

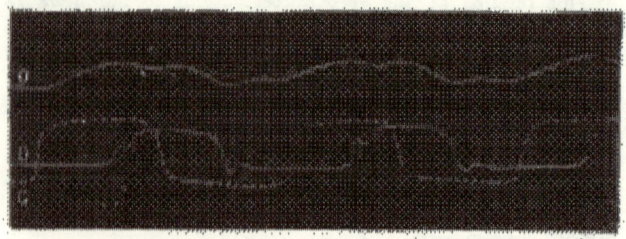

FIG. 81.—Man galloping with the right foot first. Step-curves and re-actions. There is an encroachment of one curve over the other, and then a suspension of the body. The curve O, which corresponds with the re-actions, shows the effect of the two successive impulses exerted on the body by the feet.

4. *Of leaping.*—Although *leaping* is not a sustained mode of progression in human locomotion, we will say a few words about it, in order to complete the series of the movements which man is able to execute.

The two feet being joined together, we can make a series of leaps, and advance thus, by imitating the mode of locomotion of some birds, or of certain quadrupeds, as the kangaroo.

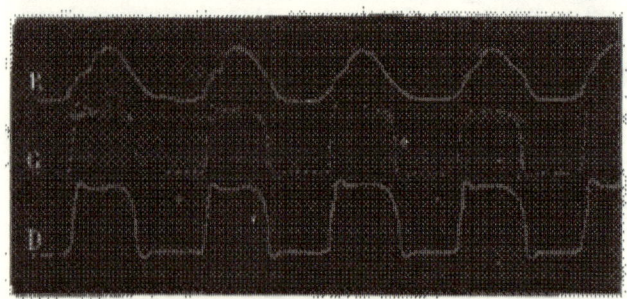

FIG. 82.—Leap on two feet at once, D and G. The line R, the curve of re-actions, shows that the maximum of elevations corresponds with the middle of the pressure of the feet.

The apparatus intended to illustrate the vertical oscillations of the body, being placed on the head of the experimenter,

we get three tracings at once; those of the pressures of the two
feet, and that of the re-actions; these furnish fig. 32.

We see here that the maxima of the curve of re-actions
(line R) coincide with the pressures. Thus, by their united
energy, the two legs raise the body, and then let it fall again at
the moment when they bend and prepare to act afresh.

Hopping on one foot gives the tracings (fig. 33) which
only consist in the pressure and rise of a single foot. The
elevations of the body coincide with the step-curves In fact,
when the speed of the leap is lessened, it is prolonged more
especially at the period of the pressure of the foot on the
ground, that of suspension remaining very nearly constant.

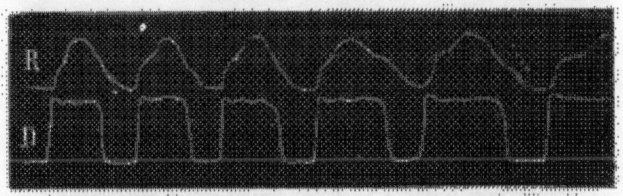

Fig. 33.—D, series of hops on the right foot. The duration of the time
of suspension remains evidently constant, even when that of the pressure
of the foot varies.

In certain species of animals, successive leaps constitute
the ordinary mode of locomotion; it will be interesting to
study by the graphic method the various paces of these
animals.

NOTATION OF RHYTHM IN DIFFERENT MODES OF PROGRESSION.

Among the characters of various modes of progression, it
is the rhythm of the impact of the feet which is the most
striking. The strokes of the feet upon the ground give rise
to sounds, the order of whose succession is sufficient for a person with an ear accustomed to them to recognise the kind of
pace which originates them. We will, therefore, endeavour
to establish the classification of the various paces by attending
to this order of succession.

In order to give the figure of each of these rhythms, we shall
employ the musical notation, modified so as to furnish at the

same time the notion of the duration of each pressure, that of
the foot to which this pressure belongs, and also the length of
time during which the body is suspended. This notation of
rhythms is constructed in a very simple manner from the
tracings furnished by the apparatus.

Fio. 34.

Let us return (fig. 34) to the curve which corresponds with
the act of running in man. Below this figure let us draw
two horizontal lines—1 and 2; these will form the *staff* on
which will be written this simple music, consisting only of
two notes, which we shall call right foot, left foot. From the
commencement of the ascending part of one step-curve belonging to the right foot, let us let fall upon the staff a perpendicular (*a*); this line will determine the commencement of
the pressure of the right foot. A perpendicular (*b*) let fall
from the end of the curve will determine where the pressure
of this foot ends. Between these two points, let us trace a
broad white line; it will express, by its length, the duration
of the pressure of the right foot.

A similar construction made on the step-curve (No. 1) will
give the notation of the pressure of the left foot. The notations of the left foot have been shaded with oblique lines to
avoid all confusion.

Between the pressure of the two feet there is found to be *silence*
in the rhythm; that is to say, the expression of that instant
of the course when the body is suspended above the ground.

If we note in this manner the rhythms of all the *paces* used by man, we shall obtain a synoptical table which will much facilitate the comparison of these varied rhythms. Fig. 25 represents the *synoptical notation* of the four kinds of progression, or paces, which are regularly rhythmical, and in which the two feet act alternately.

Line 1 represents the *notation of the rhythm of the walking pace*. This is the principle of the representation.

The pressure of the right foot on the ground is represented by a thick white stroke, a sort of rectangle, the length of which corresponds with the duration of that pressure. For the left foot there is a greyish rectangle shaded with oblique lines.

These alternations of grey and white express, by their succession, that in walking the pressure of one foot succeeds the other without allowing any interval between the two.

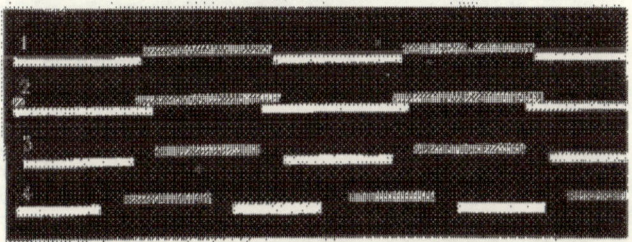

Fig. 25.—Synoptical notation of the four kinds of progression used by man.

Line 2 is the notation which corresponds with the *ascent of a staircase*. It is seen, agreeably with what has been already explained (fig. 29), that the step-curves encroach on each other, and that, consequently, the body during an instant rests on both feet at once.

Line 3 corresponds with the *rhythm of running*. After a shorter step-curve of the right foot than in the walking pace, an interval is seen which corresponds with the suspension of the body; then a short impulse of the left foot, followed by a fresh suspension, and so on continually.

Line 4 answers to a more *rapid rate of running*. We find in it a shorter duration of the pressures, a longer time of the

suspension of the body, and a more rapid succession of the
various movements

FIG. 36.—Notations of the gallop.   1. Left gallop.   2. Right gallop.

Fig. 36 is the notation of the *gallop of children*, a mode of
progression in which both the feet do not move in the same
manner. In this figure, line 1 represents the left gallop—that
is, with the left foot always forward. It is seen that the right
foot presses on the ground first; then the left falls and touches
the ground for a shorter time.

Then, there occurs a suspension of the body, after which
the right foot falls afresh, and so on. The time of the simultaneous pressure of both feet is measured according to the
space by which the shaded rectangle rests on the white one.

Line 2 is the notation of the *right gallop*; that is to say,
when the right foot is always in advance, reaching the ground
later than the left. Thus, in the gallop, the body is sometimes
in the air, sometimes on one foot, and sometimes supported
by two.

Finally, the notations represented in fig. 37 would be:
upper line, a series of *jumps* on two feet; lower line, a series
of *hops* on the right foot only.

FIG. 37.—(Upper line), notation of a series of jumps on two feet. (Lower
line), notation of hops on right foot. It is seen that there is constancy
in the durations of suspension, notwithstanding the variability of the
pressures.

This method of representation is less complete than the

curves given before, for it does not indicate the phases of
variable pressure exerted by the foot upon the ground; but it
is much more simple, and allows the two modes of progression
to be compared much more easily than the other. It will be
seen farther on, when speaking of quadrupedal locomotion,
that the complication of the subject renders it indispensable
to employ this very simple notation of the rhythm of movement.

Definition of a pace in any kind of progression.—It is usually
considered that a pace is produced by the series of movements
which are executed between the action of one foot and that
of the other, whether we choose for the commencement of
the pace the instant that the feet reach the ground, or that
when they rise from it. Thus, in measuring a pace on the
ground, we usually take as its length the distance which
separates one portion of the print of the right foot from
a similar point of the impression made by the left.

We shall be obliged to depart from this usage. Although
we regret any innovation, yet we shall consider the standard
pace only as *half a pace*, and we shall thus define it : *A pace
is the series of movements executed between two similar positions of
the same foot*—between the two successive treads of the right
foot, for example, or two successive elevations of the left
foot, &c.

In the same manner the extent of a pace on the ground
will be the distance which separates two homologous points
taken in the two successive impressions of the same foot.
The pace is estimated in this manner in Mexico. This is the
only method of counting which will prevent errors in the very
complicated moments of quadrupedal progression.

SYNTHETIC REPRODUCTION OF THE MODES OF PROGRESSION EMPLOYED BY MAN.

Since we have completed the analysis of a phenomenon of
which we now seem to understand all the details, it is by
synthesis that we will endeavour to construct a counter-proof.
This method has proved very useful in verifying our theories
concerning certain physiological actions, as, for instance, the
circulation of the blood. It consisted in representing, by arti-

ficial means, the movements and the sounds of the heart, the
arterial pulsations, &c., and we thus proved the correctness
of our theories as to the nature of these phenomena. The
same method will serve hereafter to verify our theories of the
flight of insects and birds. In the present case it is necessary
to represent, according to the data afforded by analysis, the
movements of walking and of the other paces employed by
man.

Every one knows the ingenious optical instrument invented
by Plateau, and called by him "Phénakistoscope." This
instrument, which is also known by the name of Zootrope,
presents to the eye a series of successive images of persons or
animals represented in various attitudes. When these attitudes are co-ordinated so as to bring before the eye all the
phases of a movement, the illusion is complete; we seem to
see living persons moving in different ways.

This instrument, usually constructed for the amusement of
children, generally represents grotesque or fantastic figures
moving in a ridiculous manner. But it has occurred to us
that, by depicting on the apparatus figures constructed with
care, and representing faithfully the successive attitudes of the
body during walking, running, &c., we might reproduce the
appearance of the different kinds of progression employed
by man.

Mons. Carlet, whose remarkable studies of walking we have
before quoted, and Mons. Mathias Duval, professor of anatomy
at the École des Beaux-arts, have carried out this plan, and,
after many attempts, have arrived at excellent results.

Mons. Duval is engaged in perfecting his diagram, which
furnishes to the eye sixteen successive positions for each kind
of locomotion employed by man. Each figure is carefully
drawn according to the results afforded by the graphic method.
When rotated with suitable speed, the instrument shows, with
perfect precision, the different movements of walking or running. But its principal advantage is that, by turning it less
quickly, we cause it to represent the movements much more
slowly, so that the eye can ascertain with the greatest facility
these actions, the succession of which cannot be apprehended in
ordinary walking.

CHAPTER IV.

QUADRUPEDAL LOCOMOTION STUDIED IN THE HORSE.

Insufficiency of the senses for the analysis of the paces of the horse—
Comparison of Dugès—Rhythms of the paces studied by means of the
ear—Insufficiency of language to express these rhythms—Musical
notation—Notation of the *amble*, of the *walking pace*, of the *trot*—
Synoptical table of paces noted according to the definition of each of
them by different authors—Instruments intended to determine by the
graphic method the rhythms of the various paces, and the *re-actions*
which accompany them.

THERE is scarcely any branch of animal mechanics which
has given rise to more labour and greater controversy than the
question of the paces of the horse. The subject is one of
great importance to a large number of persons engaged in
special pursuits, but its extreme complexity has caused in-
terminable discussions. Any one who proposed at the present
time to write a treatise on the paces of the horse, would have
to discuss many different opinions put forward by a great
number of authors.

While reading these works, on which so much sagacity of
observation and such rigorous reasoning have been expended,
one is astonished to find that the greater number of these
writers are not agreed in their definitions of the paces. This
disagreement in similar observers can only be accounted for
on the principle of the insufficiency of the means at their
disposal to enable them to analyse the very complex and rapid
movements of the horse. The difficulty of expressing in
words the rhythms and the durations of these various movements adds still more to the confusion. When a horse is
running, and passing from one kind of motion to another;
when he moves his limbs with a rapidity which makes one
dizzy, and according to the most varied rhythms, how can we
appreciate and describe faithfully all these actions? It would
be as easy a task, after looking at the fingers of a pianist

when running over the keys, to try and describe the movements which have just been executed.

Still, in the midst of this confusion, it has been found possible, by observation alone, to establish certain divisions which singularly simplify the study. Thus, certain paces give to the ear a rhythm in which the strokes of the hoofs succeed each other at sufficiently regular intervals; others, such as the different kinds of gallop, offer an irregular rhythm, recurring at periodical times. These latter paces are the most difficult to analyse.

But if we observe a horse either at a *walking pace*, *ambling*, or *trotting*, and if we concentrate our attention on the anterior limbs alone, or on the posterior ones, we perceive that the rhythm of the impacts and elevations of the right and left foot entirely resemble those of the feet of a man walking or running more or less quickly. The alternation of the strokes of the feet is perfectly regular, if the horse be not lame of one of the limbs under observation.

If we then pass to the comparison of the movements in the two fore and hind legs on the same side, we see that the two feet on the right side, for example, make the same number of steps, and that if one of them strikes the ground at a greater or less interval before the other, this is preserved as long as the same pace is continued. Add to this that the length of the step is the same for both the fore and hind limbs, of which fact we may convince ourselves by seeing that these two feet always leave on the ground prints situated at the same distance from each other. In general, the hind-foot covers the print left by the corresponding fore-foot; if the prints be not covered, they preserve always the same distance from each other. Thus, the steps of the fore and hind legs are of the same number and the same extent; these facts have not escaped former observers.

Dugès has compared the quadruped when walking to two men placed one before the other, and following each other. According as these two persons (who ought both to take the same number of steps) move their limbs simultaneously, or alternately; according as the man in front executes his movements more quickly or more slowly than the one behind, we see all the rhythms of the movements which characterise the different paces of the horse reproduced.

Every one has seen in the circus or the masquerade those figures of animals whose legs are formed by those of two men with their bodies concealed in that of the horse. This grotesque imitation bears a striking resemblance to the animal, when the movements of the two men are well co-ordinated, so as to reproduce the rhythms of the paces of a real quadruped.

In the examination of the tracings furnished by the graphic method when applied to the paces of the horse, we may have recourse to the theory propounded by Dugès; we shall then find the curves furnished by human locomotion twice repeated. We shall see that the difference between one pace and another consists in the manner in which the footfalls of the hind leg of a horse succeed each other, with relation to those of the fore leg on the same side. But this determination of the order of the succession of footfalls presents singular difficulties, even for the most skilful observers.

Many attempts have been made to bring to perfection the means of observation, and to remedy the insufficiency of language in the description of the observed phenomena. Long since, the rhythm of the steps according to the sounds which they produce has been substituted for their examination by means of the eye. The ear, in fact, is better adapted than the eye to distinguish the rhythms or relations of succession. To ascertain the order in which each limb strikes the ground, certain experimenters have attached to the legs of the horse bells of different tones, which can be easily distinguished from each other.

A point which has been better ascertained with respect to the locomotion of the horse, is the determination of the space passed over on the ground during each of the various kinds of paces. This space has been directly measured by means of the distance between the prints of the feet left on the ground. To render the distinction between the footprints more easy, each of the animal's feet has been shod in a different manner. Besides this, observers have studied the proportion which exists between the height of the animal and the length of its various paces. All those who have made any progress in this interesting study have arrived at it by the employment of rigorous methods of observation.

On the other hand, the manner of expressing the observed phenomena has occupied the attention of different authors. Almost all have had recourse, with great advantage, to the use of drawings, but have agreed but little in their mode of representing the successive actions which characterise the different paces. The most perfect kind of representation is that employed during the last century by Vincent and Goiffon.* A sort of musical staff, composed of four lines, served to note the instant of each impact of the four feet, and the duration of the succeeding pressures on the ground. This notation resembles, to a certain degree, that which we have employed to represent the different rhythms of human loco-motion, and which will hereafter serve to explain the various paces of the horse. But we must not forget that the method of Vincent and Goiffon only expressed a succession of move-ments observed by the sight or the ear, and that it realised no greater exactitude than that of the individual observer.

Our registering instruments resolve the double problem of analysing with fidelity the acts which the senses could not accurately appreciate, and expressing clearly the result of this analysis.

Before we describe our experiments, we shall, in order that the reader may understand their utility, try to present a summary of the present state of the science, and to show what disagreement exists on various points among different authors. As the standard definitions are not always easy to be under-stood, we shall add to them the notation of each of the paces, trusting that this method of representation will render them more intelligible, and especially more easy to be compared with each other.

Notation of the various paces of the horse.—Recurring to the comparison used by Dugès, let us represent the horse as com-posed of two bipeds walking one behind the other. We must determine the manner in which the rise and fall of the feet

* Mémoire artificielle des principes relatifs à la fidèle représentation des animaux, tant en peinture qu'en sculpture. Alford, 1769.

succeed each other, in each of the persons supposed to be walking.

Of the amble.—Let us take the simplest case, in which the two persons walking steadily go through the same movements at the same time. If we represent, by the notation before employed, the movements of these two men, placing at the top the notation which belongs to the foremost, and below it that of the hindmost, we shall have the following figure :—

FIG. 38.—Notation of a horse's amble.

The footfalls of the right and left foot being produced at the same time by the person walking in front and by him who follows, must be represented by similar signs placed exactly over each other. Thus, in the paces of the horse, this agreement between the movements of the fore and hind limbs belongs to the *amble*. The notation (fig. 38) will be that of a horse's amble; the upper line referring to the movements of the fore quarters of the animal, and the lower line to the hind limbs.

The standard definition is the following : "The amble is a kind of pace characterised by the alternate and exclusive action of two lateral *bipeds*." Authors are entirely agreed on this point. Let us add that in the amble the ear perceives only *two beats* at each pace, the two limbs on the same side striking the ground at the same instant. In the notation these two sounds are marked by vertical lines joining the two synchronous impacts.

In the amble the pressure of the body on the ground is said to be *lateral*, as the two limbs on one side only are in contact with the ground at the same time.

Of the walking pace.—According to the definition of the greater number of authors, the *walking pace* consists in an equal succession of impacts of the four feet, which strike the ground in the following order : if the right foot be considered as moving first, we shall have the following succession—*right fore-foot, left hind-foot, left fore-foot,* and then *right hind-foot.*

To express this succession of movements of the two persons walking, it is only necessary to alter the place of the signals of the hind feet with respect to those of the fore feet. We shall obtain the rhythm indicated by authors by causing the signals of the hind feet to slip towards the left, which will give the following figure :—

Fig. 39.—Notation of the horse's walking pace

It is seen, therefore, that when compared with the amble, the walking pace consists in an anticipation of the hinder limbs, whose footfalls precede those of the corresponding fore limbs by the half of the duration of one of their pressures on the ground.

If the notations be read from left to right, like ordinary writing, it is evident that each sign situated farther to the left than another precedes it in order of succession. Thus, in fig. 39, the impact of the right hind-foot precedes that of the right fore-foot. But as it is of little consequence, in the series of successive acts of the same kind of pace, whether we choose one instant rather than another as the point of departure, we shall always take as the commencement the impact of the right fore-foot.

The ear distinguishes *four beats*, separated by regular intervals, each of which is indicated in the notation by a vertical line. Finally, the body rests on the ground *twice laterally and twice diagonally* during one entire pace. It is easy to ascertain this by looking at fig. 39, in which, after the first impact, the body rests on the right feet (lateral biped L) ; after the second impact, on the right foot in front, and the left foot behind (diagonal biped D), &c.

But this notation only expresses the theory of the most extended pace. The equality of intervals between the strokes of the feet is not admitted by all writers. We shall see, in the course of our experiments, that the walking pace, in fact, may present different rhythms.

Of the trot.—The notation of the trot is obtained by a more decided anticipation of the hinder limbs, each of which will have entirely completed its pressure on the ground, and begun to rise at the moment when the fore-leg on the same side has completed its stroke. Fig. 40 expresses the absolute alternation of the two persons supposed to be walking.

Fig. 40.—Notation of a horse's trot.

Authors agree also on this point, that in the trot, the limbs which act together are associated in diagonal pairs.

The ear perceives but *two sounds* of the hoofs, as in the amble, but with this difference, that it is always a right and left foot together, and not two feet on the same side, which produce each sound.

The notation also shows that the pressure of the body on the ground is always diagonal. What it does not express is, that between successive pressures, the body of the animal is, for an instant, suspended in the air. This suspension arises from the fact that the trot is not a *walking*, but a *running* pace, and that to represent it faithfully we must place together two notations similar to that which is represented in fig. 34.

We have designedly omitted the time of suspension in the former notation ; it would have rendered a difficult subject still more complicated. Besides, this suspension does not always take place ; certain horses have a *low trot*, which has nothing to characterise it except its rhythm in double time and the diagonal impacts of the feet.

We will not fatigue the reader by detailing the definition of all the paces admitted by different authors. We shall merely present in a synoptical table the series of notations which correspond with them. In this table (fig. 41) it is seen, that all the *lower paces* may be considered as derived from the amble, and that if we wished to make a methodical classification, we should group them in a series of which the amble would be the first term, and all the other terms would be obtained by means of an increasing anticipation of the movements of the hinder limbs. Fig. 41 represents this series. In the notation of each kind of pace, we have left on the same vertical the impact of the right fore-foot, which we shall choose as the commencement of each pace, and which will serve as a point of reference to characterise each kind of locomotion.

This table, prepared from *different treatises on the horse*, represents as faithfully as we have been able to depict it, that which each author admits as constituting each particular kind of pace. The explanatory notes show the disagreement which exists between the various theories relative to the succession of movements which characterise each of them. Thus we see, that with the exception of the amble, on which all are agreed, all the other kinds of paces are defined in a different manner by various authors. Thus, the notation No. 2, which, according to Merche, would correspond with the broken amble, would be, according to Bouley, the expression of the high step, or the pace of Norman ponies; while this same Norman pace would be, according to Lecoq, that which is represented in No. 9. We also see that the notation of No. 3 would correspond, according to Merche, with the *ordinary step of a pacing horse*, while Bouley would consider it as a *broken amble*, and Lecoq the *traquenade*; which *traquenade*, according to Merche, would not differ from the pace represented by the notation No. 10. The ordinary *walking pace* itself is not understood in the same manner by different writers, and if the greater part of them, with Vincent and Goiffon, Colin, Bouley, &c., admit in this pace a succession of impacts at unequal intervals, it is to be observed that the theory of Lecoq and Raabe, concerning the *normal pace*, is different.

This disagreement can easily be explained: first, the observation of these movements is very difficult; then, each pace must naturally present, according to the conditions under which it is studied, the different forms which each writer has arbitrarily taken as the type of the normal walking

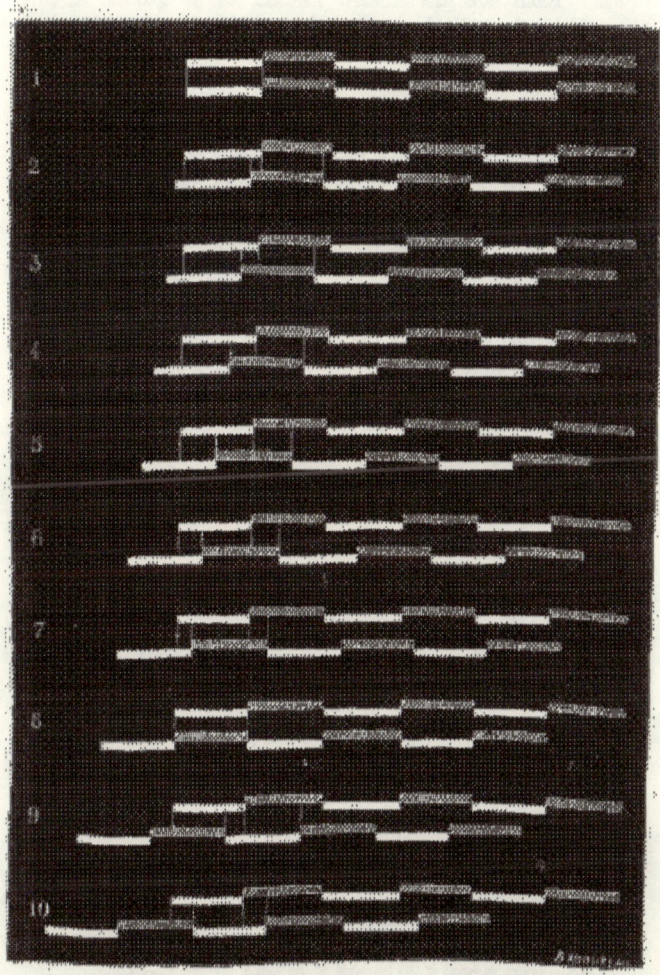

FIG. 41.—Synoptical notations of the paces of the horse, according to various writers.—See Description at the foot of page 147.

pace. Each one has suffered himself to be guided in this respect by theoretical considerations. Those who admit equal intervals between the four footfalls, have thought that they found in this type more clearness and a more decided distinction between the amble and the trot. The other writers have attempted the realisation of a certain ideal in the kind of pace which served them as a type. For Raabe, it was the maximum of stability, which, according to his theory, is obtained when the weight of the body rests longer on the two diagonal feet than on the two lateral feet; whence arises the choice of the type represented by the notation No. 6. Lecoq, thinking, on the contrary, that the most rapid pace is the best, has chosen as his type the pace in which the body rests longer on the two lateral feet than on the diagonal ones (notation No. 4).

Whatever may be the value of these considerations, of which practical men alone can judge, it seems to us that the physiologist must first of all endeavour to search for facts, and must take simply such types as experiment may reveal to him. It is for this purpose that the investigations have been made with registering apparatus, the result of which will now be given.

APPARATUS INTENDED FOR THE STUDY OF THE MODES OF LOCOMOTION OF THE HORSE.

For the *experimental shoe* employed in the experiments made on man has been substituted, on the horse, a ball of india-rubber filled with horsehair, and attached to the horse's hoof by a contrivance which adapts it to the shoe.

DESCRIPTION OF FIG. 41.

No. 1. Amble, according to all writers.
No. 2. { Broken amble, according to Merche.
        { High step, according to Bouley.
No. 3. { Ordinary step of a pacing horse, according to Marura.
        { Broken amble, according to Bouley.
        { Traquenade, according to Lecoq.
No. 4. Normal walking pace, according to Lecoq.
No. 5. Normal walking pace (Bouley, Vincent and Goiffon, Sallsysel, Colin).
No. 6. Normal walking pace, according to Raabe.
No. 7. Irregular trot (trot décousu).
No. 8. Ordinary trot. (In the figure, it is supposed that the animal trots without leaving the ground, which occurs but rarely. The notation only takes into account the rhythm of the impacts of the feet.)
No. 9. Norman pace, from Lecoq.
No. 10. Traquenade, from Merche.

L 2

By turning an adjusting screw

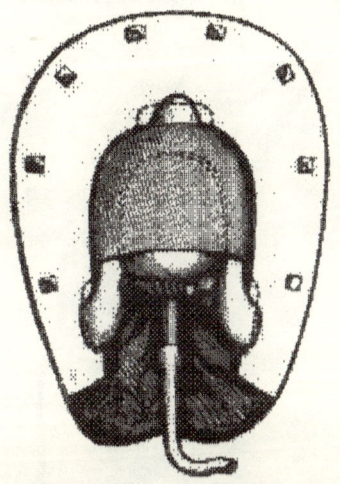

we fix it to the horse-shoe by three catches, which keep the instrument securely fastened. A strong band of india-rubber passes over the apparatus (fig. 42), and keeps in its place the ball filled with horse-hair, so as to allow it to rise slightly above the lower surface of the hoof. When the foot strikes the ground, the india-rubber ball is compressed, and drives a part of the confined air into the registering instruments. When the foot is raised, the ball recovers its form, and draws again into its interior the air which the pressure had expelled. These instruments soon wear out on the road, but will last during some time on the artificial soil of the riding-school.

For experiments which we have made on ordinary roads, we have had recourse to an instrument represented in fig. 43.

To the leg of the horse just above the fetlock-joint is attached a kind of leather bracelet fastened by straps. In front of this bracelet, which furnishes a solid point of resistance, are placed various pieces of apparatus. There is, first, a flat box of india-rubber firmly fixed in front of the bracelet; this box communicates, by a transmission tube, with the registering apparatus. Every pressure exerted on the box moves the corresponding registering lever. It is evident that all the movements of the horse's foot are shown by pressures on the india-rubber box, and are immediately signalled by the registering levers.

For this purpose, a plate of copper, inclined about 45°, is

connected at its upper extremity with a kind of hinge, whilst its lower end is fastened by a solid wire to the upper face of the india-rubber box, on which it presses by means of a flat disc. On a wire parallel to the slip of copper slides a ball of lead, the position of which can be varied in order to increase or diminish the pressure which this jointed apparatus exerts on the india-rubber box.

The function of this apparatus is analogous with that of the instrument represented in fig. 28, intended to show the reactions which are produced in various kinds of locomotion; only the inclination of the oscillating portions allows them to act on the membrane during the movement of the elevation, the descent, and the horizontal progress of the foot.

When the hoof meets the ground the ball has a tendency to continue its motion, and compresses with force the india-rubber box. When the foot rises,

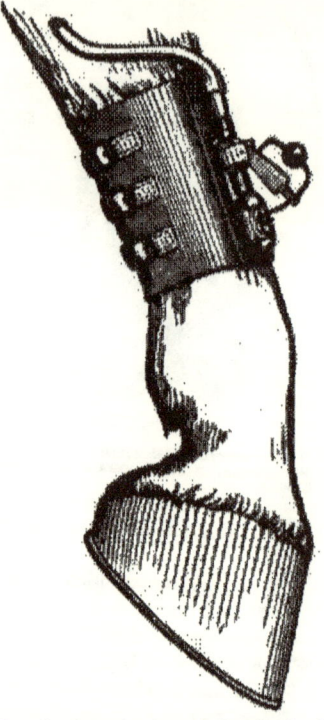

Fig. 43.—Apparatus to give the signals of the pressure and rise of the horse's hoof.

the inertia of the ball produces in its turn a compression by a kind of mechanism already described with reference to fig. 28.

Through the kindness of Mons. Pellier, we have been able to experiment on several horses, ridden by himself, while holding in his hand the registering instruments.

When the horse had his feet furnished with the india-rubber boxes which have just been described, thick transmitting tubes not easily crushed were fitted to these receptacles. These tubes are usually fastened by flannel bands to the legs of the animal, and thence directed to a point of attachment at the level of the withers; they are then continued to the registering apparatus, which has been already described in the experiments on biped locomotion.   The registrar now

Fig. 44.—This figure represents a trotting horse, furnished with the different experimental instruments; the horseman carrying the register of the pace. On the withers and the croup are instruments to show the reactions.

carries a great number of levers; he must have four at least—one for each of the legs, and usually two other levers which receive their movements of re-action from the withers and the croup. Similar kinds of apparatus to those represented in fig. 28 are employed for this purpose.

The rider carries by the handle a portable registering instrument, to which all the levers give their signals at once; the hand which holds the reins is also ready to compress a ball of india-rubber at the moment when the horseman wishes the tracings to commence. Fig. 44 represents the general arrangement of the apparatus at the moment when the rider is about to collect the graphic signals of any particular pace.

CHAPTER V.

EXPERIMENTS ON THE PACES OF THE HORSE.

Double aim of these experiments: determination of the movements under the physiological point of view, and of the attitudes with reference to art.
Experiments on the trot—Tracings of the pressures of the feet and of the re-actions—Notation of the trot—*Piste* of the trot—Representation of the trotting horse.
Experiments on the walking pace—Notation of this kind of motion; its varieties—*Piste* of the walking pace—Representation of a pacing horse.

THE aim of these experiments is twofold; as far as physiology is concerned, we derive from them the expression of the duration, actions, and re-actions of each pace, the energy and duration of each movement, and the rhythm of their succession. But the artist is no less interested in knowing exactly the attitude which corresponds with each movement, in order to represent it faithfully with the various *poses* which characterise it. All these details are furnished by the registering apparatus; the artist need fear no error if he conform his sketches to the indications furnished by the tracings made by the instrument.

The remarkable work of Vincent and Goiffon was expressly intended to establish principles relative to the faithful representation of the horse. We shall borrow some things from this book, which seems to have been too much forgotten, and not to have exercised upon art the influence that might have been expected. This is doubtless owing, in some degree, to a certain obscurity in the mode of explanation, and still more to the fact that the writers, having had recourse only to direct

observation in order to analyse the paces of the horse, have
not been able to give all the details. We trust that we shall
be more fortunate in our treatment of the subject; but we are
assured, at least, of the perfect exactitude of the data furnished by the apparatus which we have used.

Colonel Duhousset has been kind enough to offer us his
assistance in representing the horse in its various paces; it is
to his skilful pencil that we owe the figures represented in this
chapter, which are the faithful translation of the notation
which accompanies them. We are also indebted to Mons.
Duhousset for some documents relating to the representation
of the paces.

The knowledge of the *pistes*—that is to say, the impressions
which the feet of the horse leave on the ground—is of great
importance; they enable an experienced eye to recognise the
pace of the animal which has marked them.

These *pistes* are of extreme value to the artist; they
alone can represent to him the limbs as they strike the ground,
with the true distances which they ought to preserve from
each other according to the size of the horse and the speed of
the pace. We refer the reader to the works of Vincent and
Goiffon, of Baron Curnieu, of Colin, &c., on this subject, con-
tenting ourselves with giving merely, from these writers, the
piste which characterises each pace.

The first series of experiments, the results of which we are
about to analyse, were made in the riding school of Mons.
Pellier, *fils*. The horses were furnished, on each foot, with
an instrument for determining pressures, similar to that which
is represented in fig. 42. We shall first discuss the experiments on the trot; the tracings which they give are easy to
be understood; the study of these will serve as a preparation
for the more complicated analysis of the other paces.

OF THE TROT.

Experiments on the trot.—An old and very quiet horse furnished the tracing represented in fig. 45. In this plate are
shown at the same time the tracings of the pressures of the
four feet with their notations, and on the other side, the re-
actions produced on the horse by this kind of pace.

Let us analyse the details of these curves. Above are the re-actions taken from the withers for the fore part of the

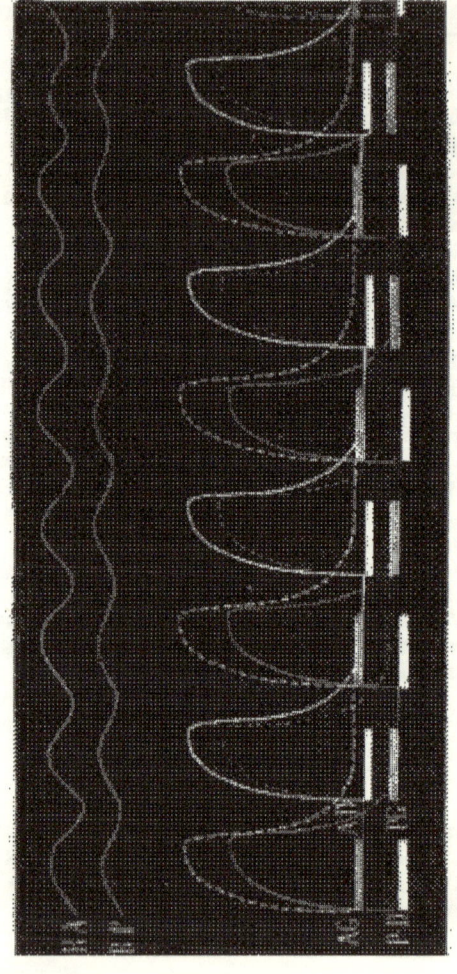

FIG. 43.—Graphic curves and notation of the horse's trot—R A, re-actions of the fore-limbs. R F, re-actions of the hind-limbs. A G & A U, curves and notation of fore-limbs. F D & F G, curves and notation of hind-limbs.

animal, which are given by the line R A (anterior re-actions),
and from the croup for the hinder part, which correspond
with the line R P (posterior re-actions).

Below are given the curves of pressure of the four feet;
they are drawn at two different levels; above are the curves
of the anterior, below those of the posterior limbs. In each
of these series the curves of the left foot are drawn with
dotted lines, those of the right with full lines. Whether
dotted or full, these lines have been made thicker for the
fore-limbs than for the hinder ones; this difference, though
of little use in curves as simple as those of the trot, will
serve to render the more complicated tracings much more
intelligible.

The moment when the curve begins its rise, represents the
commencement of the pressure of the foot on the ground.
The instant when the curve descends again gives the signal
of the rise of the foot.* It is seen from these tracings
that the feet A G and P D, left fore-foot and right hind-foot,
strike the ground at the same time. The simultaneous lowering of the curves of the two feet shows that they also rise from
the ground simultaneously. Under these curves is the notation which represents the pressure of the left diagonal biped.†

The second impact is given by the feet A D and P G (right
diagonal biped), and so on through all the length of the
tracing.

This experiment confirms the correctness of the standard
theory of the trot, and at the same time affords additional
information on some points. Thus, all writers agree in
choosing, as the type of the free trot, the pace in which all the
four feet give but two strokes, and in which the ground is
struck in turn by the two diagonal bipeds. It is admitted

---

* The duration of the pressure ought to be marked by a horizontal line,
but we have made the tube somewhat narrow in order to lessen the force
of the shocks given to the registering lever; the narrowing of the tube
has slightly affected the curve, which, however, produces no inconvenience
in studying the rhythms.

† Each diagonal biped is named after the anterior foot of which it forms
a part; the left diagonal biped means, therefore, left fore foot, right hind
foot.

also that the trot is a *high* pace, and that, in the interval
between two successive strokes, the animal is for an instant
raised above the ground.

But we find disagreement when we come to estimate the
duration of this suspension. Thus, according to Bouley, it is
very short in proportion to the duration of the pressure;
whilst Raabe thinks, on the contrary, that the pressure is
very short, so that the animal is a longer time in the air than
on the ground.

In the notation of the tracing (fig. 45), it is seen that the
pressures are twice as long as the periods during which the
body is suspended above the ground. This experiment, therefore, would confirm the opinion of Bouley in opposition to
that of Raabe; but it appears to us that there is a great
variety in the relative duration of the pressures, and of the
periods of suspension above the ground during the trot.
Thus, certain horses running in harness have furnished
tracings in which the phase of suspension was scarcely
visible; so that this form of trot resembled the *low* paces,
only preserving that characteristic of the free type which
arises from the perfect synchronism of the diagonal strokes of
the feet. We have not yet been able to study the movements
of rapid trotters; in these perhaps we should see, in an
inverse ratio, the time of suspension increase over that of the
duration of pressures.

If we seek to ascertain the correspondence between the
re-actions (R A and R P) and the movements of the limbs, we
see that the moment when the body of the animal is at the
lowest part of its vertical oscillation coincides precisely with
that at which its feet touch the ground. The time of suspension does not depend on the fact that the body of the horse is
projected into the air, but that all four legs are bent during
this short period. The maximum height of the suspension of
the body corresponds, on the contrary, with the end of the
pressure of the limbs on the ground. It seems, according to
the tracings, that the elevation of the body does not commence till after each double impact, and that it continues
during the whole time of the pressure.

It is also seen, in the same figure, that the re-actions of the fore-limbs are much more considerable than those of the hinder ones. This fact appears to us to be constant; and the inequality of the re-actions is still more marked in the walking pace, because the apparatus placed on the withers almost always gives appreciable re-actions, while that on the croup gives scarcely any.

Of the irregular trot (*trot décousu*).—We call that a free trot which gives two distinct sounds to the ear for each pace, and we name that irregular, each sound of which is in a certain degree divided by the want of synchronism in the strokes of each diagonal biped. The irregular trot has been met with in many of our experiments. Occasionally this pace was continued, and then the want of synchronism existed sometimes in the impacts of the two diagonal bipeds, and sometimes in one pair only; at other times, on the contrary, the trot was irregular only for an instant, at the moment of the passage from one kind of pace to another. In all the experiments which we have hitherto made, the want of synchronism depended on the hinder limb being behind the anterior limb which corresponded diagonally with it.

Fig. 46 represents the notation of an *irregular trot*, in which the diagonal impacts leave between them an appreciable interval of time. We can recognise this by the obliquity of the dotted line which unites with each other the impacts of the two diagonal bipeds.

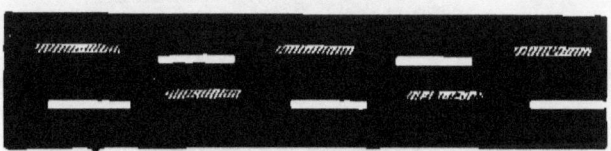

Fig. 46.—Notation of the irregular trot.

The *piste* of the trot is represented in fig. 47, according to Vincent and Goiffon. All the prints are double, for the hinder-foot always comes up to take the place of the fore-foot on the same side.

In fig. 47 we have rendered this superposition imperfect

in order to avoid confusion; for the same purpose, we have represented the prints of the fore-feet by dotted lines, those of the hind-feet by full lines. In the trot, the prints of the left feet alternate perfectly with those of the right feet.

Fig. 47.—Piste of the trot according to Vincent and Goiffon.

According to the speed of the trot, and the size of the horse, the *piste* varies much with respect to the space which separates the prints on the same side.

Fig. 48.—Horse trotting with a low kind of pace. The instant corresponding with the attitude represented in this figure, is marked with a white dot on the notation.

In the representation of the trotting horse we must distinguish the different forms of this pace.

The *low and short trot* is represented in fig. 48. We usually make our observations at the start of the animal, or at the moment when he passes from the walking pace to the trot. The diagonal impacts succeed each other without interval, as is seen in the notation placed below the figure. The animal has been depicted from the notation.

The instant which the artist has chosen is that which is marked in the notation by a white dot. At this moment, as the superposition indicates, the left fore-foot is at the end of its pressure; the right fore-foot is about to reach the ground; the right hind-foot is finishing its pressure; the left hind-foot is about to fall. The inclination of the limbs is that which corresponds with each of the phases of the pressures and the rise of the feet. The distance separating the feet is that which is indicated by the prints on the ground. Thus, in fig. 48, it is seen that the trot is *shortened*, for the hind-foot

Fig. 48.—Horse at full trot. The dot placed in the notation corresponds with the attitude represented.

on the point of striking the ground, will not reach the place
of the fore-foot on the same side.

The *elevated and lengthened trot* is represented in fig. 49,
which has already served to show the rider and his horse
furnished with the instruments for the purpose of forming
tracings of the various paces. The animal is depicted at the
instant which, in the notation, is represented by a dot; that
is to say, during the time of suspension, at the moment when
the left diagonal biped has just risen and the right diagonal
biped is about to descend.

OF THE WALKING PACE.

Experiments on the walking pace.—The explanations into
which we have entered in order to analyse the tracings of a
trot, will facilitate the interpretation of that of the walking
pace, represented in fig. 50. These tracings have been obtained
from the same horse as the preceding ones.

If we let fall a perpendicular from the points at which the
curves commence, we shall have the position of the successive
impacts of the four legs. On account of the thickness of the
style employed to trace these curves, the foot corresponding
with each of them is easily recognised, therefore we can
mark on each of these perpendicular lines the initial letters
of the foot which at this moment reaches the ground. The
order of succession of impacts is represented by the letters
A D, P G, A G, P D; that is to say, *right fore-foot, left hind-
foot, left fore-foot, right hind-foot,* which is the succession
admitted by writers on the subject.

There remains to be determined the greater or less regularity in the succession of these impacts, and the relative
extent of the intervals which separate them. For this purpose
it is sufficient to construct the notation of the rhythm of the
pressure of each foot according to the registered curves.
This notation for fig. 50 shows that the interval which separates the impacts is always the same, and, consequently, that
the horse rests during the same time on the lateral as on the
diagonal bipeds. But this is not always the case.

That we may render the successive positions of the centre
of gravity easily understood, we will explain in few words the

manner in which the notation of fig. 50 has been constructed. If we let fall perpendiculars corresponding with each of the

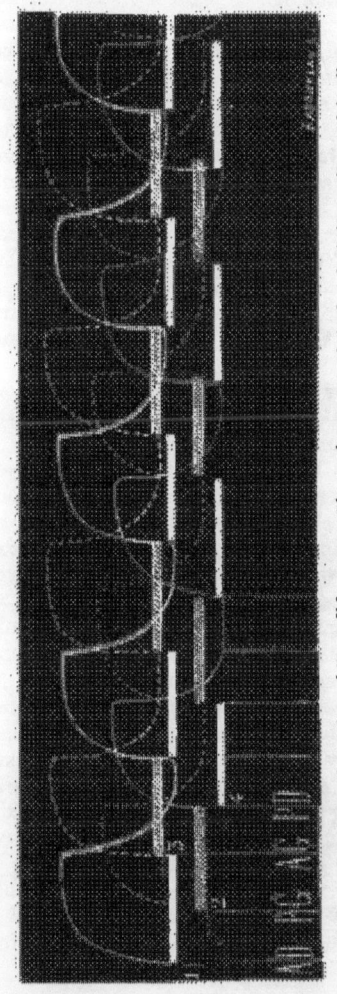

Fig. 50.—Tracings and notations of the walking pace, with equal pressure of the foot, both diagonally and laterally.

Fig. 51.—Notation of the walking pace, with predominance of the lateral pressure.

footfalls, beginning with that of the right fore-foot, which is marked No. 1, we shall divide the figures into successive portions, in which will be found the impacts, sometimes of two legs on the same side (lateral biped), at others, of two placed diagonally (diagonal biped).   Thus, from 1 to 2, the horse will rest on the right lateral biped ; from 2 to 3, on the right diagonal biped (that is to say, on that in which the *right* foot *comes first*) ; from 3 to 4, on the left lateral biped; from 4 to 5, on the left diagonal biped ; again, from 5 to 6, the horse would find himself, as at the beginning, on the right lateral biped.

This experiment has reference entirely to the standard theory of the pace (see No. 5 of the synoptical table), but some horses walk in a manner somewhat different.

Fig. 51 is the notation of the walking pace of a horse which rested longer on the lateral than on the diagonal pressures.

Sometimes the contrary is observed ; in the transitions from the walk to the trot, for instance, we have found the duration of the diagonal pressures predominate.

This study, in order to be complete, ought to have been carried on under more favourable conditions than those which we have hitherto been able to meet with.   It would be desirable to obtain many horses belonging to different breeds ; to study their movements when led by the hand, mounted, or harnessed ; to vary the load which they carry or draw ; to experiment on level or sloping ground, &c.   All this can only be effected by men especially interested in these inquiries, and placed in favourable circumstances to undertake them.

While making observations on draught horses, it has seemed to us that when the animal strives to re-act against the weight of the carriage pressing upon him, he may have *three feet on the ground* at once.   This Borelli considered to be the normal walking pace; we have just seen, on the contrary, that in the natural walking pace there are never more than two feet on the ground at a time.

As to the *re-actions* during the walking pace, they are not represented in fig. 50.   We have ascertained generally that the re-actions of the fore-limbs are the only ones of any im-

M

portance; we are led to suppose, by the extremely slight re-
actions of the hinder parts, that their action consists chiefly
in a forward propulsion, but with very slight impulsion of
the body in an upward direction. This agrees with the theory
somewhat generally admitted, by which the fore-legs would
have little to do in the normal pace except to support alternately the fore part of the body, while to the hind limbs
would belong the propulsive action and the tractive force
developed by the animal.

The *piste* of the walking pace, according to Vincent and
Goiffon, is analogous with that of the trot, except that it presents a shorter interval between the successive footprints on
the same side.

Fig. 52.—Piste of the walking pace, after Vincent and Goiffon.

In the ordinary walk, this distance would be equal to the
height of the horse, measured at the withers. As in the trot,
the prints are covered at each pace; those of the right foot
alternate perfectly with those of the left. This character of
the *piste* of the walking pace is, however, observed only under

Fig. 53.—Piste of the amble, after Vincent and Goiffon: it differs from that
of the walking pace, only by the non-superposition of the footprints on
the same side. The hind foot is placed on the ground beyond the impression of the fore foot.

certain conditions of speed, and on level ground. On rising
ground the prints of the hind-feet are usually behind those of
the fore-feet; in a descent, on the contrary, they may possibly
pass beyond them, which would give the *piste* of the walk
some resemblance to that of the amble.

Representation of a pacing horse. The representation of a horse at the walking pace has been given by Mons. Duhousset in fig. 54. The instant chosen is marked in the notation by a dot. We shall not give an enumeration of the positions of the limbs of the animal as shown in the notation, as we have already done so in the representation of the trot.

FIG. 54.—Representation of the horse at a walking pace.

CHAPTER VI.

EXPERIMENTS ON THE PACES OF THE HORSE.
(Continued.)

Experiments on the gallop—Notation of the gallop—Re-actions—Bases of support—Plates of the gallop—Representation of a galloping horse in the various times of this pace.

Transitions, or passage, from one step to the other—Analysis of the paces by means of the notation rule—Synthetic reproduction of the different paces of the horse.

OF THE GALLOP.

SEVERAL different paces, the common character of which is that irregular impacts return at regular intervals, are comprehended under this name. Most of the writers distinguish three kinds of gallop by the rhythm of the impacts, and name them, according to this rhythm, gallop in *two, three,* and *four time.* The most ordinary kind is the gallop in three-time; this we shall study in the first place.

Experiments on the gallop. Fig. 55 has been obtained from a horse which galloped in three-time. At first sight, the notation of this pace reminds us of that which we have represented when speaking of human gallop (fig. 36, p. 134), a pace used by children when "playing at horses." It appears that the notation of the horse's gallop has been obtained by placing one over another two of these notations of the biped gallop; so that, in fact, the comparison used by Dugès is perfectly just, even when it is applied to the gallop.

Analysis of the tracing. At the commencement of the figure, the animal is suspended above the ground; then comes the impact P G, which announces that the left hind-foot touches the ground. This is the foot diagonally opposed to that which the horse places forward in the gallop, and whose impact A D will be produced the last. Between these two impacts, and distinctly in the middle of the interval which separates them, comes the simultaneous impact of the two feet forming the left diagonal biped. The superposition of the notations A G, P D, clearly shows this synchronism.

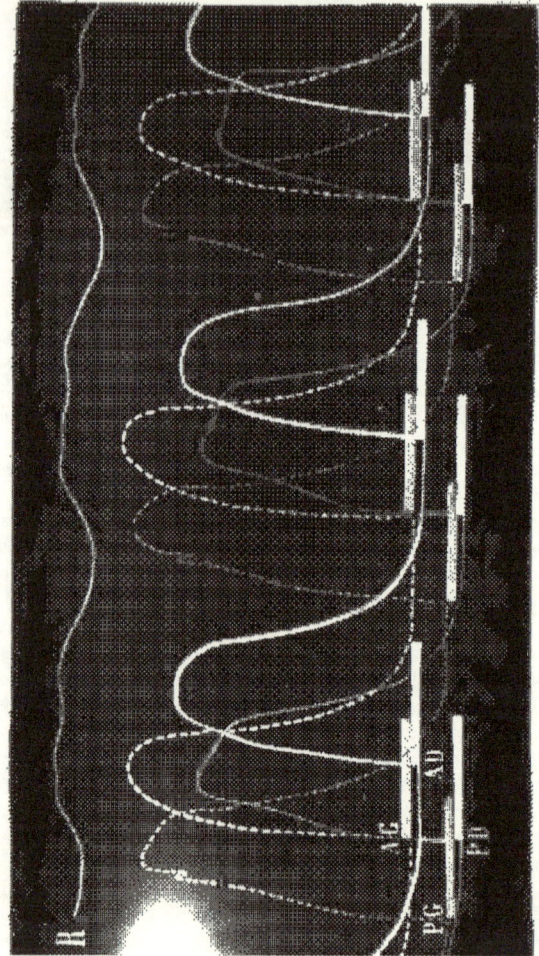

FIG. 56.—Tracings and notation of the gallop in three-time. R, curve of reactions taken at the withers. The curves of the reactions of the feet have a considerable extent, which shows the force of the pressure on the ground. The horse used for this experiment galloped with the right foot, as seen in the notation.

In this series of movements the ear has, therefore, distinguished three *sounds*, at nearly equal intervals. The first sound is produced by a hinder foot, the second by a diagonal biped, the third by a fore-foot. Between the single impact of the fore-foot, which constitutes the third sound, and the first beat of the pace which follows, reigns a silence whose duration is exactly equal to that of the three impacts taken together; then the series of movements recommences.

By the inspection of the curves, we see that the pressure of the feet on the ground must be more energetic in the gallop than in the other paces already represented, for the height of the curves is evidently greater than for the trot, and especially so as compared with the walk. In fact, the animal must not only support the weight of its body, but give it violent forward impulses. The greatest energy seems to belong to the first impact. At this moment, the body, raised for an instant from the ground, falls again, and one leg alone sustains this shock.

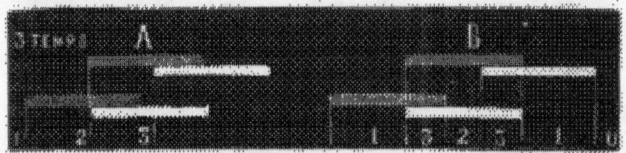

Fig. 56.—Gallop in three-time. (A) Indication of three-time. B. Indication of the number of feet which form the support of the body at each instant of the gallop in three-time.

If we wish to take account of the successive *pressures* which sustain the body during each of the steps in the gallop, we have only to divide the duration of this pace into successive instants in which the body is sometimes supported on one or on several feet, and sometimes suspended. The notation (fig. 56) allows us to follow in (A) the succession of impacts, and shows in (B) the succession of the limbs which cause these pressures on the ground.

If we wish to ascertain what are the *re-actions* produced at the withers, we see them represented in fig. 55 (upper line R). We find an undulatory elevation, which lasts all the time that the animal touches the ground; in this elevation are recognised the effects of the three impacts, which give it a triple undulation. The minimum elevation of the curve corresponds, as in the trot, with the moment when the feet do not touch the ground. Therefore, it is not a projection of the body into the air which constitutes the time of suspension in the gallop. Lastly, by comparing the re-actions of the gallop with those of the trot (fig. 45), we see that in the gallop the rise and fall of the body are effected in a less sudden manner. These re-actions are, therefore, less jarring to the rider. though they may, in fact, present a greater amplitude.

Piste of the gallop in three-time.—According to Curnieu, this piste is the following :—

Fig. 57.—Piste of the short gallop in three-time. The hinder feet, whose prints have the form of an U, reach the ground in front of the prints of the fore feet. The latter have been represented by a form somewhat like an O.

The piste of the gallop varies according to the speed. In the *short* gallop of the riding school, the hind-feet leave their prints behind those of the fore-feet; in the rapid gallop, on the contrary, they come in front of the prints of the fore-feet. A horse which, in the pace of the riding school, gallops almost entirely within his own length, will, when started at full gallop, cover an enormous space. According to Curnieu, the famous *Eclipse* covered 22 English feet. The following is the piste which this very rapid pace leaves on the ground :—

Fig. 58.—Piste of Eclipse's gallop, from Curnieu. The prints of the hind-feet are very far before those of the fore-feet.

Representation of a horse galloping.—For this representation we will give three attitudes, differing much from each other, and corresponding nearly with the three kinds of time found in this pace.

Fig. 59.—Horse galloping in the first time (right foot advancing), the hind left foot only on the ground. The white dot, in the notation, corresponds with the instant at which the horse is represented.

In the first time, fig. 59, the left hind-foot, on which the horse has just descended, alone rests on the ground.

In the second time, fig. 60, the left diagonal biped has just finished its impact, the right fore-foot is about to reach the ground, the left hind-foot has just risen.

The third time of the gallop, fig. 61, has been drawn as well as the others by Mons. Duhousset according to the notation; the moment chosen is that in which the right foot alone rests on the ground, and is about to rise in its turn.

Fig. 60.—Horse galloping in the second time (right foot forward).

Fig. 61.—Horse galloping in the third time (right foot forward).

The figure which represents it is rather strange; the eye is but little accustomed to see this time of the gallop, which is doubtless very rare. When considering this ungraceful figure, we are tempted to say with De Curnieu, "the province of painting is what one sees, and not what really exists."

The gallop in four-time differs from 'that which has just been described only in this point, that the impacts of the diagonal biped, which constitute the second time, are disunited and give distinct sounds; we see an example of this in fig. 62.

Fig. 62.—Notation of the gallop in four-time. (A) determination of each of the successive times. (B) determination of the number of feet which support the body at each instant.

According to this notation, the body, at first suspended, is borne successively on one foot, on three, on two, on three, and on one, after which a new suspension recommences.

Of the full gallop.—This very rapid pace could not be studied by means of the apparatus which we have employed hitherto. It was necessary to construct a special registering instrument, and new experimental apparatus.

To leave the two hands of the rider free, the registering instrument was enclosed in a flat box, attached to the back of the horseman by straps like the knapsack of the soldier. We shall not attempt the detailed description of this instrument, which carried five levers, tracing on smoked glass the curves of the action of the four legs, and the reaction of the withers. The violence of the impacts on the ground is such that they would instantly have broken the apparatus before employed. We have substituted for this a copper tube, in which moves a leaden piston, suspended between two spiral springs. The shocks given to this piston at each footfall, produce an effect like that of an air-pump acting on the registers. A ball of india-rubber, which can be pressed between the teeth, sets the register going, and allows the tracing to be taken at a suitable time.

Through the kindness of Mons. H. Delamarre, who placed at our disposal his stables at Chantilly, we have been able to procure tracings of the full gallop, of which the following is the notation :—

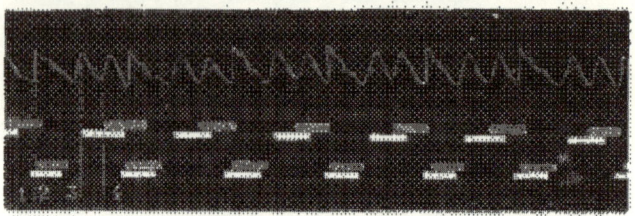

Fig. 63.—Notation of full gallop; re-actions of this pace.

It is seen that this pace is, in reality, a gallop in four-time. The impacts of the hinder limbs, however, follow each other at such short intervals, that the ear can only distinguish one of them; but those of the fore-legs are noticeably more dissociated, and can be heard separately. Another character of the full gallop is, that the longest period of silence takes place during the pressure of the hinder limbs. The time of suspension appears to be extremely short.

To get the best possible results from these experiments, it would be necessary to repeat them on a great number of horses, and to ascertain whether there may not be some relation between the rhythm of the impacts and the other characters of the pace. We must leave this task to those who especially addict themselves to the study of the horse.

Lastly, let us add, that the *re-actions*, in full gallop, reproduce with great exactness the rhythm of the impacts. Thus, it is observed, that at the moment of the almost synchronous impacts of the two hinder limbs, there is a sharp and prolonged re-action, after which two less sudden re-actions take place, each of which corresponds with the impact of one of the fore-legs.

The line placed above fig. 63 is the tracing of the re-actions

of the withers. This curve, being placed above the notation,
enables us, by the superposition of its various elements, to
notice with which impact of the limbs each re-action corresponds.

An observer finds great difficulty in ascertaining how one
kind of pace passes into another. The graphic method furnishes a very easy means of following these transitions; this
will perhaps be not one of the least advantages of the employment of this method of studying the paces of the horse.

In order thoroughly to understand what takes place in these
transitions, we must refer again to the comparison made by
Dugès, and represent to ourselves two persons walking, and
following each other's footsteps, both in the trot and the
gallop. In these continued paces, these two persons present
a constant rhythm in the relation of their movements; while,
in the transitions, the foremost or hindermost person, as the
case may be, quickens or moderates his movements so as to
change the rhythm of the footfalls. Some examples will
render this more evident.

The principal transitions are represented in page 174.

Fig. 64 is the notation of the *transition from the walking
pace to the trot*. The dominant character of this change, inde-
pendently of the increase of rapidity, consists in the hinder
impacts gaining upon those of the fore-limbs; so that the
impact of the left hind-foot, P G, for instance, which, during
the walking pace, took place exactly in the middle of the
duration of the pressure of the right fore-foot, A D, gradually
advances till it coincides with the commencement of the
pressure A D, and with the impact also, at which time the
trot is established.

Fig. 65 indicates, on the contrary, the *transition from the
trot to the walk*. We see here, in an inverse manner, the
diagonal impacts, synchronous at first, become more and more
separated. A dotted line, which unites the left diagonal
impacts, is vertical at the commencement of the figure in the
part which corresponds with the pace of the trot; by degrees

this line becomes oblique, showing that the synchronism is disappearing. The direction of the obliquity of this line proves that the hinder limbs grow slower in their movements in passing from the trot to the walk.

In the *passage from the trot to the gallop* the transition is very curious; it is represented by the notation, fig. 66. We see, from the very commencement of the figure, that the trot is somewhat irregular; the dotted line which unites the left diagonal impacts A G, P D, is at first rather oblique, and indicates a slight retardation of the hind-foot. This obliquity constantly increases, but only for the left diagonal biped; the right diagonal biped A D, P G, remains united, even after the gallop is established. The transition from the trot to the gallop is made, not only by the retardation of the hind-foot, but by the advance of the fore-foot, so that two of the diagonal impacts, which were synchronous in the trot, leave the greater interval between them; that which in the *ordinary gallop* constitutes the great silence. An opposite change produces the *transition from the gallop to the trot*, as is seen in fig. 67. The transition from the gallop in four-time to that in three-time is made by an increasing anticipation of the impacts of the hinder limbs.

SYNTHETIC STUDY OF THE PACES OF THE HORSE.

The analytical method to which we have hitherto had recourse in describing the paces of the horse may have left many things obscure in this delicate question. We hope to clear them up by recurring to the synthetic method.

When tracing, at the commencement of this study, the synoptical table of the different paces, we classed their notations in a natural series, the first term of which is the amble, and in which the difference between one step and the next consists in an anticipation of the action of the hinder limbs. This transition is just what is observed in animals. A dromedary, for instance, whose normal pace is the broken amble,*

---

* Through the kindness of Mons. Geoffroy St. Hilaire, director of the "Jardin d'Acclimatation," we have been permitted to study the paces of different quadrupeds, and especially those of the large dromedary which that garden possesses.

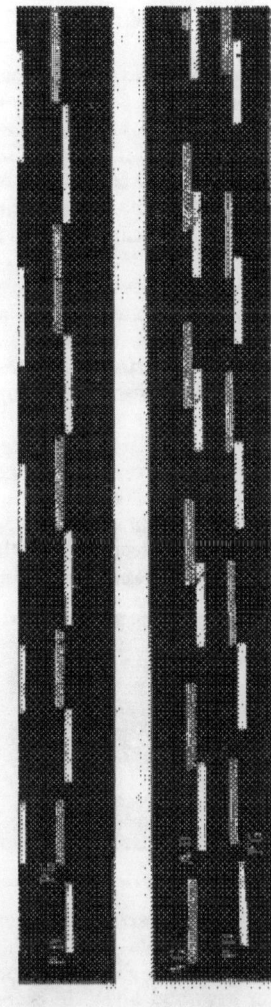

FIG. 65.—
Transition from
the trot to the
walk.

FIG. 66.—
Transition from
the trot to the
gallop.

has given us the whole series of notations, which, in our synoptical table, separate No. 2 from No. 8. When urging on the animal and forcing him to trot, he first broke his amble in an exaggerated manner, then he began to walk, and afterwards commenced an irregular trot, which soon became a free trot. We have just seen that the paces of the horse are formed in the same order when the animal passes from the walk to the trot.

When a horse begins to move more slowly, the change of pace is effected in an inverse manner; the paces succeed each other by running up the series represented in the plate.

The greater or less anticipation of the action of the hinder limbs is represented in the plate by a sliding backward of the notation towards the left of the figure. This fictitious sliding may become real by using a little instrument, which enables us to understand and explain very simply the formation of the different paces. It consists of a little rule, somewhat analogous to the sliding rule used in calculation, and which carries the notations of the four limbs on four little slips, which can glide side by side, and be arranged in various positions.

FIG. 68.—Notation rule, to represent the different paces.

Figs. 68 and 69 show the arrangement of this little instrument. Let us imagine a rule made of black wood, having four narrow grooves, in which slip sliding portions, alternately black and white, or grey and black, in order to represent the notation of the amble, as in No. 1 of the plate. If we push towards the left the two lowest slides simultaneously (fig. 68), we shall form, according to the amount of displacement, one or other of the notations in the table of regular paces. A scale, marked 1, 2, 3, 4, &c., up to which we can bring the mark representing the left hinder impact, allows us to form without hesitation any notation whatever.

To form the notations of the gallop, it is necessary to shift the slides corresponding with the fore-legs, so as to make them encroach on each other as is seen in notation, fig. 69.

FIG. 69.—Notation rule forming the representation of the gallop in three-time.

The notation rule is thus used. When we are sure that the pace is regular, it is sufficient, for instance, to examine the impacts of the two right feet, in order to construct the whole notation. According as the hinder impact is synchronous with that in front, or precedes it by a quarter, half, three-quarters, or the whole of the duration of a pressure, we place the two lower slides in the position which they ought to occupy, and the notation is thus simply constructed; it shows the rhythms of the impacts, the duration of the lateral and diagonal pressures, &c. The construction of the various paces of the gallop is effected in the same manner.

The artist who wishes to represent a horse at any instant of a particular pace, can thus easily determine the corresponding attitude. He forms on his rule the notation of the pace of the horse which is to be represented. Then, on the length which corresponds with the extent of a single pace in this notation, he erects a perpendicular line at any point. This line corresponds with a certain instant of the pace. Thus, as he can trace, on the length corresponding with a single pace, an indefinite number of perpendicular lines, it follows that the artist may choose in the duration of any pace, in any kind of locomotion, an indefinite number of different attitudes. Suppose him to have made his choice, and that he wishes to represent in the kind of pace (fig. 68), the instant which is marked by the vertical line 7, the notation will show him that the right fore-foot has just been placed upon the ground, that the left fore-foot is therefore beginning to rise, that the right hind-foot is almost at the end of its pressure on the ground, and that the left hind-foot is near the end of its rise. All that is necessary, in order to represent the animal exactly, is to know the attitude of each limb at the different instants of its rise, fall, or pressure, which is a comparatively easy matter. But the artist, guided by this method, will thus inevitably avoid altogether those false attitudes which often cause representations of horses to be so utterly unnatural.

FIGURES ARRANGED TO SHOW THE PACES OF THE HORSE.

Mons. Mathias Duval has undertaken to make, in order to illustrate the locomotion of the horse, a series of pictures, which, seen by means of the zootrope, represent the animal as if in motion in the various kinds of paces. This ingenious physiologist formed the idea of reproducing in an animated form, as it were, that which notation has done for the rhythm of the movements. The following is the arrangement which he employed. He first drew a series of figures of the horse taken at different instants of an ambling pace. Sixteen successive figures enabled him to represent the series of positions which each limb successively assumes in a pace belonging to this kind of locomotion. This band of paper, when placed in the instrument, gives to the eye the appearance of an ambling horse in actual motion.

We have said that all the walking paces may be considered as derived from the amble, with a more or less anticipation of the action of the hind limbs. Mons. Duval has realised this in his pictures in the following manner. Each plate, on which has been drawn the series of pictures of the ambling horse, is formed of two sheets of paper placed the one on the other. The upper one has in it a number of slits or openings, so that each horse is drawn half on this sheet, and the other half on that which is placed beneath. The hind quarters, for example, having been drawn on the upper sheet, the fore quarters are drawn on the under sheet, and are visible through the portion cut out of the upper sheet. Let us suppose that we cause the upper paper to slide as far as the interval which separates two figures of the horse, we shall have a series of images in which the fore limbs will fall back a certain distance towards the hind limbs. We shall thus represent, under the form of pictures, what is obtained under the form of notation, by slipping the two lower slides of the notation rule one degree. And as this displacement to the distance of one degree for each of the movements of the hinder limbs gives the notation of the broken amble, we shall obtain, in the figures thus drawn, the series of the successive positions of the paces of the broken amble. If the paper be made to slip a greater number of degrees, we shall have the series of attitudes of the horse at his walking pace. A still greater displacement will give the attitudes of the trot.

In all these cases, these figures, when placed in the instrument, make the illusion complete, and show us a horse which ambles, walks, or trots, as the case may be. Then, if we regulate the swiftness of the rotation given to the instrument, we render the movements which the animal seems to execute more or less rapid, which will permit the inexperienced observer to follow the series of positions of each kind of pace, and soon enable him to distinguish with the eye a series of movements in the living animal which appear at first sight to be in absolute confusion.

We hope that these plates, though still somewhat defective, will soon be sufficiently perfect to be of real use to those who are engaged in the artistic representation of the horse.

After these studies of terrestrial locomotion, we ought to explain the mechanism of *aquatic locomotion*. Some recent experiments of Mons. Ciotti have thrown great light on the propulsive action of the tails of fishes; not that they have overthrown the theory held ever since the time of Borelli, concerning the mechanism of swimming, but they have approached the question in another manner, that of the synthetic reproduction of this phenomenon. This method will certainly permit us to determine, with a precision hitherto unknown, both the motive work and resistant work in aquatic locomotion. It will, therefore, be advisable to wait for the results of experiments which are now being made, and which will be of equal service both to mechanicians and to physiologists.

BOOK THE THIRD.

AËRIAL LOCOMOTION.

CHAPTER I.

OF THE FLIGHT OF INSECTS.

Frequency of the strokes of the wing of insects during flight; acoustic determination; graphic determination—Influences which modify the frequency of the movements of the wing—Synchronism of the action of the two wings—Optical determination of the movements of the wing; its trajectory; changes in the plane of the wing; direction of the movement of the wing.

In terrestrial locomotion we have been able to measure by experiment the pressure of the feet on the ground, and hence we have deduced the intensity of the re-actions on the body of the animal. These two forces were easily ascertained by direct measurement. In the problem which is now to occupy us, the conditions are very different. The air gives a certain resistance to the wings which strike upon it, but it is a resistance every instant yielding, for it is only in proportion to the rapidity with which it is displaced, that the air resists the impulse of the wing. When we study the phenomena of flight, it is therefore necessary to know the movement of the wing in all the phases of its speed, in order to estimate the resistance which the air presents to that organ. We will propound in the following order the questions which must be resolved.

1. What is the frequency of the movements of the wing of insects?

2. What are the successive positions which the wing occupies during its complete revolution?

3. How is the motive force which sustains and transports the body of the animal developed?

I. *Frequency of the movements of the wing of insects.*—The frequency of the movements of the wing varies according to species. The ear perceives an acute sound during the flight of mosquitos and certain flies; there is a graver sound during the flight of the bee and the drone fly; still deeper in the macroglossæ and the sphingidæ. As to the other lepidoptera, they have, in general, a silent flight on account of the few strokes which they give with their wings.

Many naturalists have endeavoured to determine the frequency of the strokes of the wing by the musical note produced by the animal as it flies. But in order that this determination should be thoroughly reliable, it must be clearly established that the sound produced by the wing depends exclusively on the frequency of its movements, in the same manner as the sound of a tuning-fork results from the frequency of its vibrations. But opinions differ on this subject; certain writers have thought that during flight there is a movement of the air through the spiracles of insects, and that the sound which is heard depends on these alternate movements.

Without giving our adherence to this opinion, which seems to be contradicted by many facts, we think that the acoustic method is insufficient to furnish an estimate of the frequency with which the wing moves. The reason which would induce us not to employ this method, is that the musical note produced by the flying insect is varied by other influences besides the changes in the strokes of the wing.

When we observe the buzzing of an insect flying with a uniform rapidity, we perceive that the tone does not continue constantly the same. As the insect approaches the ear, the tone rises; it sinks as it goes farther from us. Something of an analogous kind happens when we cause a vibrating tuning-fork to pass before the ear; the note at first becomes more shrill and then more grave, and the difference may attain to a quarter or even to half a tone. We must, therefore, take care that the insect on which we experiment should be always at the same distance from the observer. This disturbing phenomenon, however, presents no real difficulty of interpretation; Pisko, the German writer on acoustics, has perfectly explained it. There is no doubt that the vibrations always follow each other after the same interval of time; when a vibrating plate remains at the same distance from the ear, the vibrations require the same time to reach us, and the phenomenon, uniform for the instrument, is uniform also for our organ. On the contrary, if the instrument be brought rapidly nearer, the vibration which is produced every instant has less space to traverse before it reaches the tympanum; it thus approximates to that which preceded it, and the sound grows sharper. If the instrument be removed to a greater distance the vibrations are more extended, and the tone becomes more grave. Every one has remarked, when travelling on a railroad, that if a locomotive passes us while the driver is sounding the whistle, the sharpness of the tone increases as the engine comes nearer, and becomes graver when it has passed by us, and the whistle is rapidly carried to a greater distance.

From these considerations we must be convinced that it is very difficult to estimate from the musical tone produced by a flying insect, the absolute frequency of the strokes of its wings. This depends to some extent on the variation of the tone thus produced, which passes at each instant from grave to sharp, according to the rapidity and the direction of the flight. Besides this, it is not easy to assign to each wing the part which it plays in the production of the sound. We have also to take into consideration that the wing of an insect may, by brushing through the air as it flies, be subjected to sonorous vibrations much more numerous than the complete revolutions which it accomplishes.

The graphic method furnishes a simple and precise solution of the question; it enables us to ascertain almost to a single beat the number of movements made per second by an insect's wing.

Experiment.—A sheet of paper blackened by the smoke of a wax-candle, is stretched upon a cylinder. This cylinder turns uniformly on itself at the rate of a turn in a second and a-half.

The insect, the frequency of the movement of whose wings

is to be studied, is held by the lower part of the abdomen, in a delicate pair of forceps; it is placed in such a manner that one of its wings brushes against the blackened paper at every movement. Each of these contacts removes a portion of the black substance which covers the paper, and, as the cylinder revolves, new points continually present themselves to the wing of the insect. We thus obtain a perfectly regular figure, if the insect be held in a steadily fixed position. These figures, of which we give some examples, differ according as the contact of the wing with the paper has been more or less extended. If the contact be very slight, we obtain a series of points or short cross-lines, as in fig. 70.

FIG. 70.—Showing the frequency of the strokes of the wing of a drone-fly (the three upper lines), and of a bee (the lower dotted line). The fourth line is produced by the vibrations of a chronographic tuning-fork, furnished with a style which registers 250 double vibrations per second.

Knowing that the cylinder revolves once in a second and a-half, it is easy to see how many revolutions of the wing are thus marked on the whole circumference of the cylinder. But it is still more convenient and accurate to make use of a chronographic tuning-fork, and to register, near the figure traced by the insect, the vibrations of the style with which the tuning-fork is furnished.

Fig. 70 shows, by the side of the tracing made by the wing of a drone-fly, that of the vibrations of a tuning-fork, which executes a double oscillation 250 times in a second. This instrument, enabling us to give a definite value to any portion of the tracing, shows that the wing of the drone performed from 240 to 260 complete revolutions per second.

Influences which modify the frequency of the movements of the wing.—Since we know the influence of resistance to the rapidity of the movements of animals, we may suppose that the wing which rubs on the cylinder has not its normal rate of motion, and that its revolutions are less numerous in proportion as the friction is greater. Experiment has confirmed this opinion. An insect performing the movements of flight by rubbing its wings rather strongly against the paper gave 240 movements per second; by diminishing more and more the contacts of the wing with the cylinder, we obtained still greater numbers —282, 305, and 321. This last number may perhaps express with sufficient accuracy the rapidity of the wing when moving freely, for the tracing was reduced to a series of scarcely-visible points. On the contrary, as the wing rubbed more strongly, the frequency of its movements was reduced below 240.

Another modifying cause of the frequency of movement in the wing is the *amplitude* of these movements. We must compare this cause with the preceding, for it is natural to admit that great movements meet with greater resistance in the air than smaller ones.

When we hold a fly or a drone by the forceps, we see that the animal executes sometimes strong movements of flight; we then hear a grave sound; but occasionally, when its wing is only slightly agitated, we perceive only a very shrill tone. That which the ear reveals to us with regard to the difference in the frequency of the strokes which the insect gives with its wings, is entirely confirmed by the experiments which we have made graphically.

Choosing the instants when the insect is at its strongest flight, and also when it gently flutters its wing, we find that the frequency varies within very extensive limits, nearly in the proportion of one to three—the least frequency belonging to the movements of greatest amplitude.

The *different species* of insects on which we have experimented, presented also very great variations in the rapidity of the movements of their wings. We have endeavoured as far as possible to compare the different species under similar conditions, during their swiftest flight, and with slight friction on the cylinder. The following are the results obtained as the expressions of the number of movements of the wing per second in each species :—

Common fly	330
Drone-fly	240
Bee	190
Wasp	110
Humming-bird moth (Macroglossa)	72
Dragon-fly	28
Butterfly (Pontia Rapæ)	9

Synchronism of the action of the two wings.—By holding the insect in a suitable position we can make both wings rub on the cylinder at the same time. It is then seen, on the tracing, that the two wings act simultaneously, and that both perform the same number of movements. Independantly of this, we may easily convince ourselves that there must necessarily be a similar motion in both wings.

If we move one of the wings of an insect recently killed, we shall find that a similar movement is given, in a certain degree, to the other corresponding wing; if we extend one wing laterally, the other is also extended, if we raise one up, the other rises. The wasp is well suited for this experiment.

Still, in captive flight, certain insects can perform great movements with one of their wings, while the other only executes slight vibrations. The dung-fly, for instance, usually affects this kind of alternate flight; when it is held with the forceps, its two wings rarely move together. The suddenness and the unforeseen condition of these alternations, and the violent deviations which they give to the axis of the body, have prevented us from taking the simultaneous tracings of the movement of its two wings, and from ascertaining whether the synchronism continues under these conditions, in spite of the unequal amplitude of the movements.

The preceding figures show the regular periodicity of the movements of insect flight, but they also prove that the graphic method cannot represent the whole course of the wing, for this organ can only be tangential to a certain portion of the surface of the cylinder. Whatever may be the movements

which the wing describes, its point evidently moves on the
surface of a sphere, the radius of which is the length of the
wing, and the centre at the point of attachment of this organ
with the mesothorax.   But a sphere can only touch a plane or
convex surface at one point; thus, we only obtain a number
of points for a series of revolutions of the wing, if the turning cylinder be only tangential to the extremity of the wing.
More complicated tracings can only be obtained by more
extensive contacts, in which the wing bends, and thus rubs
a portion of its surfaces or its edges on the blackened paper.

We will explain the means by which the graphic method
can serve to determine the movements of the wing, but let
us first show the results obtained by another method, in
order to render the explanation more clear.

2. *Optical method of the determination of the movements of
the wing.*—Having being convinced by the former experiments, of the regular periodicity of these movements, we have
thought it possible to determine their nature by the eye.   In
fact, if we can attach a brilliant spot to the extremity of the
wing, this spot passing continually through the same space
would leave a luminous trace which would produce a figure
completely regular, and free from the deformity incident to
that effected by the friction on the cylinder.   This optical
method has already been employed for a similar purpose by
Wheatstone, who placed brilliant metallic balls on rods producing complex vibrations, and thus obtained luminous
figures varying according to the different combinations of the
vibrating movements.

By fixing a small piece of gold-leaf at the extremity of the
wing of a wasp, and throwing upon it a ray of the sun while
the insect was executing the movements of flight, we have
obtained a brilliant image of the successive positions of the
wing, which gave nearly the appearance represented in
fig. 71.

This figure shows that the point of the wing describes a
very elongated figure 8; sometimes, indeed, the wing seems
to move entirely in one plane, and the instant afterwards the
terminal loops which form the 8 are seen to open more and
more.   When the opening becomes very large, one of the

loops usually predominates over the other; it is generally the lower one which increases while the upper diminishes. Indeed, by a still greater opening, the figure is occasionally transformed into an irregular ellipse, at the extremity of which we can recognise a vestige of the second loop.

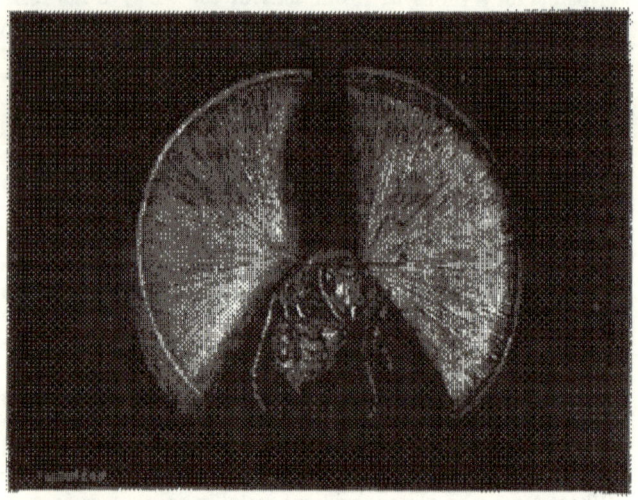

Fig. 71.—Appearance of a wasp, the extremity of each of whose larger wings has been gilded. The insect is supposed to be placed in a sunbeam.

We thought that we had been the first to point out the form of the trajectory of the wing of the insect, but Dr. J. B. Pettigrew, an English author, informs us that he had already mentioned this figure of 8 appearance described by the wing, and had represented it in the plates of his work.[*] It will be seen presently that, notwithstanding this apparent agreement, our theory and that of Dr. Pettigrew differ materially from each other.

Changes of the plane of the wing.—The luminous appearance given during flight by the gilded wing of an insect, shows

* On the Mechanical Appliances by which Flight is Maintained in the Animal Kingdom. Transact. of Linnean Society, 1867, p. 233.

besides, that during the alternate movements of flight, the plane of the wing changes its inclination with respect to the axis of the insect's body, and that the upper surface of the wing turns a little backward during the period of ascent, whilst it is inclined forward a little during its descent.

If we gild a large portion of the upper surface of a wasp's wing, taking precautions that the gold-leaf should be limited to this surface only, we see that the animal, placed in the sun's rays, gives the figure of 8 with a very unequal intensity in the two halves of the image, as represented in fig. 71. The figure printed thus ❸ gives an idea of the form which is then produced, if we consider the thick stroke of this character as corresponding with the more brilliant portion of the image, and the thin stroke as representing the part which is less bright.

It is evident that the cause of the phenomenon is to be found in a change in the plane of the wing, and consequently in the incidence of the solar rays; being favourable to their reflection during the period of ascent, and unfavourable during the descent. If we turn the animal round, so as to observe the luminous figure in the opposite direction, the 8 will then present the unequal splendour of its two halves, but in the inverse direction; it becomes bright in the portion before relatively obscure, and *vice versâ*.

We shall find in the employment of the graphic method, new proofs of changes in the plane of the wing during flight. This phenomenon is of great importance, for in it we seem to find the proximate cause of the motive force which urges forward the body of the insect.

In order to verify the preceding experiments, and to assure ourselves still more of the reality of the displacement of the wing, which the optical method has revealed to us, we have introduced the extremity of a small pointer into the interior of the figure 8 described by the wing, and we have proved that in the middle of these loops there really exist free spaces of the form of a funnel, into which the pointer penetrates without meeting the wing, whilst, if we try to pass the intersection where the lines cross each other, the wing immediately strikes against the pointer, and the flight is interrupted.

*Graphic method employed for the determination of the move-
ments of the wing.*—The preceding experiments throw great light
on the traces which we obtain by the friction of the insect's
wing against the blackened cylinder. Although the figures
thus produced are for the most part incomplete, we are able,
by means of their scattered elements, to reconstruct the figure
which has been shown by the optical method.

It is to be remarked that without sensibly interfering with
the movements of the wing, we can obtain traces of seven or
eight millimetres when the wing is rather long. The slight
flexure to which the wing is subjected allows it to remain in
contact with the cylinder to that extent; we thus obtain a
partial tracing of the movement; so that if we are careful to
produce the contact of the wing with the cylinder in different
parts of the course passed through by the limb, we obtain a
series of partial tracings which are complementary to each
other, and thus allow us to deduce from them the form of a
perfect curve of the revolution of a wing. Suppose, then,
that in fig. 71, the curve described by the gilded wing is
divided by horizontal lines into three zones: the upper one,
formed by the upper loop; that in the middle, comprehending
the two branches of the 8, crossing each other and forming a
sort of X; the lower one including the lower loop.

By registering the movement of the middle zone, we get

Fig. 72.—Tracing of the middle region of the course of the wing of a bee,
showing the crossing of the two branches of the 8. One of the branches
is prolonged rather far, but still the tracing of the lower loop has not been
produced.

figures somewhat resembling each other, in which the lines,
placed obliquely with respect to each other, cut each other.
This is the case in fig. 72, the middle region of the tracing
of a bee, and in fig. 73, the middle portion of that of a
humming-bird moth.

The upper zone of the revolution of the wing gives tracings analogous with that of fig. 74, in which the upper loops of the 8 are plainly visible.   The tracings of the zone which corre-

Fig. 73.—Tracing of the middle zone in the course described by the wing of a humming-bird moth. The numerous strokes of which this tracing is formed, arise from the extremity of the wing being fringed and presenting a rough surface.

sponds with the lower course of the wing give also loops like those of the upper arch (fig. 75 shows a specimen of them); so that the figure 8 of the tracing can be reproduced by

Fig. 74.—This figure shows, in the tracing made by a wasp, the upper loop, and all the extent of one branch of the 8. The middle part of this branch is merely dotted because of the feeble friction of the wing.

bringing together the three fragments of its course successively obtained.

If we could only once procure the entire tracing formed by the wing of an insect, we should then get a figure identical with that which our learned writer on acoustics, Kœnig, was the first to obtain with a Wheatstone rod tuned to the octave, that is to say, describing an 8 in space. This typical form is represented in fig. 76. We shall see that the graphic method

is adapted to other experiments intended to verify those which
we have already made by other means. By varying the incidence of the wing on the revolving cylinder, we can foretell
what will be the figure traced, if it be true that the wing
really describes the form of an 8. Thus, if we obtain a figure

Fig. 75.—Tracings of the wing of a wasp; several of the lower loops are
distinctly seen. This tracing was obtained by holding the insect so as
to rub the cylinder by the hinder point of the wing, which gives very extended curves.

conformable to that which we have foreseen, it will be an
evident proof of the reality of these movements.

Fig. 76.—Tracing of a Wheatstone's kaleidophone rod, tuned to the octave,
that is to say, vibrating twice transversely for each longitudinal vibration.
(This figure is taken from R. Kœnig.) The slackening speed of the
cylinder produces an approximation of the curves towards the end of the
figure.

Let us suppose that the wing of the insect, instead of
touching the cylinder with its point, as we have seen just
now, brushes it with one of its edges; and let us admit for
an instant that the 8 described by the wing is so lengthened
that it departs but slightly from the plane passing through
the vertical axis of this figure. If we press the wing slightly
against the cylinder the contact will be continuous, and the
tracing uninterrupted; but the figure obtained will no
longer be an 8; if the cylinder be immovable it will be an
arc of a circle, whose concavity will be turned towards the
point of insertion of the wing, a point which will occupy precisely the centre of the curve described.

If the cylinder revolve, the figure will be spread out like
the oscillation of a tuning-fork registered under the same
conditions, and we shall obtain a tracing more or less approaching in form to that which is represented in fig. 77.

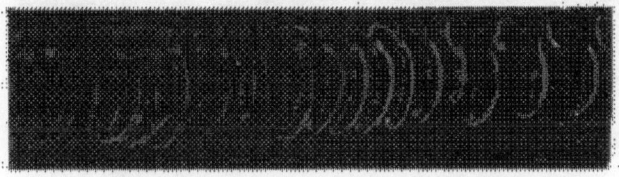

Fig. 77.—Tracing obtained with the wing of a bee, oscillating in a plane
which is sensibly tangential to the generatrix of the registering cylinders.

This form, which theory enables us to predict, is always
produced when the plane in which the wing moves is tangential to the generatrix of the cylinder.

But in examining these tracings we easily recognise *changes
in the thickness of the stroke*—parts which appear to have been
made by a greater or less friction of the wing on the cylinder; we here find a new and certain proof of the existence of
a movement in the form of an 8, as we now propose to show
by a synthetic method.

Let us take a Wheatstone's rod tuned to the octave; let us fix
on it the wing of an insect as a style, and let us trace the vibrations which it executes. We shall obtain, if the cylinder be
motionless, figures of 8 when the wing touches the paper by
its point applied perpendicularly to its surface; and if the
cylinder revolve, we shall have lengthened figures of 8.

We may obtain, with a rod tuned to the octave, tracings
identical with those given by the insect; of which a proof is
afforded by the comparison of the two following figures:—

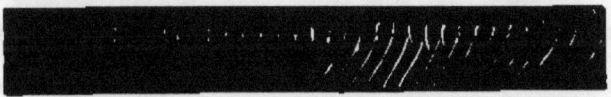

Fig. 78.—Tracings of a wasp; the insect is held so that its wing touches
the cylinder by its point, and traces especially the upper loop of the 8.

The graphic method also furnishes us with the proof of changes in the plane of the wing of the insect during the various instants of its revolutions.

Fig. 79.—Tracings of a Whetstone rod tuned to the octave, furnished with the wing of a wasp, and arranged so as to register especially the upper loop of the 8.

Fig. 80 shows the tracing furnished by a wing of a humming-bird moth, arranged so as to touch the cylinder with its posterior edge. By bringing the insect not too near, we can succeed in producing only intermittent contacts; these take place at the moment when the wing describes that part of the loops of the 8 whose convexity is tangential to the cylinder. The contacts which occupy the upper half of the figure alternate with those occupying the lower half. It is seen, besides, that it is not the same surface of the wing which produces these two kinds of friction. In fact, it is evident that the

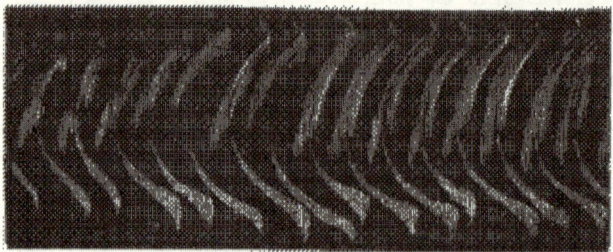

Fig. 80.—Tracings of the movements of the wing of a humming-bird moth (macroglossa) rubbing on the cylinder by its lower edge.

marks of the upper half, each formed of a series of oblique strokes, are produced by the contact of a fringed border, while the contacts of the lower part are produced by another portion of the wing which presents a region unprovided with fringes, and leaves a whiter trace with boundaries better defined.

o

These changes of plane are only found in great movements
of the wing.   This is an important fact, for it will explain to
us the method of their production.   Fig. 81 was furnished
like fig. 80 by the movements of the wing of a moth (macroglossa); but on account of its fatigue these movements had
lost nearly all their amplitude.

FIG. 81.—Tracing of the wing of a fatigued macroglossa.   The figure 8 is
no longer to be seen, but only a simple pendular oscillation.

We see only in this figure a series of pondular oscillations,
showing that the wing merely rose and fell without changing
its plane.   The bright line which borders the ascending and
upper parts of these curves is explained by the alternate
flexions of the wing as it rubs upon the paper, and shows
that the upper surface was rough, and left a distinct trace,
while the lower surface presented no similar roughness.

3. *Direction of the movement of the wing.*—One more very
important element is required to give us a complete knowledge
of the movements which the insect's wing executes in its flight.
The optical method, while it shows us all the points in the
curve described by the gilded extremity of the wing, does not
indicate the direction in which this revolution is accomplished;
whatever may be the direction in which the wing moves in its
orbit, the luminous image which it affords must be always
the same.

A very simple method has furnished a solution of this new
question.   Let fig. 82 be the luminous image furnished by
the movements of the right wing of an insect.   The direction
of these movements which the eye cannot follow is indicated
by arrows.

To determine the direction of these movements, we take a
small rod of polished glass and blacken it with the smoke of
a wax taper; when holding the rod at right angles to the
direction in which the wing moves, we present the blackened

end to (*a*), that is to say, in front of the lower loop. We endeavour to pass this point into the interior of the course described by the wing; but as soon as it enters this region, the rod receives a series of shocks from the wing, which rubs on its surface, and wipes off the soot which covered it. When we examine the surface of the glass, we see that the soot has been removed only on the upper part, which shows that at the point (*a*) of its course, the wing is descending. The same experiment being repeated in (*a'*), that is to say, in the hinder part of the orbit of the wing, it is found that the rod has been rubbed beneath; so that the wing at *a'* was ascending. In the same manner it may be shown that the wing rises at *b* and descends at *b'*.

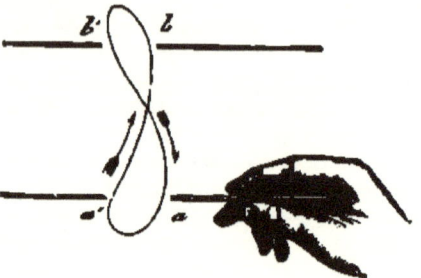

Fig. 82.—Determination of the direction of the movements of an insect's wing.

We now know all the movements executed by an insect's wing during its revolution, as well as the double change of plane which accompanies them. The knowledge of this change of plane was given to us by the unequal brightness of the two branches of the luminous 8. Thus we may feel assured that in the course of the descending wing, that is from *b'* to *a* in fig. 82, the upper surface of the wing turns slightly forward, while from *a'* to *b*, that is, in ascending, this surface turns a little backwards.

CHAPTER II.

MECHANISM OF THE FLIGHT OF INSECTS.

Causes of the movements of the wings of insects—The muscles only give
a motion to and fro, the resistance of the air modifies the course of
the wing—Artificial representation of the movements of the insect's
wing—Of the propulsive effect of the wings of insects—Construction of an artificial insect which moves horizontally—Change in the
plane in flight.

1. *Causes of the movements of the wing.*—These exceedingly
complicated movements would induce us to suppose that there
exists in insects a very complex muscular apparatus, but
anatomy does not reveal to us muscles capable of giving rise
to all these movements. We scarcely find any but elevating
and depressing forces in the muscles which move the wing;
besides this, when we examine more closely the mechanical
conditions of the flight of the insect, we see that an upward
and downward motion given by the muscles is sufficient to produce all these successive acts, so well co-ordinated with each
other; the resistance of the air effecting all the other movements.

If we take off the wing of an insect (fig. 83), and holding
it by the small joint which connects it with the thorax, expose
it to a current of air, we see that the plane of the wing is

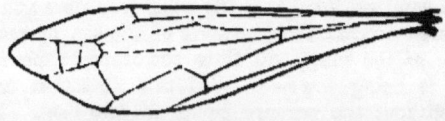

Fig. 83.—Structure of an insect's wing.

inclined more and more as it is subjected to a more powerful
impulse of the wind. The anterior nervure resists, but the
membranous portion which is prolonged behind bends on
account of its greater pliancy. If we blow upon the upper sur-

face of the wing, we see this surface carried backwards, while by blowing on it from beneath, we turn the upper surface forwards. In certain species of insects, according to Félix Plateau, the wing resists the pressure of the air acting from below upwards, more than that exerted in an opposite direction.

Is it not evident, that in the movements which take place during flight, the resistance of the air will produce upon the plane of the wing the same effects as the currents of air which we have just employed? The changes in the plane, caused by the resistance of the air under these conditions, are precisely those which are observed in flight. We have seen that the descending wing presents its anterior surface forwards, which is explained by the resistance of the air acting from below upwards; while the ascending wing turns its upper surface backwards, because the resistance of the air acts upon it from above downwards.

It is, therefore, not necessary to look for special muscular actions to produce changes in the plane of the wing; these, in their turn, will give us the key to the oblique curvilinear movements which produce the figure of 8 course followed by the insect's wing.

Let us return to fig. 82 : the wing which descends has at the same time a forward motion ; therefore, the inclination taken by the plane of the wing, under the influence of the resistance of the air, necessarily causes the oblique descent from b' to a. An inclined plane which strikes on the air has a tendency to move in the direction of its own inclination.

Let us suppose, then, that the wing only rises and falls by its muscular action ; the resistance of the air, by pressing on the plane of the wing, will force the organ to move forward while it is being lowered. But this deviation cannot be effected without the nervure being slightly bent. The force which causes the wing to deviate in a forward direction necessarily varies in intensity according to the rapidity with which the organ is depressed. Thus, when the wing towards the end of its descending course moves more slowly, we shall see the nervure, as it is bent with less force, bring the wing backwards in a curvilinear direction. Thus we explain

naturally the formation of the descending branch of the 8
passed through by the wing.

The same theory applies to the formation of the ascending
branch of this figure. In short, a kind of pendular oscillation executed by the nervure of the wing is sufficient, together with the resistance of the air, to give rise to all the
movements revealed to us by our experiments.

2. *Artificial representation of the movements of the insect's wing.*
—These theoretical deductions require experimental verification, in order that they may be thoroughly borne out. We
have succeeded in obtaining the following results :—

Let fig. 84 be an instrument, which, by means of a multiplying wheel and a connecting rod, gives to a flexible shaft
rapid to and fro movements in a vertical plane. Let us take
a membrane similar to that in the wings of insects, and fix it
to this shaft, which will then represent the main rib of the
wing; we shall see this contrivance execute all the movements which the wing of the insect describes in space.

If we illuminate the extremity of this artificial wing, we
shall see that its point describes the figure 8, like a real wing;
we shall observe also that the plane of the wing changes
twice during each revolution in the same manner as in the
insect itself. But in the apparatus which we now employ,
the movement communicated to the wing is only upwards
and downwards. Were it not for the resistance of the air,
the wing would only rise and fall in a vertical plane; all
these complicated movements are due therefore only to the
resistance presented by the air. Consequently, it is this
which bends the main rib of the wing, turning it in a direction perpendicular to the plane in which its oscillation is
effected.

But if the wing be pushed aside from its main-rib at each
of its alternate movements, it is evident that the air, acted
upon by this wing, will receive an impulse in an opposite
direction; that is to say, it will escape at the side of the
flexible portion of the wing, and cause in this direction a
current of air. It is seen, in figure 84, that a candle placed
by the side of the thin edge of the wing, is strongly blown
by the current of air which is produced. In front of the wing,

on the contrary, the air will be drawn forwards, so that the flame of another candle placed in front of the nervure will be strongly drawn towards it.

Fig. 54.—Artificial representation of the movements of an insect's wing.

3. *Of the propulsive action of the wings of insects.*—In the same manner as the squib moves in the opposite direction to the jet of flame which it throws out, the insect propels itself in the course opposed to the current of air produced by the movement of its wings.

Each stroke of the wing acts on the air obliquely, and neutralizes its resistance, so that a horizontal force results, which impels the insect forwards. This resultant acts in the descent of the wing, as well as in its upward movement, so that each part of the oscillation of the wing has an action favourable to the propulsion of the animal.

An effect is produced analogous with that which takes place when an oar is used in the stern of a boat in the action of sculling. Each stroke of the oar, which presents an inclined plane to the resisting water, divides this resistance into two forces: one acts in a direction opposed to the motion of the oar, the other, in a direction perpendicular to that movement, and it is the latter which impels the boat.

Most of the propellers which act in water overcome the resistance of the fluid by the action of an inclined plane. The tail of the fish produces a propulsion of this kind; that of the beaver does the same, with this difference, that it oscillates in a vertical plane. Even the screw may be considered as an inclined plane, whose movement is continuous, and always in the same direction.

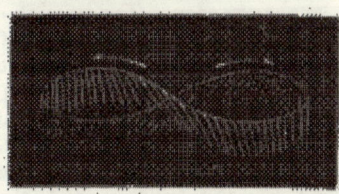

FIG. 85.—Representation of the changes in the plane of the insect's wing.

If we wish to represent the inclination of the plane of the wing at the different parts of its course, we shall obtain fig. 85, in which the arrows indicate the direction of the course of the wing, and the lines, whether dotted or full, show the inclination of its plane.

After this, we need only show the figure traced by Dr. Pettigrew in his work on flight, to prove how far the ideas of this English writer differ from ours.

The trajectory of the wing is represented by Dr. Pettigrew by means of fig. 86. Four arrows indicate, according to this writer, the direction of movements in the different portions of this trajectory. These arrows are in the same direction, and this first fact is opposed to the experiment described in page 195, where we have investigated the direction of the movement of the wing, and have found it pass in opposite directions in the two branches of the 8. In order to explain the form which he assigns to this trajectory, Dr. Pettigrew admits that in its passage from right to left, the wing describes by its thicker edge the thick branch of the 8, and the

FIG. 86.—Trajectory of the wing.

thin branch by its narrow edge. The crossing of the 8 therefore would be formed by a complete reversal of the plane of the wing during one of the phases of its revolution. In fact, the author seems to perceive in this reversal of the plane, an action similar to that of a screw, of which the air would form the nut. We will not dwell any longer on this theory, but we have deemed it necessary to bring it forward, in consequence of the appeal which has been made to us.

4. *Artificial representation of an insect's flight.*—In order to render the action of the wing and the effects of the resistance of the air more intelligible, we have made use of the following apparatus :—

Let fig. 87 represent two artificial wings composed of a rigid main-rib connected with a flexible membrane, composed of gold-beater's skin, strengthened by fine nervures of steel; the plane of these wings is horizontal; a system of bent levers raises or lowers them without giving them any lateral motion.

The movement of the wings is caused by a little copper drum, in which the air is alternately condensed and rarefied by the action of a pump. The circular surfaces of this drum

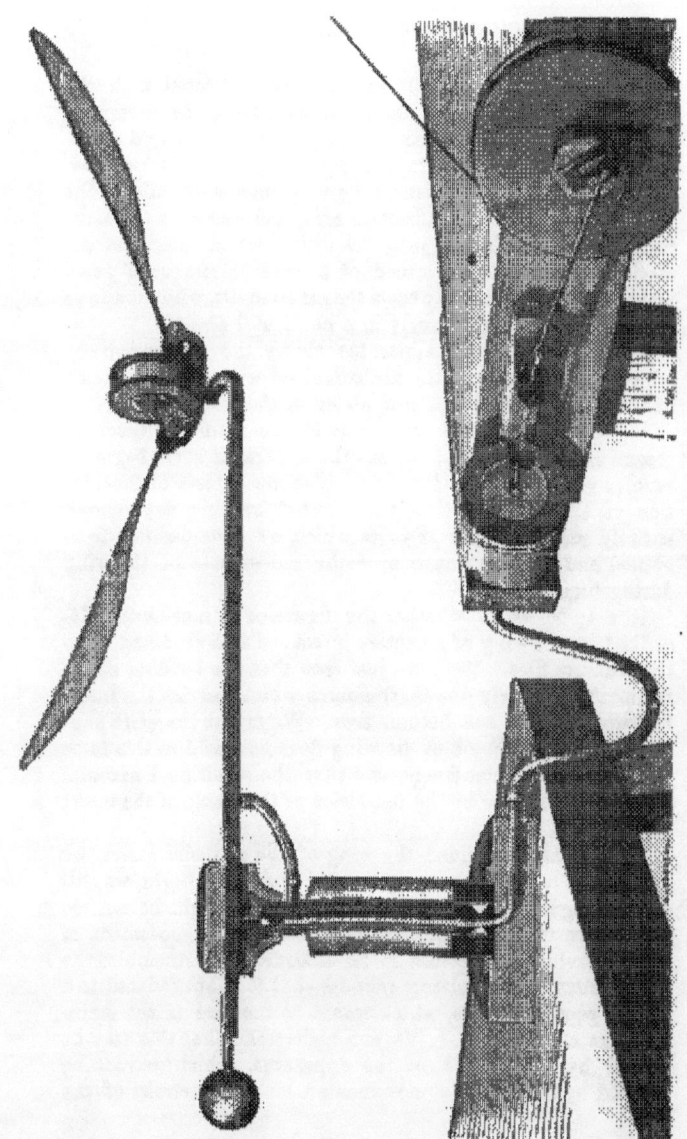

FIG. 67.—Representing the artificial insect, or instrument to illustrate the flight of insects.

are formed of india-rubber membranes connected with the two wings by bent levers; the air when compressed or rarefied gives to these flexible membranes powerful and rapid movements, which are transmitted to both wings at the same time.

A horizontal tube, balanced by a counterpoise, allows the apparatus to turn upon a central axis, and serves at the same time to conduct the air into the drum, which produces the motion. This axis is formed of a kind of mercurial gasometer, which hermetically seals the air conduits, while it allows the instrument to turn freely in a horizontal plane.

Thus arranged, the apparatus shows the mechanism by which the resistance of the air, combined with the movements of the wing, produces the propulsion of the insect.

If we set in motion the wings of the artificial insect by means of the air-pump, we see the apparatus soon begin to revolve rapidly around its axis. The mechanism of the motion of the insect is clearly illustrated by this experiment, entirely confirming the theories which we have deduced from optical and graphic analysis of the movements of the wing during flight.

It may be asked whether the figure of 8 movements described by the wing of a captive insect are also produced when the creature flies. We have just seen that the bending of the main-rib is entirely due to the force which carries the insect forward when it has become free. We might therefore suppose that the main-rib of the wing does not yield to this force when the insect flies freely, and that the resulting horizontal force is shown only by the impulsion of the whole of the insect forwards.

If, after having gilded the wing of the artificial insect, we look at the luminous image produced during its flight, we still see the figure of 8 remaining, provided the flight be not too rapid. In fact, this figure is modified by the movement of the apparatus; it becomes more extended, and resembles the 8 registered on a revolving cylinder, but it is not reduced to a simple pendular curve, which would be the case if the main-rib were always rigid. We can understand that this may be caused by the inertia of the apparatus, which cannot be affected by the variable movements which each stroke of the wing tends to bring to bear upon it. The artificial insect, when once set in motion, is sometimes before, and at others behind the horizontal force developed by the wing: on this account the rib of the wing is forced to bend, because the mass to be moved does not obey instantaneously the resulting horizontal force which the wing derives from the resistance of the air. The same phenomenon must take place in the flight of a real insect.

5. *Plane of oscillation of an insect's wing.*—The apparatus which has just been described does not yet give a perfect idea of the mechanism of insect flight. We have been compelled, for the sake of explaining the movements of the wing more easily, to suppose that its oscillation is made from above downwards; that is to say, from the back of the insect towards its lower surface, when lying horizontally in the air.

But we need only observe the flight of certain insects, the common fly, for instance, and most of the other diptera, to see that the plane in which the wings move is not vertical, but, on the contrary, very nearly horizontal. This plane directs its upper surface somewhat forward, and therefore the main-rib of the wing corresponds with this surface. Consequently, it is from below upwards, and a little forward that the propulsion of the insect is effected. The greater part of the force exerted by the wing will be employed in supporting the insect against the action of its weight; the rest of this impulse will carry it forward.

By changing the inclination of the plane of oscillation of its wings, which can be done by moving the abdomen so as to displace the centre of gravity, the insect can, according to its wishes, increase the rapidity of its forward flight, lessen the speed acquired, retrograde, or dart toward the side.

It is easily to be seen that, when a hymenopterous insect flying at full speed, stops upon a flower, this insect directs the plane of the oscillation of its wings backwards with considerable force.

Nothing is more variable, in fact, than the inclination of the plane in which the wings of different species of insects oscillate.

The diptera appear to us to have this plane of oscillation

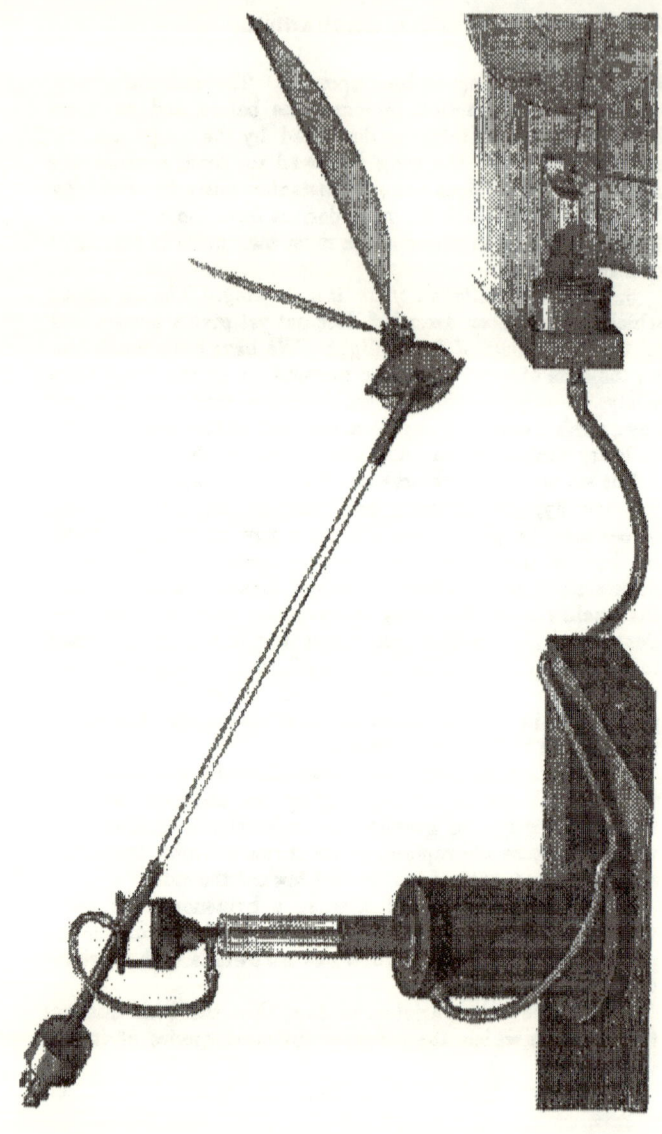

Fig. 88.—Arrangement of the artificial insect, to obtain the change of plane, or ascending flight.

very nearly horizontal; in the hymenoptera, the wing moves
in a plane of nearly 45°, but the lepidoptera flap their wings
almost vertically, after the manner of birds.

In order to render the influence of the plane of oscillation more evident, and to show that the force derived from the
resistance of the air has the double effect of raising the insect
and directing its course, we must arrange the *flight-instrument*
in a peculiar manner. It will be necessary, in the first place,
to be able to change the plane of oscillation of the wings,
which is effected by placing the drum on a pivot at the extremity of the horizontal tube, at the end of which it turns.
To show the ascensional force which is developed in this new
arrangement, the instrument must no longer be confined to a
simple movement of rotation in the horizontal plane, but it
must be able to oscillate in a vertical plane like the scale beam
of a balance.

Fig. 88 shows the new arrangement which we have given
to the instrument in order to obtain this double result.

In this modification of the apparatus, the air-pump which
constitutes the moving force is retained; as is also the turning column which moves in the mercurial gasometer. But
above the disc which terminates this column at the upper end,
is fixed a new joint, which allows the horizontally-balanced
tube at the end of which the artificial insect is placed, to
oscillate in the vertical plane like a scale-beam. In order to
establish a communication between the revolving column and
the tube carrying the insect, we make use of a little india-
rubber tube, sufficiently flexible not to interfere with the
oscillatory movements of the apparatus.

Other accessory modifications may be seen in fig. 88; one
consists in employing a glass tube to convey the air from the
pump which moves the insect; the other in a change of the
mechanism by which motion is imparted to the wings. The
most important alteration is the introduction of a joint which
allows us to give every possible inclination to the plane in
which the wings oscillate.

The apparatus being arranged so that the counterpoise,
having been brought nearer to the point of suspension, does
not exactly balance the weight of the insect, the latter is

placed so that its wings may move in a horizontal plane, the main-rib being uppermost. Thus all the motive force is directed from below upwards, and as soon as the pump begins to act, we see the insect rise vertically. We can easily estimate the weight raised by the flapping of the wings, and as we can vary the weight of the insect by altering the position of the counterpoise, we can determine the effort which is developed according to the frequency or the amplitude of the strokes.

By turning the insect half way round, so that its wings, still oscillating in a horizontal plane, should turn their main-rib downwards; we develop a descending vertical force which may be measured by removing the counterpoise to a greater or less distance, and causing it to be raised by the descent of the insect.

If we adjust the plane of oscillation of the wings vertically, the insect turns horizontally round its point of support in the same manner as has been previously described and represented in fig. 87.

Lastly, if we give to the plane of oscillation of the wings, the oblique position which it presents in the greater number of insects; that is to say, so that the main-rib turns at once upwards and slightly forward, we see the insect rise against its own weight, and turn at the same time round the vertical axis; in a word, the apparatus represents the double effect which is observed in a flying insect, which obtains from the stroke of its wings, both the force which sustains it in the air, and that which directs its course in space.

The first of these forces is by far the more considerable; thus, when an insect hovers over a flower, and we see it illuminated obliquely by the setting sun, we may satisfy ourselves that the plane of oscillation of its wings is nearly horizontal. This inclination must evidently be modified as soon as the insect wishes to dart off rapidly in any direction, but then the eye can scarcely follow it, and detect the change of plane, the existence of which we are compelled to admit by the theory and the experiments already detailed.

A curious point of study would be the movements prepara-

tory to flight. We speak not only of the spreading of the
wings, which in the coleoptera precedes flight, a movement
which is sometimes so slow as to be easily observed, nor of
the unfolding of the first pair of wings, as wasps do before
they fly.   Other insects, the diptera, turn their wings as on
a pivot around its main-rib in a very remarkable manner,
at the moment when the wings which were previously extended on the back in the attitude of repose start outwards
and forwards before they begin to fly. Flies, tipulæ and
many other kinds, show this preparatory movement very clearly
when the insect, being exhausted, has no longer any energy
in its flight. We see the main-rib of the wing remain sensibly immovable, and around it turns the membranous portion
whose free border is directed downwards.   This position
having been obtained, the insect has only to cause its wing
to oscillate in an almost horizontal direction from backwards
forwards, and from forwards backwards. If this motion as on
a pivot did not exist, the wing would cut the air with its edge,
and would be utterly incapable of producing flight. In other
species, as in the agrion, a small dragon-fly, for instance, the
four wings, during repose, are laid back to back one against
the other above the abdomen of the animal. Their main-
ribs are upwards, and keep their position when the wings pass
downwards and forwards; here no preparation for flight is
necessary. In these insects, as in butterflies, the wing has
only to set itself in motion when the creature flies.

It is interesting to follow throughout the series of insects
the variations presented by the mechanism of flight.

The confirmation of the theory just propounded is found in
the experiments which certain naturalists have made by
means of vivisection. For the most interesting of these we
are indebted to Professor M. Giraud. All these experiments
prove that the insect needs for the due function of flight a
rigid main-rib and a flexible membrane. If we cover the
flexible part of the wing with a coating which hardens as it
dries, flight is prevented. We hinder it also by destroying
the rigidity of the anterior nervure.

If we only cut off, on the contrary, a portion of the flexible
membrane, parallel to its hinder edge, the power of flight

is preserved, for the wing retains the conditions essential to this function—namely, a rigid main-rib and a flexible surface. Lastly, in some species the combination of two wings is indispensable to flight; a kind of pseudo-elytron constitutes the nervure, and behind this is extended a membranous wing, which is locked in with the posterior border of the anterior one. This second wing does not present sufficient rigidity to enable it to strike the air with advantage, and in these insects flight is rendered impossible, if we cut off the false wing-case; it is as if we had destroyed the main-rib of a perfect wing.

CHAPTER III.

OF THE FLIGHT OF BIRDS.

Conformation of the bird with reference to flight—Structure of the wing, its curves, its muscular apparatus—Muscular force of the bird; rapidity of contraction of its muscles—Form of the bird; stable equilibrium; conditions favourable to change of plane—Proportion of the surface of the wings to the weight of the body in birds of different size.

THE plan by which we have been guided in the study of insect flight must also be followed in investigating that of birds. It will be necessary to determine, by a delicate mode of analysis, the movements produced by the wing during flight; from these movements we may draw a conclusion as to the resistance of the air which affords the bird a fulcrum on which to exert its force. Then, having propounded certain theories respecting the mechanism of flight, the force required for the work affected by the bird, &c., we will undertake to represent these phenomena by means of artificial instruments, as we have already done with respect to insects.

But, before we enter methodically on this study, it will be useful to prepare ourselves for it by some general observations on the organization of the bird, the structure of its wings, the force of its muscular system, its conditions of equilibrium in the air, &c.

P

Conformation of the bird.—By the simple inspection of a
bird's wing, it is easy to see that the mechanism of its flight
is altogether different from that of an insect. From the
manner in which the feathers of its wing lie upon each other,
it is evident that the resistance of the air can only act from
below upwards, for in the opposite direction the air would
force for itself an easy passage by bending the long barbs of
the feathers, which would no longer sustain each other. This
well-known arrangement, so carefully described by Prechlt,*
has caused persons to suppose that the wing only needed to
oscillate ·in a vertical plane in order to sustain the weight of
the bird, because the resistance of the air acting from below upwards is greater than that which it exerts in the
opposite direction.

This writer has been wrong in basing on the inspection of
the organ of flight all the theory of its function. We shall find
that experiment contradicts in the most decided manner these
premature inductions.

If we take a dead bird, and spread out its wings so as to
place them in the position represented in fig. 89, we see that at

FIG. 89.—Various curves of the wing of a bird at different points in its
length.

different points in its length, the wing presents very remarkable changes of plane. At the inner part, towards the body,
the wing inclines considerably both downwards and backwards, while near its extremity, it is horizontal and sometimes slightly turned up, so that its under surface is directed
somewhat backward.

Dr. Pettigrew thought that he could find in this curve a
surface resembling a left-handed screw propeller; struck with
the resemblance between the form of the wing and that of
the screw used in navigation, he considered the wing of a

* Untersuchungen über den Flug der Vogel. 8vo. Vienna : 1846.

bird as a screw of which the air formed the nut. We do
not think that we need refute such a theory. It is too evident that the alternating type which belongs to every muscular
movement cannot tend to produce the propulsive action of a
screw; for while we admit that the wing revolves on an axis,
this rotation is confined to the fraction of a turn, and is followed by rotation in the opposite direction, which in a screw
would entirely destroy the effect produced by the previous
movement. And yet the English writer to whose ideas we
refer has been so fully convinced of the truth of his theory
that he has wished to extend it to the whole animal kingdom.
He proposes to refer locomotion in all its forms, whether
terrestrial, aquatic, or aerial to the movements of a screw
propeller. Let us only seek in the anatomical structure of
the organs of flight the information which it can afford us;
that is to say, that which refers to the forces which the bird
can develop in flight, and the direction in which these forces
are exerted.

Comparative anatomy shows us in the wing of birds an
analogue of the fore limb of mammals. The wing when
reduced to its skeleton, presents, as in the human arm, the
humerus, the two bones of the fore-arm, and a rudimentary
hand, in which we still find metacarpal bones and phalanges.
The muscles also present many analogies with those of the
anterior limb of man; some parts of these bear such a resemblance both in appearance and in function, that they have
been designated by the same name.

In the wing of the bird, the most strongly developed muscles
are those whose office it is to extend or bend the hand upon
the fore-arm, the fore-arm on the humerus, and also to move
the humerus, that is say, the whole arm, round the articulation of the shoulder.

In the greater number of birds, especially of the larger
kinds, the wing seems to remain always extended during flight.
Thus, the extensor muscles of the different portions of this
organ would serve to give this organ the position necessary
for rendering flight possible, and for maintaining it in this position; as to motive work, it would be executed by other muscles,
much stronger than the preceding—namely, the *pectorals*.

All the anterior surface of the thorax of birds is occupied by powerful muscular masses, and especially by a large muscle, which by its attachments to the sternum, to the ribs and the humerus, is analogous with the *large pectoral* muscle in man and the mammals; its office is evidently to lower the wing with force and rapidity, and thus to gain from the air the fulcrum necessary to sustain, as well as to move the mass of the body. Underneath the large pectoral is found the *medium pectoral*, whose action is to raise the wing. On the exterior, the *small pectoral*, acting as accessory to the large one, extends from the sternum to the humerus.

Since the force of a muscle is in proportion to the volume of this organ, when we consider that these pectoral muscles represent about one-sixth part of the whole weight of the bird, we shall immediately understand that the principal function of flight devolves on these powerful organs.

Borelli endeavoured to deduce from the volume of the pectoral muscles the energy of which they are capable; he concluded that the force employed by the bird in flight was equal to 10,000 times its weight. We will not here refute the error of Borelli; many others have undertaken to combat his notions, and have substituted for the calculations of the Italian physiologist others whose correctness it would be difficult to prove. Such great contradictions as are to be found in the different estimates formed of the muscular force of birds have arisen from the fact that those attempts at measurement were premature.

Navier, depending on calculations which were not based on experiment, considered himself authorized in admitting that birds develop enormous mechanical work: seventeen swallows would exert work equal to a horse-power. "As easy would it be," said M. Bertrand, facetiously, "to prove by calculation that birds could not fly—a conclusion which would rather compromise mathematics."

Besides, we find that Cagniard Latour admitted, basing his assertion on theory, that the wing is lowered eight times more quickly than it rises. Experiment, however, proves that the wing of the bird is raised more quickly than it descends.

Estimate of the muscular force of the bird.—We must at the present day measure mechanical force under the form of work. It is necessary for this purpose to know what resistance is met with by the wing at each instant of its movements, and the direction in which it repels from it this resisting medium.

Such an estimate requires a previous knowledge of the resistance of air against surfaces of different curvature moving with various degrees of velocity; it supposes at the same time that we know the movements of the wing as well as their velocity and direction at every instant.

This problem will perhaps be the last which we may hope to solve, but we may even now study from other points of view the force exerted by the muscles of the bird, and estimate some of its characteristics.

Thus, we may obtain experimentally a measure of the maximum effort which these muscles can exert. This measure may not really correspond with the real effort displayed in flight, but it may keep us from forming exaggerated estimates.

. If the calculations of Borelli, or even those of Navier were correct, we ought to find in the muscles of the bird a very considerable statical force. Experiments show, however, that these muscles do not seem capable of more energetic efforts than those of other animals.

   Experiment.—Our first experiment was made upon a buzzard. The creature being hoodwinked was stretched upon its back, with its wings held on the table by bags filled with small shot. The application of the hood plunges these birds into a sort of hypnotism, during which we can make any number of experiments upon them, without their evincing any pain.

We laid bare the great pectoral muscle and the humeral region, we placed a ligature on the artery, disarticulated the elbow-joint, and took away all the rest of the wing. A cord was fixed to the extremity of the humerus, and at the end of this cord was placed a scale-pan, into which small shot was poured. The trunk of the bird being rendered perfectly immovable, we excited the muscle by means of interrupted induced currents; while the artificial contraction was produced, an assistant poured into the pan the small shot, until the force of contraction of the muscle was counteracted. At this

movement, the weight supported was 2 kilogrammes 380
grammes (about 6·38 lbs. troy).

If we take into account the unequal length of the arms of
the lever, on the side of the power and that of the resistance,
we find that the pectoral muscle had been able to produce a
total effort of 12 kilogrammes 600 grammes (about 33·78 lbs.
troy), which would correspond with a traction of 1298
grammes (3·66 lbs. troy) for each square centimetre of the
transverse section of the muscle.

A pigeon placed under the same conditions has given, as its
entire effort, a weight of 4860 grammes, which, according to
the transverse section of its muscle, raised to 1400 grammes
the effort which each muscular bundle could develop for every
square centimetre of section.

If we admit that the electrical action employed in these
experiments to make the muscles contract, develops an effort
less than that which is caused by the will, it is not less true
that these estimates, which are less than those which we
generally obtain in the muscles of mammals under the same
conditions, do not authorize us in recognizing in the bird any
special muscular power.

Lastly, if we were to take into account in this estimate
the laws of thermo-dynamics, we might affirm that the bird
would not develop in flight a very especial amount of work.

All work, in fact, can only be performed with a certain
waste of substance, and if the act of flying involved a great
expenditure of work, we ought to find a notable diminution
of weight in a bird when it returns from a long flight. Nothing
of this kind is observed. Persons who train carrier pigeons
have given us information on this point, from which we gather
that a bird which has traversed in a single flight a distance of
fifty leagues (which it seems to do without taking any food),
weighs only a few grammes less than at its departure. It
would be interesting to make these experiments again with
greater exactitude.

Of the rapidity of the muscular actions of birds.—One of the
most striking peculiarities in the action of a bird's muscles
is the extreme rapidity with which force is engendered in
them. Among the different species of animals whose muscular

acts we have determined, the bird is that which, after the insect, has given the most rapid movements.

This rapidity is indispensable to flight. In fact, the wing when lowered, can meet with a sufficient resistance in the air only when it moves with great velocity. The resistance of the air against a plane surface which strikes upon it and repels it, evidently increases in the ratio of the square of the velocity with which this plane is displaced. It would be of no use for the bird to have energetic muscles, capable of effecting considerable work, if they could only give slow movements to the wing; their force could not be exerted for want of resistance, and no work could be produced. It is otherwise with terrestrial animals which run or creep on the ground, with a speed more or less rapid according to the nature of their muscles, but which in every case utilize their muscular force by means of the perfect resistance of the ground. The necessity of velocity in the movements of fishes has been already observed, since the water in which they swim resists more or less, according to the rapidity with which their tails or their fins act upon it. Thus the muscular action of fishes is rapid, but much less so than that of birds, which move in a medium far more yielding.

In order to understand the rapid production of movements in the muscles of the bird, we must remember that these movements are connected with chemical action, produced in the very substance of the muscle, where they give rise, as in machines, to heat and motion. We must therefore admit that these actions are excited and propagated more readily in the muscles of birds than in those of any other species of animals. In the same manner the different kinds of powder used in war differ much from each other in the rapidity of their explosion, and consequently give very different velocities to the projectiles which they impel.

Lastly, the *form of movement* presents in different species of birds peculiarities which we have already noticed. We have seen in Chapter VIII. how much the dimensions of the pectoral muscles vary according as the strokes of the wing are required to have much force or great extent; therefore we shall not recur again to this subject.

Form of the bird.—All those who have studied the flight of birds have very properly paid great attention to the form of these creatures, as rendering them eminently adapted to flight. They have recognised in them perfect stable equilibrium in the aerial medium. They have thoroughly understood the part played by the large surfaces formed by the wings, which may sometimes act as a parachute, to produce a very slow descent; while at other times these surfaces glide through the air, and following the inclination of their plane, allow the bird to descend very obliquely, and even to rise, or to hover while keeping its wings immovable. Some observers have gone so far as to admit that certain species of birds play an entirely passive part in flight, and that giving up their wings to the impulse of the wind, they derive from it a force capable of carrying them in every direction, even against the wind. It seems to us interesting to discuss, in a few words, this important question in the theory of flight.

The stable equilibrium of the bird has been well explained; there is nothing for us to add to the remarks which have been made on this subject. The wings are attached exactly at the highest part of the thorax, and consequently when the outstretched wings act upon the air as a fulcrum, all the weight of the body is placed below this surface of suspension. We know also that in the body itself, the lightest organs, the lungs and the air vessels, are in the upper part; while the mass of the intestines, which is heavier, is lower; also that the thoracic muscles, which are so voluminous and heavy, occupy the lower part of the system. Thus the heaviest part is placed as low as possible beneath the point of suspension.

The bird, as it descends with its wings outspread, will thus present its ventral region downwards, without its being necessary to make an effort to keep its equilibrium; it will take this position passively, like a parachute set free in space, or like the shuttlecock when it falls upon the battledore.

But this vertical descent is an exceptional case; the bird which allows itself to fall is almost always impelled by some previous horizontal velocity; it therefore glides obliquely upon the air, as every light body of large surface does when placed under the conditions of stable equilibrium which we have just described. Mons. J. Pline has carefully studied the different kinds of sliding movement which may take place; he has even represented them by means of small pieces of apparatus which imitate the insect or the bird when they fly without moving their wings.

If we take a piece of paper of a square form, and fold it in

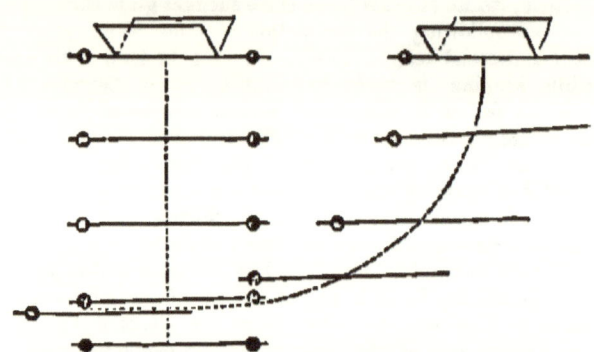

Fig. 90.—Representing, on the left, a contrivance intended to imitate the hovering of birds; it is placed in equilibrium by two equal weights attached to the extremities of a wire which is fixed in the lower part of the angle formed by the folded paper. This piece of apparatus falls vertically, as shown by the successive positions of the two weights. On the right is seen the same contrivance connected with one weight only. Its fall is parabolic, as shown by the dotted trajectory.

the middle, so as to form a very obtuse angle (fig. 90); then, at the bottom of this angle, let us fix with a little wax a piece of wire attached to two masses of the same weight; we shall have a system which will maintain stable equilibrium in the air. If the centre of gravity pass exactly through the centre of the figure, we shall see it descend vertically when we let it go, the convexity of its angle being directed downwards.

If we take away one of the weights, so as to alter the position of the centre of gravity, the apparatus, instead of descending vertically, will follow an oblique trajectory, and will glide through the air with an accelerated motion (fig. 90, to the right).

The trajectory passed through by this little instrument will
be situated in a vertical plane, if the two halves of the apparatus are perfectly symmetrical; but if they are not, it will
turn towards the side in which while it cuts the air it finds
the greater resistance. These effects, which are easily understood, are identical with those which the resistance of the
rudder causes in the advancing motion of a ship. They can
also be produced in a vertical direction; so that the trajectory
of the apparatus may be a curve with its concavity above or
below, as the case may be.

Every thin body which is curved tends to glide upon the
air according to the direction of its own curvature.

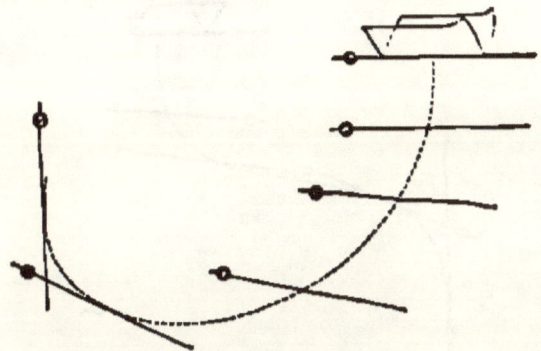

Fig. 91.—We have turned back the right hand corner of the two planes
which form the angle. After a descent in a parabolic curve, the apparatus
rises again, as shown by the dotted trajectory.

If we turn back either the anterior or posterior edge of our
little apparatus, we shall see it at a given moment of its
descent rise in opposition to its own weight, but it will soon
lose its upward movement (fig. 91). Let us consider what
has taken place.

So long as the paper descended with but slight rapidity,
the effect of its curvature was not perceptible, because the
air resists surfaces only in the ratio of the velocity with which
they move. But when the rapidity was sufficiently great, an

effect was produced similar to that of a rudder, which turned up the anterior extremity of the little apparatus, and gave it an ascending course. Immediately, the weight which was the generating force of its gliding movement through the air began to retard it; in proportion as it rose, it lost its velocity until it reached the point of rest. After that, a downward movement commenced, then an ascent in the opposite direction, so that the paper descended to the ground by successive oscillations.

If we give the apparatus a slight concavity downwards, the opposite effect is produced; we see (fig. 92), at a certain

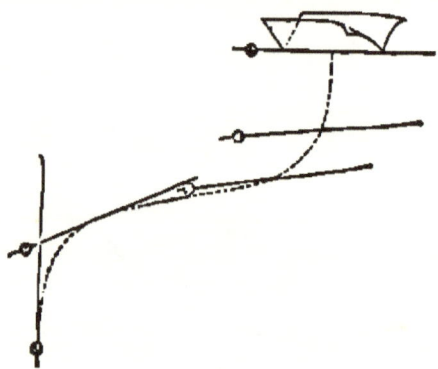

Fio. 92.—The right hand corner of the plane of the angle has been bent downwards. After a parabolic descent, the apparatus falls very rapidly in a perpendicular direction.

moment, the trajectory turns abruptly downwards, and the falling body strikes the ground with considerable violence. In this second case, when the rudder-like effect is produced, the new direction has in its favour the weight which hastens the fall of the little instrument, as in the former experiment it rendered the re-ascent more slow.

We have dwelt upon these effects, because they often occur in the flight of birds. They are mentioned in the old treatises on falconry, which describe the evolutions of birds used in

hawking. Without going further back, we find in Huber* the
description of these curvilinear movements of falcons, to which
they gave the name of *passades*, and which consisted of an
oblique descent of the bird, followed by a re-ascent, which
they called *ressource* (from the Latin, *resurgere*). " The bird,"
says Huber, " carried forward by its own velocity, would dash
itself against the ground, were it not that it exercises a certain power which it possesses of stopping when at its utmost
speed, and turning directly upwards to a sufficient height to
enable it to make a second descent. This movement is able
not only to arrest its descent, but also to carry it without any
further effort, as high as the level from which it started."

Surely, there is some exaggeration in saying that the bird
can rise, without any active effort, to the height from which
it stooped; the resistance of the air must destroy a portion of
the force which it had acquired during its descent, and which
must be transformed into a rising impulse. We see, however, that the phenomenon of the *ressource* has been noticed
by many observers, and that it has been considered by them
as, to a certain extent, a passive motion in which the bird
has to employ no muscular force.

The act of *hovering* presents, in certain cases, a great analogy with the phenomena just described. When a bird—a
pigeon, for example—has traversed a certain distance by flapping its wings, we see it suspend all these movements for
some instants, and glide on either horizontally, ascending or
descending. The latter kind of hovering motion is that which
is of longest duration; in fact, it is only an extremely slow
fall, but in which the weight assists the movement, while
it checks it in the horizontal or ascending course. In the last
two forms, the wing, directed more or less obliquely, derives
its point of resistance from the air, like the child's plaything
called a kite, but with this difference, that the velocity is
given to the kite by the tractile force exerted on the string
when the air is calm, while the bird when it hovers utilizes
the speed which it has already acquired, either by its oblique
fall or by the previous flapping of its wings.

We have already said, that observers had admitted that

* 8vo. Geneva, 1784.

certain birds which they called "sailing birds" could sustain and direct themselves in the air solely by the action of the wind. This theory has all the appearance of a paradox; we cannot understand how the bird, when in the wind, and using no exertion, should not be affected by its force.

If the *passades*, or the changes which it effects in the plane of its wings, can sometimes carry it in a direction contrary to that of the wind, these can be only transient effects, compensated afterwards by a greater force driving them before the wind.

Nevertheless, this theory of *sailing flight* has been advocated with great talent by certain observers, and especially by Count d'Esterno, the author of a remarkable memoir on the flight of birds.

"Every one," says this author, "must have seen certain birds practise this kind of sailing flight; to deny it, is to contradict evidence."

We know so little yet of the resistance of the air, especially with reference to the resolution of this force when it acts against inclined planes under different angles, that it is impossible to decide on this question as to sailing flight. It would be rash absolutely to condemn the opinion of observers, by depending on a theory or on notions as vague as those which we possess on this subject.

Ratio of the surfaces of the wings to the weight of the body.— One of the most interesting points in the conformation of birds consists in the determination of the ratio borne by the surface of the wings to the weight of the bird. Is there a constant relation between these two quantities? This question has been the cause of many controversies.

It has already been shown that, if we compare birds of different species and of equal weight, we may find that some have their wings two, three, or four times more extended than the others. The birds with large wing surfaces are those which usually give themselves up to a kind of hovering flight, and have been called sailing birds; while those whose wing is short or narrow are more usually accustomed to a flight which resembles rowing. If we compare together two "rowing" or two "sailing" birds; if, to be more

exact, we choose them from the same family, in order to have
no difference between them except that of size, we shall find
a tolerably constant ratio between the weight of these birds
and the surface of their wings. But the determination of this
ratio must be based upon certain considerations which have
been long disregarded by naturalists.

Mons. de Lucy has endeavoured to compare the surface of
the wings with the weight of the body in all flying animals.
Then, in order to establish a common unit between creatures
of such different species and size, he referred all these estimates to an ideal type, the weight of which was always one
kilogramme. Thus, having ascertained that the gnat, which
weighs three milligrammes, possesses wings of thirty square
millimetres of surface, he concluded that in the gnat type
each kilogramme of the animal was supported by an alar surface of ten square millimetres.

Having drawn up a comparative table of measurements
taken in animals of a great number of different species
and sizes, Mons. de Lucy has arrived at the following results :—

Species.	Weight of Animal.	Surface of Wings.	Surface per Kilogramme.
Gnat . . .	3 milligr.	30 sq. millim.	10 sq. millim.
Butterfly. .	20 centigr.	1663 ,, ,,	8½ ,, ,,
Pigeon . .	290 grammes.	750 sq. centim.	2566 sq. centim.
Stork . .	2285 ,,	4506 ,, ,,	1968 ,, ,,
Australian Crane.	9500 ,,	8543 ,, ,,	899 ,, ,,

From these measurements we obtain the following important consideration, that animals of large size and great
weight sustain themselves in the air with a much less proportionate surface of wing than those of smaller size.

Such a result plainly shows that the part played by the
wing in flight is not merely passive, for a sail or a parachute
ought always to have a surface in proportion to the weight
which it has to support; but, on the contrary, when considered in its proper point of view, as an organ which strikes
the air, the wing of the bird ought, as we shall see, to pre-

sent a surface relatively less in birds of large size and of great weight.

The surprise which we feel at the result obtained by Mons. de Lucy disappears when we consider that there is a geometrical reason why the surface of the wing cannot increase in the ratio of the weight of the bird. In fact, if we take two objects of the same form—two cubes, for example—one of which has a diameter twice as large as the other, each of the surfaces of the larger cube will be four times as large as that of the smaller one, but the weight of the large cube will be eight times that of the small one.

Thus, for all similar geometrical solids, the linear dimensions being in a certain ratio, the surfaces will increase in proportion to their squares, and the weights in that of their cubes. Two birds similar in form, one of which has an extent of wing twice as large as the other, will have wing surfaces in the proportion of one to four, and weights in that of one to eight.

Dr. Hureau de Villeneuve, basing his enquiries on these considerations, has determined the surface of wing which would enable a bat having the weight of a man to fly; and he has found that each of the wings need not be three metres in length.

In a remarkable work on the relative extent of wing and weight of pectoral muscles in different species of flying vertebrate animals,[*] Hartings shows that in a series of birds we can establish a certain relation between the surface of the wing and the weight of the body. But we must be careful only to compare elements which admit of comparison; for instance, the length of the wings, the square roots of their surfaces, and the cube roots of the weights of different birds.

Let l be the length of the wing; a, its area or surface; and p the weight of the body; we can compare together l, $\sqrt{a}$, and $\sqrt{p}$.

Making observations on different types of birds, Hartings ascertained their measurements and weights, from which he obtained the following table :—

* Archives Néerlandaises, Vol. XIV., p. 1869.

Name of Species.	Weight. p	Surface. a	Ratio. $\frac{\sqrt{a}}{\sqrt[3]{p}}$
1. Larus argentatus . . .	565·0	541	2·82
2. Anas nyroca . . .	508·0	321	2·26
3. Fulica atra . . .	495·0	262	2·05
4. Anas crecca . . .	275·5	144	1·84
5. Larus ridibundus . .	197·0	331	3·13
6. Machetes pugnax . .	190·0	164	2·23
7. Hallus aquaticus . .	170·5	101	1·81
8. Turdus pilaris . . .	103·4	101	2·14
9. Turdus merula . . .	88·8	106	2·31
10. Sturnus vulgaris . .	86·4	85	2·09
11. Bombicilla garrula . .	60·0	44	1·69
12. Alauda arvensis. . .	32·2	75	2.69
13. Parus major . . .	14·5	31	2·29
14. Fringilla spinus . .	10·1	25	2·33
15. Parus cœruleus . . .	9·1	24	2·34

To this list of Hartings we will add another which we have prepared by the same method (p. 225). All the experiments have been made on birds killed by the gun, and a few instants after death. We have taken the surface of the two wings instead of only one, as Hartings had done; this modification, which appeared necessary, is the principal cause of the difference which the reader will find between our numbers and those of the Dutch physiologist. To compare the two tables, it will be necessary to multiply by $\sqrt{2}$ the number obtained by Hartings as the expression of the ratio $\frac{\sqrt{a}}{\sqrt[3]{p}}$

The variations that we find in the ratio of the weight of the body to the surface of the wings in different species of birds, depends in a great degree on the form of the wings. In fact, it is not immaterial whether the surface which strikes the air has its maximum near the body or near the extremity; these two points have very different velocities. For an equal extent of surface the resistance will be greater at the point of the wing than at its base. It follows from this, that two birds of unequal surface of wing may find in the air an equal resistance, provided that these surfaces are differently arranged.

The weight of the pectoral muscles is, on the contrary, in a simple ratio to the total weight of the bird, and notwith-

standing variations which correspond with the different aptitudes for flight with which each species is endowed, we find
that it is about one-sixth of the whole weight in the greater
number of birds.

Name of Species.	Weight = p. Grammes	Surface of Wings = 2a. Square centimetres.	Ratio = $\frac{\sqrt{2a}}{\sqrt[3]{p}}$
Vultur	1663·94	3131	4·722
Vultur cinereus . . .	1535·00	3233	4·029
Falco tinnunculus . .	128·94	642	5·015
„ „ minor . .	147·36	546	4·424
Falco Kobek . . .	282·44	970	4·747
Falco sublatio (?) . .	509·62	1684	5·138
Falco palustris . . .	208·76	1188	5·810
Falco milvus . . .	620·14	1904	5·117
Strix passerina . . .	122·80	394	3·993
„ „	128·94	442	4·162
Saxicola œnanthe . .	56·05	125	2·922
Alauda cristata . . .	36·80	202	4·273
Corvus cornix . . .	374·54	1156	4·717
Upupa epops . . .	49·12	329	4·952
Merops apiaster . . .	18·30	117	4·105
Alcedo ispida . . .	82·89	270	3·769
Alcedo afra (?) . . .	85·96	288	3·845
Columba vinacea . .	112·00	292	3·545
Vanellus spinosus . .	159·64	636	4·649
Glareola	95·17	343	4·058
Buteo vulgaris . . .	785·00	1651	4·495
Perdix cinerea . . .	280·00	320	2·734
Sturnus vulgaris . .	78·00	202	3·326
Corvus pica . . .	212·00	540	3·906
„ „ . . .	275·00	690	4·039
Hirundo urbica . . .	18·00	120	4·180
Turdus merula . . .	94·00	230	3·335

In conclusion, each animal which sustains itself in the air
must develop work proportionate to its weight; it ought, for
this purpose, to possess muscular mass in proportion to this
weight; for, as we have already seen, if the actions performed
by the muscles of birds are always of the same nature, these
actions and the work which they perform will be in proportion
to the mass of the muscles.

But how is it that wings whose surfaces vary as to the square of their linear dimensions are sufficient to move the weights of birds which vary in the ratio of the cubes of these dimensions?

It can be proved that, if the strokes of the wing were as frequent in large as in small birds, each stroke would have a velocity whose value would increase with the size of the bird; and as the resistance of the air increases for each element of the surface of the wing, according to the square of the velocity of that organ, a considerable advantage would result to the bird of large size, as to the work produced upon the air.

Hence it follows, that it would not be necessary for large birds to give such frequent strokes of the wing in order to sustain themselves as would be required for those of smaller size.

Observers have not, hitherto, been able to determine very accurately the number of the strokes of the wing, in order to ascertain whether their frequency is in an exact inverse ratio to the size of birds; but it is easy to see that the number of strokes varies in birds of different size in a proportion of this kind.

CHAPTER IV.

OF THE MOVEMENTS OF THE WING OF THE BIRD DURING FLIGHT.

Frequency of the movements of the wing—Relative durations of its rise and fall—Electrical determination—Myographical determination. Trajectory of the bird's wing during flight—Construction of the instruments which register this movement—Experiment—Elliptical figure of the trajectory of the point of the wing.

In the general remarks on the form of the bird, and on the deductions to be drawn from it, the reader must have seen that many hypotheses await experimental demonstration. For this reason, we have been anxious to apply to the flights of the bird the method which has enabled us to analyse the other modes of locomotion.

Frequency of the strokes of the wing.—The graphic method which enabled us so easily to determine the frequency of the strokes of the insect's wing cannot be employed under the same conditions when we experiment on the bird. It will be necessary to transmit signals between the bird as it flies and the registering apparatus. We have here to deal with a problem similar to that which we solved with respect to terrestrial locomotion, when we registered the number and the relative duration of the pressures of the feet upon the ground. We must now estimate the duration of the impacts of the wing upon the air, and the time which it occupies in its rising motion.

Electrical method.—We made use at first of the electric telegraph. The experiments consist in placing on the extremity of the wing a kind of apparatus which breaks or closes an electric circuit at each of the alternate movements which it is induced to make. In this circuit is placed an electro-magnetic arrangement which writes upon a revolving cylinder. Figure 94 shows this mode of telegraphy applied to the study of a pigeon's flight, simultaneously with the transmission of signals of another kind, to be hereafter described. In this figure the two conducting wires are separated from each other.

The writing point will trace a wavy line, the elevations and depressions of which will correspond with each change in the direction of the movement of the wing. In order that the bird may fly as freely as possible, a thin flexible cable, containing two conducting wires, establishes a communication between the bird and the telegraphic tracing point. The two ends of the wires are fastened to a very small light instrument which acts like a valve under the influence of the resistance of the air. When the wing rises, the valve opens, the current is broken, and the line of the telegraphic tracing rises. When the wing descends, the valve closes, the current closes at the same time, and the tracing made by the telegraph is lowered.

This instrument, when applied to different kinds of birds, enables us to ascertain the frequency peculiar to the movements of each. The number of species which we have been

able to study is very small as yet; the following are the
results obtained :—

	Revolutions of wing per second.
Sparrow .	13
Wild duck	9
Pigeon .	8
Moor buzzard	5½
Screech owl	5
Buzzard	3

The frequency of the strokes of the wing varies also, according
as the bird is first starting, in full flight, or at the end of its
flight. Some birds, as we know, keep their wings perfectly
still for a time; they glide upon the air, making use of the
velocity already acquired.

Relative duration of the depression and elevation of the wing.—
Contrary to the opinion entertained by some writers, the
duration of the depression of the wing is usually longer than
that of its rise. The inequality of these two periods is more
distinctly seen in birds whose wings have a large surface, and
which beat slowly. Thus, while the durations are almost
equal in the duck, whose wings are very narrow, they are
unequal in the pigeon, and still more so in the buzzard.
The following are the results of our experiments :—

	Total duration of a revolution of the wing.		Ascent.	Descent.
Duck .	11½ hundreds of a second	.	5	6½
Pigeon .	12½ ,,	,,	4	8½
Buzzard .	32½ ,,	,,	12½	20

It is more difficult than would have been expected, to determine
the precise instant when the direction of the line traced by the
telegraph changes. The periods during which the soft iron
is first attracted and then set free, have an appreciable duration
when the blackened cylinder turns with sufficient rapidity to
enable us to measure the rapid movements which are the
subjects of this inquiry. The inflections of the line traced by
the telegraph then become curves, the precise commencement

of each of which it is difficult to discover.   There is therefore
some limit to the precision of the measurements which we can
take by the electric method ; we can still, however, estimate
by this means the duration of a movement with a tolerably
accurate approximation.

Myographic method.—We have seen that a dilatation accompanies the contraction of the muscles, and follows it through
all its phases.   A shortening of the muscle, either rapid or
slow, feeble or energetic, as the case may be, will therefore be
accompanied by a lateral dilatation which will have similar
characters of rapidity or intensity.   At each depression of the
wing of a bird, the *large pectoral* muscles will be subject to a
dilatation which it will be necessary to transmit to the registering apparatus.

We shall have recourse, for this purpose, to the apparatus
which we have employed in determinations of the same kind,
when treating of human locomotion.   Some slight modifications will enable them to give signals of the alternate phases
of dilatation and relaxation of the large pectoral muscle.

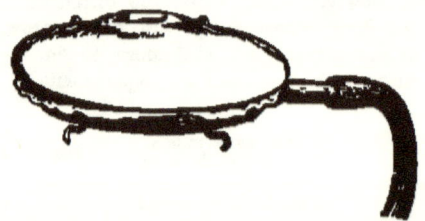

Fig. 93.—Apparatus to investigate the contraction of the thoracic muscles
of the bird. The upper convex surface is formed of a membrane of india-
rubber supported by a spiral spring ; this part is applied to the muscles.
The lower surface, in contact with the corset, carries four small hooks
which are fastened in the stuff and keep the instrument in its place.

The bird flies in a space fifteen metres square and eight
metres high.   The registering apparatus being placed in the
centre of the room where the experiment is made, twelve
metres of india-rubber tubing are sufficient to establish a
constant communication between the bird and the apparatus.

A sort of corset is fixed on a pigeon (see figure 94).   Under
this corset, between the stuff, which is tightly stretched, and

the pectoral muscles, a small instrument is slipped, which is intended to show the dilatation of the muscles, and is constructed in the following manner:

A little metal pan (fig. 93), containing within it a spiral spring, is closed by a membrane of india-rubber. This closed pan communicates with a tube transmitting air.

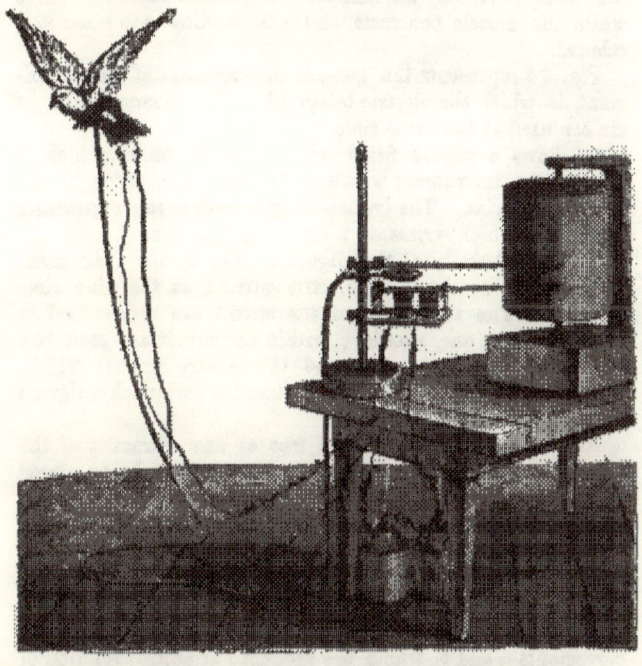

Fig. 94.—Experiment to determine by the electrical and myographical methods, at the same time, the frequency of the movements of the wing and the relative durations of its elevation and depression.

Each pressure on the india-rubber membrane depresses it, and the spring gives way; the air is driven out of the pan, and escapes by the tube. When the pressure ceases, the air is returned to the instrument by the elasticity of the spring

which raises the membrane.   Alternate outward and inward
currents of air are thus established in the tube, and this
movement transmits to the registering apparatus the signals
of the less or greater pressures exerted on the membrane of
the small pan.

The registering instrument is the lever drum, with which
the reader is already acquainted.   It gives an ascending curve
while the muscle contracts, and a descending one when it is
relaxed.

Fig. 94 represents the general arrangement of the experiment, in which the electric telegraph and the transmission of
air are used at the same time.

It shows a pigeon fitted with a corset, under which is
slipped the instrument which is to show the action of the
pectoral muscles.   The transmitting tube ends in a registering
apparatus, which writes on a revolving cylinder.

At the extremity of the pigeon's wing is the instrument
which opens or closes an electric current, as the wing rises
or sinks.   The two wires of the circuit are represented as
separated from one another; within the circuit are seen two
elements of Bunsen's pile, and the electro-magnet which,
being furnished with a lever, registers the telegraphic signals
of the movements of the wing.

Experiment.—The bird is set free at one extremity of the
room, the dove-cot in which it is usually kept being placed
at the opposite end.   The bird as it flies naturally seeks its
nest in which to rest.   During its flight we obtain the tracings
represented by fig. 95.

It is seen that the tracings differ according to the kind of
bird on which the experiment is made.   However, we observe in each of the tracings the periodical return of the two
movements a and b, which are produced at each revolution of
the wing.

On what do these two muscular acts depend?   It is easy
to discover that the undulation a corresponds with the muscle
that elevates the wing, and b with that which depresses it.
This can be proved: first, by collecting, at the same time as
the muscular tracing, those of the ascending and descending
movements of the wing transmitted by electricity.   When

these two tracings are placed over each other, they show that the time of the elevation of the wing agrees with the duration of the undulation *a*, and the time of its depression coincides with the undulation *b*.

From this we may see how the undulations *a* and *b* are produced in all the muscular tracings obtained from birds. In fact, close by the portion of the bird's breast on which the experiment is made, and near the projecting edge of the sternum, there are two distinct layers of muscle; the more superficial one is formed by the large pectoral, the depressor of the wing; the deeper one by the middle pectoral, or elevator of the wing, whose tendon passes behind the forked part of the sternum to attach itself to the head of the humerus.

These two muscles, being superposed, will act by their dilatation on the apparatus applied to them; the elevator of the wing, swelling as it contracts, gives its signal by the undulation *a*; the great pectoral signals the depression of the wing by the undulation *b*.

We may verify the correctness of this explanation by means of a very simple experiment. Anatomy shows us that the muscle which elevates the wing is narrow, and only covers the depressor in its most inward part, situated along the ridge of the sternum; so that if we displace the little apparatus which shows the movement of the muscles, and remove it a little outwards, it will occupy a part where the depressor of the wing is not covered by the elevator, and the tracing will only present a simple undulation, corresponding with *b* in the curves of fig. 95. It is thus plainly shown that the undulations *a* and *b* in the muscular tracings of the birds on which we have experimented correspond exactly with the actions of the principal muscles which elevate and depress the wing; but we cannot attach great importance to the form of the tracings, in order to deduce from them the precise nature of the movement performed by the muscle. These movements seem, in fact, to encroach on each other; so that the relaxation of the elevator of the wing is probably not completed when the depressor begins to act.

We expect nothing more from these tracings than that

Fig. 96.—Showing the differences of amplitude and frequency of the strokes of a pigeon's wing, during a flight of 15 metres in length. To the left of the figure, we see great movements within must the beginning of its flight. This tracing has been obtained on a cylinder whose rotation was not very rapid, which allowed us to collect a great number of movements in a small space.

which they more readily furnish; namely, the number of the revolutions of the wing, the greater or less regularity of these movements, and the equality or inequality of each of them.

Confining the question within these limits, experiment shows that the strokes of the bird's wing differ in amplitude and in frequency from one moment to another as they fly. When they first start, the strokes are rather fewer, but much more energetic; they reach, after two or three strokes of the wing, a rhythm almost regular, which they lose again when they are about to settle (fig. 96).

TRAJECTORY OF THE WING OF THE BIRD DURING FLIGHT.

We have seen, when treating of the mechanism of insect flight, that the fundamental experiment was that which revealed to us the course of the point of the wing throughout each of its revolutions. Our knowledge of the mechanism of flight naturally flowed, if we may so say, from this first notion.

The same determination is equally necessary for the flight of birds; but the optical method is unsuitable for this purpose. In fact, the movement of the bird's wing, although too rapid to be appreciable by the eye, is not sufficiently so to furnish such a persistent impression on the retina as to show its whole course.

The graphic method, with its transmission of signals, which we have hitherto employed, only furnishes the expression of movements which take place in a straight line, such as the contraction or lengthening of a muscle, the vertical and horizontal oscillations of the body during the act of walking, &c. It is only by combining this rectilinear movement with the uniform advance of the smoked surface that receives the tracing, that we obtain the expression of the velocity with which the movement at each instant is effected.

The action of the wing during flight does not consist merely of alternate elevations and depressions. We have only to look at a bird as it flies over our head to ascertain that the wing is carried also forward and backward at each stroke. From this double action must result a curve which it is necessary to describe.

It can be geometrically shown that every plane figure, that is to say, every figure susceptible of being described upon a plane surface, can be produced by the rectangular combination of two rectilinear movements. The tracings obtained by Koenig by arming with a style Wheatstone's vibrating rods, and the luminous figures of musical chords which Lissajous produced by the reflection of a pencil of light upon two mirrors vibrating perpendicularly to each other, are well-known examples of the formation of a plane figure by means of two rectilinear movements at right angles to each other.

Thus, if we can transmit at the same time the movements of elevation and depression executed by the wing of the bird, as well as those which the organ makes forwards and backwards; then, supposing that a tracing point can receive simultaneously the impulse of these two movements at right angles to each other, this point will describe on the paper the exact tracing of the movements of the bird's wing.

We have endeavoured first to construct an instrument which would thus transmit to a distance any movement whatever, and register it on a plane surface, without attending to the method by which this machine, which may be more or less heavy, might be adapted to the body of the bird. Fig. 97 represents our first experimental instrument, the description of which is indispensable in order to enable our readers to

understand the construction of the machine which we finally
employed.

On two solid feet carrying vertical supports, we placed
two horizontal arms parallel to each other. These were two
aluminium levers, which, by means of the apparatus we are
about to describe, will both execute the same movements.
Each of these levers is mounted on a Cardan joint, that is to
say, a universal joint which allows every kind of movement;
so that each lever can be carried upwards, downwards, to
the right or the left; it can describe with its point the base
of a cone of which the Cardan forms the apex; in fact it will
execute any kind of movement which the experimenter may
please to give it.

It was requisite to effect the transmission of the movements of one of these levers to the other, and that at a distance of ten or fifteen metres. This is done by a method with
which the reader is already acquainted—the employment of
air-drums and tubes.

The lever, which in fig. 97 is seen to the left hand, is
fastened by a vertical metallic wire to the membrane of a
drum placed underneath it. In the vertical movements of
the lever, the membrane of the drum, alternately depressed
and raised, will produce a current of air, which will be transmitted by a long air-tube to the membrane of a similar drum
belonging to the apparatus on the right hand. The second
drum, placed above the lever which corresponds with it, and
is fastened to it, will faithfully transmit all the vertical
movements which have been given to drum No. 1 (that on
the left). The motion of the two levers will be in the same
direction, on account of the inversion of the position of the
drums.

Let us suppose that we lower the lever No. 1; we compress the membrane of the drum beneath it; a current of
air is produced which raises the membrane of the second
drum, and consequently lowers lever No. 2. On the contrary,
the elevation of lever No. 1 will produce an inward current of
air, which will raise the membrane and the lever of No. 2.

Proceeding in the same manner for the transmission of
movements in the horizontal plane, we place to the right of

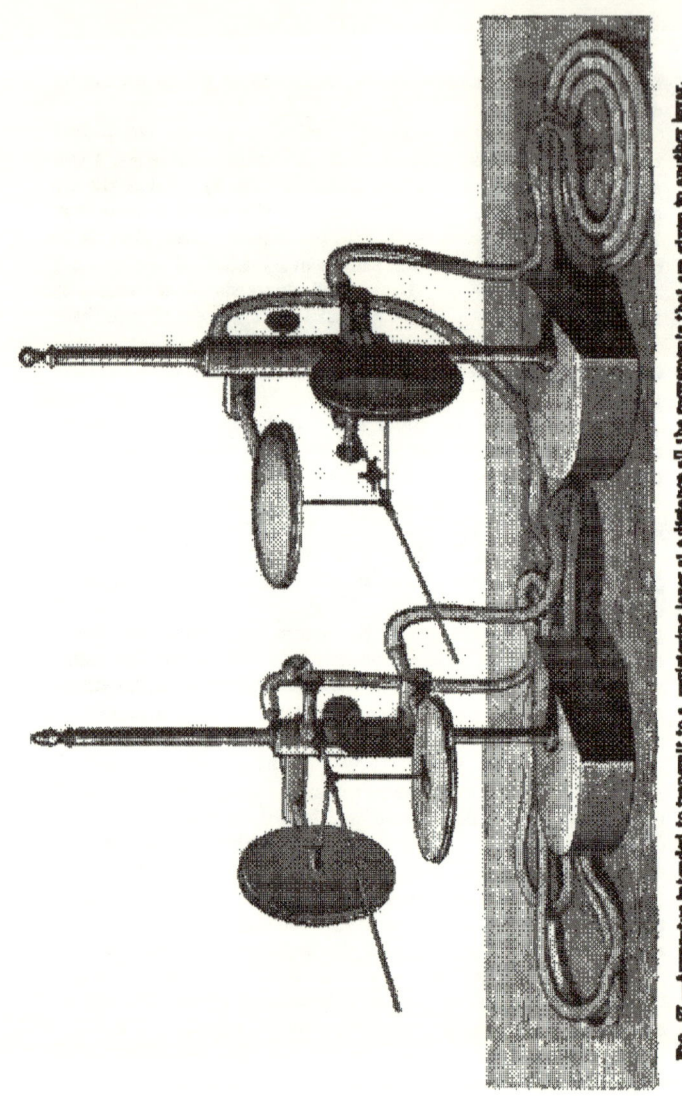

Fig. 97.—Apparatus intended to transmit to a registering lever at a distance all the movements that are given to another lever.

one of the levers and to the left of the others, a drum whose
membrane, situated in the vertical plane, acts in a lateral
direction; the transmission of these movements is made by a
special tube, as in the case of the vertical movements.

The apparatus having been thus constructed, if we take in
our fingers the extremity of one of the levers, and give it any
motion whatever, we shall see the other lever repeat it with
perfect fidelity.

All the difference consists in a slight diminution of the amplitude of the movements in the second lever. This is because
the air contained in each of the systems of tubes and drums
is slightly compressed, and consequently does not transmit
completely the movement which it receives. It would be easy
to remedy this inconvenience, if it were found to be one, by
giving to the receiving apparatus a greater sensibility, which
might be effected by placing the Cardan joint a little nearer
the point where the movement is transmitted to the lever of
the second instrument. But it is better not to seek to amplify
the movements too much when we wish to register them by
tracings, since we then augment the friction, and diminish the
force by which it must be overcome.

After having ascertained that the transmission of any movement whatever is effected in a satisfactory manner by this apparatus, we sought for a means of tracing this movement on a
plane surface. The difficulty which occurred in the application
of the graphic method to the study of the movement of the
insect's wing, again presents itself here; but in this case there
are no means of avoiding it by taking only partial tracings.

The point of the lever No. 2 describes in space a spherical
figure incapable of becoming tangential, except in a single
point, to the smoked surface which is to receive the tracing.
Consequently, it has been necessary to register the projection
of this figure on a plane surface, and to arrange the lever in
such a manner that it may lengthen or shorten itself as required, in order to keep always in contact with the smoked
glass. This result was obtained by means of a spring which
served as a writing point.

Fig. 98 shows the spring in question, at the extremity of a
lever. It is wide at the base, in order to resist any tendency

to lateral deviations under the influence of the friction; this base is fixed to a vertical piece of aluminium, which is attached by its lower part to the extremity of the lever.   In this manner, the point of the spring which acts as a style is considerably in front of the lever whose movements it is to register.   Let us suppose the lever to rise, and take the position indicated by the dotted line in figure 98; while traversing this space, it will have described an arc of a circle, and its extremity will no longer be in the same plane as before, but the elasticity of the spring will have carried the writing point more forward; it will still continue, therefore, to be

FIG. 98.—Elastic point tracing on a smoked glass.

in contact with the plane on which it is to trace.   Thus the lever lengthens or shortens, as required, and its point always presses on the plane.   The surface on which the tracing is received is a well-polished glass, and the spring which forms the style is so flexible, that the elastic pressure which it exerts upon the glass rubs it but slightly.

The apparatus being thus arranged, it must be submitted to a verifying process, to ascertain if movements are faithfully transmitted and registered.

For this purpose, arming the two levers of fig. 97 with similar styles, we placed their points against the same piece of smoked glass; we directed with the hand one of the levers so as to trace any figure, to sign one's name for instance; the other lever ought to trace the same figure, to reproduce the same signature.

It generally happens that the transmission is not equally easy in both directions; we perceive a slight deformity in the transmitted figure, which is lengthened more or less both in height and in width.   This fault can always be corrected; it arises from the fact, that the membrane of one of the drums, being more stretched than that of the other, obeys less easily. We soon succeed, by various trials, in giving the same sensibility to the two membranes, which is ascertained, when we find that the figure traced by the first lever is identical with that of the second.

Experiment to determine graphically the trajectory of the wing. —The following are the modifications which allow us to apply this mode of transmission to the study of the movements of the wing of a flying bird.

As the apparatus must necessarily be of considerable weight, we chose a large bird to carry it; strong full-grown buzzards were employed in these experiments. By means of a kind of corset which left both the wings and the legs at liberty, we fixed on the back of the bird a thin piece of light wood on which the apparatus was placed.

In order that the lever might execute faithfully the same movements as the wing, it was necessary to place the Cardan joint of this lever in contact with the humeral articulation of the buzzard. Therefore, as the presence of the drums by the side of the lever did not permit this immediate contact, we had recourse to a parallelogram, which transmitted to the lever of the apparatus the movements of a long rod, the centre of motion in which was very near the articulation of the bird's wing. Then, in order to obtain perfect correspondence between the movements of the rod and those of the buzzard's wing, we fixed on the outer edge of the wing—that is to say, on the metacarpal bone of the thumb of the bird, a very tight screw clip, furnished with a ring, through which slipped the steel rod, of which we have before spoken.

Fig. 99 represents the buzzard flying with the apparatus just described; underneath it hang the two transmitting tubes which are fixed to the registering instrument.

After a great many fruitless attempts and changes in the construction of the apparatus, which, being too fragile, broke

FIG. 91.—Buzzard flying with the apparatus which gives the signal of the movements described by the extremity of its wing

R

at almost every flight of the bird, we succeeded in obtaining satisfactory results. During the whole of the bird's flight the registering lever described a kind of ellipse. This ellipse, registered on a plate having an advancing movement from right to left, gave figure 100. In order to understand this figure, we must imagine the bird flying from left to right (as the tracing is to be read), and rubbing the extremity of its left wing against a wall blackened with smoke; the tracing which its wing would leave under these conditions would be identical with that represented in fig. 100. This curve is a kind of ellipse spread out by the advancing motion of the plate which receives the tracing. Except some tremblings of the line, which arose from the imperfection of the apparatus, the trajectory of the bird's wing may be compared to the tracing given under the same conditions by a Wheatstone's rod, tuned in unison, and giving an elliptical vibration.

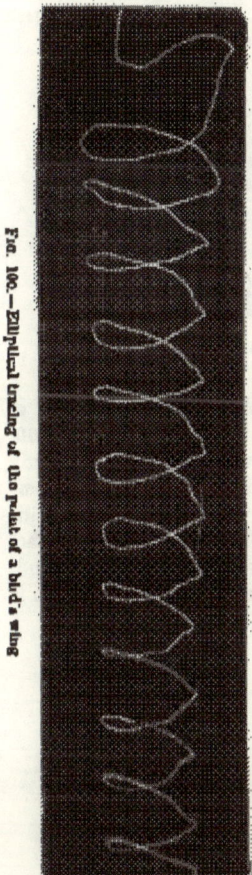

Fig. 100.—Elliptical tracing of the point of a bird's wing

Fig. 101 represents a tracing of this kind.

The determination of the course of the wing, with the different phases of its velocity, is so important, that we resolved to verify by various methods the reality of this elliptical form. All our experiments have furnished results which agree with each other; they have shown that birds of different species describe with their wings an elliptical trajectory.

D'Esterno had already determined by his experiments that this trajectory existed; and he has even figured, in his work, the curve described; but, in his opinion, the larger axis of the ellipse would be directed downwards and backwards, which is entirely opposed to the result of our experiments.

Fig. 101.—Ellipse formed by a Wheatstone's rod tuned in unison, and tracing on a revolving cylinder.

We remark also the unequal amplitude of the strokes of the wing from the commencement to the end of fig. 100. This variation in size agrees with what we have already stated concerning fig. 96. This showed that at the commencement of its flight, the bird gives stronger strokes with its wing. It is at that moment, in fact, that it has to effect the maximum of work, in order to rise from the ground. After this, it will only need to remain at the height which it has attained.

CHAPTER V.

OF THE CHANGES IN THE PLANE OF THE BIRD'S WING AT DIFFERENT POINTS IN ITS COURSE.

New determination of the trajectory of the wing—Description of apparatus
—Transmission of a movement by the traction of a thread Instrument and apparatus to suspend the bird—Experiment on the flight of
a pigeon—Analysis of the curves—Description of the apparatus
intended to give indications of the changes in the plane of the wing
during flight—Relation of these changes of plane with the other
movements of the wing.

NEW DETERMINATION OF THE TRAJECTORY OF THE WING.

THE simultaneous analysis of the changes in the plane of
the wing, and of the various phases of its course, would have
presented great difficulties, if we had not discovered a new
arrangement of the apparatus, which allowed us to examine,
at the same time, an almost infinite number of different
movements.

This simplification of the method consists in the employment of threads to transmit the movement of any point
whatever to the experimental apparatus, which in its turn,
sends it by the ordinary means to the registering instrument.

Description of apparatus.—Let fig. 102 be two lever-drums
connected together, similar to those already represented in
fig. 21.

The lever L belongs to the experimental apparatus, that on
which the movement to be studied is to act. On the frame
of this first instrument let us place an arm of bent wire, from
the extremity of which an india-rubber thread, F, will pass to
the lever L. From the same lever hangs a cord of twisted
silk, C C, to which is suspended a leaden ball.

Let us suppose the ball to be at its lowest position—at
the point A—the lever L occupies the place marked by a dotted
line, while in the registering instrument the air driven out
raises the lever L', which traces the movement.

Now let us raise the ball to the position B; the elasticity of the india-rubber thread will cause the lever to rise. Thus it is acted upon alternately by two forces, sometimes by the traction exerted by the silk thread, which lowers it; at others, by the retraction of the india-rubber, which re-acts as soon as the tractile force ceases. Thus the lever will follow faithfully all the movements which are given to the extremity of the thread which draws it down.

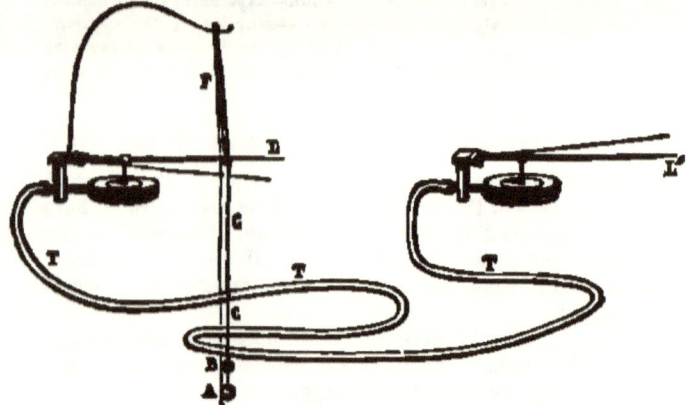

Fig. 102.—Transmission of a to-and-fro movement by means of a simple traction-cord.

The lever L', which is to trace on the cylinder the movements transmitted to it, moves in an opposite direction to the course of the cord C C. The tracing will thus be reversed, and if it were important to obtain it in the same direction, it would be necessary to turn the registering drum, so as to place the membrane downwards.*

With two instruments of this kind, one acted upon by the

* As many instruments of this kind are required as there are movements to be studied. But three connected levers will always be sufficient to ascertain the movements of a point in space, since each of the positions of this point is defined when it has been determined with reference to three axes at right angles to each other.

vertical tractions of a thread attached to the wing of the bird,
and the other by the horizontal tractile force of a second
thread also fastened to its wing, we can verify the experiment
which has furnished us with the trajectory of this organ, and
obtain with much greater accuracy the curve illustrating its
movements. This we have perfectly succeeded in doing, as
we shall show further on.

But this is not all that we wished to obtain. We might
have made the bird carry the apparatus which we have just
described, and put it in communication with the registers by
means of tubes, as in the experiment represented in fig. 99.
But while seeking to render the analogies of the movements
of flight perfect, we wished also to discover a plan which
would be equally applicable to the living bird, and to every
kind of machine intended to represent artificially aerial locomotion.

In this project we must endeavour to copy Nature in her
functions, as the artist does in her form. We must give more
rapidity to movements which are too slow, and render those
slower which are too rapid, until they have absolutely the same
characters and the same mechanical effects as those of the
bird.

This incessant comparison requires us to place ourselves
under new conditions. Hitherto, our analytical studies have
been directed to a bird flying at liberty; for since we have
never been able to imitate flight exactly by mechanical
methods, it would be impossible to leave an artificial instrument to itself; it would be broken at each experiment.

The comparison of the movements of the bird with those
of imitative instruments does not require these movements to
be effected under the conditions of free flight. Provided that
the bird, although restrained in its movements, should flap
its wings with the intention of flying, we shall be able to
study these muscular actions with reference to their characters
of force, extent, and duration. A bird suspended by a cord
and allowed to flap its wings might, for example, be compared with an artificial apparatus suspended in the same
manner.

We have tried a less imperfect mode of suspension which

allows the bird to fly under conditions almost normal, and at the same time will permit the artificial instruments to make attempts at flight, without any fear of letting them fall, if the movements which they produce should be insufficient to sustain them in the air.   We will now describe this suspensory apparatus.

There is a sort of frame-work of six or seven metres in diameter, in which the bird moves continuously, being thus able to furnish us with an observation of a circular flight of long duration.   We give the instrument a large radius, that its curve, being less abrupt, should modify less the nature of the movement which the bird may make.   Harnessed to some extent to the extremity of a long arm which turns on a central pivot, the bird ought to be as free as possible to go through its movements of vertical oscillation.   We shall presently see that a bird passes through a double oscillatory movement in a vertical plane for each revolution of its wings.

Arrangement of the frame.—The conditions to be fulfilled are the following : in the first place, a great mobility of the instrument, that the bird may have the least possible resistance to overcome in its flight ; then, a perfect rigidity of the arm of the machine, to prevent any vibrations peculiar to itself, which might render unnatural the movements executed by the bird.

Fig. 103 shows the general arrangement of the apparatus. A steel pivot, resting on a solidly-cast socket of great weight, is placed on the platform of a photographic table.   This table is raised by means of rack-work, so that the operator, after having arranged his apparatus so as to suit the experiment, may place the platform sufficiently high for the instrument to turn freely above his head.

The frame-work, properly so called, is a bow formed of a long piece of fir-wood slightly curved.   The string of this bow is an iron wire, which is fixed by the middle to a cage of wood traversed by the central pivot.   Care is taken to balance the two ends of the apparatus, by gradually adding weights to the arm not carrying the bird which is the subject of the experiment.

If we did not take this precaution, the apparatus, as it

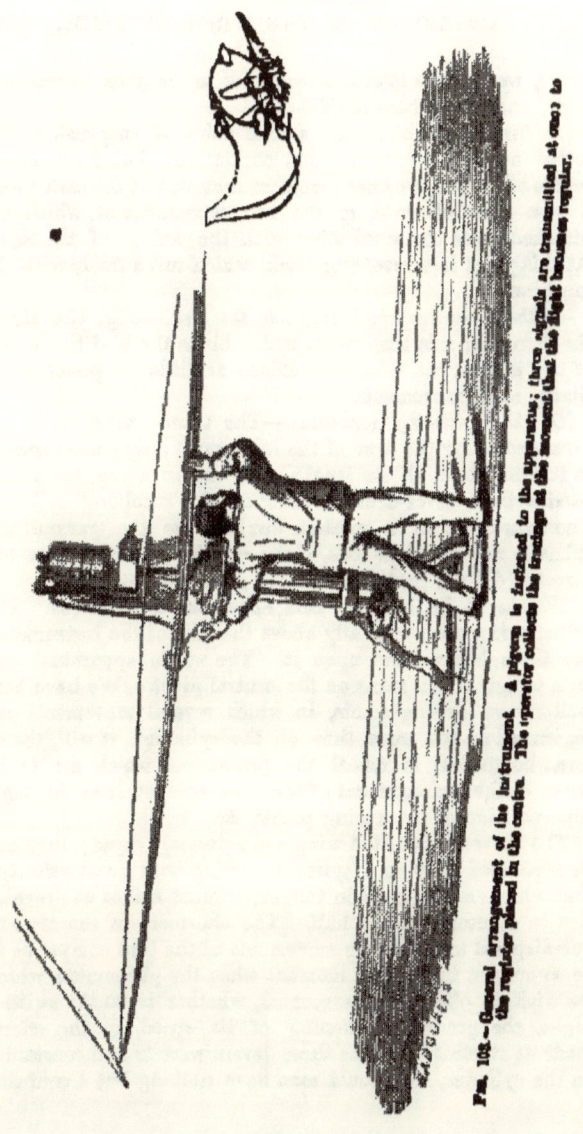

Fig. 103.—General arrangement of the instrument. A pigeon is fastened to the apparatus; three signals are transmitted at once; to the register placed in the centre. The operator collects the tracings at the moment that the flight becomes regular.

turns, would give lateral movements to the pivot on which it rests, and to the base itself.

To furnish the bird with a solid point of suspension, protected not only from vertical oscillations, but from movements of torsion, we have placed at each end of the instrument a cross piece of wood, to the two extremities of which are attached cords communicating with the ceiling of the room. At this point is a revolving hook, which turns freely with the machine.

·*Of the apparatus which suspends the bird.*—Fig. 104 shows the details of this suspension which binds the bird to the arm of the instrument, while it confines as little as possible the liberty of its movements.

Of the registering apparatus.—The transmitting tubes are arranged along the arm of the instrument; they are fastened to it throughout all its length, and end in a register which carries three lever-drums tracing on the revolving cylinder. The instrument in its rotation would cause the transmitting tubes to roll round its axis, if the register to which they are directed did not participate in the general rotation.

We see in fig. 103 how this apparatus is arranged. The cylinder is placed vertically above the axis of the instrument; the three levers trace upon it. The whole apparatus rests on a tablet, which turns on the central pivot. We have here well-known arrangements, in which several movements are registered at the same time on the cylinder; it will, therefore, be useless to repeat the precautions which are to be taken in the management of the apparatus, such as the exact superposition of the tracing points, &c.

The movements of the wing are extremely rapid; they can be registered only on a cylinder turning with great velocity; that which is employed in this experiment makes one revolution in a second and a half. The shortness of the time at our disposal to trace the movements of the bird compel us to do so only at the precise moment when the phenomena which we wish to observe are presented, whether it be the swiftest flight, the gradual slackening of its speed, or the efforts made at starting. If the three levers were to rub constantly on the cylinder, we should soon have nothing but a confused

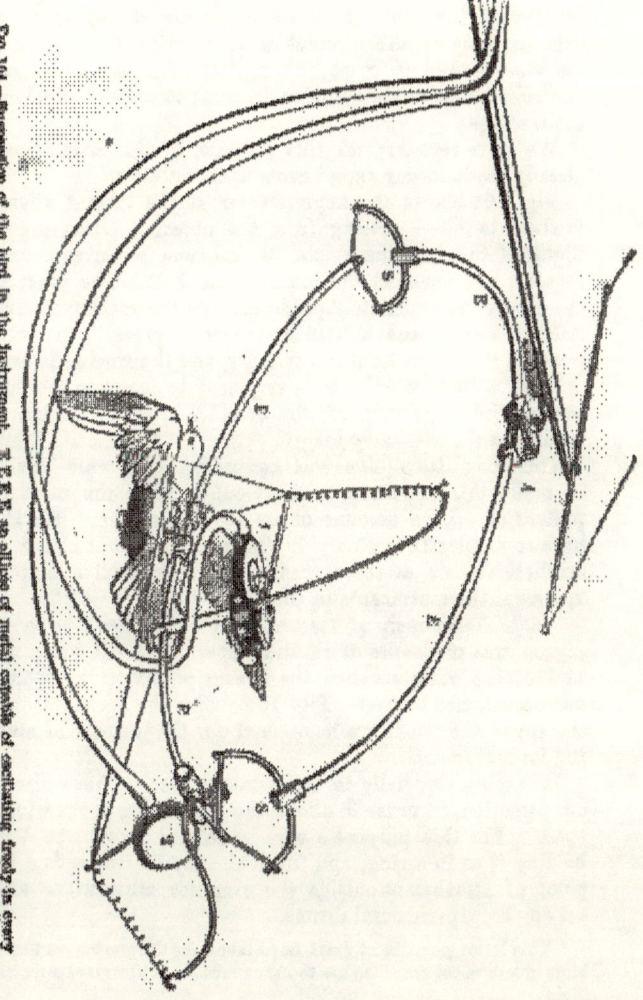

FIG. 104.—Suspension of the bird in the instrument. The metal support is an ellipse allowing the upper part of the ellipse to oscillate freely in every direction, by means of the double suspension A. B, C, D, E, F. The suspensory apparatus is fixed on the back of the pigeon. The lever-drum (I) receives the movements executed by the wing in a vertical direction. The lever-drum (I) receives those of the horizontal movements.

scrawl. It is indispensably necessary so to arrange tho instrument that the points of the levers should touch the cylinder only at the moment when we wish to register the phenomena, and to cease this contact after one, or at most two revolutions of the cylinder, in order to avoid confusion in the tracings.

We have recourse, for this purpose, to the arrangements already made in our experiments upon walking.

Fig. 103 shows the experimenter at the instant when he is about to take a tracing from the pigeon. Observing the flight of the bird, he seizes the moment when it becomes regular, and squeezes the india-rubber ball. The contact of the levers is immediately produced, and the tracing is made. After a second and a half he ceases to press it, the spring removes the levers from the cylinder, and the tracing is over.

With a little practice it is very easy to ascertain the duration of the revolution of the cylinder, and to confine the tracing to the necessary length.

This long description was necessary, as we were anxious to make this apparatus understood, it being the most important of all, on account of its double function. We shall have to employ it, not only in the analytical, but also in the synthetical part of these studies, when we shall attempt to represent the movements in the bird's flight.

New determination of the trajectory of a bird's wing.—A pigeon was made use of in this experiment. It was a male bird of the variety called the *Roman pigeon*, very vigorous, and accustomed to fly.* Fig. 104 shows the arrangement of the apparatus which we have used for the purpose of studying its movements.

It is more especially to the humerus that we have directed our attention, in order to obtain the movements of the wing in space. For this purpose a wire is twisted round the bone, holding it as in a ring, and furnishing by its free ends a firm point of attachment outside the wing for other wires which act on the experimental drums.

* This latter point is of great importance, for the greater part of the birds in a dove-cot are of no use to us, on account of their inexperience in flight.

The movements of the two wings being perfectly symmetrical in regular flight, we cause two wires, which pass symmetrically from the wings, to converge to each of the experimental drums.   Thus, drum No. 1, intended to give signals of the elevation and depression of the wing, receives two wires, each of which proceeds from one of the humerus bones of the pigeon, at about 3 centimetres outside the articulation of the shoulder. These wires rise and converge, and are attached to the point of the lever No. 1; while from the same point proceeds an india-rubber thread,* which serves as a counter-spring, and rises vertically to a hook above, which holds it.

We have before seen (fig. 102) how the lever of the experimental drum receives, under these conditions, all the movements of elevation and depression executed by the humerus of the bird.

Two other wires, each attached to the humerus of the pigeon on each wing, and starting from the same point of the bone to which were fastened the wires of drum No. 1, converge also, turning backwards, and proceed to the lever of drum No. 2. This is the drum which receives the movements executed by the wing in the antero-posterior direction. The two drums send their signals by air tubes to the register situated in the centre of the apparatus.

Experiment.—After having ascertained that the two levers intended to trace have their points situated on the same vertical, the pigeon is allowed to fly. The bird goes through the movements of flight, and soon carries round with considerable rapidity the instrument to which it is attached. The operator, placed in the centre of the apparatus, has only to follow for a few paces the rotation of the instrument. During this time he holds in his hand the india-rubber ball, and has only to compress it, in order that the two levers may rest with their points against the blackened paper, and that the tracing may commence. As soon as the flight is well established, and seems to be carried on under satisfactory

---

* In fig. 104 a spiral spring has been substituted for this india-rubber thread.

conditions, he compresses the ball, and produces the tracing represented in fig. 105.

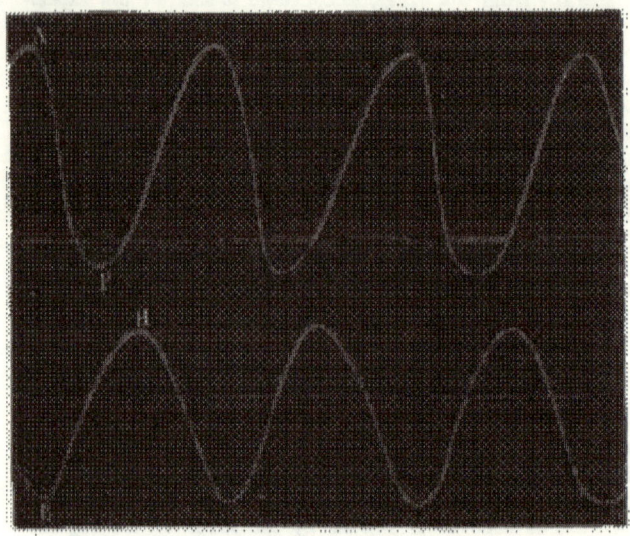

Fig. 105.—Tracing of the movements of a pigeon's wing. The upper line, A P, shows the movements forwards and backwards, The lower line H H, the movements up and down.

Interpretation of the tracings.—The curves are read from left to right, like ordinary writing. The upper curve is that described by the humerus of a bird in its movements forwards and backwards; the direction of these movements is indicated by the letters A and P, which signify that all the tops of the curves, as well as that at A, correspond with the time when the wing has reached the most forward part of its course; the lower parts of the curves, on the contrary, indicate, as well as that at the point P, the moment when the wing has reached the hinder part of its movement.

The horizontal line which cuts this curve has been traced in a previous experiment by the point of the lever at the instant when the wings of the bird, kept motionless by an assistant, may be considered as horizontally extended, tending neither forwards nor backwards. This line represents, therefore, to some extent, the *zero* of the scale of the movements of the wing in its antero-posterior direction. The inspection of the curve shows us also, that the pigeon's wing was carried more especially in the direction of the upper parts, similar to the point A; in other terms, that the forward predominated over the backward movement.

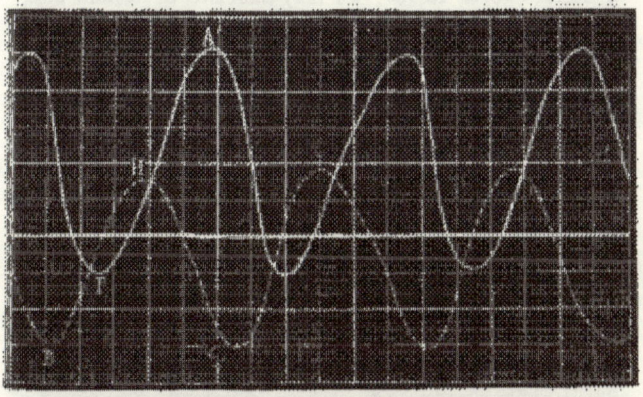

Fig. 106.—Superposition of the preceding curves on paper divided in millimetres. The two curves have a common direction with reference to the axis of the abscissæ.

The same explanations would apply to the lower curve H P, which expresses the movements of the wing upwards and downwards.

In order to ascertain if the course of the pigeon's wing in the present experiment is apparently the same as that of the buzzard recorded before, we have constructed the complete curve of the wing during one of its revolutions, making use for this purpose of the two partial curves of fig. 105.

The following is the method employed in this construction:

In order to give more facility to the measurement of the positions of the different points of these curves, we have copied them both on a paper graduated in centimetres and

millimetres. We have traced in full line one of these curves,
that of the movements in the antero-posterior direction, the
course of which is indicated by the letters A and P; then we
have represented, by a dotted line, the curve of the upward
and downward motions with the letters H and B.   We have
placed these two tracings over each other, so as to make the
zero-lines of each coincide.   We have also taken care to
preserve the vertical superposition of the corresponding points
of each of these curves; we may therefore be certain that,
wherever any vertical line cuts the two curves, the inter-
sections correspond with the position which the humerus of
the bird occupies, at that instant, with reference to two planes
at right angles to each other. The intersection with the dotted
line will express, by the length of the ordinate drawn from
this point to the axis of the abscissæ, the position which the
wing then occupies with reference to an horizontal plane; the
intersection with the full line will express the position of the
wing as referred to a vertical plane.

This determination is realised in fig. 107 for the trajectory
of the wing, which has been constructed by successive points
in the following manner:—

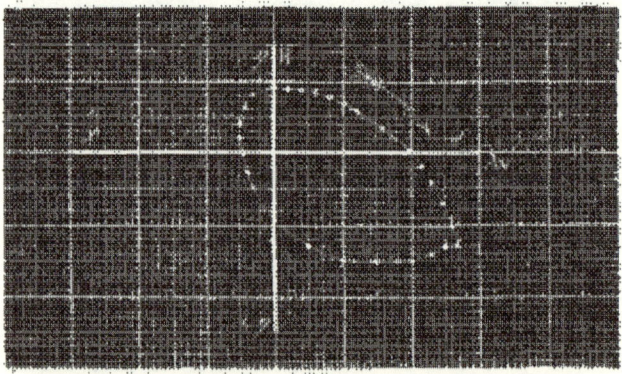

FIG. 107 —Constructed from the preceding curves. An arrow indicates the
direction of the movement. The separation of the dots expresses the
rapidity of the movements of the wing at the different parts of its
course.

Let there be two lines, $x\, x$, forming the axis of the
abscissæ, and y y that of the ordinates. Let us assume, that
all which is above the line of zeros, in the full curve—that is
to say, that which corresponds with a movement in a forward
direction, ought to point to the right of the line y y. Inversely, that all which is below the zeros, in the full curve,
will point to the left of the axis of y y. The position with
reference to this axis will be reckoned, parallel to it, by
means of millimetric divisions.

On the other hand, the different measurements taken on
the dotted curve (that which expresses the upward motion of
the wing) must point to the corresponding elevation, reckoned
above or below the line $x\, x$, according as these points in the
curve of the elevations are removed a certain number of
millimetres either above or below the zero line.

Let us take as our point of departure, in the construction
of the new curve, the point c (fig. 107), chosen on the dotted
line, at one of the times when the wing has arrived at one of
its anterior limits.

This point, according to the millimetric scale, shows us
that the wing is depressed 13 divisions beneath the horizontal
line. Let us follow the vertical line which passes through
the point c, till it meets with the curve of movement in the
antero-posterior direction: the intersection of this vertical
line with the curve shows us that the wing at this moment
had been carried forward 26 divisions; on the new curve,
therefore, the point a ought to be marked at a well-ascertained
position c, which will be found at the intersection of the thir-
teenth division below the axis $x\, x$, with the twenty-sixth to the
right of the axis y y, which according to what we have assumed, corresponds with 26 divisions in the forward direction.

To determine a second point in our curve, let us proceed,
in reading the tracings, one millimetric division farther to
the right; we shall find, as before, the intersection of the
vertical at this point with the two curves, and we shall thus
have a second point in the new construction determined.

The series of successive points obtained in this manner
form a curve which shows the course of the wing; the arrow
indicates the direction of the movement.

By constructing thus the whole figure, we see that this curve, after proceeding downwards and forwards, rises and returns back again.

By comparing this figure with that which we have obtained by means of another apparatus (fig. 100), on another kind of bird, and by examining the movement of another part of the wing, we shall find striking resemblances between the two curves, which show that birds proceed in their flight by movements which are almost identical. In fact, the bone of the wing in each describes a kind of irregular ellipse, with its greater axis inclined downward and forward. The importance of this determination is so great, that we trust we shall be pardoned for the long and minute details of the experiments which have furnished these results.

OF THE CHANGES IN THE PLANE OF THE WING.

We have seen in Chapter I. that the wing of the insect is subject to torsions under the influence of the resistance of the air, and that the inclination of the plane of its wing is changed at every moment. These movements, which are entirely passive, constitute the essence of the mechanism of the insect's flight; the wing, in each of its alternate movements, acts on the resistance of the air, and gains from it a force which is exerted on the membrane by the side of the main-rib, thus serving to sustain the insect and propel it forward. The structure of the bird's wing does not allow the existence of a similar mechanism. Its wing during its ascent does not present to the air a resisting plane, because the feathers which fold over each other would open to allow it to pass through. The depression of the wing is therefore the only phase in the flight of the bird which has any analogy with that of the insect. Besides, the curve described by the point of the bird's wing is sufficiently different from that of the insect, to prove that their mechanical conditions are very dissimilar.

It was indispensable to determine by experiment the different inclinations of the plane of the bird's wing at each phase of its revolutions. In fact, to estimate the resistance which the air presents at each moment of the flight, we must know the two elements of this resistance: first, the angle

under which the plane of the wing strikes the air, and
secondly, the velocity with which it is lowered. Nothing is
more easy than to obtain the second data of the problem;
we can reduce them from the curve which represents the
position of the wing at each instant, a curve of which we
have an example in fig. 108, as obtained from a pigeon. But
the difficulty which presents itself, is to obtain the indication
of the changes which take place in the plane of the wing
during flight. · For this purpose we have had recourse to the
following mechanism.

We have seen, in fig. 99, that a rod connected with a
Cardan universal joint, whose centre of rotation is near the
scapulo-humeral articulation, can be made to represent accurately the circular movements of the wing. But Cardan's
joint, though it obeys the rotary motions of every kind which
are given to the rod, does not allow any movements of torsion
with reference to the axis of this rod.

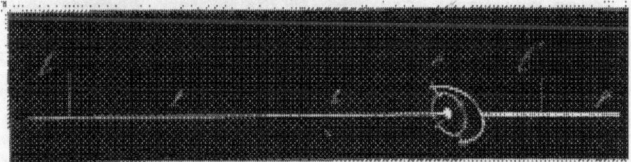

Fig. 193.—Theoretical figure of the apparatus to investigate the torsion of
the wing.

Let fig. 108 be a kind of apparatus of this sort: we can
give the rod *t t* every kind of motion in the vertical or horizontal direction; it will follow all the impulses which it
receives. But if we take hold of the extremity of the rod,
near the lever *l* which is perpendicular to it, and try to give
the lever a movement of torsion, as if we were turning a screw,
the Cardan does not allow this movement to be made, and the
rod resists the impulse brought to bear upon it. Let us
suppose that behind the Cardan joint, and on the prolonga-
tion of the rod *t t*, there is another cylindrical rod, *p*, turning
in a tube; this rod will turn under the influence of the torsion
exercised by the hand holding the lever *l*, and if the rod *p*
carries a lever *l'*, at right angles to it, and situated in the

same plane as *l*, we shall see that these levers correspond with each other, and that every change of plane undergone by the first will be transmitted to the second.

Under these conditions, if we cause the lever *l* to signal the changes of plane which the wing undergoes in the various phases of its revolution, these changes will be communicated to the lever *l'*, which can in its turn act on an experimental apparatus, and transmit the signal under the form of a tracing. This is precisely the method which we have employed in our experiments. The lever *l* was placed upon the wing of the bird, and was held in a horizontal position. The lever *l'*, also horizontal, was fastened by a wire to the lever of an experimental drum placed above it, and arranged in the same manner as in the experiments described in the former chapter.

When we caused the plane of the wing to oscillate, so as to turn its upper surface more or less backwards, the registered curve was depressed; it rose, on the contrary, when we turned the wing so as to carry its upper surface forwards.

Still a difficulty presented itself. It was not possible to fix the lever *l* at one point of the rod *t t*; and, at the same time, to render it immovable at a single point in the bird's wing. In fact, the Cardan joint, not having the same centre of motion as the articulation of the wing, it followed that in the vertical movements the rod slipped upon the wing. It was necessary, therefore, for the lever *l*, while fixed to the feathers of the bird, to glide freely on the rod in the direction of its length, and yet that it should cause it to receive, under the form of torsion, all the changes of inclination that are transmitted to it by the wings of the bird. We see in fig. 109 how this result has been obtained.

Let *t t* be the rod which is to follow all the circular movements executed by the bird. This rod has in it deep longitudinal grooves, which give its section the appearance of a star; it glides freely in a tube which is applied to its external surface. But at one of the extremities of the tube is a metallic sliding casting, the interior part of which is grooved like a star, through which passes the rod whose grooves slide in those of the star-shaped opening. Then the lever *l* is soldered to this tube, and is able to move with it to any point along the rod, thus allowing full liberty to the movements of flight, while no change of plane can be effected without communicating a movement of torsion to the rod.

After some experiments, it became necessary to make improvements in this apparatus. Thus, the lever *l* had a tendency to get twisted on account of the displacement of the feathers during flight; it was replaced (fig. 109) by a piece with three

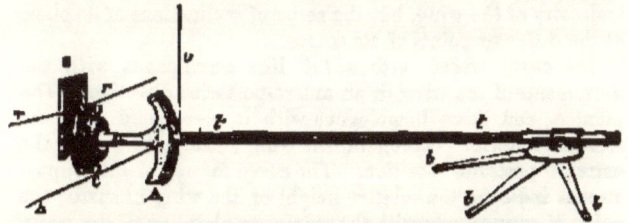

Fɪɢ. 109.—Actual arrangement of the apparatus intended to experiment upon the movements of the wing, and its change of plane.

movable levers, *b b b*, turning in the same plane round a common centre, like the blades of a fan. Each of these little branches terminated in a hook. After having attached the sliding tube to the *false wing* of the bird, the extremity of each of these three blades was tied to one of the long feathers of the wing. This ligature, made with india-rubber, gave excellent results.

The lever *l* (fig. 109) was also defective on account of its unequal action. In its stead was substituted a pulley of short radius, placed on the rod prolonged behind the Cardan joint. The thin cord *r r*, which was to transmit the torsions of the rod, passed round the wheel of this pulley. In this manner the rotation of the pulley, resulting from the torsion of the rod, always faithfully transmitted this torsion to the experimental lever.

To put an end to this long description of the instrument intended to transmit the signals of the elevation and depression of the wing, let us only say that the piece situated at the base of the lever *t t* is intended to transmit the vertical and horizontal movements by two systems of cords.   For the vertical ones, a cord v goes to the lever of the experimental drum.   The cord h transmits to another apparatus the movements in the horizontal, that is, in the antero-posterior direction.

Experiment.—A buzzard to which this apparatus has been adapted is harnessed to the instrument and allowed to fly: we obtain at the same time the three curves represented in fig. 110.   With these three data, we can construct, not only the trajectory of the wing, but the series of inclinations of its plane at the different points of its course.

The curve traced with a full line corresponds with the movements of the wing in an antero-posterior direction.   The point A, and those homologous with it, correspond with the extreme anterior position of the wing ; the point P with the extreme posterior position.   The curve formed of interrupted strokes indicates the relative height of the wing in space ; the point H corresponds with the maximum elevation of the wing, and the point B with its greatest depression.

These two first curves enable us to construct, by means of points, the closed curve* (fig. 111) representing the trajectory of the buzzard's wing.   It is by this trajectory that we shall determine the inclination of the plane of the wing at every part of its elliptical course.

For this purpose, we must return (fig. 110) to the dotted curve S, which is the expression of the torsions of the wing at different instants.   The positive and negative ordinates of this curve correspond with the trigonometrical tangents of the angles† which the wing makes with the axis of the body.‡

* This curve is not always closed ; this is the case only when the flight is extremely regular.

† We must subtract algebraically from the angle found, a constant quantity, the angle of 30° which the wing, during repose, makes with the horizon.

‡ We cannot positively affirm that this axis is horizontal ; it seems rather that it is inclined so that the beak of the bird turns slightly upwards.   This inclination of the axis would necessitate a correction in the absolute inclinations of the wing at the different points of its revolution.

They enable us, therefore, to trace in fig. 111 a series of
lines, each of which expresses, by its inclination with respect

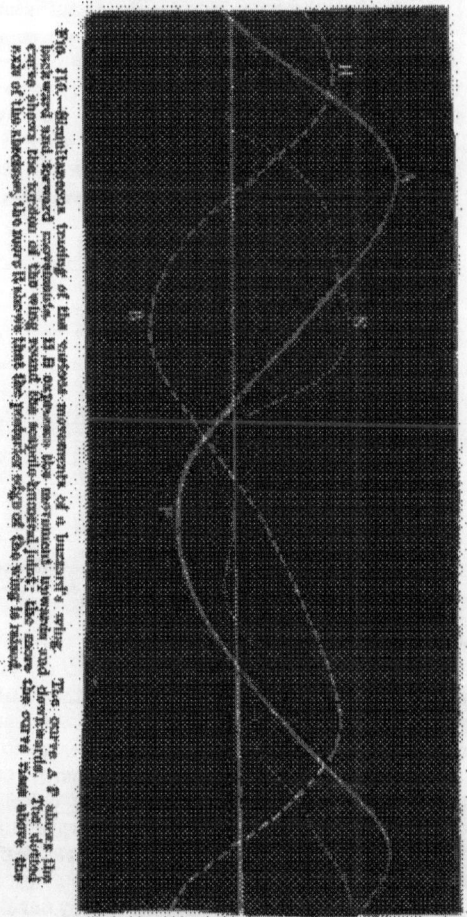

FIG. 110.—Simultaneous tracing of the various movements of a buzzard's wing. The curve A B above the
backward and forward movements. H A expresses the movement upwards and downwards. The curve A B above the
curve shows the torsion of the wing round the longitudinal axis; the more the curve rises above the
axis of this abscissa, the more it shows that the posterior edge of the wing is raised.

to the horizontal axis, that which the plane of the wing
presented to the horizon at this same portion of its course.

The direction of the movement of the wing is read from above and forward, from II to Av.

Fig. 111 shows that the wing during its ascent assumes an inclined position which allows it to cut the air so as to meet with the minimum of resistance; while in its descent, on the contrary, the position of its plane is reversed, so that its lower surface turns downwards and slightly backwards. It follows, that in its period of depression, the wing, by its obliquity, acts upon the resistance of the air, and while raising the body of the bird, carries it forward. We see, also, that

Fig. 111.—Inclinations of the plane of the wing with reference to the axis (Av) of the body during flight.

the inclination of the wing changes gradually, in the different phases of its elevation and of its descent. Especially in this latter phase, the influence of the air in shaping the course of the wing is more evidently seen; it is, in fact, at the moment when the rapidity of its depression attains its maximum that we see the posterior edge of the wing turn up the more strongly.

The wing, when it has reached the end of its descending course, changes its plane very suddenly. The explanation of this movement is very natural. As soon as the resistance of the air ceases to raise the feathers, these, by their elasticity, return to their ordinary position, which they occupy during all the phase of elevation.

Even the ellipse which forms the trajectory of the wing can

be explained by the resistance of the air. The muscular
apparatus of the bird, like that of the insect, has nothing to
do with the course of the wing; elevation and depression are
almost all the movements that it can produce. But the
resistance of the air during the phase of descent gives rise to
the anterior convexity of the curve passed through, by means
of a mechanism which we already understand. The posterior
convexity which belongs to the ascensional phase is also
explained by the action of the air on the lower surface of the
wing, which it carries backward at the same time as it raises
it. We must seek for the demonstration of this theory in the
artificial representation of these different movements.

CHAPTER VI.

RE-ACTIONS OF THE MOVEMENTS OF THE WING ON THE
BODY OF THE BIRD.

Re-actions of the movements of the wing—Vertical re-actions in different
species ; horizontal re-actions or changes in the rapidity of flight ;
simultaneous study of the two orders of re-actions—Theory of the
flight of the bird—Passive and active parts of the wing—Reproduction of the mechanism of the flight of the bird.

In order that we may follow, in studying the flight of the
bird, the same plan which has guided our researches on the
other kinds of locomotion, we must determine what are the
reactionary effects of each of the movements of the wing on
the body of the animal.

Two distinct effects are produced during flight: by one, the
bird is sustained in opposition to its weight; by the other, it
is subjected to a propulsive force which carries it from one
place to another. But do we find that the bird, when sustained in the air, keeps at a constant level, or does it pass
through oscillations in the vertical plane ?　Does it not
experience, by the intermittent effect of the flapping of its
wings, rising and falling motions, of which the eye can detect

neither the frequency nor the extent? Again, does not the bird advance in its onward course with variable rapidity? Shall we not find in the action of its wings a series of impulses, which give to its advancing course a jerking motion?

These queries can be answered experimentally in the following manner.

Since we have at our disposal the means of sending the signals of movements to a distance, and recording them by tracings, when these movements are made to produce a pressure on the membrane of a drum filled with air, we must endeavour to reduce to a pressure of this kind the movements which we desire to study.

The oscillations which can be effected by the bird in a horizontal plane must be made to exert on the membrane of the drum pressures alternately strong or feeble, in proportion as the bird mounts or descends. The same kind of experiment must be made on the variations in its horizontal rapidity.

The question has been already solved for the vertical re-actions, by means of the apparatus represented in fig. 28, when we were treating of terrestrial locomotion; a slight modification will allow us to employ the same method to ascertain whether vertical oscillations are produced during flight.

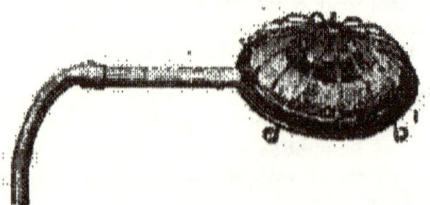

Fig. 112.—Apparatus intended to transmit to the registering instrument all the vertical oscillations of the bird.

Fig. 112 shows the arrangement that we have adopted. The mass of lead is applied directly to the membrane; some wire-work protects the upper surface of the apparatus from the friction of the feathers of the bird, which, without this precaution, might sometimes affect the form of the tracing.

FIG. 118.—Line 1. Tracing of a chronographic tuning-fork, making sixty vibrations in a second. Line 2. Vertical oscillations of a wild duck during flight. Line 3. Oscillations of the moor buzzard. Line 4. Those of the screech owl. Line 5. Those of the common buzzard.

After having convinced ourselves that the apparatus transmits faithfully the movements which are communicated to it, we connect it with the registering instrument by means of a long tube, and place it on the back of a bird, which is then allowed to fly. Experiments made on many different species, pigeons, wild ducks, buzzards, moor-buzzards, screech owls, have shown that there are very varied types of flight with respect to the intensity of the oscillations in the vertical plane.

Fig. 113 shows the tracings furnished by different species of birds. All these tracings, collected on a cylinder revolving with a constant rapidity, and referred to a chronographic tuning-fork vibrating 60 times in a second, enable us to ascertain the absolute and relative duration of the oscillations during the flight of different species of birds.

We find from this figure, that the frequency and amplitude of the vertical oscillations vary much according to the species of the bird. In order to ascertain the cause of each of these movements with greater accuracy, let us register at the same time the vertical oscillations of the bird, and the action of the muscles of the wing. If we make this double experiment on two birds which differ much in their manner of flight, such as the wild duck and the buzzard, we obtain the tracings represented in fig. 114.

The duck (upper line) presents at each elevation of its wing two energetic oscillations; that at *b*, at the moment when the wing is lowered, is easy to be understood, as well as that at *a*, at the moment that the wing begins to rise again. To explain the ascent of the bird during the time of the elevation of the wing, it seems indispensable to refer to the effect of the child's kite, to which we have before alluded. The bird having acquired a certain velocity, presents its wings to the air as inclined planes; an effect is immediately produced, similar to the ascent of the hovering apparatus which transform their acquired velocity into ascensional force. The flight of the buzzard shows also, but in a less degree, the ascent which accompanies the upward movement of the wing.

Determination of variations in the rapidity of flight.—The

second question which we have to solve relates to the determination of the various phases in the rapidity of flight. It
may receive its solution by the employment of the same
method. If the drum, loaded with a piece of lead, be placed
on the back of the bird so as to present its membrane in a
vertical plane—that is, at right angles to the direction of flight,

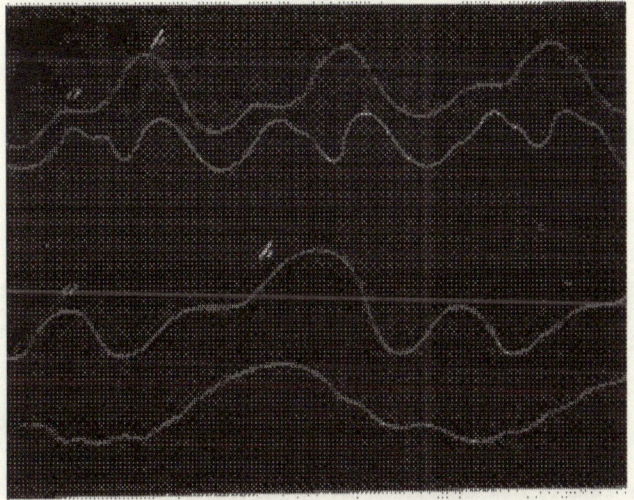

Fig. 114.—In the upper part we see, placed above each other, the muscular
tracing (see p. 232), and that of the vertical oscillations in a wild duck.
Under the undulation a, which shows the elevation of the wing, is seen a
vertical oscillation; another is seen under b, the tracing corresponding
with the depression of the wing. In the lower half of the figure are
tracings collected from a buzzard; the oscillation at o, which corresponds
with the elevation of the wing, is less marked than that from the duck.

the apparatus would be insensible to vertical oscillations, and
would only give the signal of those which are made backwards
and forwards. Let us turn the membrane of the drum in
front; it is evident that if the bird quickens its speed, the
retarding influence of the inertia of the mass of lead will
produce a pressure on the membrane of the drum; the air
will be compressed, and the registering lever will rise; while

the slackening of the bird's speed will cause a descent of the lever by an inverse action.

Experiments tried upon the species of birds before mentioned, have furnished us with tracings analogous with those of the vertical oscillations.

If it be true, as we have supposed, that the vertical oscillation of the bird, at the moment of the ascent of the wing, is due to the transformation of speed into elevation, we shall have the means of verifying this supposition, by collecting simultaneously the tracings of the vertical oscillations and those of the variations of rapidity.

Thus, by registering at the same time the two orders of oscillation in the flight of a buzzard, we find that the phase of depression of the wing produces at the same time the elevation of the bird and the acceleration of its horizontal swiftness. This effect is the natural consequence of the inclination of the plane of the wing at the moment of its descent; this we already know from having obtained it in the flight of the insect. As to the elevation of the wing, it is found that during the slight ascent which accompanies it, the swiftness of the bird diminishes. In fact, the curve of the variations of rapidity is depressed at the moment when the bird rises. This is, therefore, a confirmation of the theory which we have propounded concerning the transformation of the horizontal rapidity of the bird into ascensional force. Thus by this mechanism, the stroke of the descending wing produces the force which will cause the two oscillations of the bird in the vertical plane. It produces directly the ascent which is synchronous with it, and indirectly prepares the second vertical oscillation of the bird by creating rapidity.

Simultaneous tracing of the two orders of the oscillations of the bird.—Instead of representing separately the two kinds of oscillation executed by the bird as it flies, it is more instructive to seek to obtain a single curve representing together the movements which the body of the bird makes as it advances in space.

The method which we have employed to obtain the movements of the point of the wing may, with certain modifications, furnish the simultaneous tracing of the two orders of movement which we wish to investigate. For this purpose, the two drums combined rectangularly must be connected with the same inert mass.

Let us refer to fig. 97 (p. 237), where we see the two levers connected together and communicating with each other by tubes, which transmit to one all the movements executed by the other. When we give the first lever any kind of movement, we see it reproduced by the second lever in the same direction.

Now, let each of these levers be loaded with a piece of lead, and taking in our hand the support of the apparatus, let us cause it to describe any kind of movement in a plane perpendicular to the direction of the lever. We shall see that the lever No. 2 executes movements of exactly an opposite kind. In fact, since the motive force which acts on the membrane of the drums is nothing more than the inertia of the mass of lead, and the movements of this mass are always later than those given to the apparatus, it is clear that if we raise the whole system, the mass will keep the lever down, while if we lower the instrument the mass will retain the lever above; that if we carry it forward, the inertia will keep the lever back, &c. Therefore, the lever No. 2, only going through the same movements as No. 1, will give curves which will be absolutely opposed to the movement which has been given to the stand of the apparatus. This being assumed, let us pass to the experiment; for this, let us employ the apparatus represented in fig. 99 on the back of the buzzard as it flies; let us remove the rod which received the movements of the wing, as well as the parallelogram which transmitted them to the lever; we will only retain the lever fastened to the two drums, and the contrivance which fixes the whole instrument on the back of the buzzard; lastly, let us adapt a piece of lead to this lever, and let the bird fly. The tracing procured is represented in fig. 115. The analysis of this curve is at first sight extremely difficult; we hope, however, to succeed in showing its signification.

Analysis of the curve illustrating the oscillations of the bird.— This curve is described on the cylinder in the same manner as in fig. 100, which shows the different movements of the point of the wing; the glass plate moves from right to left; the tracing must be read from left to right. The head of the bird is turned towards the left, its flight is in the direction pointed out by the arrow.

We may divide this figure into a series of portions by means of vertical lines passing through homologous points, whether we let fall these perpendiculars from the top of the loops, or from that of the simple curves, as has been done at the points *a* and *c*. Each of these portions will enclose tolerably similar elements, with the exception of their unequal development in the different points of the figure: let us neglect this detail for the present.

It is evident that the periodical return of similar forms corresponds with the return of the same phases in a revolution of the bird's wing. The portion *a c* will, therefore, represent the different movements of the bird in one and the same revolution.

Let us remember that in the curves which we analyse, all the movements are contrary to those really performed by the bird. The

two vertical oscillations of the bird, the greater and the less, must thus be represented by two curves, of which the summit will be placed downwards. It is easy to recognise their existence in the large curve, *a b c*, and the smaller one *c d e*. The bird was, therefore, rising from *a* to *b*, descending from *b* to *c*; it rose again from *c* to *d*, and descended from *d* to *e*.

But these two oscillations encroach on each other, which produces the loop *c d*; the oscillation *c d e* partly covers the first by turning towards the head of the bird. Since the indications of the curve are in a direction contrary to the real motion, this is a proof that the bird, at this moment, was either carried backwards, or at least slackened the rapidity of its flight.

This figure, therefore, recalls all that the former experiments have taught us concerning the movements of the bird in space. We see from them, that at each revolution of its wing it rises twice, followed by two descents; that these oscillations are unequal: the larger one, as we know, corresponds with the lowering of the wing, the smaller one with its elevation. We see, also, that the ascent of the bird, while the wing is rising, is accompanied by the slackening of its speed, which justifies the theory that this re-ascent is made at the expense of the velocity acquired by the bird.

But this is not all: fig. 115 shows us, also, that the movements of the bird are not the same at the commencement as at the end of its flight. We have already seen (figs. 95 and 100) that the strokes of the wing at its departure are more extended; we see here that the oscillations produced at its departure by the descent of the wing (shown at the left hand of the figure) are also more extended. But theory enables us to foresee that the oscillation of the ascent of the wing, being produced by the velocity of the bird, must be very feeble at the commencement of its flight, when the bird has, as yet, but little rapidity. This figure shows us that this is actually the case, and that at the beginning of the flight, the second oscillation of the wing (that which forms the loop) is but slight.

We are now, therefore, in possession of the principal

notions on which may be established the mechanical theory of flight.

From all these experiments we may deduce that it is during the descent of the wing that the bird acquires all the motive force which sustains and directs it in space.

Theory of the flight of the bird.—On this subject, as on almost all those that belong to this discussion, nearly everything has been already said; so that we must not expect to find an entirely new theory arise from the experiments which have been described. In the works of Borelli we find the first correct idea of the mechanism of flight. The wing, says this writer, acts on the air like a wedge. Developing still farther the thought of the learned Neapolitan physiologist, we should now say that the wing of the bird acts on the air after the manner of an inclined plane, in order to produce a re-action against this resistance which impels the body of the bird upward and forward. This theory, confirmed by Strauss-Durkheim, has been completed by Lisis, who noticed the double action of the wing; first, that which in the phase of depression of this organ, raises the bird and gives it an impulse in a forward direction; then, the action of the ascending wing, which is guided in the same manner as a boy's kite, and sustains the body of the bird until the following stroke of the wing.

We have been reproached for relying on a theory which had its origin more than two centuries ago; we much prefer an old truth to the most modern error; therefore we must be allowed to render to the genius of Borelli the justice which is due to him, and only claim for ourselves the merit of having furnished the experimental demonstration of a truth already suspected.

But the theories which had been propounded up to the present time neglected many important parts which experiments reveal, and which we are about to endeavour to bring clearly forward.

Thus, the manner in which the change in the plane of the wing is effected in every part of the flight was necessary to be known, in order to explain the re-actions which tend always to sustain the body of the bird, sometimes by accelerating the rapidity of its flight, sometimes by slackening it.* Fig. 111 shows this change of plane.

As to the re-actions to which the body of the bird is subjected, experiment has clearly demonstrated them; it has furnished us with the means of estimating their absolute force. We have seen that these re-actions differ according to the species of bird which is observed. They are powerful and sudden in birds which have a small surface of wing; longer and more gentle in birds formed for hovering; the re-action of the period of the re-ascent of the wing disappears almost entirely in the latter kind.

If we could compare terrestrial locomotion with the flight of birds, and assimilate alternate with simultaneous movements, we might find certain analogies between the walk of man and the flight of the bird. In both, the body is urged forward by an intermittent impulse; man, like the bird, raises himself by borrowing the necessary *work* from the *dynamic energy* which he has acquired by his muscular efforts.

As to the estimation of the work expended in flight, we must, before we can undertake it, have a perfect knowledge of the resistance which the air presents to surfaces of every form, inclined at different angles, and possessing varied velocities. We only know as yet the movements of the wings;

---

* We ought to beg the reader to remark that the inclinations represented in fig. 111 are referred to a line which probably is not horizontal during flight. In fact, this line does not correspond with the axis of the body of the bird, for it was suspended in the apparatus by a corset placed behind its wings, and thus had its centre of gravity in front of the point of suspension, which caused its beak to hang slightly down. In free flight, on the contrary, the axis of the bird is horizontal—or rather turned somewhat upward. Restored to this proper position, a fresh direction would be given to each of the positions of the wing (fig. 111), which would alter them all by the same number of degrees. Then, probably, we should see that the wing always presents its lower surface to the air, as the only one which can find in it a point of resistance. This supposition requires for its verification some fresh experiments, which we hope to be soon able to make.

the resistance which they meet with in the air has yet to be determined. Our experiments on this subject are still being pursued. When once we have these two elements, the measure of work will be obtained from the resistance which is presented to the wing by the air at every instant, multiplied by the distance passed over. This will give us the measure of work brought to bear upon the air.

For its horizontal advance the bird will be obliged only to furnish the quantity of work equivalent to the resistance presented by the air in front of it, multiplied by the distance passed through. A part of this resistance, namely, that which is applied to the lower surface of the wing, is utilised to sustain the bird, by the kind of action which we have compared to that of a child's kite.

It appears that this action is of primary importance in the flight of the bird. In fact, among the researches on the resistance of the air there is one which we owe to Mons. du Louvrié, which seems to prove that if the wing make a very small angle with the horizon, nearly all the work obtained from the *dynamic energy* of the bird is employed to sustain it; according to this writer, an angle of 6° 30′ would be the most favourable to the utilisation of its energy. The important part played by the gliding of the wing upon the air seems also proved by the shape of that organ. The wing being alternately active when it strikes the air, and passive when it glides through it, is not, in all its parts, equally adapted to this double function.

When a surface strikes the air, it must move with rapidity in order to find resistance. Thus the wing, turning around the point by which it is attached to the body, shows unequal and gradually-increasing velocity in different points according as they are nearer to the body, so that being almost nothing at the point of attachment of the wing, the velocity will be very great at the free end.

Let us imagine the wing of an insect as large at the base as at the extremity; this size would be useless in the part nearest to the body, for the wing, at this point, has not sufficient rapidity to strike the air with effect. Thus we find, in the greater part of insects, the wing reduced to a strong

nervure towards its base. The membranous part commences
only at the point where rapidity of movement begins to be
of some use, and the membrane goes on increasing in breadth
till near the extremity of the wing. Such is (fig. 116) the
type of the wing essentially active—that is, intended only to
strike the air.

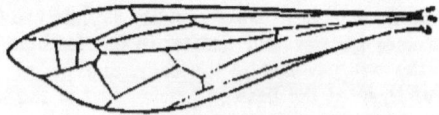

Fig. 116.—Wing of an insect.

In the bird, on the contrary, one of the phases of the
movement of the wing is, to a certain extent, passive; that
is to say, it receives the pressure of the air on its lower surface, when the bird is projected rapidly forward by its
acquired velocity. Under these conditions, the whole bird
being carried forward into space, all the parts of the wing
are moved with the same rapidity; the regions near to the
body are as useful as the others to take advantage of the
action of the air which presses on them as on a kite.

Fig. 117.—Active and passive parts of the bird's wing.

Thus, the base of the wing in the bird, far from being reduced, as in the insect, to a rigid but bare rib, is very wide,
and furnished with *feathers* and *wing coverts* which constitute
a large surface, under which the air presses with force, and
in a manner very efficacious to sustain the bird. Fig. 117
gives an idea of the arrangement of the wing of the bird, at
the same time active and passive.

The inner part, deprived of sufficient velocity, may be

considered, while it is being lowered, as the passive part of the
organ, while the external part, that which strikes the air, is
the active portion.

By its very great velocity, the point of the wing must meet
with more resistance from the air than any other part of this
organ; whence the extreme rigidity of the large feathers of
which it is formed.

The conditions of decreasing rapidity explain the flexibility
which becomes greater and greater in the feathers of those
parts of the wing nearer to the body, and at last the great
thinness of those at the base or passive part of the wing.

Let us add that the effect of the kite must be produced at
the base of the wing, even while the point strikes the air, so
that the bird, as soon as it has acquired its velocity, would
be constantly lightened of part of its weight, on account of
this inclined plane.

The reproduction of the mechanism of flight now occupies the
minds of many experimenters, and we hesitate not to own
that we have been sustained in this laborious analysis of the
different acts in the flight of the bird, by the assured hope of
being able to imitate, more or less imperfectly, this admirable
type of aërial locomotion. We have already met with some
success in our attempts, which have been interrupted during
the last two years.

Winged apparatus has been seen in our laboratory, which
when adapted to the frame-work which had held the bird,
gave it a rather rapid rotation. But this was only a very
imperfect imitation, which we hope shortly to improve.
Already a young and ingenious experimentalist, Mons.
Alphonse Pénaud, has obtained much more satisfactory results
in this direction. The problem of aërial locomotion, formerly
considered a Utopian scheme, is now approached in a truly
scientific manner.

The plan of the experiments to be made is all traced out :
they will consist in continually comparing the artificial instruments of flight with the real bird, by submitting them both
to the modes of analysis which we have described at such
length; the apparatus will, from time to time, be modified
till it is made to imitate these movements faithfully. For

this purpose we are about to undertake a new series of experiments; some new apparatus is being constructed, which will soon be finished.

We hope that we have proved to the reader that nothing is impossible in the analysis of the movements connected with the flight of the bird: he will no doubt be willing to allow that mechanism can always reproduce a movement, the nature of which has been clearly defined.

INDEX.

THE END.

A Classified Catalogue of

Henry S. King & Co.'s Publications.

CONTENTS.

HISTORY AND BIOGRAPHY.

MRS. GILBERT, FORMERLY ANN TAYLOR, AUTOBIO-GRAPHY AND OTHER MEMORIALS OF. By Josiah Gilbert, Author of "Cadore and the Titian Country," &c. In 2 vols. Post 8vo. With Steel Portrait, and several Wood Engravings.

A. B. GRANVILLE, M.D., F.R.S., &c., AUTOBIOGRAPHY OF. Edited, with a brief account of the concluding years of his life, by his youngest Daughter. 2 vols. Demy 8vo. With a Portrait. Price 32s.

SAMUEL LOVER, THE LIFE AND UNPUBLISHED WORKS OF. By Bayle Bernard. In 2 vols. Post 8vo. With a Steel Portrait.

THE LIFE & LETTERS of ROWLAND WILLIAMS, D.D., a Memoir of, with selections from his Note-books. Edited by Mrs. Rowland Williams. With a Photographic Portrait. In 2 vols. Large post 8vo.

WILLIAM GODWIN, AUTOBIOGRAPHY, MEMOIR, AND CORRESPONDENCE OF. 2 vols, demy 8vo. *(Preparing.)*

JOHN GREY (of Dilston), MEMOIRS OF. By his Daughter, Josephine Butler. New and Cheaper Edition.

A CLUSTER OF LIVES. Biographical Sketches. By Alice King. Crown 8vo, cloth.

POLITICAL WOMEN. By Sutherland Menzies. 2 vols. Post 8vo. 24s. "Has all the information of history, with all the interest that attaches to biography."—*Scotsman.*

Third Edition, Revised and Corrected. With Index.

SARA COLERIDGE, MEMOIR AND LETTERS OF. Edited by her Daughter. 2 vols. Crown 8vo. With 2 Portraits. Price 24s.

"Sara Coleridge, as she is revealed, or rather reveals herself, in the correspondence, makes a brilliant addition to a brilliant family reputation."—*Saturday Review.*

"These charming volumes are attracting as a memorial of a most amiable woman of high intellectual mark."—*Athenæum.*

HISTORY AND BIOGRAPHY—*continued.*

THE LATE REV. F. W. ROBERTSON, M.A., LIFE AND LETTERS OF. Edited by the Rev. Stopford Brooke, M.A., Chaplain in Ordinary to the Queen.

   I. In 2 vols., uniform with the Sermons. With a Steel Portrait. Price 7s. 6d.
   II. Library Edition, in demy 8vo, with Two Steel Portraits. Price 12s.
   III. A Popular Edition, in 1 vol. Price 6s.

NATHANIEL HAWTHORNE, A MEMOIR OF, with Stories now first published in this country. By H. A. Page. Large post 8vo. Price 7s. 6d.

   "Seldom has it been our lot to meet with a more appreciative delineation of character than this Memoir of Hawthorne."—*Morning Post.*

   "Exhibits a discriminating enthusiasm for one of the most fascinating of novelists."—*Saturday Review.*

LEONORA CHRISTINA, MEMOIRS OF, Daughter of Christian IV. of Denmark: Written during her Imprisonment in the Blue Tower of the Royal Palace at Copenhagen, 1663–1685. Translated by F. E. Bunnett. With an Autotype Portrait of the Princess. Medium 8vo. Price 12s. 6d.

   "A valuable addition to the tragic romance of history."—*Spectator.*

   "A valuable addition to history."—*Daily News.*

LIVES OF ENGLISH POPULAR LEADERS. No. 1.—STEPHEN LANGTON. By C. Edmund Maurice. Crown 8vo. Price 7s. 6d.

   "Very well and honestly executed."—*John Bull.*
   "In style it is characterised by the greatest fairness and ability, and the picture of the archbishop

   is vigorously and firmly drawn."—*Churchman's Shilling Magazine.*
   "Well worth a careful study."—*Jewish World.*

CABINET PORTRAITS. BIOGRAPHICAL SKETCHES OF STATESMEN OF THE DAY. By T. Wemyss Reid. 1 vol. Crown 8vo. Price 7s. 6d.

   "We have never met with a work which we can more unreservedly praise. The sketches are absolutely impartial."—*Athenæum.*

   "We can heartily commend this work."—*Standard.*
   "Drawn with a master hand."—*Yorkshire Post.*

THE CHURCH AND THE EMPIRES: Historical Periods. By the late Henry W. Wilberforce. Preceded by a Memoir of the Author by John Henry Newman, D.D., of the Oratory. Post 8vo. With Portrait. 10s. 6d.

   "The literary relics presented by Dr. Newman are varied in subject and in character. They comprise an eloquent, though somewhat empirical, treatise on the formation of Christendom; two masterly reviews of Champagny's too little known

   works. ... Henry William Wilberforce was a man of strong opinions, and in all he wrote gave expression to the judgments of a powerful, if possibly an undetermined mind."—*Standard.*

HISTORY OF THE ENGLISH REVOLUTION OF 1688. By C. D. Yonge, Regius Professor, Queen's Coll., Belfast. Crown 8vo. Price 6s.

   "A fair, succinct, useful, and modestly written of the main causes, circumstances, and history of

   the Revolution, and not without some striking comments on its effects."—*Standard.*

ALEXIS DE TOCQUEVILLE. Correspondence and Conversations with Nassau W. Senior, from 1833 to 1859. Edited by M. C. M. Simpson. In 2 vols. Large post 8vo. Price 21s.

   "A book replete with knowledge and thought."—*Quarterly Review.*

   "An extremely interesting book."—*Saturday Review.*

JOURNALS KEPT IN FRANCE AND ITALY. From 1848 to 1852. With a Sketch of the Revolution of 1848. By the late Nassau William Senior. Edited by his Daughter, M. C. M. Simpson. In 2 vols. Post 8vo. Price 24s.

   "The book has a genuine historical value."—*Saturday Review.*
   "No better, more honest, and more readable

   view of the state of political society during the existence of the second Republic could well be looked for."—*Examiner.*

PERSIA; ANCIENT AND MODERN. By John Piggot, F.S.A. Post 8vo. Price 10s. 6d.

   "A very useful book."—*Mark.*
   "That Mr. Piggot has spared no pains or research in the execution of his work is apparent in the list of authorities, classic and modern, which he

   continually quotes; his style also, when not recounting history, is lively and pleasant, and the anecdotes which he culls from the writings of travellers are frequently amusing."—*Hour.*

HISTORY AND BIOGRAPHY—*continued.*

New Edition Revised.

THE HISTORY OF JAPAN. From the Earliest Period to the Present Time. By Francis Ottiwell Adams, H.B.M.'s Secretary of Embassy at Berlin, formerly H.B.M.'s Chargé d'Affaires, and Secretary of Legation at Yedo. Volume I. Demy 8vo. With Map and Plans. Price 21s.

"He translates his facts with skill and judgment; and he writes with an elegance worthy of a very skilful craftsman in literary work. . . We hope Mr. Adams will not keep the public long waiting the second volume, for the appearance of which all who read the first will anxiously look."—*Standard.*

"As a diplomatic study, and as referring to a deeply interesting episode in contemporary history, it is well worth reading. The information it contains is trustworthy, and is carefully compiled, and the style is all that can be desired."—*Saturday Review.*

"A most valuable contribution to our knowledge of an interesting people."—*Examiner.*

THE HISTORY OF JAPAN. Volume II. completing the Work. By F. O. Adams. From the year 1865 to present time. Demy 8vo. with Map. Price 21s. *Preparing.*

THE NORMAN PEOPLE, AND THEIR EXISTING DESCENDANTS IN THE BRITISH DOMINIONS AND THE UNITED STATES OF AMERICA. 8vo. Price 21s.

"A very singular work. . . We do not accept the consequences to their full extent, but we can cordially recommend the volume as one which is emphatically extraordinary."—*Notes and Queries.*

"The author has given us a valuable list of mediæval surnames, and their origin which demands our best gratitude."—*Standard.*

THE RUSSIANS IN CENTRAL ASIA. A Critical Examination, down to the present time, of the Geography and History of Central Asia. By Baron F. von Hellwald. Translated by Lieut.-Col. Theodore Wirgman, LL.B. In 1 vol. Large post 8vo, with Map. Price 12s.

"A learned account of the geography of this still little known land, of the characteristics of its main divisions, of the nature and habits of its numerous races, and of the progress through it of Russian influence. . . It contains a large amount of valuable information."—*Times.*

"A lucidly written, and apparently accurate account of Turkestan, its geographical features and its history. Its worth to the reader is further enhanced by a well-executed map, based on the most recent Russian surveys."—*Glasgow News.*

BOKHARA: ITS HISTORY AND CONQUEST. By Professor Arminius Vámbéry, of the University of Pesth, Author of "Travels in Central Asia," &c. Demy 8vo. Price 18s.

"We conclude with a cordial recommendation of this valuable book."—*Saturday Review.*

"Almost every page abounds with composition of peculiar merit."—*Morning Post.*

THE RELIGIOUS HISTORY OF IRELAND: PRIMITIVE, PAPAL, AND PROTESTANT: including the Evangelical Missions, Catholic Agitations, and Church Progress of the last half Century. By James Godkin, Author of "Ireland: her Churches," &c. 1 vol. 8vo. Price 12s.

"These latter chapters on the statistics of the various religious denominations will be welcomed."—*Evening Standard.*

"Mr. Godkin writes with evident honesty, and the topic on which he writes is one about which an honest book is greatly wanted."—*Examiner.*

THE GOVERNMENT OF THE NATIONAL DEFENCE. From the 30th June to the 31st October, 1870. The Plain Statement of a Member. By Mons. Jules Favre. 1 vol. Demy 8vo. Price 10s. 6d.

"A work of the highest interest. The book is most valuable."—*Athenæum.*

"Of all the contributions to the history of the late war, we have found none more fascinating and,

perhaps, none more valuable than the 'apology,' by M. Jules Favre, for the unsuccessful Government of the National Defence."—*Times.*

ECHOES OF A FAMOUS YEAR. By Harriet Parr, Author of "The Life of Jeanne d'Arc," "In the Silver Age," &c. Crown 8vo. Price 8s. 6d.

"Miss Parr has the great gift of charming simplicity of style; and if children are not interested in her book, many of their seniors will be."—*British Quarterly Review.*

VOYAGES AND TRAVEL.

SOME TIME IN IRELAND; A Recollection. Crown 8vo. 7s. 6d.

"The author has got a genuine Irish gift of | The little volume will give to strangers a more
wit, and graceful writing, and has produced a | faithful idea of Irish society and tendencies will
clever and entertaining book."—*Examiner.* | working in that unhappy island than any other we
"Clever, brilliant sketches of life and character | know.—*Literary Churchman.*
among the Irish gentry of the last generation. .

WAYSIDE NOTES IN SCANDINAVIA. Being Notes of Travel in the North of Europe. By **Mark Antony Lower**, F.S.A., M.A. Crown 8vo. 9s.

⁎⁎ This Volume is an Account of Researches prosecuted, during a Tour in Scandinavia, in the Summer of 1873. It contains illustrations of the History, Antiquities, Legendary Lore, and Social Condition of Denmark, Sweden, and Norway, from Ancient to Modern Times.

ON THE ROAD TO KHIVA. By **David Ker**, late Khivan Correspondent of the *Daily Telegraph.* Illustrated with Photographs of the Country and its Inhabitants, and a copy of the Official Map in use during the Campaign, from the Survey of CAPTAIN LEUSILIN. 1 vol. Post 8vo. Price 12s.

"Though it is a graphic and thoughtful sketch, | "Very interesting reading . . . a really good
we refer to it, in some degree, for reasons apart | book full of quaint, vivid writing."—*Echo.*
from its intrinsic merits. . . He (the author) has | "He is a clever and decent writer. . . The book
satisfied us that he was not the impudent impostor | is smartly written."—*Saturday Review.*
he seemed to be; and though he did not witness | "A pleasant book of travels. It is exceedingly
the fall of Khiva, he travelled through a great | smart and clever, full of amusing anecdotes and
part of Central Asia, and honestly tried to accom- | graphic descriptions."—*Vanity Fair.*
plish his task. . . His work, we have said, is an | "Mr. Ker knows Russian peasant life very well
able résumé of genuine observation and reflection, | indeed, and his little about the Cossacks are full of
which will well repay a reader's attention."— | character."—*Athenæum.*
Times.

VIZCAYA; or, Life in the Land of the Carlists at the Outbreak of the Insurrection, with some account of the Iron Mines and other characteristics of the country. With a Map and 8 Illustrations. Crown 8vo. Price 9s.

"A neat and chatty little volume."—*Hour.* | scriptions of ordinary Spanish life are extremely
"A pleasant little volume . . . evidently | graphic."—*Liverpool Albion.*
genuine and accurate. . The author's de-

ROUGH NOTES OF A VISIT TO BELGIUM, SEDAN, AND PARIS, in September, 1870-71. By **John Ashton**. Crown 8vo. Price 3s. 6d.

"The author does not attempt to deal with mili- | forward simplicity with which it is written."—
tary subjects, but writes sensibly of what he saw in | *Graphic.*
1870-71."—*John Bull.* | "An interesting work by a highly intelligent ob-
"Possesses a certain freshness from the straight- | server."—*Standard.*

THE ALPS OF ARABIA; or, Travels through Egypt, Sinai, Arabia, and the Holy Land. By **William Charles Maughan.** Demy 8vo. with Map. 12s.

"Deeply interesting and valuable."—*Edinburgh* | "Very readable and instructive. . . . . A work
Review. | far above the average of such publications."—
"He writes freshly and with competent know- | *John Bull.*
ledge."—*Standard.*

THE MISHMEE HILLS: an Account of a Journey made in an Attempt to Penetrate Thibet from Assam, to open New Routes for Commerce. By **T. T. Cooper**, Author of "The Travels of a Pioneer of Commerce." Demy 8vo. With Four Illustrations and Map. Price 10s. 6d.

"The volume, which will be of great use in India | It is especially rich in sporting incidents."—
and among Indian merchants here, contains a good | *Standard.*
deal of matter that will interest ordinary readers.

GOODMAN'S, CUBA THE PEARL OF THE ANTILLES. By **Walter Goodman**. Crown 8vo. Price 7s. 6d.

"A series of vivid and miscellaneous sketches. | "The whole book deserves the heartiest com-
We can recommend this whole volume as very | mendation. . . . sparkling and amusing from be-
amusing reading."—*Pall Mall Gazette.* | ginning to end."—*Spectator.*

VOYAGES AND TRAVEL—*continued.*

FIELD AND FOREST RAMBLES OF A NATURALIST IN NEW BRUNSWICK.
With Notes and Observations on the Natural History of Eastern Canada. By **A. Leith Adams, M.A.** 8vo, cloth. Illustrated. 14*s.*

"Both sportsmen and naturalists will find this work replete with anecdote and carefully-recorded observation, which will entertain them."—*Nature.*
"Will be found interesting by those who take a | pleasure either in sport or natural history."—*Athenæum.*
"To the naturalist the book will be now valuable. . . . To the general reader most interesting."—*Evening Standard.*

ROUND THE WORLD IN 1870.
A Volume of Travels, with Maps. By **A. D. Carlisle, B.A.,** Trin. Coll., Camb. Demy 8vo. Price 16*s.*

"We can only commend, which we do very heartily, an eminently sensible and readable book."—*British Quarterly Review.*
"Mr. Carlisle's account of his little outing is exhilarating and charming."—*Spectator.*
"Rarely have we read a more graphic description of the countries named, India, China, Japan, California, and South America . . . The chapters about Japan are especially replete with information."—*John Bull.*

Third Edition. Revised and Corrected.

TENT LIFE WITH ENGLISH GIPSIES IN NORWAY.
By **Hubert Smith.** In 8vo, cloth. Five full-page Engravings, and 31 smaller Illustrations, with Map of the Country showing Routes. Price 21*s.*

"Written in a very lively style, and has throughout a smack of dry humour and satiric reflection which shows the writer to be a keen observer of | men and things. We hope that many will read it and feel in it the same amusement as ourselves."—*Times.*

FAYOUM; OR, ARTISTS IN EGYPT.
A Tour with M. Gérôme and others. By **J. Lenoir.** Crown 8vo, cloth. With 13 Illustrations. Price 3*s.* 6*d.*

"The book is very amusing. . . . Whoever may take it up will find he has with him a bright and pleasant companion."—*Spectator.*
"A pleasantly written and very readable book."—*Examiner.*

SPITZBERGEN—THE GATEWAY TO THE POLYNIA; OR, A VOYAGE TO SPITZBERGEN.
By **Captain John C. Wells, R.N.** 8vo, cloth. With numerous Illustrations and Map. Price 21*s.*

"Straightforward and clear in style, securing our confidence by its unaffected simplicity and good sense."—*Saturday Review.*
"A charming book, remarkably well written and well illustrated."—*Standard.*

AN AUTUMN TOUR IN THE UNITED STATES AND CANADA.
By **Lieut.-Col. J. G. Medley.** Crown 8vo. Price 5*s.*

"Colonel Medley's little volume is a pleasantly written account of a two months' visit to America."—*Hour.*
"May be recommended as manly, sensible, and pleasantly written."—*Globe.*

Second Edition.

THE NILE WITHOUT A DRAGOMAN.
By **Frederic Eden.** In 1 vol. Crown 8vo, cloth. Price 7*s.* 6*d.*

"Should any of our readers care to imitate Mr. Eden's example, and wish to see things with their own eyes, and shift for themselves, next winter in | Upper Egypt, they will find this book a very agreeable guide."—*Times.*
"It is a book to read during an autumn holiday."—*Spectator.*

IRELAND.
A Tour of Observation, with Remarks on Irish Public Questions. By **Dr. James Macaulay.** Crown 8vo. Price 7*s.* 6*d.*

"We have rarely met a book on Ireland which for impartiality of criticism and general accuracy of information could be so well recommended to the Liberal-minded Irish reader."—*Evening Standard.*
"A careful and instructive book. Full of facts, full of information, and full of interest."—*Literary Churchman.*

A WINTER IN MOROCCO.
By **Amelia Perrier.** Crown 8vo. With 4 Illustrations. Price 10*s.* 6*d.*

"Well worth reading, and contains several excellent illustrations."—*Hour.*
"Miss Perrier is a very amusing writer. She has a good deal of humour, sees the oddity and quaint- | ness of Oriental life with a quick observant eye, and evidently turned her opportunities of sarcastic examination to account."—*Daily News.*

SCIENCE.

EUCLID SIMPLIFIED IN METHOD AND LANGUAGE. Being a Manual of Geometry on the French System. By J. R. Morell.

The chief features of the work are :—The separation of Theorems and Problems—The Natural Sequence of reasoning ; areas being treated by themselves and at a later page— The simpler and more natural treatment of ratio—The legitimate use of arithmetical applications, of transposition, and superposition—The general alteration of language to a more modern form—Lastly, if it be assumed to be venturesome to supersede the time-hallowed pages of Euclid it may be urged that this attempt is made under the shelter of very high authorities.

THE PHYSICS AND PHILOSOPHY OF THE SENSES ; OR THE MENTAL AND THE PHYSICAL IN THE MUTUAL RELATION. By R. S. Wyld, F.R.S.E. Illustrated by Several Plates.

The author's object is twofold : first, to supply a Manual of the Senses, embracing the more important discoveries of recent times ; second, in discussing the subject of Life, Organisation, Sensibility, and Thought, to demonstrate in opposition to the materialistic Theory, that the Senses, no less than Reason, furnish proof that an immaterial and spiritual element is the operative element in nature.

THE QUESTIONS OF AURAL SURGERY. By James Hinton, late Aural Surgeon to Guy's Hospital. Post 8vo. Price 12s. 6d.

AN ATLAS OF DISEASES OF THE MEMBRANA TYMPANI. With Descriptive Text. By James Hinton, late Aural Surgeon to Guy's Hospital. Post 8vo. Price £6 6s.

PHYSIOLOGY FOR PRACTICAL USE. By various Writers. Edited by James Hinton. 2 vols. Crown 8vo. With 50 Illustrations. Price 12s. 6d.

"A more clear, valuable, and well-informed set of treatises we never saw than these, which are bound up into two compact and readable volumes. And they are pleasant reading, too, as well as useful reading."—*Literary Churchman.*

"We can heartily recommend these instructive essays to our readers, being sure that no one who begins them will lay them down without having gained some knowledge."—*Liverpool Albion.*

"We never saw the popular side of the science

of physiology better explained than it is in these two thin volumes."—*Standard.*

"It has certainly been edited with great care. Physiological treatises we have had in great number, but not one work, we believe, which so thoroughly appeals to all classes of the community as the present. Everything has apparently been done to render the work really practical and useful."—*Civil Service Gazette.*

THE PRINCIPLES OF MENTAL PHYSIOLOGY. With their Applications to the Training and Discipline of the Mind, and the Study of its Morbid Conditions. By W. B. Carpenter, LL.D., M.D., F.R.S., &c. 8vo. Illustrated. Price 12s.

". . . We have not dealt with the two main views elaborated in this valuable book, from the first of which, together with the inferences which Dr. Carpenter draws as to the sources of our knowledge of necessary truth, we mainly dissent, but with the latter of which we cordially agree. Let us add that nothing we have said, or in any limited space could say, would give no adequate

conception of the valuable and curious collection of facts bearing on morbid mental conditions, the learned physiological exposition, and the treasure-house of useful hints for mental training which make this large and yet very amusing, as well as instructive book, an encyclopædia of well-classified and often very startling psychological experiences."—*Spectator.*

SENSATION AND INTUITION. By James Sully. Demy 8vo. 10s. 6d.

"Though the series of essays is by no means devoid of internal connection, each presents so many new points of interest that it is impossible here to note more than one or two particulars. The first essay of all, wherein the author considers the relation of the Evolution-hypothesis to human

psychology, may be cited as an excellent specimen of his style of work."—*Examiner.*

". . . In conclusion, we beg to thank Mr. Sully for a meritorious and successful attempt to popularise valuable and not very tractable departments of science."—*Academy.*

Second Edition.

THE EXPANSE OF HEAVEN. A Series of Essays on the Wonders of the Firmament. By R. A. Proctor, B.A. With a Frontispiece. Crown 8vo. 6s.

"A very charming work ; cannot fail to lift the reader's mind up through nature's work to nature's God."—*Standard.*

"Full of thought, readable, and popular."—*Brighton Gazette.*

SCIENCE—*continued.*

STUDIES OF BLAST FURNACE PHENOMENA. By **M. L.
Gruner.** Translated by **L. D. B. Gordon, F.R.S.E., F.G.S.** Demy 8vo.
Price 7s. 6d.

" The whole subject is dealt with very copiously | appreciation at the hands of practical men, for
and clearly in all its parts, and can scarcely fail of | whose use it is designed."—*Iron.*

Second Edition Revised.

A LEGAL HANDBOOK FOR ARCHITECTS. By Edward
Jenkins and John Raymond, Esqrs., Barristers-at-Law. Crown 8vo. 6s.

" We can confidently recommend this book to all | "Architects, builders, and especially the building
engaged in the building trades."—*Edinburgh* | public, will find the volume very useful."—*Freeman's
Daily Review.* | *Journal.*

CONTEMPORARY ENGLISH PSYCHOLOGY. From the French of
Professor Th. Ribot. Large post 8vo. Price 9s. An Analysis of the Views and
Opinions of the following Metaphysicians, as expressed in their writings :—

James Mill, Alexander Bain, John Stuart Mill, George H. Lewes, Herbert
Spencer, Samuel Bailey.

" The task which M. Ribot set himself he has | "We can cordially recommend the volume."—
performed with very great success."—*Examiner.* | *Journal of Mental Science.*

**HEREDITY : a Psychological Study on its Phenomena, its Laws, its Causes,
and its Consequences.** By **Th. Ribot,** Author of " Contemporary English Psychology."
1 vol. Large crown 8vo.

It is generally admitted that "Heredity '—or | devotes his work to the study of the question.
that biological law which all living creature tend | " Does the law also hold in regard to the mental
to reproduce themselves in their descendants—is | faculties?"
the rule in all forms of vital activity. The author |

THE HISTORY OF CREATION, a Popular Account of the Develop-
ment of the Earth and its Inhabitants, according to the theories of Kant, Laplace,
Lamarck, and Darwin. By **Professor Ernst Haeckel,** of the University of Jena.
Translated by E. Ray Lankester, M.D., &c. With Coloured Plates and
Genealogical Trees of the various groups of both plants and animals. 2 vols. Post 8vo.
[*Preparing.*

A New Edition.

CHANGE OF AIR AND SCENE. A Physician's Hints about Doctors,
Patients, Hygiene, and Society : with Notes of Excursion for health in the Pyrenees,
and amongst the Watering-places of France (Inland and Seaward), Switzerland, Corsica,
and the Mediterranean. By **Dr. Alphonse Donne.** Large post 8vo. Price 9s.

"A very readable and serviceable book . . . . | taken on the continents for their mineral waters."
The real value of it is to be found in the accurate | —*Pall Mall Gazette.*
and minute information given with regard to a | " A singularly pleasant and chatty as well as
large number of places which have gained a repu- | instructive book about health."—*Guardian.*

New and Enlarged Edition.

MISS YOUMANS' FIRST BOOK OF BOTANY. Designed to
cultivate the observing powers of Children. With 300 Engravings. Crown 8vo. Price 5s.

" It is but rarely that a school-book appears | First Book of Botany . . . . It has been everywhere
which is at once so novel in plan, so successful in | welcomed as a timely and invaluable contribution
execution, and so suited to the general want, as to | to the improvement of primary education."—*Bell
command universal and unqualified approbation, | Mall Gazette.*
but such has been the case with Miss Youmans' |

A DICTIONARY AND GLOSSARY OF THE KO-RAN. With
copious Grammatical References and Explanations of the Text. By **Major J.
Penrice, B.A.** 4to. Price 21s.

"The book is likely to answer its purpose in smoothing a beginner's road in reading the
Ko-ran."—*Academy.*

MODERN GOTHIC ARCHITECTURE. By T. G. Jackson.
Crown 8vo. Price 5s.

" The reader will find some of the most impor- | "This thoughtful little book is worthy of the
tant doctrines of eminent art teachers practically | perusal of all interested in art or architecture."
applied in this little book, which is well written and | —*Standard.*
popular in style."—*Manchester Examiner.*

A TREATISE ON RELAPSING FEVER. By R. T. Lyons,
Assistant-Surgeon, Bengal Army. Post 8vo. Price 7s. 6d.

" A practical work, thoroughly supported in its views by a series of remarkable cases."—*Standard.*

SCIENCE—*continued.*

WORKS BY DR. EDWARD SMITH.

I. HEALTH AND DISEASE, as influenced by the Daily, Seasonal, and other Cyclical Changes in the Human System. A New Edition. Price 7s. 6d.

II. FOODS. Third Edition. Profusely Illustrated. Price 5s.

III. PRACTICAL DIETARY FOR FAMILIES, SCHOOLS, AND THE LABOURING CLASSES. A New Edition. Price 3s. 6d.

IV. CONSUMPTION IN ITS EARLY AND REMEDIABLE STAGES. A New Edition. Price 7s. 6d.

CHOLERA: HOW TO AVOID AND TREAT IT. Popular and Practical Notes by Henry Blanc, M.D. Crown 8vo. Price 4s. 6d.

"A very practical manual, based on experience and careful observation, full of excellent hints on a most dangerous disease."—*Standard.*

THE INTERNATIONAL SCIENTIFIC SERIES.

Fourth Edition.

I. THE FORMS OF WATER IN CLOUDS AND RIVERS, ICE AND GLACIERS. By J. Tyndall, LL.D., F.R.S. With 26 Illustrations. Crown 8vo. Price 5s.

Second Edition.

II. PHYSICS AND POLITICS; OR, THOUGHTS ON THE APPLICATION OF THE PRINCIPLES OF "NATURAL SELECTION" AND "INHERITANCE" TO POLITICAL SOCIETY. By Walter Bagehot. Crown 8vo. Price 4s.

Third Edition.

III. FOODS. By Dr. Edward Smith. Profusely Illustrated. Price 5s.

Third Edition.

IV. MIND AND BODY: THE THEORIES OF THEIR RELATIONS. By Alexander Bain, LL.D., Professor of Logic at the University of Aberdeen. With Four Illustrations. Price 4s.

Third Edition.

V. THE STUDY OF SOCIOLOGY. By Herbert Spencer. Crown 8vo. Price 5s.

Third Edition.

VI. ON THE CONSERVATION OF ENERGY. By Professor Balfour Stewart. With Fourteen Engravings. Price 5s.

Second Edition.

VII. ANIMAL LOCOMOTION; or, Walking, Swimming, and Flying. By J. B. Pettigrew, M.D., F.R.S. With 119 Illustrations. Price 5s.

Second Edition.

VIII. RESPONSIBILITY IN MENTAL DISEASE. By Dr. Henry Maudsley. Price 5s.

Second Edition.

IX. THE NEW CHEMISTRY. By Professor Josiah P. Cooke, of the Harvard University. With Thirty-one Illustrations. Price 5s.

Second Edition.

X. THE SCIENCE OF LAW. By Professor Sheldon Amos. Price 5s.

XI. ANIMAL MECHANICS. A Treatise on Terrestrial and Aerial Locomotion. By E. J. Marey. With 117 Illustrations. Price 5s.

XII. THE CHEMISTRY OF LIGHT AND PHOTOGRAPHY. By Professor Vogel (Polytechnic Academy of Berlin).

XIII. ON PARASITES IN THE ANIMAL KINGDOM. By Mons. Van. Beneden.

XIV. THE THEORY OF DESCENT AND DARWINISM. By Professor Oscar Schmidt (Strasburg University).   [*In the Press.*

SCIENCE—*continued.*

FORTHCOMING VOLUMES.

Prof. LOMMEL (University of Erlangen).
Optics. [*In the Press.*]

Rev. M. J. BERKELEY, M.A., F.L.S., and M. COOKE, M.A., LL.D.
Fungi; their Nature, Influence, and Uses. [*In the Press.*]

Prof. W. KINGDOM CLIFFORD, M.A.
The First Principles of the Exact Sciences explained to the non-mathematical.

Prof. T. H. HUXLEY, LL.D., F.R.S.
Bodily Motion and Consciousness.

Dr. W. B. CARPENTER, LL.D., F.R.S.
The Physical Geography of the Sea.

Prof. WILLIAM ODLING, F.R.S.
The Old Chemistry viewed from the New Standpoint.

W. LAUDER LINDSAY, M.D., F.R.S.E.
Mind in the Lower Animals.

Sir JOHN LUBBOCK, Bart., F.R.S.
The Antiquity of Man.

Prof. W. T. THISELTON DYER, B.A., B.SC.
Form and Habit in Flowering Plants.

Mr. J. N. LOCKYER, F.R.S.
Spectrum Analysis.

Prof. MICHAEL FOSTER, M.D.
Protoplasm and the Cell Theory.

Prof. W. STANLEY JEVONS.
Money: and the Mechanism of Exchange.

H. CHARLTON BASTIAN, M.D., F.R.S.
The Brain as an Organ of Mind.

Prof. A. C. RAMSAY, LL.D., F.R.S.
Earth Sculpture: Hills, Valleys, Mountains, Plains, Rivers, Lakes; how they were produced, and how they have been Destroyed.

Prof. RUDOLPH VIRCHOW (Berlin Univ.)
Morbid Physiological Action.

Prof. CLAUDE BERNARD.
Physical and Metaphysical Phenomena of Life.

Prof. H. SAINTE-CLAIRE DEVILLE.
An Introduction to General Chemistry.

Prof. WURTZ.
Atoms and the Atomic Theory.

Prof. DE QUATREFAGES.
The Negro Races.

Prof. LACAZE-DUTHIERS.
Zoology since Cuvier.

Prof. BERTHELOT.
Chemical Synthesis.

Prof. J. ROSENTHAL.
General Physiology of Muscles and Nerves.

Prof. JAMES D. DANA, M.A., LL.D.
On Cephalization; or, Head-Characters in the Gradation and Progress of Life.

Prof. S. W. JOHNSON, M.A.
On the Nutrition of Plants.

Prof. AUSTIN FLINT, Jr. M.D.
The Nervous System and its Relation to the Bodily Functions.

Prof. W. D. WHITNEY.
Modern Linguistic Science.

Prof. BERNSTEIN (University of Halle).
Physiology of the Senses.

Prof. FERDINAND COHN (Breslau Univ.).
Thallophytes (Algæ, Lichens, Fungi).

Prof. HERMANN (University of Zurich).
Respiration.

Prof. LEUCKART (University of Leipsic).
Outlines of Animal Organization.

Prof. LIEBREICH (University of Berlin).
Outlines of Toxicology.

Prof. KUNDT (University of Strasburg).
On Sound.

Prof. REES (University of Erlangen).
On Parasitic Plants.

Prof. STEINTHAL (University of Berlin).
Outlines of the Science of Language.

P. BERT (Professor of Physiology, Paris).
Forms of Life and other Cosmical Conditions.

E. ALGLAVE (Professor of Constitutional and Administrative Law at Douai, and of Political Economy at Lille).
The Primitive Elements of Political Constitutions.

P. LORAIN (Professor of Medicine, Paris).
Modern Epidemics.

Prof. SCHÜTZENBERGER (Director of the Chemical Laboratory at the Sorbonne).
On Fermentations.

Mons. FREIDEL.
The Functions of Organic Chemistry.

Mons. DEBRAY.
Precious Metals.

Mons. ALFRED GRANDIDIER.
Madagascar.

ESSAYS AND LECTURES.

A CLUSTER OF LIVES. By Alice King, Author of "Queen of Herself," &c. Crown 8vo.

CONTENTS.—Vittoria Colonna—Madame Récamier—A Daughter of the Stuarts—Dante—Madame de Sévigné—Geoffrey Chaucer—Edmund Spenser—Captain Cook's Companion—Ariosto—Lucrezia Borgia—Petrarch—Cervantes—Joan of Arc—Galileo—Madame Cottin—Song of the Bird in the Garden of Armida.

Second Edition.

IN STRANGE COMPANY; or, The Note Book of a Roving Correspondent. By James Greenwood, "The Amateur Casual." Crown 8vo. 6s.

"A bright, lively book."—*Standard.*
"Has all the interest of romance."—*Queen.*

"Some of the papers remind us of Charles Lamb on beggars and chimney-sweeps."—*Echo.*

MASTER-SPIRITS. By Robert Buchanan. Post 8vo. 10s. 6d.

"Good Books are the precious life-blood of Master-Spirits."—*Milton.*

"Full of fresh and vigorous writing, such as can only be produced by a man of keen and independent intellect."—*Saturday Review.*
"Written with a beauty of language and a spirit of vigorous enthusiasm rare even in our best living word-painters."—*Standard.*

"A very pleasant and readable book."—*Examiner.*
"Mr. Buchanan is a writer whose books the critics may always open with satisfaction ... both manly and artistic."—*Hour.*

GLANCES AT INNER ENGLAND. A Lecture delivered in the United States and Canada. By Edward Jenkins, M.P., Author of "Ginx's Baby," &c. Crown 8vo. Price 5s.

"These 'glances' exhibit much of the author's characteristic discrimination and judgment."—*Edinburgh Courant.*
"Cleverly written, full of terse adages and

raplerlike epigram it is a thoughtful and just it is in many respects."—*Echo.*
"Eloquent and epigrammatic."—*Illustrated Review.*

SHORT LECTURES ON THE LAND LAWS. Delivered before the Working Men's College. By T. Lean Wilkinson. Crown 8vo, limp cloth. 2s.

"A very handy and intelligible epitome of the general principles o existing land laws."—*Standard.*

AN ESSAY ON THE CULTURE OF THE OBSERVING POWERS OF CHILDREN, especially in connection with the Study of Botany. By Eliza A. Youmans. Edited, with Notes and a Supplement, by Joseph Payne, F.C.P., Author of "Lectures on the Science and Art of Education," &c. Crown 8vo, 2s. 6d.

"This study, according to her just notions on the subject, is to be fundamentally based on the exercise of the pupil's own powers of observation. He is to see and examine the properties of plants and

flowers at first hand, not merely to be informed of what others have seen and examined."—*Pall Mall Gazette.*

THE GENIUS OF CHRISTIANITY UNVEILED. Being Essays by William Godwin, Author of "Political Justice," &c. Never before published. 1 vol. Crown 8vo. 7s. 6d.

"Few have thought more clearly and directly than William Godwin, or expressed their reflections with more simplicity and unreserve."—*Examiner.*

"The deliberate thoughts of Godwin deserve to be put before the world for reading and consideration."—*Athenæum.*

MILITARY WORKS.

RUSSIA'S ADVANCE EASTWARD. Based on the Official Reports of Lieutenant Hugo Stumm, German Military Attaché to the Khivan Expedition. To which is appended other Information on the Subject, and a Minute Account of the Russian Army. By **Captain C. E. H. Vincent, F.R.G.S.** Crown 8vo. With Map. 6s.

THE VOLUNTEER, THE MILITIAMAN, AND THE REGULAR SOLDIER; a Conservative View of the Armies of England, Past, Present, and Future, as Seen in January, 1874. By **A Public School Boy.** 1 vol. Crown 8vo. Price 5s.

THE OPERATIONS OF THE GERMAN ENGINEERS AND TECHNICAL TROOPS IN THE FRANCO-GERMAN WAR OF 1870-71. By Capt. **A. von Goetze.** Translated by Col. **G. Graham.**   [*In the Press*

THE OPERATIONS OF THE FIRST ARMY, UNDER GEN. VON STEINMETZ. By **Major von Schell.** Translated by **Captain E. O. Hollist.** Demy 8vo. Uniform with the other volumes in the Series. Price 10s. 6d.

"A very complete and important account of the investment of Metz."

"The volume is of somewhat too technical a character to be recommended to the general reader, but the military student will find it a valuable and important contribution to the history of the great struggle; and its utility is increased by a capital general map of the operations of the First Army, and also plans of Spicheren and of the battle-field round Metz."—*Morning Advertiser.*

THE OPERATIONS OF THE FIRST ARMY UNDER GEN. VON GOEBEN. By **Major von Schell.** Translated by Col. **C. H. von Wright.** Four Maps. Demy 8vo. Price 9s.

"In concluding our notice of this instructive work, which, by the way, is enriched by several large-scale maps, we must not withhold our tribute of admiration of the manner in which the translator has performed his task. So thoroughly, indeed, has he succeeded, that it might really be imagined that the book had been originally composed in English. . . The work is decidedly valuable to a student of the art of war, and no military library can be considered complete without it."—*Hour.*

THE OPERATIONS OF THE FIRST ARMY UNDER GEN. VON MANTEUFFEL. By Col. **Count Hermann von Wartensleben,** Chief of the Staff of the First Army. Translated by **Colonel C. H. von Wright.** In demy 8vo. Uniform with the above. Price 9s.

"Very clear, simple, yet eminently instructive, is this history. It is not overladen with useless details, is written in good taste, and possesses the inestimable value of being in great measure the record of operations actually witnessed by the author, supplemented by official documents."—*Athenæum.*

THE GERMAN ARTILLERY IN THE BATTLES NEAR METZ. Based on the official reports of the German Artillery. By **Captain Hoffbauer,** Instructor in the German Artillery and Engineer School. Translated by **Capt. E. O. Hollist.** Demy 8vo. With Map and Plans. Price 21s.

"Contains much solid and valuable information . . . We can commend this work to all students of military history, while the historian will find in it much valuable matter."—*Court Circular.*

"Captain Hoffbauer's style is much more simple and agreeable than those of many of his comrades and fellow authors, and it suffers nothing in the hands of Captain Hollist, whose translation is close and faithful. He has given the general public a readable and instructive book; whilst to his brother officers, who have a special professional interest in the subject, its value cannot well be overrated."—*Academy.*

THE OPERATIONS OF THE BAVARIAN ARMY CORPS. By **Captain Hugo Helvig.** Translated by **Captain G. S. Schwabe.** With 5 large Maps. In 2 vols. Demy 8vo. Price 24s.

"It contains much material that may prove useful to the future historian of the war; and it is, on the whole, written in a spirit of fairness and impartiality . . . It only remains to say that the work is enriched by some excellent large scale maps, and that the translator has performed his work most creditably."—*Athenæum.*

"An instructive work."—*Westminster Review.*

"Captain Schwabe has done well to translate it, and his translation is admirably executed."—*Pall Mall Gazette.*

MILITARY WORKS—*continued.*

AUSTRIAN CAVALRY EXERCISE. From an Abridged Edition compiled by CAPTAIN ILLIA WOINOVITS, of the General Staff, on the Tactical Regulations of the Austrian Army, and prefaced by a General Sketch of the Organisation, &c., of the Cavalry. Translated by Captain **W. S. Cooke.** Crown 8vo, cloth. Price 7*s.*

"Among the valuable group of works on the military system of the chief States of Europe which Messrs. King are publishing, a small treatise on 'Austrian Cavalry Exercise' will hold a good and useful place."—*Westminster Review.*

"Well and clearly written, and contains a vast amount of very useful information."—*Edinburgh Daily Review.*

History of the Organisation, Equipment, and War Services of

THE REGIMENT OF BENGAL ARTILLERY. Compiled from Published Official and other Records, and various private sources, by **Major Francis W. Stubbs,** Royal (late Bengal) Artillery. Vol. I. will contain WAR SERVICES. The Second Volume will be published separately, and will contain the HISTORY OF THE ORGANISATION AND EQUIPMENT OF THE REGIMENT. In 2 vols. 8vo. With Maps and Plans. [*Preparing.*]

VICTORIES AND DEFEATS. An Attempt to explain the Causes which have led to them. An Officer's Manual. By Col. **R. P. Anderson.** 8vo. 14*s.*

"The young officer should have it always at hand to open anywhere and read a bit, and we warrant him that let that bit be ever so small it will give him material for an hour's thinking."—*United Service Gazette.*

"The present book proves that he is a diligent student of military history, his illustrations ranging over a wide field, and including ancient and modern Indian and European warfare."—*Standard.*

THE FRONTAL ATTACK OF INFANTRY. By Capt. **Laymann,** Instructor of Tactics at the Military College, Neisse. Translated by Colonel **Edward Newdigate.** Crown 8vo, limp cloth. Price 2*s. 6d.*

"An exceedingly useful kind of book. A valuable acquisition to the military student's library. It recounts, in the first place, the opinions and tactical formations which regulated the German army during the early battles of the late war; it ex-

plains how these were modified in the course of the campaign by the terrible and unanticipated effect of the fire; and how, accordingly, troops should be trained to attack in future wars."—*Naval and Military Gazette.*

ELEMENTARY MILITARY GEOGRAPHY, RECONNOITRING, AND SKETCHING. Compiled for Non-Commissioned Officers and Soldiers of all Arms. By **Lieut. C. E. H. Vincent,** Royal Welsh Fusiliers. Square cr. 8vo, 2*s. 6d.*

"This manual takes into view the necessity of every soldier knowing how to read a military map, in order to know in what posses in an enemy's country to direct his attention; and provides for this necessity by giving, in terse and sensible

language, definitions of varieties of ground and the advantages they present in warfare; together with a number of useful hints in military sketching."—*Naval and Military Gazette.*

THREE WORKS BY LIEUT.-COL. THE HON. A. ANSON, V.C., M.P.

THE ABOLITION OF PURCHASE AND THE ARMY REGULATION BILL OF 1871. Crown 8vo. Price One Shilling.

ARMY RESERVES AND MILITIA REFORMS. Crown 8vo. Sewed. Price One Shilling.

THE STORY OF THE SUPERSESSIONS. Crown 8vo. Price Sixpence.

STUDIES IN THE NEW INFANTRY TACTICS. Parts I. & II. By **Major W. von Scherff.** Translated from the German by Colonel **Lumley Graham.** Demy 8vo. Price 7*s. 6d.*

"The subject of the respective advantages of attack and defence, and of the methods in which each form of battle should be carried out under the fire of modern arms, is exhaustively and ad-

mirably treated; indeed, we cannot but consider it to be decidedly superior to any work which has hitherto appeared in English upon this all-important subject."—*Standard.*

Second Edition. Revised and Corrected.

TACTICAL DEDUCTIONS FROM THE WAR OF 1870—71. By Captain **A. von Boguslawski.** Translated by Colonel **Lumley Graham,** late 18th (Royal Irish) Regiment. Demy 8vo. Uniform with the above. Price 7*s.*

"We must, without delay, impress, brain and forethought into the British Service; and we cannot commend the good work too soon, or better, than by placing the two books ('The Operations of

the German Armies' and 'Tactical Deductions'). We have here criticised in every military library, and introduced them as class-books in every tactical school."—*United Service Gazette.*

MILITARY WORKS—*continued.*

THE OPERATIONS OF THE SOUTH ARMY IN JANUARY AND FEBRUARY, 1871. Compiled from the Official War Documents of the Head-quarters of the Southern Army. By **Count Hermann von Wartensleben**, Colonel in the Prussian General Staff. Translated by **Colonel C. H. von Wright.** Demy 8vo, with Maps. Uniform with the above. Price 6s.

THE ARMY OF THE NORTH-GERMAN CONFEDERATION. A Brief Description of its Organization, of the different Branches of the Service, and their "Rôle" in War, of its Mode of Fighting, &c. By a **Prussian General.** Translated from the German by **Col. Edward Newdigate.** Demy 8vo, Price 5s.

"The work is quite essential to the full use of the other volumes of the 'German Military Series,' which Messrs. King are now producing in handsome uniform style.—*United Service Magazine.*

"Every page of the book deserves attentive

study.... The information given on mobilization, garrison troops, keeping up establishment during war, and on the employment of the different branches of the service, is of great value."—*Standard.*

THE OPERATIONS OF THE GERMAN ARMIES IN FRANCE, FROM SEDAN TO THE END OF THE WAR OF 1870-71. With large Official Map. From the Journals of the Head-quarters Staff, by **Major William Blume.** Translated by **E. M. Jones**, Major 20th Foot, late Professor of Military History, Sandhurst. Demy 8vo, Price 9s.

"The book is of absolute necessity to the military student.... The work is one of high merit."—*United Service Gazette.*

"The work of Major von Blume is in English dress forms the most valuable addition to our stock

of works upon the war that our press has put forth. Our space forbids our doing more than commending it earnestly as the most authentic and instructive narrative of the second section of the war that has yet appeared."—*Saturday Review.*

HASTY INTRENCHMENTS. By Colonel A. Brialmont. Translated by Lieut. Charles A. Empson, R.A. With Nine Plates. Demy 8vo, Price 6s.

"A valuable contribution to military literature."—*Athenæum.*

"In seven short chapters it gives plain directions for forming shelter-trenches, with the best method of carrying the necessary tools, and it offers practical illustration of the use of hasty intrenchments on the field of battle."—*United Service Magazine.*

"It supplies that which our own text-books give but imperfectly, viz., how as to how a position can best be strengthened by means ... of such extemporised intrenchments and batteries as can be thrown up by infantry in the space of four or five hours ... deserves to become a standard military work.—*Standard.*

STUDIES IN LEADING TROOPS. By Colonel von Verdy Du Vernois. An authorised and accurate Translation by Lieutenant H. J. T. Hildyard, 71st Foot. Parts I. and II. Demy 8vo. Price 7s.

"*** General BEAUCHAMP WALKER says of this work:—'I recommend the first two numbers of Colonel von Verdy's 'Studies' to the attentive perusal of my brother officers. They supply a want which I have often felt during my service, in this country, namely, a minuter detail of the minor operations of war than any but the most

observant and fortunately-placed staff-officer is in a position to give. I have read and re-read them very carefully, I hope with profit, certainly with great interest, and believe that practice, in the sense of these 'Studies,' would be a valuable preparation for manœuvres on a more extended scale.'—*Berlin, June, 1872.*

CAVALRY FIELD DUTY. By Major-General von Mirus. Translated by Captain Frank S. Russell, 14th (King's) Hussars. Cr. 8vo, cloth limp, 7s. 6d.

"We have no book on cavalry duties that at all approaches in this, either for completeness in details, clearness in description, or for manifest utility. In its pages will be found plain instructions for every portion of duty before the enemy that a combatant horseman will be called upon to perform, and if a dragoon but studies it well and

intelligently, his value to the army, we are confident, must be increased one hundredfold. Skirmishing, scouring, patrolling, and vedetting are now the chief duties demanded in peace should be practised at, and how to perform these duties effectively is what the book teaches."—*United Service Magazine.*

DISCIPLINE AND DRILL. Four Lectures delivered to the London Scottish Rifle Volunteers. By Captain S. Flood Page. New and Cheaper Edition. Crown 8vo, cloth, limp. Price 1s.

"The very useful and interesting work."—*Volunteer Service Gazette.*

"An admirable collection of lectures."—*Times.*

INDIA AND THE EAST.

THE THREATENED FAMINE IN BENGAL; How it may be Met, and the Recurrence of Famines in India Prevented. Being No. 1 of "Occasional Notes on Indian Affairs." By Sir H. Bartle E. Frere, G.C.B., G.C.S.I., &c. &c. Crown 8vo. With 3 Maps. Price 5s.

THE ORIENTAL SPORTING MAGAZINE. A Reprint of the first 5 Volumes, in 2 Volumes, demy 8vo. Price 28s.

"Lovers of sport will find ample amusement in the varied contents of these two volumes."—*Allen's Indian Mail.*
"Fullest interest for the sportsman and naturalist. Full of thrilling adventures of sportsmen who have attacked the fiercest and most gigantic specimens of the animal world in their native jungle. It is seldom we get so many exciting incidents in a similar amount of space . . . Well suited to the libraries of country gentlemen and all those who are interested in sporting matters."—*Civil Service Gazette.*

Second Edition, Revised and Corrected.

THE EUROPEAN IN INDIA. A Hand-book of Practical Information for those proceeding to, or residing in, the East Indies, relating to Outfits, Routes, Time for Departure, Indian Climate, &c. By Edmund C. P. Hull. With a MEDICAL GUIDE FOR ANGLO-INDIANS. Being a Compendium of Advice to Europeans in India, relating to the Preservation and Regulation of Health. By R. S. Mair, M.D., F.R.C.S.E., late Deputy Coroner of Madras. In 1 vol. Post 8vo. Price 6s.

"Full of all sorts of useful information to the English visitor or traveller in India."—*Standard.*
"One of the most valuable books ever published in India—valuable for its sound information, its careful array of pertinent facts, and its sterling common sense. It supplies a want which few persons may have discovered, but which everybody will at once recognise when once the contents of the book have been mastered. The medical part of the work is invaluable."—*Calcutta Englishman.*

THE MEDICAL GUIDE FOR ANGLO-INDIANS. Being a Compendium of Advice to Europeans in India, relating to the Preservation and Regulation of Health. By R. S. Mair, M.D., F.R.C.S.E., late Deputy Coroner of Madras. Reprinted, with a Supplement on the Management of Children in India, from "The European in India." Cr. 8vo. limp cloth. Price 3s. 6d.

EASTERN EXPERIENCES. By L. Bowring, C.S.I., Lord Canning's Private Secretary, and for many years Chief Commissioner of Mysore and Coorg. Illustrated with Maps and Diagrams. Demy 8vo. Price 16s.

"An admirable and exhaustive geographical, political, and industrial survey."—*Athenæum.*
"Interesting even to the general reader, but especially so to those who may have a special concern in that portion of our Indian Empire."—*Post.*
"This compact and methodical summary of the most authentic information relating to countries whose welfare is intimately connected with our own."—*Daily News.*

TAS-HIL UL KALAM; OR, HINDUSTANI MADE EASY. By Captain W. R. M. Holroyd, Bengal Staff Corps, Director of Public Instruction, Punjab. Crown 8vo. Price 5s.

"As clear and as instructive as possible."—*Standard.*
"Contains a great deal of most necessary infor-mation, that is not to be found in any other work on the subject that has crossed our path."—*Allen's Indian Mail.*

EDUCATIONAL COURSE OF SECULAR SCHOOL BOOKS FOR INDIA. Edited by J. S. Laurie, of the Inner Temple, Barrister-at-Law; formerly H.M. Inspector of Schools, England; Assistant Royal Commissioner, Ireland; Special Commissioner, African Settlement; Director of Public Instruction, Ceylon.

"These valuable little works will prove of real service to many of our readers, especially to those who intend entering the Civil Service of India."—*Civil Service Gazette.*

The following Works are now ready:—

	s. d.		s. d.
THE FIRST HINDUSTANI READER, stiff linen wrapper	0 6	GEOGRAPHY OF INDIA, with Maps and Historical Appendix, tracing the growth of the British Empire in Hindustan. 228 pp. cloth	1 6
THE SECOND HINDUSTANI READER, stiff linen wrapper	0 6		

In the Press.

ELEMENTARY GEOGRAPHY OF INDIA.	FACTS AND FEATURES OF INDIAN HISTORY, in a series of alternating Reading Lessons and Memory Exercises.

INDIA AND THE EAST—*continued.*

Second Edition.

WESTERN INDIA BEFORE AND DURING THE MUTINIES.

Pictures drawn from life. By **Major-Gen. Sir George Le Grand Jacob, K.C.S.I., C.B.** In 1 vol. Crown 8vo. Price 7*s.* 6*d.*

"The most important contribution to the history of Western India during the Mutinies which has yet, in a popular form, been made public."—*Athenæum.*

"Few men more competent than himself to speak authoritatively concerning Indian affairs."—*Standard.*

EXCHANGE TABLES OF STERLING AND INDIAN RUPEE CURRENCY,

upon a new and extended system, embracing Values from One Farthing to One Hundred Thousand Pounds, and at rates progressing, in Sixteenths of a Penny, from 1*s.* 9*d.* to 2*s.* 3*d.* per Rupee. By **Donald Fraser,** Accountant to the British Indian Steam Navigation Company, Limited. Royal 8vo. Price 10*s.* 6*d.*

"The calculations must have entailed great labour on the author, but the work is one which we fancy must become a standard one in all business houses which have dealings with any country where the rupee and the English pound are standard coins of currency."—*Inverness Courier.*

BOOKS for the YOUNG and for LENDING LIBRARIES.

NEW WORKS BY HESBA STRETTON.

CASSY. A New Story. Square crown 8vo, with Illustrations, uniform with "Lost Gip." Price 1*s.* 6*d.*

THE KING'S SERVANTS. Square crown 8vo, uniform with "Lost Gip." With Eight Illustrations. 1*s.* 6*d.*
Part I.—Faithful in Little. Part II.—Unfaithful. Part III.—Faithful in Much.

THE WONDERFUL LIFE. Crown 8vo. [*Preparing.*

LOST GIP. Square crown 8vo. With Six Illustrations. Price 1*s.* 6*d.*

.•. *ALSO A HANDSOMELY-BOUND EDITION, WITH TWELVE ILLUSTRATIONS, PRICE HALF-A-CROWN.*

PRETTY LESSONS IN VERSE FOR GOOD CHILDREN, with some Lessons in Latin, in Easy Rhyme. By **Sara Coleridge.** A New Edition.

DADDY'S PET. By **Mrs. Ellen Ross (Nelsie Brook).** Square crown 8vo, uniform with "Lost Gip." With Six Illustrations. Price 1*s.*

"We have been more than pleased with this simple tale of writing."—*Christian World.*

"Full of deep feeling and true and noble sentiment."—*Brighton Gazette.*

AUNT MARY'S BRAN PIE. By the Author of "St. Olave's," "When I was a Little Girl," &c. Illustrated.

SEEKING HIS FORTUNE, AND OTHER STORIES. Crown 8vo. With Four Illustrations. Price 3*s.* 6*d.*
CONTENTS.—Seeking his Fortune.—Oluf and Stephanoff.—What's in a Name?—Contrast.—Onesta.

THREE WORKS BY MARTHA FARQUHARSON.
I. ELSIE DINSMORE. Cr. 8vo. Price 3*s.* 6*d.* | III. ELSIE'S HOLIDAYS AT ROSELANDS.
II. ELSIE'S GIRLHOOD. Cr. 8vo. Price 3*s.* 6*d.* | Crown 8vo. Price 3*s.* 6*d.*
Each Story is independent and complete in itself.
They are published in uniform size and price, and are elegantly bound and illustrated.

THE LITTLE WONDER-HORN. By **Jean Ingelow.** A Second Series of "*Stories told to a Child.*" With Fifteen Illustrations. Cloth, gilt. Price 3*s.* 6*d.*

"We like all the contents of the 'Little Wonder-Horn' very much."—*Athenæum.*
"We recommend it with confidence."—*Pall Mall Gazette.*

"Full of fresh and vigorous fancy; it is worthy of the author of some of the best of our modern verse."—*Standard.*

BOOKS FOR THE YOUNG AND FOR LENDING LIBRARIES—*continued.*

Second Edition.

THE AFRICAN CRUISER. A Midshipman's Adventures on the West Coast. A Book for Boys. By **S. Whitchurch Sadler, R.N.**, Author of "Marshall Vavasour." With Three Illustrations. Crown 8vo. Price 3s. 6d.

"A capital story of youthful adventure .... Sea-loving boys will find few pleasanter gift books this season than 'The African Cruiser.'"—*Hour.*

"Sea yarns have always been in favour with boys, but this, written in a brisk style by a thorough sailor, is crammed full of adventures."—*Times.*

Second Edition.

BRAVE MEN'S FOOTSTEPS. A Book of Example and Anecdote for Young People. By the Editor of "**Men who have Risen.**" With Four Illustrations, by C. Doyle. Crown 8vo. Price 3s. 6d.

"A readable and instructive volume."—*Examiner.*

"The little volume is precisely of the stamp to

win the favour of those who, in choosing a gift for a boy, would consult his moral development as well as his temporary pleasure."—*Daily Telegraph.*

Second Edition.

PLUCKY FELLOWS. A Book for Boys. By **Stephen J. Mac Kenna**. With Six Illustrations. Crown 8vo. Price 3s. 6d.

"This is one of the very best 'Books for Boys' which have been issued this year."—*Morning Advertiser.*

"A thorough book for boys, . . . written throughout in a manly straightforward manner that is sure to win the hearts of the children."—*London Society.*

Second Edition.

GUTTA-PERCHA WILLIE, THE WORKING GENIUS. By **George Macdonald**. With Nine Illustrations by **Arthur Hughes**. Crown 8vo. Price 3s. 6d.

"The cleverest child we know assures us she has read this story through five times. Mr. Macdonald

will, we are convinced, accept that verdict upon his little work as final."—*Spectator.*

THE TRAVELLING MENAGERIE. By **Charles Camden**, Author of "Hoity Toity." With Ten Illustrations by **J. Mahoney**. Crown 8vo. 3s. 6d.

"A capital little book .... deserves a wide circulation among our boys and girls."—*Hour.*

"A very attractive story."—*Public Opinion.*

THE DESERT PASTOR, JEAN JAROUSSEAU. Translated from the French of **Eugene Pelletan**. By Colonel **E. P. De L'Hoste**. In fcap. 8vo, with an Engraved Frontispiece. New Edition. Price 3s. 6d.

"A touching record of the struggles in the cause of religious liberty of a real man."—*Graphic.*

"There is a poetical simplicity and picturesqueness; the noblest heroism; unpretentious religion;

pure love, and the spectacle of a household brought up in the fear of the Lord .... "—*Illustrated London News.*

THE DESERTED SHIP. A Real Story of the Atlantic. By **Cupples Howe**, Master Mariner. Illustrated by **Townley Green**. Cr. 8vo. Price 3s. 6d.

"Curious adventures with bears, seals, and other Arctic animals, and with scarcely more human Esquimaux, form the mass of material with which

the story deals, and will much interest boys who have a spice of romance in their composition."—*Courant.*

HOITY TOITY, THE GOOD LITTLE FELLOW. By **Charles Camden**. With Eleven Illustrations. Crown 8vo. Price 3s. 6d.

"Relates very pleasantly the history of a charming little fellow who meddles always with a kindly disposition with other people's affairs and helps

them to do right. There are many shrewd lessons to be picked up in this clever little story."—*Public Opinion.*

THE BOY SLAVE IN BOKHARA. A Tale of Central Asia. By **David Ker**, Author of "On the Road to Khiva," &c. Crown 8vo, with Illustrations. Price 5s.

SLAVONIC FAIRY TALES. From Russian, Servian, Polish, and Bohemian Sources. Translated by **John T. Naake**, of the British Museum. Crown 8vo. With Four Illustrations. Price 5s.

"A most choice and charming selection .... The tales have an original national ring in them, and will be pleasant reading to thousands besides children. Yet children will eagerly open the pages, and not willingly close them, of the pretty volume."—*Standard.*

"English readers now have an opportunity of becoming acquainted with eleven Polish and eight Bohemian stories, as well as with eight Russian

and thirteen Servian, in Mr. Naake's modest but serviceable collection of *Slavonic Fairy Tales.* Its contents are, as a general rule, well chosen, and they are translated with a fidelity which deserves cordial praise . . . Before taking leave of his prettily got up volume, we ought to mention that its contents fully come up to the promise held out in its preface."—*Academy.*

WORKS BY ALFRED TENNYSON.

THE CABINET EDITION.

Messrs. HENRY S. KING & Co. have the pleasure to announce that they are issuing an Edition of the Laureate's works, in *Ten Monthly Volumes*, foolscap 8vo, entitled "The Cabinet Edition," at *Half-a-Crown each*, which will contain the whole of Mr. Tennyson's works. The first volume is illustrated by a beautiful Photographic Portrait; and the other volumes each contain a Frontispiece. They will be tastefully bound in Crimson Cloth, and will be issued in the following order :—

Vol.	Vol.
1. EARLY POEMS.	6. IDYLLS OF THE KING.
2. ENGLISH IDYLLS & OTHER POEMS.	7. IDYLLS OF THE KING.
3. LOCKSLEY HALL & OTHER POEMS.	8. THE PRINCESS.
4. AYLMER'S FIELD & OTHER POEMS.	9. MAUD AND ENOCH ARDEN.
5. IDYLLS OF THE KING.	10. IN MEMORIAM.

Volumes I. to IV. are now ready.

Subscribers' names received by all Booksellers.

The other forms in which Mr. Tennyson's Works are published are:—

	PRICE.
	s. d.
POEMS. Small 8vo.	9
MAUD AND OTHER POEMS. Small 8vo.	5 0
THE PRINCESS. Small 8vo.	5 0
IDYLLS OF THE KING. Small 8vo.	7 0
„ „ Collected. Small 8vo.	12 0
ENOCH ARDEN, &c. Small 8vo.	6 0
THE HOLY GRAIL, AND OTHER POEMS. Small 8vo.	7 0
GARETH AND LYNETTE. Small 8vo.	3 0
SELECTIONS FROM THE ABOVE WORKS. Square 8vo, cloth extra	3 0
SONGS FROM THE ABOVE WORKS. Square 8vo, cloth extra	3 0
IN MEMORIAM. Small 8vo.	6 0
LIBRARY EDITION OF MR. TENNYSON'S WORKS. 6 vols. Post 8vo, each	10 6
POCKET VOLUME EDITION OF MR. TENNYSON'S WORKS. 11 vols., in neat case	30 0
„ gilt edges	35 0
THE WINDOW; OR, THE SONGS OF THE WRENS. A Series of Songs. By ALFRED TENNYSON. With Music by ARTHUR SULLIVAN. 4to, cloth, gilt extra	21 0
POEMS. Illustrated Edition, 4to	21 0

65, Cornhill; & 12, Paternoster Row, London.

POETRY.

FOUR ELEGANT POETICAL GIFT BOOKS:

LYRICS OF LOVE, From Shakspeare to Tennyson. Selected and arranged by W. Davenport Adams, Junr. Fcap. 8vo, cloth extra, gilt edges, 3s. 6d.

"We cannot but highly commend this work, delightful in its contents and so pretty in its outward adornings."—*Standard.*

"Carefully selected and elegantly got up . . It is particularly rich in poems from living writers."—*John Bull.*

WILLIAM CULLEN BRYANT'S POEMS. Red-line Edition. Handsomely bound. With Illustrations and Portrait of the Author. Price 7s. 6d. A Cheaper Edition, with Frontispiece, is also published. Price 3s. 6d.

These are the only complete English Editions sanctioned by the Author.

"Of all the poets of the United States there is no one who obtained the same and position of a classic earlier, or has kept them longer, than William Cullen Bryant . . . A singularly simple and straightforward fashion of verse. Very rarely has any writer preserved such an even level of merit throughout his poems. Like some other American poets, Mr. Bryant is particularly happy in translation."—*Academy.*

"We are glad to possess so neat and elegant an edition of the works of the most thoughtful, graceful, and Wordsworthian of American poets."—*British Quarterly Review.*

"Some of the purest and tenderest poetry of this generation . . . Undoubtedly the best edition of the poet now in existence."—*Glasgow News.*

ENGLISH SONNETS. Collected and Arranged by **John Dennis.** Fcap. 8vo. Elegantly bound. Price 3s. 6d.

"Mr. Dennis has shown great judgment in this selection."—*Saturday Review.*

"An exquisite selection, a selection which every lover of poetry will consult again and again with

delight. The notes are very useful. . . The volume is one for which English literature owes Mr. Dennis the heartiest thanks."—*Spectator.*

Second Edition.

HOME-SONGS FOR QUIET HOURS. By the Rev. Canon R. H. Baynes, Editor of "Lyra Anglicana," &c. Fcap 8vo. Cloth extra, 3s. 6d.

"All the pieces breathe the spirit of true poetry, and are characterised by deep religious feeling."—*Leeds Mercury.*

"A tasteful collection of devotional poetry of a very high standard of excellence. The pieces are short, mostly original, and instinct, for the most part, with the most ardent spirit of devotion."—*Standard.*

"A very valuable and attractive batch of most readable verses . . . This collection is one of considerable power, and will be certain to be appreciated by that large and increasing class which loves sacred poetry."—*Church Herald.*

"A most acceptable volume of sacred poetry; a good addition to the gift books of the season."—*Lark.*

"These are poems in which every word has a meaning, and from which it would be unjust to remove a stanza . . . Some of the best pieces in the book are anonymous."—*Pall Mall Gazette.*

** The above four books may also be had handsomely bound in Morocco with gilt edges.

THE DISCIPLES. A New Poem. By Mrs. Hamilton King. Second Edition, with same Notes. Crown 8vo. Price 7s. 6d.

"A higher impression of the imaginative power of the writer is given by the objective truthfulness of the glimpses she gives us of her master, helping us to understand how he could be regarded by some as a heartless charlatan, by others as an inspired saint."—*Academy.*

"Mrs. King can write good verses. The description of the rapture of the Cross at Mentze is extremely spirited; there is a pretty picture of the road to Rome, from the Abruzzi, and another of Palermo."—*Athenæum.*

"In her new volume Mrs. King has far surpassed her previous attempt. Even the most hostile critic

could scarcely deny to 'Ugo Bassi' the praise of being a work worthy in every way to live . . . The style of her writing is pure and simple in the last degree, and all is natural, truthful, and free from the slightest shade of obscurity in thought or diction . . . The book altogether is one that merits unqualified admiration and praise."—*Cuthy Telegraph.*

"Throughout it breathes sustained passion and lofty sentiment, which flow out now and then in a certain widening to those slip-built into powerful music."—*British Quarterly Review.*

ASPROMONTE, AND OTHER POEMS. By the same Author. Second Edition. Cloth, 4s. 6d.

"The volume is anonymous, but there is no reason for the author to be ashamed of it. The 'Poems of Italy' are evidently inspired by genuine enthusiasm in the cause espoused; and one of them,

'The Execution of Felice Orsini,' has much poetic merit, the event celebrated being told with dramatic force."—*Athenæum.*

"The verse is fluent and free."—*Spectator.*

POETRY—*continued.*

SONGS FOR MUSIC. By Four Friends. Square crown 8vo. Price 5*s.*

CONTAINING SONGS BY

Reginald A. Gatty. Stephen H. Gatty.
Greville A. Chester. Juliana H. Ewing.

"A charming gift-book, which will be very popular with lovers of poetry."—*John Bull.*

"The charm of simplicity is manifest throughout, and the subjects are well chosen and tastefully treated."—*Echo.*

"One of the most delightful books of verse of the season."—*Mirror.*

"The collection is pleasing and varied."—*Illustrated London News.*

ROBERT BUCHANAN'S POETICAL WORKS. Collected Edition, in 3 Vols., price 6*s.* each. Vol. I. contains,—"Ballads and Romances," "Ballads and Poems of Life," and a Portrait of the Author. Vol. II.—"Ballads and Poems of Life," "Allegories and Sonnets." Vol. III.—"Cruiskeen Sonnets;" "Book of Orm;" "Political Mystics."

"Holding, as Mr. Buchanan does, such a conspicuous place amongst modern writers, the reading public will be duly thankful for this handsome edition of the poet's works."—*Civil Service Gazette.*

"Taking the poems before us as experiments, we hold that they are very full of promise.... In the romantic ballad, Mr. Buchanan shows real power."—*Hour.*

"If Mr. Buchanan were an unknown poet, this volume would be amply sufficient to establish his reputation among all lovers of true poetry."—*Liverpool Albion.*

"We can conscientiously recommend this collected edition to every admirer of Mr. Buchanan's poetry."—*Glasgow News.*

THOUGHTS IN VERSE. Small crown 8vo. Price 1*s. 6d.*

This is a Collection of Verses expressive of religious feeling, written from a Theistic stand-point.

"All who are interested in devotional verse should read this tiny volume."—*Academy.*

ON THE NORTH WIND—THISTLE-DOWN. A volume of Poems. By the Hon. Mrs. Willoughby. Elegantly bound, fcap. 8vo.

PENELOPE AND OTHER POEMS. By Allison Hughes. Fcap. 8vo.

POEMS. By Annette F. C. Knight. Fcap. 8vo. Cloth. Price 5*s.*

"The pleasant writer of these pleasant pages excels chiefly in poetical imagery, in tracing the analysis of mind and matter, and in giving beautiful expression to the most beautiful feelings of our nature."—*Standard.*

COSMOS. A Poem. 8vo. 3*s. 6d.*

SUBJECT:—Nature in the Past and in the Present.—Man in the Past and in the Present.—The Future.

NARCISSUS AND OTHER POEMS. By E. Carpenter. Fcap. 8vo. 5*s.*

"In many of these graphic there is a force of fancy, a grandeur of imagination, and a power of poetical utterance not by any means common in these days."—*Standard.*

POEMS. By Augustus Taylor. Fcap. 8vo. Cloth. Price 5*s.*

A TALE OF THE SEA, SONNETS, AND OTHER POEMS. By James Howell. Fcap. 8vo. Cloth, 5*s.*

"Mr. Howell has a keen perception of the beauties of nature, and a just appreciation of the charities of life.... Mr. Howell's book deserves, and will probably receive, a warm reception."—*Pall Mall Gazette.*

METRICAL TRANSLATIONS FROM THE GREEK AND LATIN POETS, AND OTHER POEMS. By R. B. Boswell, M.A. Oxon. Crown 8vo. 5*s.*

"Most of these translations we can praise as of very high merit.... For sweetness and regularity, his verses are pre-eminent."—*Literary Churchman.*

"Mr. Boswell has a strong poetical vein in his nature, and gives us every promise of success as an original poet."—*Standard.*

EASTERN LEGENDS AND STORIES IN ENGLISH VERSE. By Lieutenant Norton Powlett, Royal Artillery. Crown 8vo. 5*s.*

"There is a rollicking sense of fun about the stories, joined to marvellous power of rhyming, and plenty of swing, which irresistibly reminds us of our old favourite, *Ingoldsby.*"

SONGS FOR SAILORS. By Dr. W. C. Bennett. Dedicated by Special Request to H. R. H. the Duke of Edinburgh. Crown 8vo. 3*s. 6d.* With Steel Portrait and Illustrations.

An Edition in Illustrated paper Covers. Price 1*s.*

WALLED IN, AND OTHER POEMS. By the Rev. Henry J. Bulkeley. Crown 8vo.

"A remarkable book of genuine poetry."—*Evening Standard.*

"Genuine power displayed."—*Examiner.*

"Poetical feeling is manifest here, and the diction of the poems is unimpeachable."—*Pall Mall Gazette.*

SONGS OF LIFE AND DEATH. By John Payne, Author of "Intaglios," "Sonnets," "The Masque of Shadows," etc. Crown 8vo. 5*s.*

"The art of verse-writing has long been lost in England, and Mr. Payne may claim to be its restorer. It is a perfect delight to meet with such a ballad as 'May Margaret' in the present volume."—*Westminster Review.*

Second Edition.

VIGNETTES IN RHYME AND VERS DE SOCIÉTÉ. By Austin Dobson. Fcap. 8vo. 5*s.*

"Clever, clear-cut, and careful."—*Athenæum.*

"As a writer of Vers de Société, Mr. Dobson is almost, if not quite, unrivalled."—*Examiner.*

"Lively, innocent, elegant in expression, and graceful in fancy."—*Morning Post.*

IMITATIONS FROM THE GERMAN OF SPITTA AND TERSTEGEN. By Lady Durand. Fcap. 8vo. 4*s.*

"A charming little volume.. Will be a very valuable assistance to peaceful, meditative souls."—*Church Herald.*

POETRY—*continued.*

ON VIGIL AND FLUTE. A New Volume of Poems, by Edmund W. Gosse. With a Frontispiece by W. B. Scott. 8vo. 5s.

"A careful perusal of his verses will show that he is a poet... His song has the grateful, murmuring sound which reminds one of the coolness and deliciousness of summer time.... There is much that is good in the volume."—*Spectator.*

EDITH; or, LOVE AND LIFE IN CHESHIRE. By T. Ashe, Author of "The Sorrows of Hypsipyle," etc. Sewed. Price 6d.

"A really fine poem, full of tender, subtle touches of feeling."—*Manchester News.*

"Progress from beginning to end with the results of careful observation and imaginative power."—*Chester Chronicle.*

GOETHE'S FAUST. A New Translation in Rime. By C. Kegan Paul. Crown 8vo, 6s.

"His translation is the most minutely accurate that has yet been produced, ..."—*Examiner.*

"Mr. Paul is a zealous and a faithful interpreter."—*Saturday Review.*

THE INN OF STRANGE MEETINGS, AND OTHER POEMS. By Mortimer Collins. Crown 8vo.

"Abounding in quiet humour, in bright fancy, in sweetness and melody of expression, and, at times, in the tenderest touches of pathos."—*Graphic.*

"Mr. Collins has an undercurrent of chivalry and romance beneath the trifling vein of goodhumoured banter which is the special characteristic of his verse."—*Athenæum.*

EROS AGONISTES. By E. B. D. Crown 8vo. 3s. 6d.

"It is not the least merit of these pages that they are everywhere illumined with moral and religious sentiment suggested, not paraded, of the brightest, purest character."—*Standard.*

CALDERON'S DRAMAS. Translated from the Spanish. By Denis Florence MacCarthy. Post 8vo, Cloth, gilt edges, 10s.

"The lambent verse flows with an easy spirit, and magic perfectly natural, liberal, and harmonious."—*Spectator.*

"It is impossible to speak too highly of this beautiful work."—*Month.*

A LEGEND OF ST. PAUL'S. By the Rev. G. B. Howard. Fcap.8vo. 3s. 6d.

SONNETS, LYRICS, AND TRANSLATIONS. By the Rev. Charles Turner. Cr. 8vo. 4s. 6d.

"Mr. Turner is a genuine poet; his song is sweet and pure, beautiful in expression, and often subtle in thought."—*Pall Mall Gazette.*

"The light of a devout, gentle, and kindly spirit, a chastened and graceful fancy, a keen intelligence irradiates these thoughts."—*Contemporary Review.*

THE DREAM AND THE DEED, AND OTHER POEMS. By Patrick Scott, Author of "Footpaths between Two Worlds," etc. Fcap. 8vo. Cloth, 5s.

"A bitter and able satire on the vice and follies of the day, literary, social, and political."—*Standard.*

"Shows real poetic power coupled with evidence of satirical energy."—*Edinburgh Daily Review.*

SONGS OF TWO WORLDS. First Series. By a New Writer. Fcap. 8vo. 5s. *Second Edition.*

"These poems will assuredly take high rank among the class to which they belong."—*British Quarterly Review, April 1st.*

"No extracts could do justice to the exquisite tones, the delicate phrasing and delicately wrought harmonies of some of these poems."—*Nonconformist.*

"A purity and delicacy of feeling like morning air."—*Graphic.*

SONGS OF TWO WORLDS. Second Series. By the Author of "Songs of Two Worlds." Fcap. 8vo. 5s. *Second Edition.*

"In tenderness and sweetness the author may be pronounced a worthy disciple of Henry Vaughan ... Instinct with a noble purpose and high ideal ... The most noteworthy poem is the 'Ode on a Spring Morning,' which has somewhat of the charm of 'L'Allegro' and 'Il Penseroso.' It is the nearest approach to a masterpiece in the collection. We cannot find too much praise for its noble assertion of man's resurrection."—*Saturday Review.*

"A real advance on its predecessor, and contains at least one poem ('The Organ Boy') of great originality, as well as many of much beauty ... As exquisite a little poem as we have read for many a day ... but not at all above its power to fair trade."—*Spectator.*

"Will be gratefully welcomed."—*Examiner.*

THE GALLERY OF PIGEONS, AND OTHER POEMS. By Theo. Marzials. Crown 8vo. 4s. 6d.

"A conceit abounding in prettiness."—*Academy.*

"The rush of fresh, sparkling fancies is too rapid, too sustained, too abundant, not to be spontaneous."—*Academy.*

THE LEGENDS OF ST. PATRICK AND OTHER POEMS. By Aubrey de Vere. Crown 8vo. 5s.

"Mr. De Vere's versification in his chief poems is characterised by great sweetness and simplicity. He is master of his instrument, and rarely offends the ear with false notes."—*Pall Mall Gazette.*

"We have but space to commend the varied structure of his verse, the carefulness of his grammar, and his excellent English."—*Saturday Review.*

ALEXANDER THE GREAT. A Dramatic Poem. By Aubrey de Vere, Author of "The Legends of St. Patrick." Crown 8vo. 5s.

"Undeniably well written."—*Examiner.*

"In some points Mr. De Vere's poetry is a model to most of his fellow singers. Its idioms and phraseology are English, thorough and correct English; his verses, with few exceptions, are symmetrical, simple, and sweet; and his diction throughout is dignified, as becomes the stately mood of tragedy, and often rises to sublime pitch, leaving all his contemporaries far behind."—*Standard.*

"A noble play.... The work of a true poet, and of a fine artist, in whom there is nothing vulgar and nothing weak ... We bear no compassion, from our knowledge of Mr. De Vere's former poems, that so much poetic power lay in him as this drama shows. It is true as well as full of beauty, nervous as well as rich in thought."—*Spectator.*

FICTION.

WOMAN'S A RIDDLE; or, Baby WARMSTREY. By Philip Sheldon, Author of "When George III. was King." 3 vols.

LISETTE'S VENTURE. By Mrs. Russell Gray. 2 vols. [*In September.*

IDOLATRY. A Romance. By Julian Hawthorne, Author of "Bressant." 2 vols. [*In September.*

BRESSANT. A Romance. By Julian Hawthorne. 2 vols. Crown 8vo.

"One of the most powerful with which we are acquainted."—*Times.*

"We shall once more have reason to rejoice whenever we hear that a new work is coming out written by one who bears the honoured name of Hawthorne.—*Saturday Review.*

VANESSA. By the Author of "Thomasina," "Dorothy," &c. 2 vols. [*In October.*

THOMASINA. By the Author of "Dorothy," "De Cressy," &c. 2 vols. Crown 8vo.

"A finished and delicate cabinet picture; no line is without its purpose."—*Athenæum.*

THE HIGH MILLS. By Katherine Saunders. Author of "Gideon's Rock," &c. 3 vols. [*In October.*

AILEEN FERRERS. By Susan Morley. In 2 vols. Crown 8vo, cloth.

"Rex rises to a level far above that which cultivated women with a facile pen ordinarily attain when they set themselves to write a story. . . . Its grammar is faultless, its style is pure, flowing, terse, and correct; there is not a trace of fine writing. . . . there is a great absence of anything like moralising, or the introduction of goody-feelings and sermons . . . it is as a study of character, worked out in a manner that is free from almost all the usual faults of lady writers, that "Aileen Ferrers" merits a place apart from its innumerable rivals."—*Saturday Review.*

LADY MORETOUN'S DAUGHTER. By Mrs. Eiloart. In 3 vols. Crown 8vo.

"Carefully written. . . . The narrative is well sustained."—*Athenæum.*

"An interesting story . . . Above the run of average novels."—*Vanity Fair.*

"Will prove more popular than any of this author's former works. . . . Interesting and readable."—*Hour.*

"A faithful and well-drawn picture of English life and character. . . . All the characters are drawn with the author's wonted niceness and truth of touch. . . . Extremely well written."—*Edinburgh Daily Review.*

"The story is well put together, and readable."—*Examiner.*

MARGARET AND ELIZABETH. A Story of the Sea. By Katherine Saunders, Author of "Gideon's Rock," &c. In 1 vol. Cloth, crown 8vo.

"Simply yet powerfully told. . . . This opening picture is so exquisitely drawn as to be a fit introduction to a story of such simple pathos and power. . . . A very beautiful story closes as it began, in a tender and touching picture of homely happiness."—*Pall Mall Gazette.*

MR. CARINGTON. A Tale of Love and Conspiracy. By Robert Turner Cotton. In 3 vols. Cloth, crown 8vo.

"A novel in so many ways good, or in a fresh and elastic diction, stout unconventionality, and happy boldness of conception and execution. His novels, though free spoken, will be some of the healthiest of our day."—*Examiner.*

TWO GIRLS. By Frederick Wedmore, Author of "A Snapt Gold Ring." 2 vols.

"A carefully-written novel of character, contrasting the two heroines of one love tale, an English lady and a French actress. Cicely is charming; the introductory description of her is a good specimen of the well-balanced sketches in which the author abounds."—*Athenæum.*

CIVIL SERVICE. By J. T. Listado, Author of "Maurice Rhynhart." 2 vols.

"A very charming and amusing story . . . The characters are all well drawn and life-like . . . It is with no ordinary skill that Mr. Listado has drawn the character of Hugh Haughton, full as he is of sympathy and quaintness . . . The plot is worked out with great skill and is of no ordinary kind."—*Civil Service Gazette.*

"A story of Irish life, free from burlesque and partisanship yet amusingly designed . . . There is plenty of 'go' in the story."—*Athenæum.*

WAITING FOR TIDINGS. By the Author of "White and Black." 3 vols.

"An interesting novel."—*Vanity Fair.*

"A very lively tale, abounding with amusing incidents."—*John Bull.*

JUDITH GWYNNE. By Lisle Carr. In 3 vols. Cr. 8vo, cloth. Second Edition.

"Mr. Carr's novel is certainly amusing. There is much variety, and the dialogue and incident never flag to the finish."—*Athenæum.*

"Displays much dramatic skill . . . It is in the skilful manipulation of much varied detail, the extensive play of a great number of differing actors, tending naturally to the conclusion reached, that the chief charm of this novel lies."—*Edinburgh Courant.*

TOO LATE. By Mrs. Newman. 2 vols.

"The plot is skilfully constructed; the characters are well portrayed; and the narrative moves to its conclusion without any waste of words. The tone is healthy, in spite of its incidents, which will please the lovers of sensational fiction. . . . The reader who opens the book will read it all through."—*Pall Mall Gazette.*

"One of the pleasant, graceful little novelettes in which the best of our lady novelists and their special readers take delight, and of its kind is good specimen."—*Standard.*

"A capital tale."—*John Bull.*

"Undeniably interesting."—*Morning Advertiser.*

"Well conceived and well told."—*Daily News.*

REGINALD BRAMBLE. A Cynic of the 19th Century. An Autobiography. 1 vol.

"There is plenty of vivacity in Mr. Bramble's narrative."—*Athenæum.*

"Written in a lively and readable style."—*Hour.*

EFFIE'S GAME; HOW SHE LOST AND HOW SHE WON. By Cecil Clayton. 2 vols. Crown 8vo.

"Well written. The characters move, and act, and, above all, talk like human beings; and we have liked reading about them."—*Spectator.*

FICTION—*continued.*

CHESTERLEIGH. By Ansley Conyers.
3 vols. Crown 8vo.
"We have gained much enjoyment from the book."—*Spectator.*

HONOR BLAKE: THE STORY OF A PLAIN
WOMAN. By Mrs. Keatinge, Author of
"English Homes in India," etc. 2 vols.
"One of the best novels we have met with for
some time."—*Morning Post.*
"A story which must do good to all, young and
old, who read it."—*Daily News.*

HEATHERGATE. A Story of Scottish
Life and Character. By a new Author.
2 vols.
"Its merit lies in the earnest naturalness of
strongly developed characters, in different ranks
of life, and resembling each other in nothing but
their marked nationality."—*Athenæum.*

THE QUEEN'S SHILLING. By Captain
Arthur Griffiths, Author of "Peccavi."
2 vols.
"Every scene, character, and incident of the
book are so life-like that they seem drawn from
the direct."—*Pall Mall Gazette.*

MIRANDA. A Midsummer Madness. By
Mortimer Collins. 3 vols.
"Not a dull page in the whole three volumes."
—*Standard.*
"The work of a man who is at once a thinker
and a poet."—*Hour.*

SQUIRE SILCHESTER'S WHIM. By
Mortimer Collins, Author of "Marquis
and Merchant," etc. 3 vols.
"We think it the best (even) Mr. Collins has
yet written. Full of incident and adventure."—
Pall Mall Gazette.
"So clever, so irritating, and so charming a
story."—*Athenæum.*

THE PRINCESS CLARICE. A Story of
1871. By Mortimer Collins. 2 vols.
"Mr. Collins has produced a readable book,
amusingly characteristic."—*Athenæum.*
"A bright, fresh, and delightful book."—*Standard.*

JOHANNES OLAF. By E. de Wille.
Translated by F. E. Bunnett. 3 vols.
"The art of description is fully exhibited;
perception of character and capacity for delineating it are obvious; while there is great breadth
and comprehensiveness in the plan of the story."
—*Morning Post.*

**THE STORY OF SIR EDWARD'S
WIFE.** By Hamilton Marshall;
Author of "For Very Life." 1 vol. Cr. 8vo.
"A quiet, graceful little story."—*Spectator.*
"Mr. Hamilton Marshall can tell a story clearly
and pleasantly."—*Pall Mall Gazette.*

HERMANN AGHA. An Eastern Narrative. By W. Gifford Palgrave. 2 vols.
Crown 8vo, cloth, extra gilt. 18s.
"There is a positive fragrance as of newly-mown
hay about it, so concocted with the artistically
perfumed passions which are detailed to us with
such gusto by our ordinary novel-writers in their
endless volumes."—*Observer.*

A GOOD MATCH. By Amelia Perrier,
Author of "Mea Culpa." 2 vols.
"Racy and lively."—*Athenæum.*
"This clever and amusing novel."—*Pall Mall
Gazette.*

LINKED AT LAST. By F. E. Bunnett.
1 vol. Crown 8vo.
"The reader who once takes it up will not be
inclined to relinquish it without concluding the
volume."—*Morning Post.*
"A very charming story."—*John Bull.*

OFF THE SKELLIGS. By Jean
Ingelow. (Her First Romance.) In 4 vols.
"Clever and sparkling."—*Standard.*
"We read each succeeding volume with increasing interest, going almost to the point of
wishing there was a fifth."—*Athenæum.*

SEETA. By Colonel Meadows Taylor,
Author of "Tara," etc. 3 vols.
"Well told, native life is admirably described,
and the petty intrigues of native rulers, and their
hatred of the English, mingled with fear but the
latter should eventually prove the victors, are
cleverly depicted."—*Athenæum.*
"Thoroughly interesting and enjoyable reading."—*Examiner.*

WHAT 'TIS TO LOVE. By the Author
of "Flora Adair," "The Value of Fosterstown." 3 vols.
"Worthy of praise: it is well written; the
story is simple, the interest is well sustained; the
characters are well depicted."—*Edinburgh
Courant.*

**MEMOIRS OF MRS. LÆTITIA
BOOTHBY.** By William Clark
Russell, Author of "The Book of
Authors." Crown 8vo, 7s. 6d.
"Clever and ingenious."—*Saturday Review.*
"Very clever book."—*Guardian.*

THE DOCTOR'S DILEMMA. By Hesba
Stretton. 3 vols. Crown 8vo.
"A fascinating story which scarcely flags in
interest from the first page to the last."—*British
Quarterly Review.*

THE SPINSTERS OF BLATCHINGTON. By Mar. Travers. 2 vols.
"A pretty story. Deserving of a favourable
reception."—*Graphic.*
"A book of more than average merits."—
Examiner.

PERPLEXITY. By Sydney Mostyn.
3 vols. Crown 8vo.
"Written with very considerable power, great
cleverness, and sustained interest."—*Standard.*
"The literary workmanship is good, and the
story capitally and graphically told."—*Daily News.*

HESTER MORLEY'S PROMISE. By
Hesba Stretton. 3 vols.
"Much better than the average novels of the
day; has much more claim to critical consideration as a piece of literary work, every clever."—
Spectator.
"All the characters stand out clearly and are
well sustained, and the interest of the story never
flags."—*Observer.*

CRUEL AS THE GRAVE. By the
Countess Von Bothmer. 3 vols.
"Jealousy is cruel as the Grave."
"Interesting, though somewhat tragic."—
Athenæum.
"Agreeable, unaffected, and eminently readable."—*Daily News.*

SEPTIMIUS. A Romance. By Nathaniel
Hawthorne. Second Edition. 1 vol.
Crown 8vo, cloth, extra gilt. 9s.
The *Athenæum* says that "the book is full of
Hawthorne's most characteristic writing."

THE CORNHILL LIBRARY OF FICTION.

3s. 6d. per Volume.

IT is intended in this Series to produce books of such merit that readers will care to preserve them on their shelves. They are well printed on good paper, handsomely bound, with a Frontispiece, and are sold at the moderate price of 3s. 6d. each.

THE HOUSE OF RABY. By Mrs. G. Hooper.

"A work of singular truthfulness, originality, and power."—*Morning Post.*

"Exceedingly well written."—*Examiner.*
"A well told and interesting story."—*Academy.*

A FIGHT FOR LIFE. By Moy Thomas.

"An unquestionable success."—*Daily News.*
"Of the vigour, the sustained energy, the ani-

mation, there cannot be two opinions."—*Athenæum.*

ROBIN GRAY. By Charles Gibbon.

"Pure in sentiment, well written, and cleverly constructed."—*British Quarterly Review.*
"A novel of tender and pathetic interest."—*Globe.*

"A pretty tale, prettily told."—*Athenæum.*
"An unassuming, characteristic, and entertaining novel."—*John Bull.*

KITTY. By Miss M. Betham-Edwards.

"Lively and clever.... There is a certain dash in every description; the dialogue is bright and sparkling."—*Athenæum.*

"Very pleasant and amusing."—*Globe.*
"A charming novel."—*John Bull.*

HIRELL. By John Saunders.

"A powerful novel... a tale written by a poet."—*Spectator.*
"A novel of extraordinary merit."—*Post.*

"We have nothing but words of praise to offer for his style and composition."—*Examiner.*

ONE OF TWO; or, The left-handed Bride. By J. H. Friswell.

"Told with spirit ... the plot is skilfully made."—*Spectator.*

"Admirably narrated, and intensely interesting."—*Public Opinion.*

READY-MONEY MORTIBOY. A Matter-of-Fact Story.

"There is not a dull page in the whole story."—*Standard.*
"A very interesting and uncommon story."—*Vanity Fair.*

"One of the most remarkable novels which has appeared of late."—*Pall Mall Gazette.*

GOD'S PROVIDENCE HOUSE. By Mrs. G. L. Banks.

"Far above the run of common three-volume novels, evincing much literary power in not a few graphic descriptions of manners and local customs. ... A genuine sketch."—*Spectator.*

"Possesses the merit of care, industry, and local knowledge."—*Athenæum.*
"Wonderfully readable. The style is very simple and natural."—*Morning Post.*

FOR LACK OF GOLD. By Charles Gibbon.

"A powerfully written nervous story."—*Athenæum.*
"There are few recent novels more powerful

and engrossing."—*Examiner.*
"A piece of very genuine workmanship."—*British Quarterly Review.*

ABEL DRAKE'S WIFE. By John Saunders.

"A striking book, clever, interesting, and original. We have seldom met with a book so thoroughly true to life, so deeply interesting in its

detail, and so touching in its simple pathos."—*Athenæum.*

OTHER STANDARD NOVELS TO FOLLOW.

THEOLOGICAL.

SERMONETTES : On Synonymous Texts, taken from the Bible and Book of Common Prayer, for the Study, Family Reading and Private Devotion. By the **Rev. Thomas Moore**, Vicar of Christ Church, Chesham; Author of "Parishioners in Council." Small crown 8vo.

SERMONS AND EXPOSITIONS. By the **Rev. R. Winterbotham.** Crown 8vo. Cloth. [*Shortly.*

SERMONS. By the late **Rev. Henry Christopherson, M.A.** Cr. 8vo, cloth.

THE SPIRITUAL FUNCTION OF A PRESBYTER IN THE CHURCH OF ENGLAND. By **John Notrege, A.M.**, for fifty-four years a Presbyter in "that pure and Apostolical Branch of Christ's Holy Catholic Church established in this Kingdom." Crown 8vo. Red edges. Price 3s. 6d.

WORDS OF FAITH AND CHEER. A Mission of Instruction and Suggestion. By the **Rev. Archer T. Gurney.** 1 vol. Crown 8vo. Price 6s.

THE GOSPEL ITS OWN WITNESS. Being the Hulsean Lectures for 1873. By the **Rev. Stanley Leathes, M.A.** 1 vol. Crown 8vo. Price 5s.

THE CHURCH AND THE EMPIRES : Historical Periods. By the late **Henry W. Wilberforce.** Preceded by a Memoir of the Author, by J. H. Newman, D.D. 1 vol. Post 8vo. With Portrait. Price 10s. 6d.

THE HIGHER LIFE. Its Reality, Experience, and Destiny. By the **Rev. J. Baldwin Brown, B.A.**, Author of " First Principles of Ecclesiastical Truth," &c. 1 vol. Crown 8vo. Price 7s. 6d.

"Very clearly and eloquently are set forth."— *Standard.*
"A volume of sermons of no ordinary character. Full of earnest expressions of truth set forth with great eloquence. . . . Most heartily do we commend it to our readers."—*Rock.*
"One of the richest volumes of sermons that

we have yet had from the pen of this eloquent preacher."—*Christian World.*
"Mr. Baldwin Brown's writings are full of thought, beauty, and power, and repay the careful study, not only of those who have a predilection for theological reading, but of all intelligent persons. We have felt this more than ever whilst perusing this noble volume."—*Baptist.*

HARTHAM CONFERENCES ; OR, DISCUSSIONS UPON SOME OF THE RELIGIOUS TOPICS OF THE DAY. By the **Rev. F. W. Kingsford, M.A.**, Vicar of S. Thomas's, Stamford Hill; late Chaplain H.E.I.C. (Bengal Presidency). "Audi alteram partem." Crown 8vo. Price 3s. 6d.

CONTENTS :—Introductory.—The Real Presence.—Confession.—Ritualism.
"Able and interesting."—*Church Times.*

STUDIES IN MODERN PROBLEMS. A Series of Essays by various Writers. Edited by the **Rev. Orby Shipley, M.A.** Vol. I. Crown 8vo. Price 5s. A Second Series is being published Monthly, price 6d. each part.

UNTIL THE DAY DAWN. Four Advent Lectures delivered in the Episcopal Chapel, Milverton, Warwickshire, on the Sunday Evenings during Advent, 1870. By the **Rev. Marmaduke E. Browne.** Crown 8vo. Price 2s. 6d.

"Four really original and stirring sermons."—*John Bull.*

Second Edition.
A SCOTCH COMMUNION SUNDAY. To which are added Discourses from a Certain University City. By **A. K. H. B.**, Author of "The Recreations of a Country Parson." Crown 8vo. Price 5s.

"Some discourses are added, which are couched in language of rare power."—*John Bull.*
"Accordingly fresh and readable."—*Glasgow News.*

"We commend this volume as full of interest to all our readers. It is written with much ability and good feeling, with excellent taste and unrivalled tact."—*Church Herald.*

EVERY DAY A PORTION : Adapted from the Bible and the Prayer Book, for the Private Devotions of those living in Widowhood. Collected and Edited by **Lady Mary Vyner.** Square crown 8vo, elegantly bound, 5s.

"Now she that is a widow indeed, and desolate, trusteth in God."

"An excellent little volume."—*John Bull.*
"Fills a niche hitherto unoccupied, and fills it with complete success."—*Literary Churchman.*
"A tone of earnest practical piety runs through

the whole, rendering the work well suited for its purpose."—*Rock.*
"The adaptations are always excellent and appropriate."—*Notes and Queries.*

THEOLOGICAL—*continued.*

ESSAYS ON RELIGION AND LITERATURE. By Various Writers.
Edited by the **Most Reverend Archbishop Manning.** Demy 8vo. 10s. 6d.

CONTENTS.—The Philosophy of Christianity.— | Press.—Christianity in relation to Society.—The
Mystical Elements of Religion.—Controversy with | Religious Condition of Germany.—The Philosophy
the Agnostics.—A Reasoning Thought.—Darwin- | of Bacon.—Catholic Laymen and Scholastic Phi-
ism brought to Book.—Mr. Mill on Liberty of the | losophy.

Fifth Edition.

WHY AM I A CHRISTIAN? By Viscount Stratford de Redcliffe,
P.C., K.G., G.C.B. Crown 8vo. Price 3s.

" Has a peculiar interest, as exhibiting the convictions of an earnest, intelligent, and practical
man."—*Contemporary Review.*

THEOLOGY AND MORALITY. Being Essays by the Rev. J. Llewellyn
Davies, M.A. 1 vol. Crown 8vo. Price 7s. 6d.

" The position taken up by Mr. Llewellyn Davies | not spare to do more with regard to the social
is well worth a careful survey on the part of philo- | essays of the work before us, than to testify to the
sophical students, for it represents the closest | likulmess of spirit, sobriety, and earnest thought
approximation of any theological system yet for- | by which they are uniformly characterised."—
mulated to the religion of philosophy. . . We have | *Examiner.*

THE RECONCILIATION OF RELIGION AND SCIENCE.
Being Essays by the Rev. T. W. Fowle, M.A. 1 vol. 8vo. Price 10s. 6d.

" A book which requires and deserves the re- | There is scarcely a page in the book which is not
spectful attention of all reflecting Churchmen. It | equally worthy of a thoughtful pause."—*Literary
is earnest, reverent, thoughtful, and courageous. | Churchman.*

HYMNS AND SACRED LYRICS. By the Rev. **Godfrey Thring,**
B.A. 1 vol. Crown 8vo. Price 5s.   [*Ready.*

HYMNS AND VERSES, Original and Translated.   By the Rev.
Henry Downton, M.A. Small crown 8vo. Price 3s. 6d.

" Considerable force and beauty characterise | " Will, we do not doubt, be welcome as a per-
some of these verses."—*Watchman.* | manent possession to those for whom they have
" Mr. Downton's 'Hymns and Verses' are worthy | been composed or to whom they have been origi-
of all praise."—*English Churchman.* | nally addressed."—*Church Herald.*

MISSIONARY ENTERPRISE IN THE EAST.   By the Rev.
Richard Collins. With Four Illustrations. Crown 8vo. Price 6s.

" A very graphic story told in lucid, simple, and | " We may judge from our own experience, no
modest style."—*English Churchman.* | one who takes up this charming little volume will
" A readable and very interesting volume."— | lay it down again till he has got to the last word."
Church Review. | —*John Bull.*

MISSIONARY LIFE IN THE SOUTH SEAS. By James Hutton.
1 vol. Crown 8vo.   [*In the Press.*

THE ETERNAL LIFE. Being Fourteen Sermons.   By the Rev. Jas.
Noble Bennie, M.A. Crown 8vo. Price 6s.

" The whole volume is replete with matter for | Sunday reading."—*English Churchman.*
thought and study."—*John Bull.* | " Mr. Bennie preaches earnestly and well."—
" We recommend these sermons as wholesome | *Literary Churchman.*

THE REALM OF TRUTH. By Miss E. T. Carne.   Cr. 8vo. 5s. 6d.

" A singularly calm, thoughtful, and philosophical | but what it cannot be told too often, that Truth is
inquiry into what Truth is, and what its authority." | something stronger and more enduring than our
—*Leeds Mercury.* | little doings, and speakings, and actings."—*Lite-
" It tells the world what it does not like to hear, | rary Churchman.*

LIFE : Conferences delivered at Toulouse.   By the Rev. **Père Lacordaire.**
Crown 8vo. Price 6s.

" Let the serious reader cast his eye upon any | a desire to know more of the teachings of this
single page in this volume, and he will find these | worthy follower of the saintly St. Dominick."—
words which will arrest his attention and give him | *Morning Post.*

Second Edition.

CATHOLICISM AND THE VATICAN. With a Narrative of the Old
Catholic Congress at Munich. By J. Lowry Whittle, A.M., Trin. Coll., Dublin.
Crown 8vo. Price 4s. 6d.

" We may carefully recommend his book to all who wish to follow the course of the Old Catholic
movement."—*Saturday Review.*

THEOLOGICAL.—*continued.*

THE PUBLIC WORSHIP REGULATION ACT. With a Classified
Statement of its Provisions, Notes, and Index. By W. G. Brooke, M.A. Barrister-
at-Law, author of "Six Privy Council Judgments," &c. *In the Press.*

Third Edition.

SIX PRIVY COUNCIL JUDGMENTS—1850-1872. Annotated by
W. G. Brooke, M.A., Barrister-at-Law. Crown 8vo. Price 9s.

"The volume is a valuable record of cases following precedents for the future."—*Athenæum.*
"A very timely and important publication. It
brings just one view the great judgments of the

last twenty years, which will constitute the un-
written law of the English Establishment."—*British
Quarterly Review.*

THE MOST COMPLETE HYMN BOOK PUBLISHED.

HYMNS FOR THE CHURCH AND HOME. Selected and Edited by
the Rev. W. Fleming Stevenson, Author of "Praying and Working."

*The Hymn-book consists of Three Parts:—*I. For Public Worship.—II. For Family
and Private Worship.—III. For Children; and contains Biographical Notices of nearly
300 Hymn-writers, with Notes upon their Hymns.

** *Published in various forms and prices, the latter ranging from 8d. to 6s. Lists and full
particulars will be furnished on application to the Publishers.*

WORKS BY THE REV. CHARLES ANDERSON, M.A.

Second Edition.

CHURCH THOUGHT AND CHURCH WORK. Edited by the Rev.
Charles Anderson, M.A., Vicar of St. John's, Limehouse. Containing articles
by the Revs. J. M. Capes, Professor Cheetham, J. Ll. Davis, Harry Jones, Brooke Lam-
bert, A. J. Ross, the Editor, and others. Demy 8vo. 7s. 6d.

"Mr. Anderson has accomplished his task well.
The brief papers with which his book is filled are
aimed at recalling sketchy, but they are none the
less valuable on that account. Those who are con-
tending with practical difficulties in Church work,
could hardly do better than study Mr. Anderson's
suggestions for themselves."—*Spectator.*
"This new series of papers, edited by Mr.
Charles Anderson, will be heartily welcomed. A

healthy moral earnestness is conspicuous in every
one of them."—*Westminster Review.*
"It is a book which may be profitably studied by
all, whether clergymen or laymen, members of the
established or other churches, who attempt any kind
of pastoral work, for it is full of what practical suggestions evidently the result of earnest observation
and long experience, and not the mere guesses of
an à priori speculator."—*Nonconformist.*

Second Edition.

WORDS AND WORKS IN A LONDON PARISH. Edited by
the Rev. Charles Anderson, M.A. Demy 8vo. Price 6s.

"It has an interest of its own for not a few of us,
to whom the question 'Is the National Church
worth preserving as such, and if so, how best is-

consider its vital power?' is of deep and grave importance."—*Spectator.*

THE CURATE OF SHYRE. By the Rev. Charles Anderson, M.A.,
Vicar of St. John's, Limehouse. Editor of "Church Thought and Church Work," and
"Words and Works in a London Parish." Demy 8vo. Cloth, 7s. 6d. *[Shortly.*

"This book is no novel, but a record of parish reform, with its attendant religious and social
problems."—*Preface.*

WORKS BY THE REV. H. R. HAWEIS, M.A.

Seventh Edition.

THOUGHTS FOR THE TIMES. Crown 8vo. Price 7s. 6d.

"Mr. Haweis writes not only fearlessly, but with
remarkable freshness and vigour. In all that he
says, we perceive a transparent honesty and single-
ness of purpose."—*Saturday Review.*

"Bear marks of much originality of thought
and individuality of expression."—*Pall Mall
Gazette.*

Second Edition.

SPEECH IN SEASON. A New Volume of Sermons. Cr. 8vo. Price 9s.

"There is in them that which will commend them
to the approval of the reading public. . . . They
are marked by a freshness and novelty of treatment, a catholicity of spirit, and an earnestness of

faith which make them pleasant and profitable
reading, even to those who may least concur in
the views of the preacher. . . . All the subjects
are treated with great power."—*Leeds Mercury.*

UNSECTARIAN FAMILY PRAYERS, for Morning and Evening for a
Week, with short selected passages from the Bible. Square crown 8vo. Price 3s. 6d.

"These prayers are tender, devotional, and
helpful, and may be used with great profit in any

household. They are brief, but very beautiful."—
Christian World.

THEOLOGICAL—*continued.*

WORKS BY THE REV. C. J. VAUGHAN, D.D.

Third Edition.

WORDS OF HOPE FROM THE PULPIT OF THE TEMPLE CHURCH. Crown 8vo. Price 5s.

"Able, bold, and thoroughly practical." — *Standard.*

"Suffice it to say that they contain the characteristics of Dr. Vaughan's other writings, and possess an attractiveness which is generally only to be derived from a telling delivery, and consequently is rarely looked for in sermons only read." — *John Bull.*

"Quiet, scholarly, ingenious, natural, spiritual, evangelical, and earnest. The charm of their pleasantness and goodness does not weary. They are the unreal products of a cultured, industrious, vigorous mind." — *British Quarterly Review.*

"Through simplicity, devoutness, and sincerity of Christian purpose, are apparent in all his pulpit utterances." — *London Quarterly Review.*

THE SOLIDITY OF TRUE RELIGION AND OTHER SERMONS PREACHED IN LONDON DURING THE ELECTION AND MISSION WEEK, FEBRUARY, 1874. Crown 8vo. 3s. 6d.

FORGET THINE OWN PEOPLE. An Appeal for Missions. Crown 8vo, 3s. 6d.

"Faithful, earnest, eloquent, tender, and largehearted." — *British Quarterly Review.*

Fourth Edition.

THE YOUNG LIFE EQUIPPING ITSELF FOR GOD'S SERVICE. Being Four Sermons Preached before the University of Cambridge, in November, 1872. Crown 8vo. Price 3s. 6d.

"Has all the writer's characteristics of devotedness, purity, and high moral tone." — *London Quarterly Review.*

"As earnest, eloquent, and as liberal as everything else that he writes." — *Examiner.*

WORKS BY THE REV. G. S. DREW, M.A.
VICAR OF TRINITY, LAMBETH.

Second Edition.

SCRIPTURE LANDS IN CONNECTION WITH THEIR HISTORY. Bevelled Boards, 8vo. Price 10s. 6d.

"Mr. Drew has invented a new method of illustrating Scripture history—from observation of the countries. Instead of narrating his travels, and referring from time to time to the facts of sacred history belonging to the different countries, he writes an outline history of the Hebrew nation from Abraham downwards, with special reference to the various points in which the geography illustrates the history. . . . He is very successful in picturing to his readers the scenes before his own mind." — *Saturday Review.*

Second Edition.

NAZARETH: ITS LIFE AND LESSONS. Crown 8vo, 5s.

"We have read the volume with great interest. It is at once succinct and suggestive, reverent and ingenious, observant of small details, and yet not forgetful of great principles." — *British Quarterly Review.*

"A very reverent attempt to elicit and develop Scripture intimations respecting our Lord's thirty years' sojourn at Nazareth. The author has wrought well at the unworked mine, and has produced a very valuable series of Scripture lessons, which will be found both profitable and singularly interesting." — *Guardian.*

THE DIVINE KINGDOM ON EARTH AS IT IS IN HEAVEN. 8vo, 10s. 6d.

"Entirely valuable and satisfactory. There is no living divine to whom the authorship would not be a credit." — *Literary Churchman.*

"Thoughtful and eloquent. . . . . Full of original thinking admirably expressed." — *British Quarterly Review.*

WORKS OF THE LATE REV. F. W. ROBERTSON, M.A.
NEW AND CHEAPER EDITIONS.

SERMONS.

Vol. I. Small crown 8vo.   Price 3s. 6d.
Vol. II. Small crown 8vo.   Price 3s. 6d.
Vol. III. Small crown 8vo.   Price 3s. 6d.
Vol. IV. Small crown 8vo.   Price 3s. 6d.

EXPOSITORY LECTURES ON ST. PAUL'S EPISTLE TO THE CORINTHIANS. Small crown 8vo. 5s.

AN ANALYSIS OF MR. TENNYSON'S "IN MEMORIAM." (Dedicated by permission to the Poet-Laureate.) Fcap. 8vo. 2s.

THE EDUCATION OF THE HUMAN RACE. Translated from the German of Gotthold Ephraim Lessing. Fcap. 8vo. 2s. 6d.

LECTURES AND ADDRESSES, WITH OTHER LITERARY REMAINS. A New Edition. With Introduction by the Rev. Stopford A. Brooke, M.A. One Vol. Uniform with the Sermons. 5s. [*Preparing.*

A LECTURE ON FRED. W. ROBERTSON, M.A. By the Rev. F. A. Noble. Delivered before the Young Men's Christian Association of Pittsburgh, U.S. 1s. 6d.

☞ The above works can also be had Bound in half morocco.

** A Portrait of the late Rev. F. W. Robertson, mounted for framing, can be had, price 2s. 6d.

THEOLOGICAL—*continued.*

WORKS BY THE REV. STOPFORD A. BROOKE, M.A.
Chaplain in Ordinary to Her Majesty the Queen.

**THE LATE REV. F. W. ROBERTSON,
M.A. LIFE AND LETTERS OF.**
Edited by Stopford Brooke, M.A.

I. In 2 vols., uniform with the Sermons.
With a Steel Portrait. 7s. 6d.

II. Library Edition, in demy 8vo, with
Two Steel Portraits. 12s.

III. A Popular Edition, in 1 vol. 6s.

Second Edition.

**THEOLOGY IN THE ENGLISH
POETS.**—Cowper, Coleridge, Wordsworth, and Burns. Post 8vo. 9s.

"Apart from its literary merits, the book may be said to possess an independent value, as tending to familiarise a certain section of the English public with more enlightened views of theology."—*Athenæum.*

"The volume is scholarlike, and evidently the result of study and discrimination."—*Hour.*

". . . . An admirable example of interpretative criticism. It is clear, adequate, eloquent, and there are many such passages of thought scattered throughout the book. We have read Mr. Brooke's volume with pleasure; it is fresh, suggestive, stimulating, and we cordially recommend it."—*Nonconformist.*

Seventh Edition.

CHRIST IN MODERN LIFE. Sermons Preached in St. James's Chapel, York Street, London. Crown 8vo. 7s. 6d.

"Nobly fearless, and singularly strong, ... carries our admiration throughout."—*British Quarterly Review.*

Second Edition.

**FREEDOM IN THE CHURCH OF
ENGLAND.** Six Sermons suggested by the Voysey Judgment. Cr. 8vo. 3s. 6d.

"A very fair statement of the views in respect to freedom of thought held by the liberal party in the Church of England."—*Westminster Review.*

"Interesting and readable, and characterised by great clearness of thought, frankness of statement, and moderation of tone."—*Church Opinion.*

Seventh Edition.

SERMONS Preached in St. James's Chapel, York Street, London. Crown 8vo. 6s.

"No one who reads these sermons will wonder that Mr. Brooke is a great power in London, that his chapel is thronged, and his followers large and enthusiastic. They are fine, energetic, instinct with life, and with the treasures of a cultivated imagination."—*Guardian.*

**FREDERICK DENISON MAURICE:
THE LIFE AND WORK OF,** A
Memorial Sermon. Crown 8vo, sewed. 1s.

SERMONS PREACHED IN ST. JAMES'S CHAPEL, YORK ST., LONDON, SECOND SERIES IS IN THE PRESS.

MISCELLANEOUS.

FOR SCEPTRE AND CROWN. A Romance of the Present Time.
By **Gregor Samarow.** Translated by **Fanny Wormald.** 2 vols. Cr. 8vo, 15s.
This is the celebrated "Am Zepterund Krone," which was published about a year ago in Germany, when it created a very great sensation among all classes. It deals with some of the prominent characters who have figured and will continue to figure in European politics, and the accuracy of its life-picture is so great that it is presented to the English public not as a novel, but as a new rendering of an important chapter in recent European history.

THE NEGLECTED QUESTION. By **E. Markewitch.** Translated from the Russian, by the **Princesses Ouronsoff,** and dedicated by Special Permission to Her Royal Highness the Duchess of Edinburgh.

THE ROMANTIC ANNALS OF A NAVAL FAMILY. By
Mrs **Arthur Traherne.** Crown 8vo. 10s. 6d.
"Some interesting letters are introduced, amongst others, several from the late King William IV."—*Spectator.* | "Well and pleasantly told."—*Evening Standard.*

A GRAMMAR OF POLITICAL ECONOMY. By **Maj.-Gen. W. F.
Marriott.** Crown 8vo, 6s. [*Shortly.*]
The author's aim in presenting this new elementary treatise to the world is, firstly, to restrict it to truly elementary considerations in each branch of the subject; secondly, to adopt a perfectly precise and unambiguous use of terms in the sense which most nearly agrees with common use; thirdly, to offer reasonable proof of every proposition; and fourthly, to use the utmost brevity consistent with proof, so as to invite and facilitate the judgment of the student as well as of the critic.

VILLAGE HEALTH. By **Horace Swete, M.D.** Small crown 8vo.
[*In the Press.*]
* This work will be a practical hand-book of sanitary knowledge for residents in the country, landowners, clergymen, &c.

MISCELLANEOUS—*continued.*

THE ASHANTEE WAR. A Popular Narrative. By **The Special Correspondent of the "Daily News."** Crown 8vo. Price 6s. [*Just Ready.*

This account of the Ashantee War does not pretend to the dignity of a HISTORY, but attempts to provide a connected narrative of what took place, with descriptions of the country and scenes passed through. Although somewhat late in appearing, it gains in value from the fact that official documents have been had recourse to in solving some of the questions which every one is still asking.

"Trustworthy and readable, and well fitted to serve its purpose as a popular narrative. . . . The *Daily News* Correspondent secures interest chiefly by bringing together suggestive incidents, and by clearing up points that his readers would naturally be desirous of knowing."—*Examiner.*

SOLDIERING AND SCRIBBLING. By **Archibald Forbes**, of the *Daily News*, Author of "My Experience of the War between France and Germany." Crown 8vo. Price 7s. 6d.

"All who open it will be inclined to read through for the varied entertainment which it affords."—*Daily News.*

"There is a great deal of instruction to outsiders touching military life, in this volume."—*Evening Standard.*

HAKAYIT ABDULLA. The Autobiography of a Malay Munshi, between the years 1808 and 1843. In which are Sketches of Men and Events connected with the English Settlements in the Straits of Malacca during that period. Translated by **J. F. Thomson, F.R.G.S.** Demy 8vo. Price 12s.

SHAKESPEARE; a Critical Study of his Mind and Art. By **Edward Dowden.** [*Preparing.*

THE SHAKESPEARE ARGOSY: containing much of the wealth of Shakespeare's Wisdom and Wit, alphabetically arranged and classified by **Capt. A. F. P. Harcourt.** Crown 8vo. Price 6s.

SOCIALISM: its Nature, its Dangers, and its Remedies considered by the **Rev. M. Kaufman, B.A.** 1 vol. Crown 8vo.

Dr. J. H. NEWMAN; CHARACTERISTICS FROM THE WRITINGS OF: Being Selections, Personal, Historical, Philosophical, and Religious, from his various Works. Arranged with the Author's personal approval. With Portrait.

CREMATION; THE TREATMENT OF THE BODY AFTER DEATH: with a Description of the Process and necessary Apparatus. Crown 8vo, sewed. Third Edition. Price 1s.

'ILÂM EN NÂS. Historical Tales and Anecdotes of the Times of the Early Khalifahs. Translated from the Arabic Originals. By **Mrs. Godfrey Clerk,** Author of "The Antipodes and Round the World." Crown 8vo. Price 7s.

"Those who like stories full of the genuine colour and fragrance of the East should by all means read Mrs. Godfrey Clerk's volume."—*Spectator.*

"As full of valuable information as it is of amusing incident."—*Evening Standard.*

THE PLACE OF THE PHYSICIAN. Being the Introductory Lecture at Guy's Hospital, 1873–74; to which is added ESSAYS ON THE LAW OF HUMAN LIFE, AND ON THE RELATION BETWEEN ORGANIC AND INORGANIC WORLDS. By **James Hinton,** Author of "Man and His Dwelling-Place." Crown 8vo, cloth. Price 3s. 6d.

"Very remarkable. There is not a sentence in them that is not pregnant with high meaning."—*Brighton Herald.*

"A thoughtful volume."—*John Bull.*

"Full of suggestive thoughts and scientific knowledge."

"To partake of this feast of reason the book must be purchased and thought over, which advice we conscientiously give to everyone who wishes to keep up with the intellectual progress of the age."—*Brighton Gazette.*

Fifth Edition.

LITTLE DINNERS; HOW TO SERVE THEM WITH ELEGANCE AND ECONOMY. By **Mary Hooper,** Author of "The Handbook of the Breakfast Table." 1 vol. Crown 8vo. Price 5s.

"We ought not to omit the mention of several very good recipes which Mrs. Hooper introduces—e.g., ramp-steak pudding, sheep's head, Scotch fashion, devilled fowl, rich plum-pudding, neck of venison cooked in a 'oven, how to cook whitebait, and how to 'scollop oysters.' She has good hints about ragôut of wild duck, and her caution on the deliberate preparation of the sauce for the same delicacy, recommends as that—given the means and the heart to put her knowledge in practice—she undeniably knows what is good."—*Saturday Review.*

"To read this book gives the reader an appetite."—*Naval and Military.*

"We should think this little book likely to be very useful."—*Echo.*

"Sensible and well written."—*Glasgow News.*

"A very excellent little book . . . Ought to be recommended as exceedingly useful, and as a capital help to any housekeeper who interests herself in her kitchen and her cook."—*Vanity Fair.*

"A thoroughly practical book."—*Church Herald.*

OUR INVALIDS: HOW SHALL WE EMPLOY AND AMUSE THEM? By **Harriet Power.** Fcap. 8vo. Price 2s. 6d.

"A very useful little brochure. . . . Will become a universal favourite with the class for whom it is intended, while it will afford many a useful hint to those who live with them."—*John Bull.*

MISCELLANEOUS—*continued.*

THE PORT OF REFUGE; OR, COUNSEL AND AID TO SHIPMASTERS IN DIFFICULTY, DOUBT, OR DISTRESS. By **Manley Hopkins,** Author of "A Handbook of Average," "A Manual of Insurance," &c. Crown 8vo. Price 6s.

SUBJECTS:—The Shipmaster's Position and Duties.—Agents and Agency.—Average.—Bottomry, and other Means of Raising Money.—The Charter-Party, and Bill-of-Lading. Stoppage in Transitu: and the Shipowner's Lien.—Collision.

"A most useful book." —*Hampshire Review.*
"Master-mariners will find it well worth while to avail themselves of his teachings." —*United Service Magazine.*

"Considers, in quite a marvellous manner, a fulness of information which will make it perfectly indispensable in the captain's bookcase, and equally suitable to the general man's library." —*Iron.*

Fifth Edition.

LOMBARD STREET. A Description of the **Money Market.** By **Walter Bagehot.** Large crown 8vo. Price 7s. 6d.

"Mr. Bagehot touches incidentally a hundred points connected with his subject, and points wherein we feel sight upon them all." —*Spectator.*
"Anybody who wishes to have a clear idea of the workings of what is called the Money Market

should procure a little volume which Mr. Bagehot has just published, and he will there find the whole thing in a nutshell." —*Saturday Review.*
"Full of the most interesting economic history." —*Athenæum.*

THE ENGLISH CONSTITUTION. By **Walter Bagehot.** A New Edition, Revised and Corrected, with an Introductory Dissertation on Recent Changes and Events. Crown 8vo. Price 7s. 6d.

"No writer before him had set out so clearly what the essence part of the English Constitution really is." —*Pall Mall Gazette.*

"A pleasing and clever study on the department of his politics." —*Guardian.*

REPUBLICAN SUPERSTITIONS. Illustrated by the Political History of the United States. Including a Correspondence with M. Louis Blanc. By **Moncure D. Conway.** Crown 8vo. Price 5s.

"A very able exposition of the most plausible fallacies of Republicanism, by a writer of remarkable vigour and purity of style." —*Standard.*

"Mr. Conway writes with ardent sincerity. He gives us some good anecdotes, and he is occasionally absent chopping." —*Examiner.*

NEWMARKET AND ARABIA; AN EXAMINATION OF THE DESCENT OF RACERS AND COURSERS. By **Roger D. Upton,** Captain late 9th Royal Lancers. Post 8vo. With Pedigrees and Frontispiece. 9s.

"It contains a good deal of truth, and it abounds with valuable suggestions." —*Saturday Review.*
"A remarkable volume. The breeder can well ponder over its pages." —*Bell's Life.*

"A thoughtful and intelligent book. . . . A contribution to the history of the horse of remarkable interest and importance." —*Baily's Magazine.*

MOUNTAIN, MEADOW, AND MERE: a Series of Outdoor Sketches of Sport, Scenery, Adventures, and Natural History. By **G. Christopher Davies.** With 16 Illustrations by BOSWORTH W. HARCOURT. Crown 8vo. Price 6s.

"Pervaded throughout by the graceful melody of a natural idyll, and the details of sport are subordinated to a dominating sense of the beautiful and picturesque." —*Saturday Review.*

"Mr. Davies writes pleasantly, graphically, with the pen of a lover of nature, a naturalist, and a sportsman." —*Field.*

STREAMS FROM HIDDEN SOURCES. By **B. Montgomerie Ranking.** Crown 8vo. Price 6s.

"We doubt not that Mr. Ranking's enthusiasm will communicate itself to many of his readers, and induce them in like manner to follow back these streamlets to their parent river." —*Graphic.*

"The effect of reading the seven tales he presents to us is to make us wish for some seven more of the same kind." —*Pall Mall Gazette.*

MODERN PARISH CHURCHES; THEIR PLAN, DESIGN, AND FURNITURE. By **J. T. Micklethwaite, F.S.A.** Crown 8vo. Price 7s. 6d.

"Any one about to build a church we strongly recommend to study it carefully." —*Notes and Queries.*
"Will be a valuable addition to all clergymen's

libraries, whether they have to build churches or not." —*Literary Churchman.*
"A fund of sound remarks and practical suggestions on Church Architecture." —*Examiner.*

Second Edition.

LONGEVITY; THE MEANS OF PROLONGING LIFE AFTER MIDDLE AGE. By **Dr. John Gardner,** Author of "A Handbook of Domestic Medicine," &c. Small crown 8vo. Price 4s.

"We are bound to say that in general Dr. Gardner's directions are sensible enough, and founded on good principles. The advice given is such that any man in moderate health might follow it with advantage, whilst no prescription or other claptrap is introduced which ought favour of quackery." —*Lancet.*
"A very interesting book—the simplicity of the language is such that the meaning is at once evident." —*Liverpool Albion.*

"Dr. Gardner's suggestions for attaining a healthy and so far a happy old age are well deserving the attention of all who think such a blessing worth trying for." —*Notes and Queries.*
"To middle-aged persons this work will be a most useful one, if only they will follow Dr. Gardner's advice." —*Surveyor's News Letter.*
"The hints here given are to our mind invaluable." —*Standard.*

MISCELLANEOUS—*continued.*

Third Edition.

THE SECRET OF LONG LIFE. Dedicated by Special Permission to Lord St. Leonards. Large crown 8vo. Price 5s.

"A charming little volume."—*Times.*
"A very pleasant little book, cheerful, genial, scholarly."—*Spectator.*
"Entitled to the warmest admiration."—*Pall Mall Gazette.*

WORKS BY EDWARD JENKINS, M.P.

Thirty-Second Edition.

GINX'S BABY: HIS BIRTH AND OTHER MISFORTUNES. Crown 8vo. Price 2s.

LUCHMEE AND DILLOO. A Story of West Indian Life. 2 vols. Demy 8vo. Illustrated. [*Preparing.*

Fourteenth Thousand.

LITTLE HODGE. A Christmas Country Carol. With Five Illustrations. Crown 8vo. Price 5s.

A Cheap Edition in paper covers, price 1s.

Sixth Edition.

LORD BANTAM. Cr. 8vo. Price 2s. 6d.

PANDURANG HARI; or, MEMOIRS OF A HINDOO. A Tale of Mahratta Life sixty years ago. With a Preface by Sir H. Bartle E. Frere, G.C.S.I., &c. 2 vols. Crown 8vo. Price 21s.

"There is a quaintness and simplicity in the roguery of the hero that makes his life as attractive as that of Gusman of Alfarache or Gil Blas, and so we advise our readers not to be dismayed at the length of Pandurang Hari, but to read it resolutely through. If they do this they cannot, we think, fail to be both amused and interested."—*Times.*

TALES OF THE ZENANA, OR A NUWAB'S LEISURE HOURS. By the Author of "Pandurang Hari." With a Preface by Lord Stanley of Alderley. In 2 vols. Crown 8vo. [*Preparing.*

A CHEQUERED LIFE: Being Memoirs of the Vicomtesse de Léoville Meilhan. Edited by the Vicomtesse Solange de Kerkadec. Crown 8vo. Price 7s. 6d.

"There are numerous passages of a strongly dramatic character, describing conventual life, trials for murder, death-bed marriages, village feudalism, revolutionary outrages, and the other familiar aspects of those times; and we may say that the transcendance is admirable."—*Standard.*
"Easy and amusing reading."—*Hour.*

GIDEON'S ROCK, and other Stories. By Katherine Saunders. In 1 vol. Crown 8vo. Price 6s.

CONTENTS.—Gideon's Rock.—Old Matthew's Puzzle.—Gentle Jack.—Uncle Ned.—The Retired Apothecary.

"The tale from which the volume derives its title, is especially worthy of commendation, and the other and shorter stories comprised in the volume are also well deserving of reproduction."—*Queen.*

JOAN MERRYWEATHER, and other Stories. By Katherine Saunders. In 1 vol. Crown 8vo. Price 6s.

CONTENTS.—The Haunted Crust.—The Flower-Girl.—Joan Merryweather.—The Watchman's Story.—An Old Letter.

MADEMOISELLE JOSEPHINE'S FRIDAYS, AND OTHER STORIES. By Miss M. Betham-Edwards, Author of "Kitty," &c.

STUDIES AND ROMANCES. By H. Schütz Wilson. Cr. 8vo, 7s. 6d.

"Open the book, at what page the reader may, he will find something to amuse and interest, and he must be very hard to please if he finds nothing to suit him, either grave or gay, stirring or romantic, in the capital stories collected in this well-got-up volume."—*John Bull.*

THE PELICAN PAPERS. Reminiscences and Remains of a Dweller in the Wilderness. By James Ashcroft Noble. Crown 8vo. Price 6s.

"Written somewhat after the fashion of Mr. Helps's 'Friends in Council.'"—*Examiner.*
"Will well repay perusal by all thoughtful and intelligent readers."—*Liverpool Leader.*

BRIEFS AND PAPERS. Being Sketches of the Bar and the Press. By Two Idle Apprentices. Crown 8vo. Price 7s. 6d.

"Written with spirit and knowledge, and give some curious glimpses into what the majority will regard as *terra incognita* and unknown territories."—*Daily News.*
"This is one of the best books to while away an hour and cause a generous laugh that we have come across for a long time."—*John Bull.*

BY STILL WATERS. A Story for Quiet Hours. By Edward Garrett, Author of "Occupations of a Retired Life," &c. Cr. 8vo. With Seven Illustrations. 6s.

COL. MEADOWS TAYLOR'S INDIAN TALES.

THE CONFESSIONS OF A THUG

Is now ready, and is the First Volume of A New and Cheaper Edition, in 1 vol. each, Illustrated, price 6s. It will be followed by "TARA" (now in the press), "RALPH DARNELL," and "TIPPOO SULTAN."